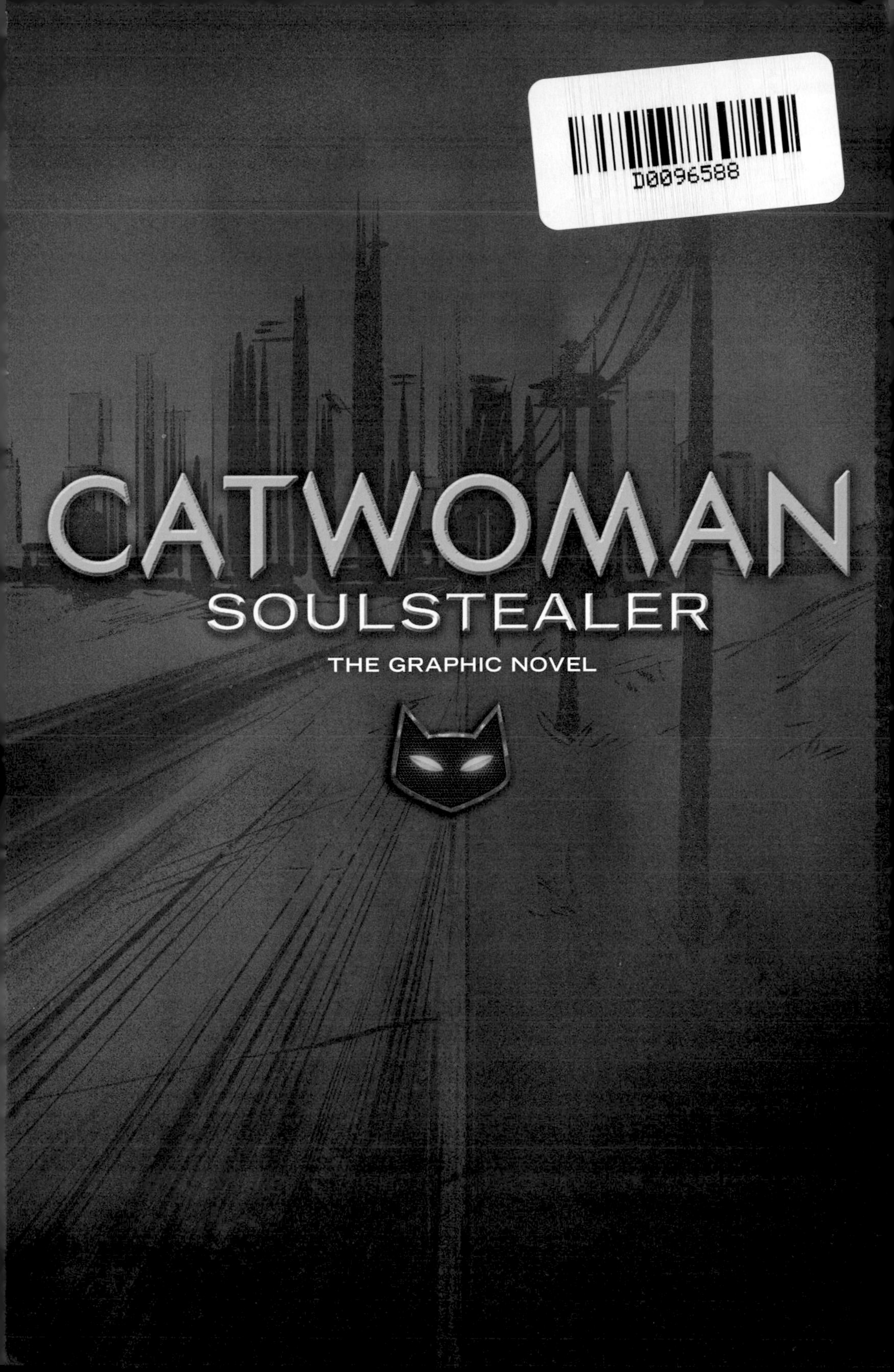

CATWOMAN

SOULSTEALER

THE GRAPHIC NOVEL

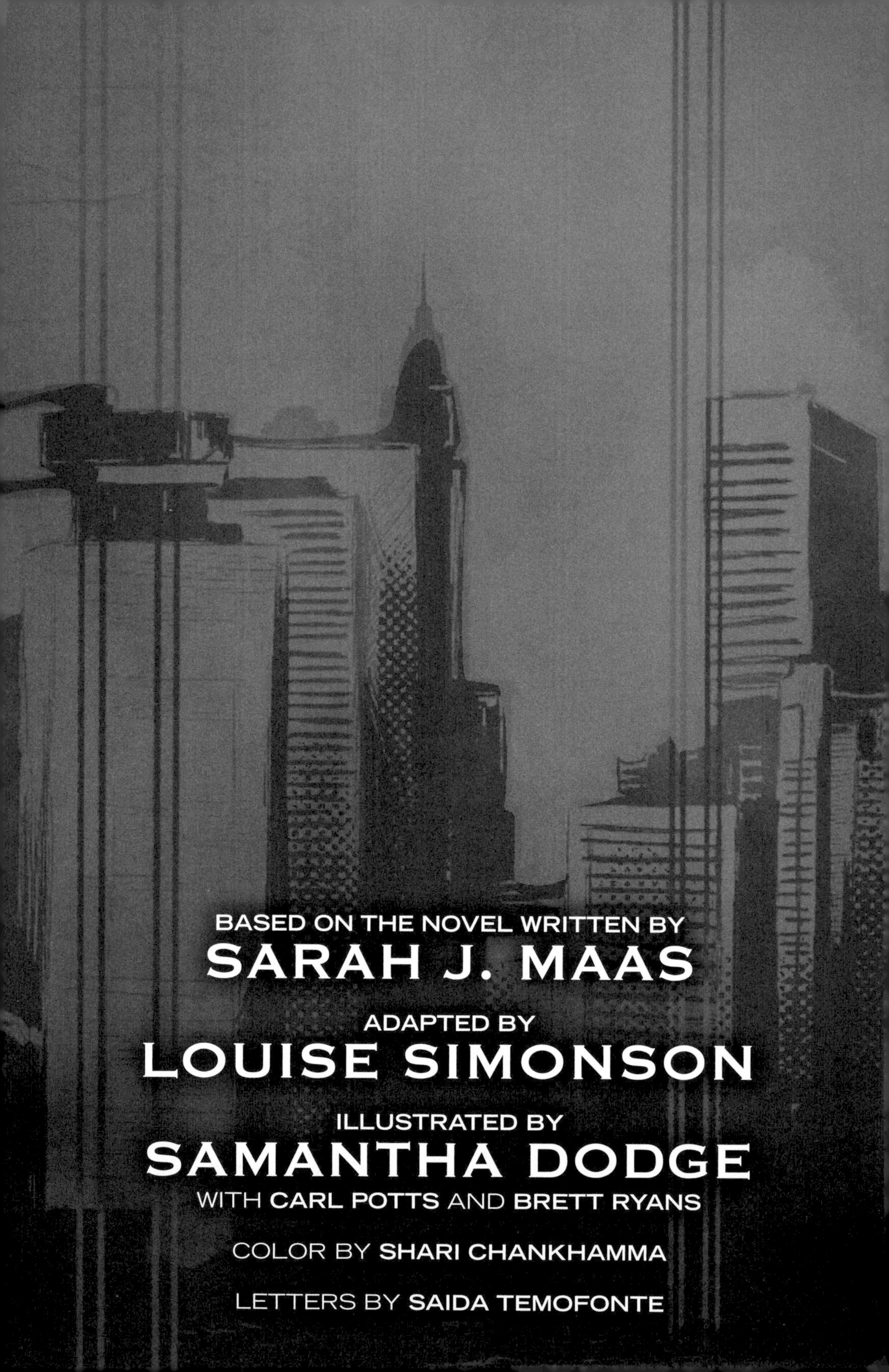

BASED ON THE NOVEL WRITTEN BY
SARAH J. MAAS

ADAPTED BY
LOUISE SIMONSON

ILLUSTRATED BY
SAMANTHA DODGE
WITH **CARL POTTS** AND **BRETT RYANS**

COLOR BY **SHARI CHANKHAMMA**

LETTERS BY **SAIDA TEMOFONTE**

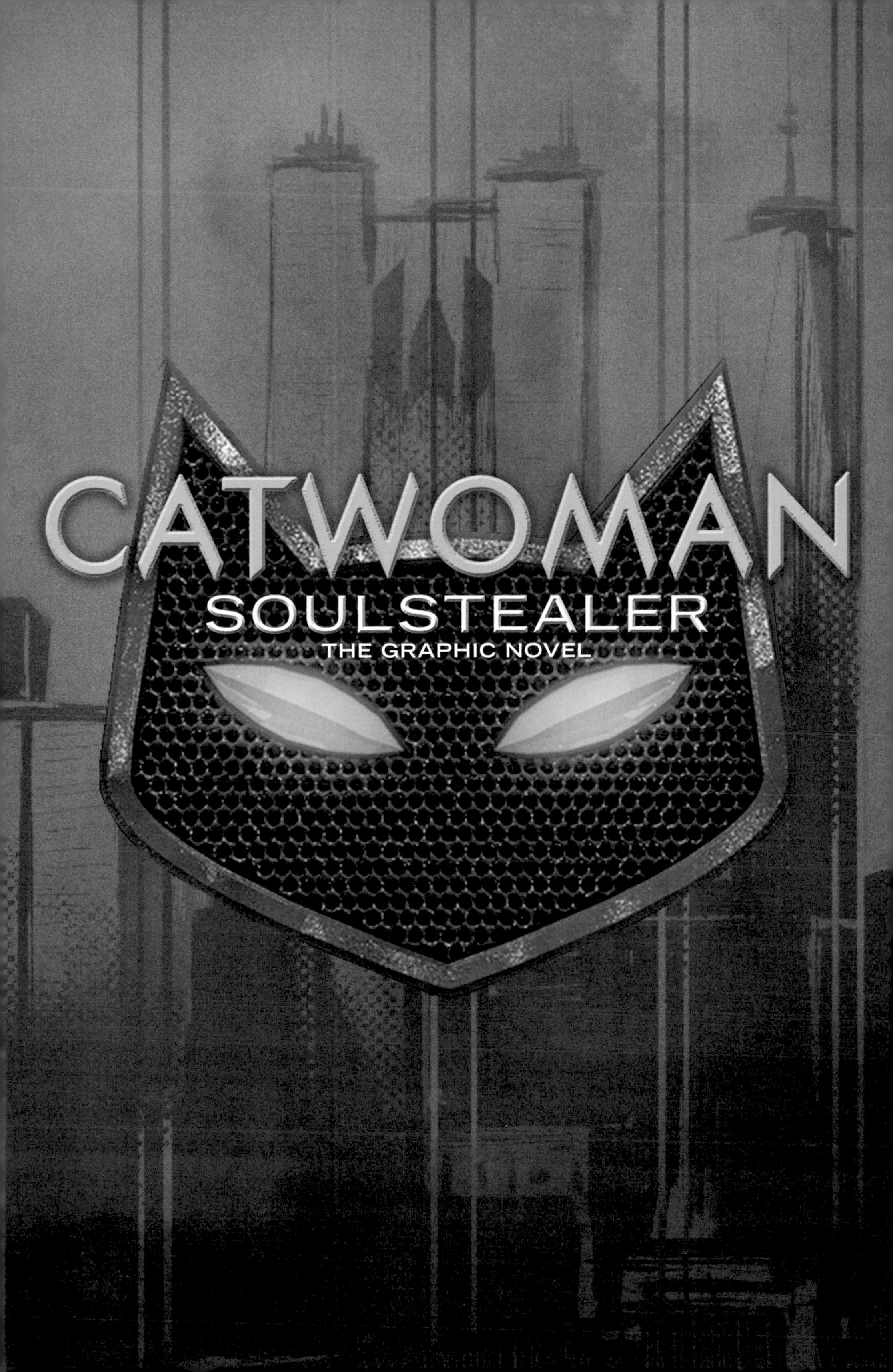
CATWOMAN
SOULSTEALER
THE GRAPHIC NOVEL

KRISTY QUINN Senior Editor

COURTNEY JORDAN Assistant Editor

STEVE COOK Design Director – Books

AMIE BROCKWAY-METCALF Publication Design

SUNNY PARADYSE Publication Production

MARIE JAVINS Editor-in-Chief, DC Comics

DANIEL CHERRY III Senior VP – General Manager

JIM LEE Publisher & Chief Creative Officer

JOEN CHOE VP – Global Brand & Creative Services

DON FALLETTI VP – Manufacturing Operations & Workflow Management

LAWRENCE GANEM VP – Talent Services

ALISON GILL Senior VP – Manufacturing & Operations

NICK J. NAPOLITANO VP – Manufacturing Administration & Design

NANCY SPEARS VP – Revenue

CATWOMAN: SOULSTEALER (THE GRAPHIC NOVEL)

DC Comics, 2900 West Alameda Ave., Burbank, CA 91505

Printed by LSC Communications, Crawfordsville, IN, USA.

4/23/21. First Printing.
ISBN: 978-1-4012-9641-4

PEFC Certified

This product is from sustainably managed forests and controlled sources

PEFC/29-31-337   www.pefc.org

Library of Congress Cataloging-in-Publication Data

Names: Simonson, Louise, adapter. I Dodge, Samantha, illustrator. I Potts, Carl, illustrator. I Ryans, Brett, illustrator. I Chankhamma, Shari, colourist. I Temofonte, Saida, letterer. I Maas, Sarah J. Catwoman, soulstealer.
Title: Catwoman, soulstealer : the graphic novel / based on the novel written by Sarah J. Maas ; adapted by Louise Simonson ; illustrated by Samantha Dodge with Carl Potts and Brett Ryans ; colors by Shari Chankhamma ; letters by Saida Temofonte.
Other titles: Soulstealer
Description: Burbank, CA : DC Comics, [2021] I Audience: Ages 13-17 I Audience: Grades 7-9 I Summary: Selina Kyle returns to Gotham City as new socialite Holly Vanderhees, but she needs to outsmart rival Batwing to rise to the top of the city's criminal underbelly.
Identifiers: LCCN 2021004260 I ISBN 9781401296414 (trade paperback)
Subjects: LCSH: Graphic novels. I CYAC: Graphic novels. I Supervillains--Fiction. I Superheroes--Fiction. I Maas, Sarah J. Catwoman, soulstealer--Adaptations.
Classification: LCC PZ7.7.S546 Cat 2021 I DDC 741.5/973--dc23
LC record available at https://lccn.loc.gov/2021004260

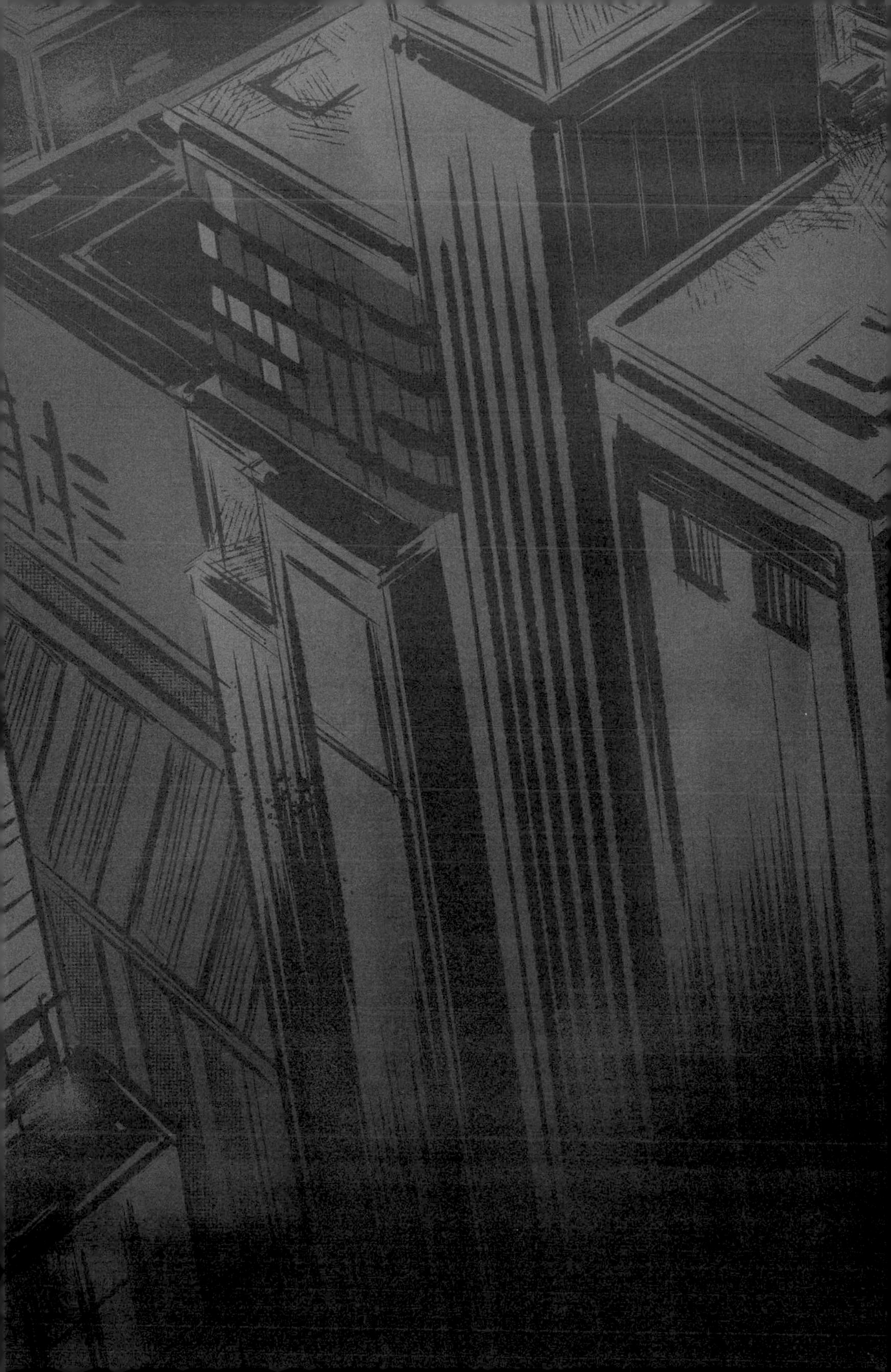

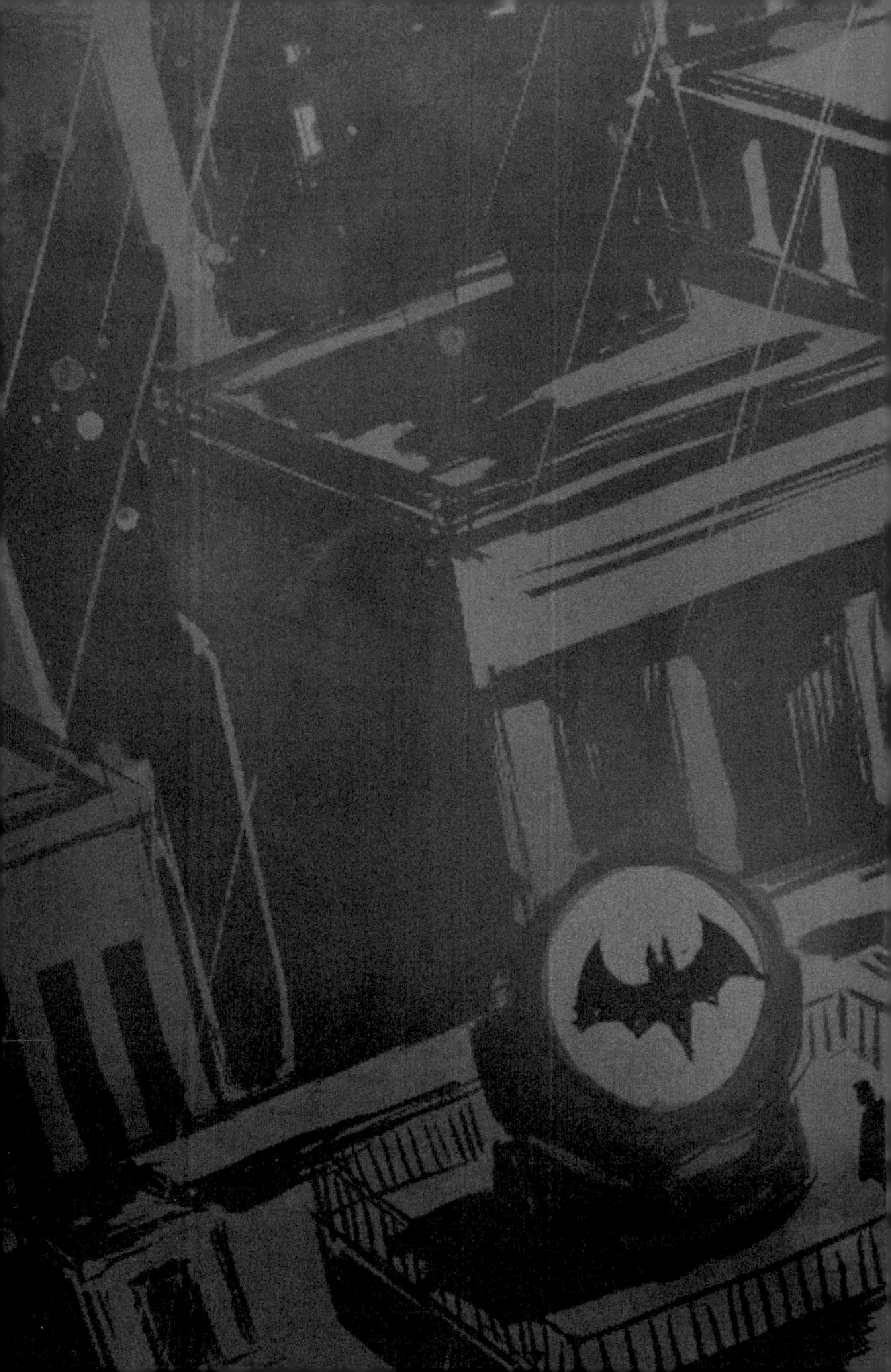

PART ONE

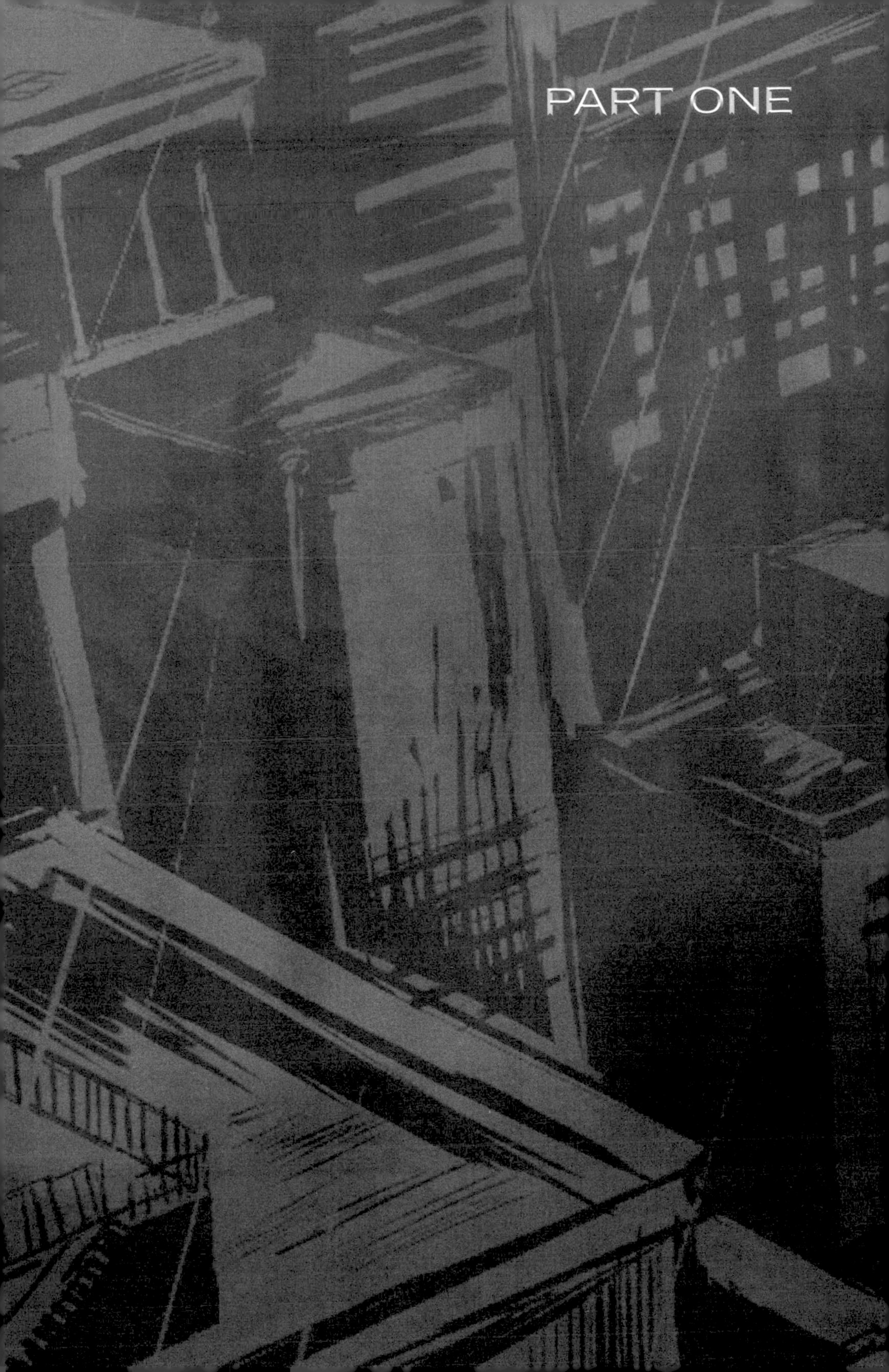

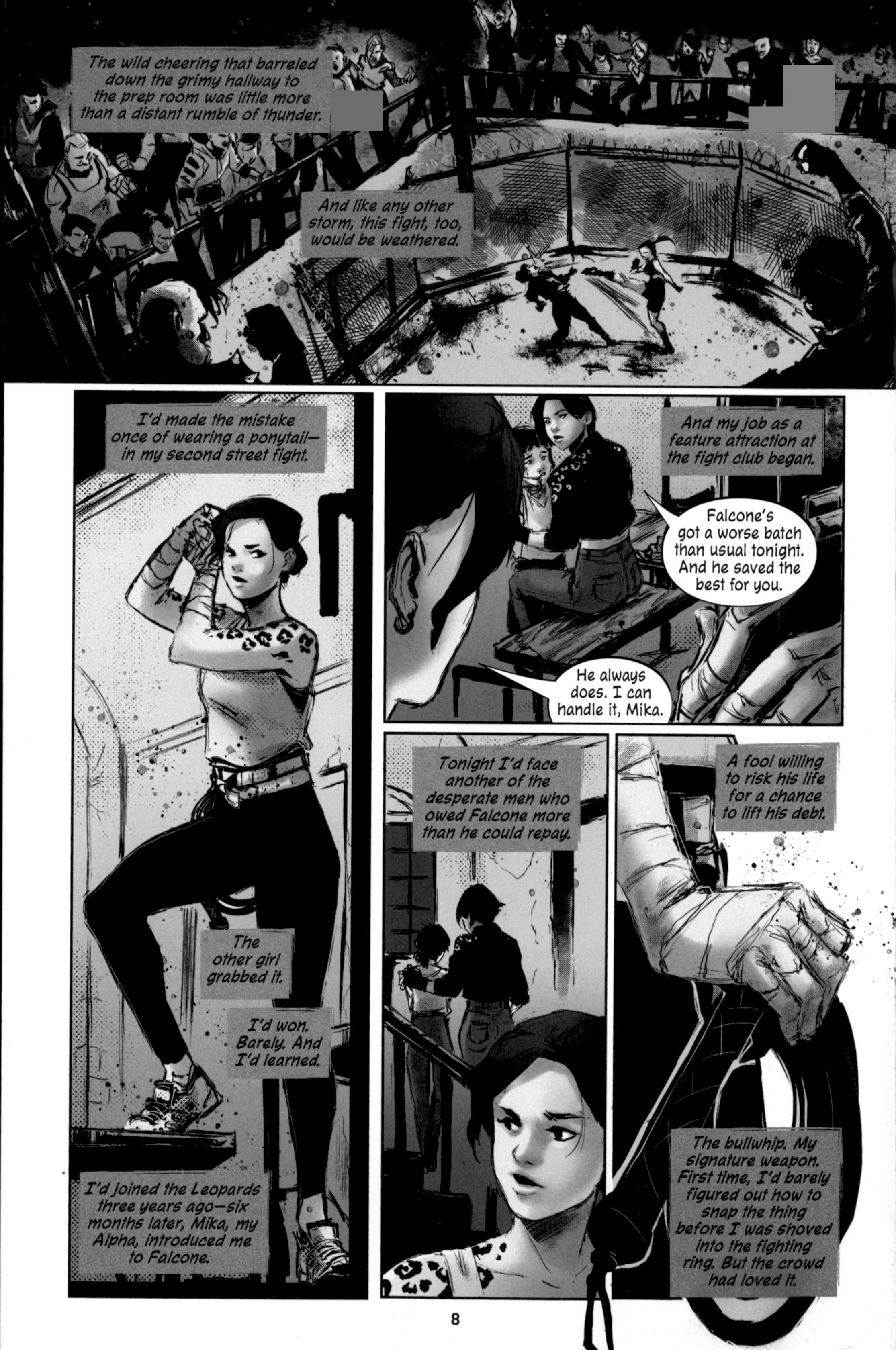

The wild cheering that barreled down the grimy hallway to the prep room was little more than a distant rumble of thunder.
And like any other storm, this fight, too, would be weathered.
I'd made the mistake once of wearing a ponytail—in my second street fight.
The other girl grabbed it.
I'd won. Barely. And I'd learned.
I'd joined the Leopards three years ago—six months later, Mika, my Alpha, introduced me to Falcone.
And my job as a feature attraction at the fight club began.
Falcone's got a worse batch than usual tonight. And he saved the best for you.
He always does. I can handle it, Mika.
Tonight I'd face another of the desperate men who owed Falcone more than he could repay.
A fool willing to risk his life for a chance to lift his debt.
The bullwhip. My signature weapon. First time, I'd barely figured out how to snap the thing before I was shoved into the fighting ring. But the crowd had loved it.

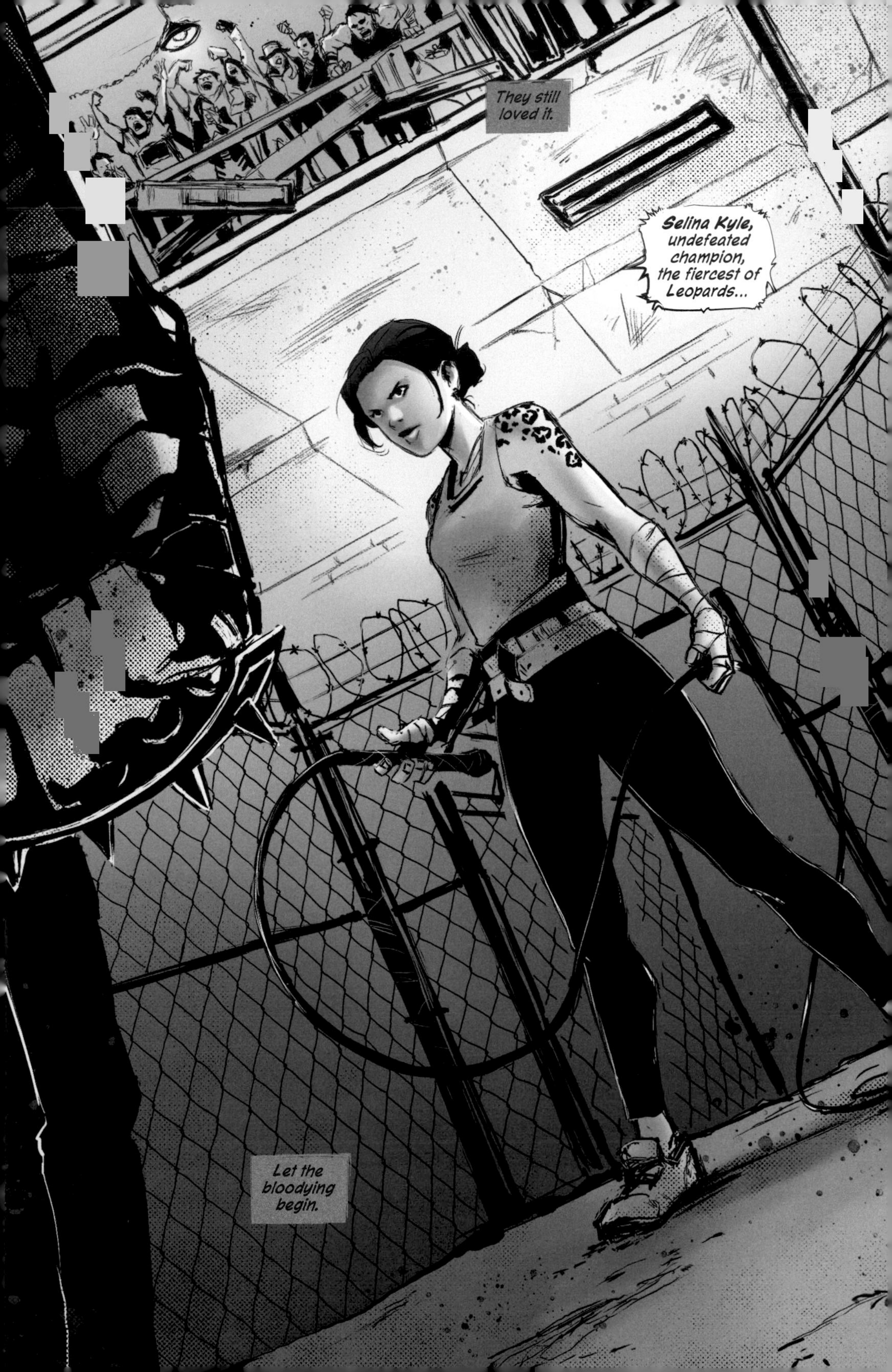
They still loved it.
Selina Kyle, undefeated champion, the fiercest of Leopards...
Let the bloodying begin.

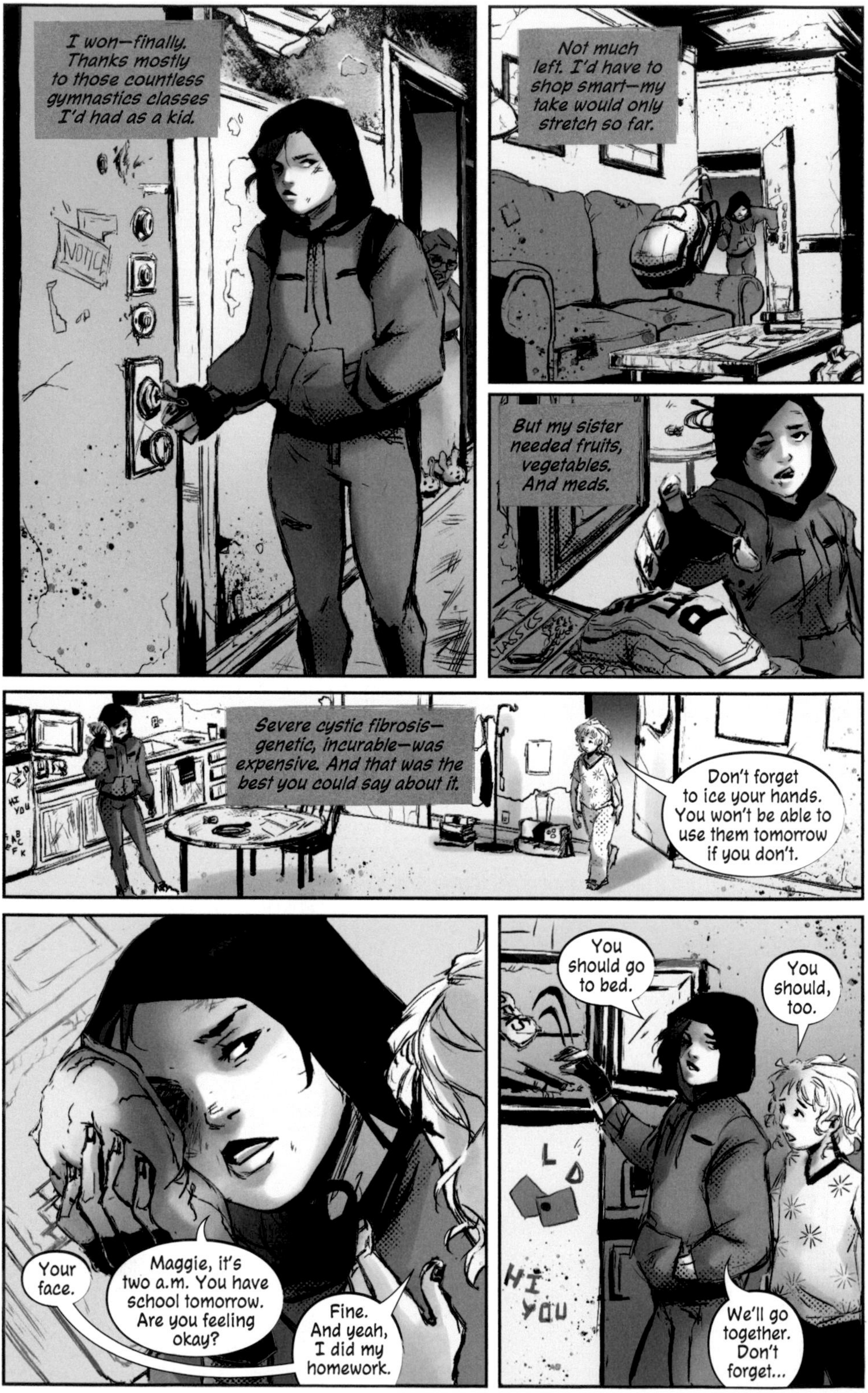
I won—finally. Thanks mostly to those countless gymnastics classes I'd had as a kid.
NOTICE
Not much left. I'd have to shop smart—my take would only stretch so far.
But my sister needed fruits, vegetables. And meds.
Severe cystic fibrosis—genetic, incurable—was expensive. And that was the best you could say about it.
Don't forget to ice your hands. You won't be able to use them tomorrow if you don't.
Your face.
Maggie, it's two a.m. You have school tomorrow. Are you feeling okay?
Fine. And yeah, I did my homework.
You should go to bed.
You should, too.
HI YOU
We'll go together. Don't forget...

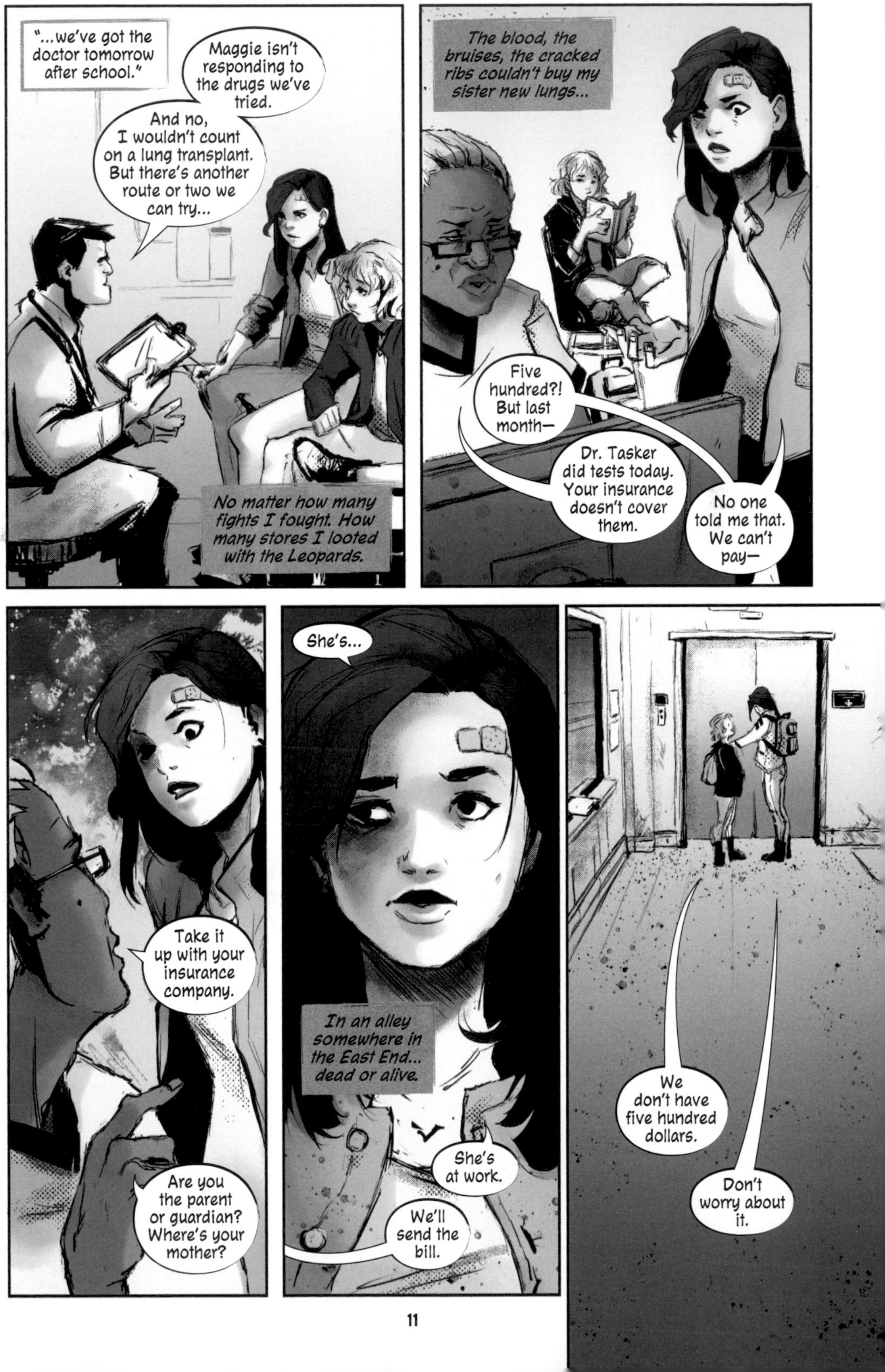
"...we've got the doctor tomorrow after school."
Maggie isn't responding to the drugs we've tried.
And no, I wouldn't count on a lung transplant. But there's another route or two we can try...
No matter how many fights I fought. How many stores I looted with the Leopards.
The blood, the bruises, the cracked ribs couldn't buy my sister new lungs...
Dr. Tasker did tests today. Your insurance doesn't cover them.
Five hundred?! But last month—
No one told me that. We can't pay—
Take it up with your insurance company.
Are you the parent or guardian? Where's your mother?
She's...
In an alley somewhere in the East End... dead or alive.
She's at work.
We'll send the bill.
We don't have five hundred dollars.
Don't worry about it.

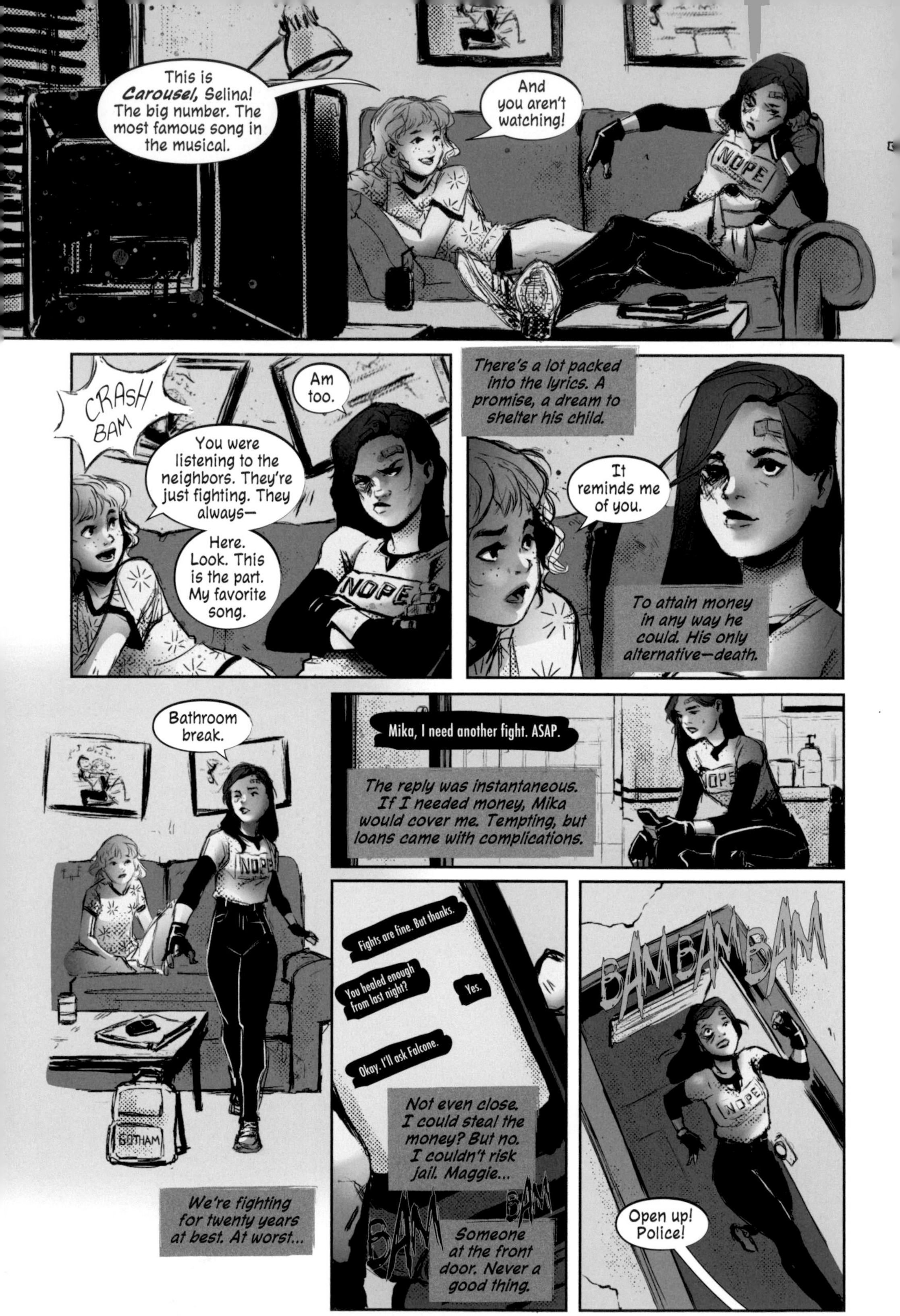
This is Carousel, Selina! The big number. The most famous song in the musical.
And you aren't watching!
NOPE
CRASH BAM
Am too.
You were listening to the neighbors. They're just fighting. They always—
Here. Look. This is the part. My favorite song.
There's a lot packed into the lyrics. A promise, a dream to shelter his child.
It reminds me of you.
To attain money in any way he could. His only alternative—death.
Bathroom break.
We're fighting for twenty years at best. At worst...
GOTHAM
Mika, I need another fight. ASAP.
The reply was instantaneous. If I needed money, Mika would cover me. Tempting, but loans came with complications.
Fights are fine. But thanks.
You healed enough from last night?
Yes.
Okay. I'll ask Falcone.
Not even close. I could steal the money? But no. I couldn't risk jail. Maggie...
BAM
BAM
Someone at the front door. Never a good thing.
BAMBAMBAM
Open up! Police!

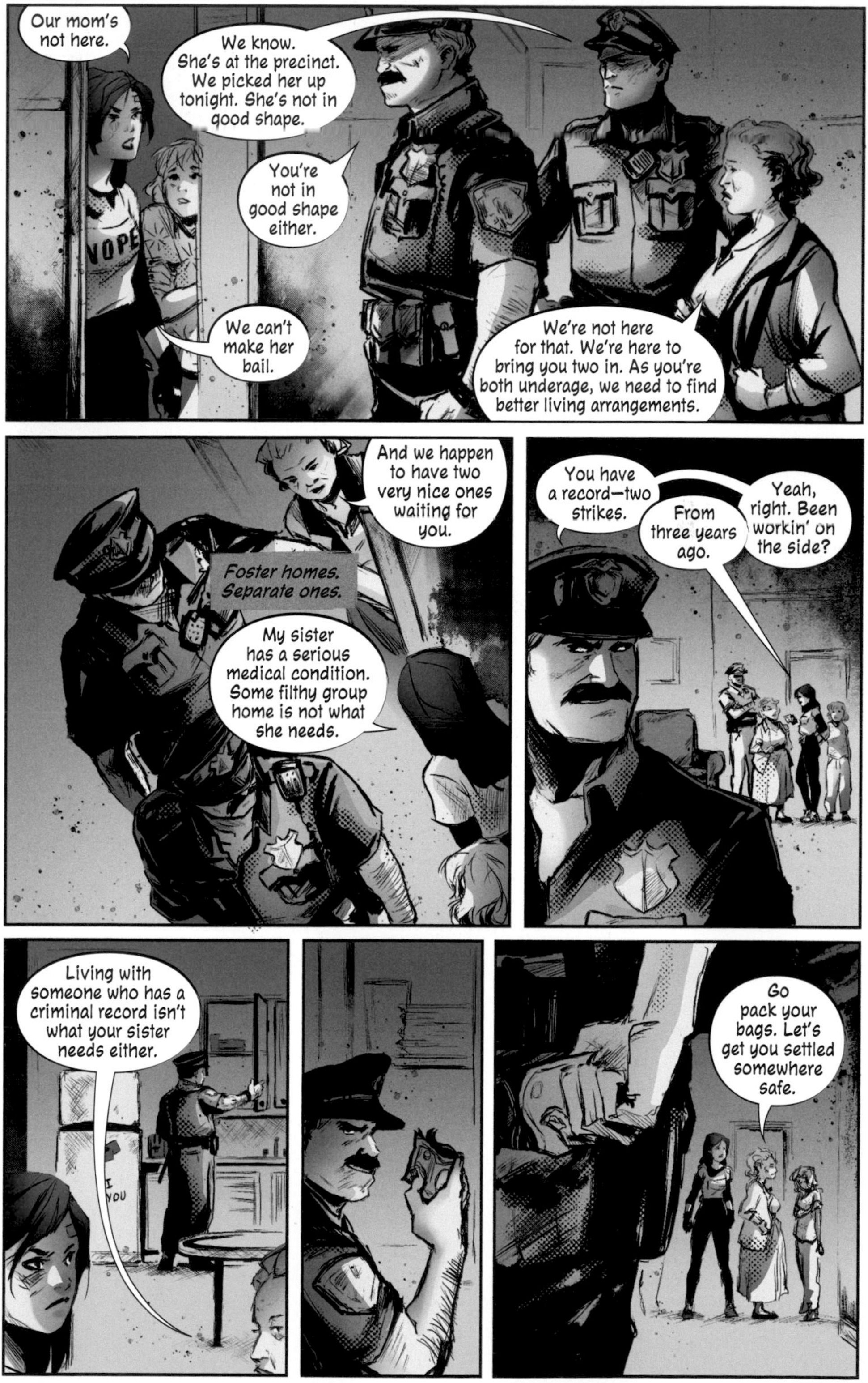

Our mom's not here.
We know. She's at the precinct. We picked her up tonight. She's not in good shape.
You're not in good shape either.
We can't make her bail.
We're not here for that. We're here to bring you two in. As you're both underage, we need to find better living arrangements.
And we happen to have two very nice ones waiting for you.
Foster homes. Separate ones.
My sister has a serious medical condition. Some filthy group home is not what she needs.
You have a record—two strikes.
From three years ago.
Yeah, right. Been workin' on the side?
Living with someone who has a criminal record isn't what your sister needs either.
Go pack your bags. Let's get you settled somewhere safe.

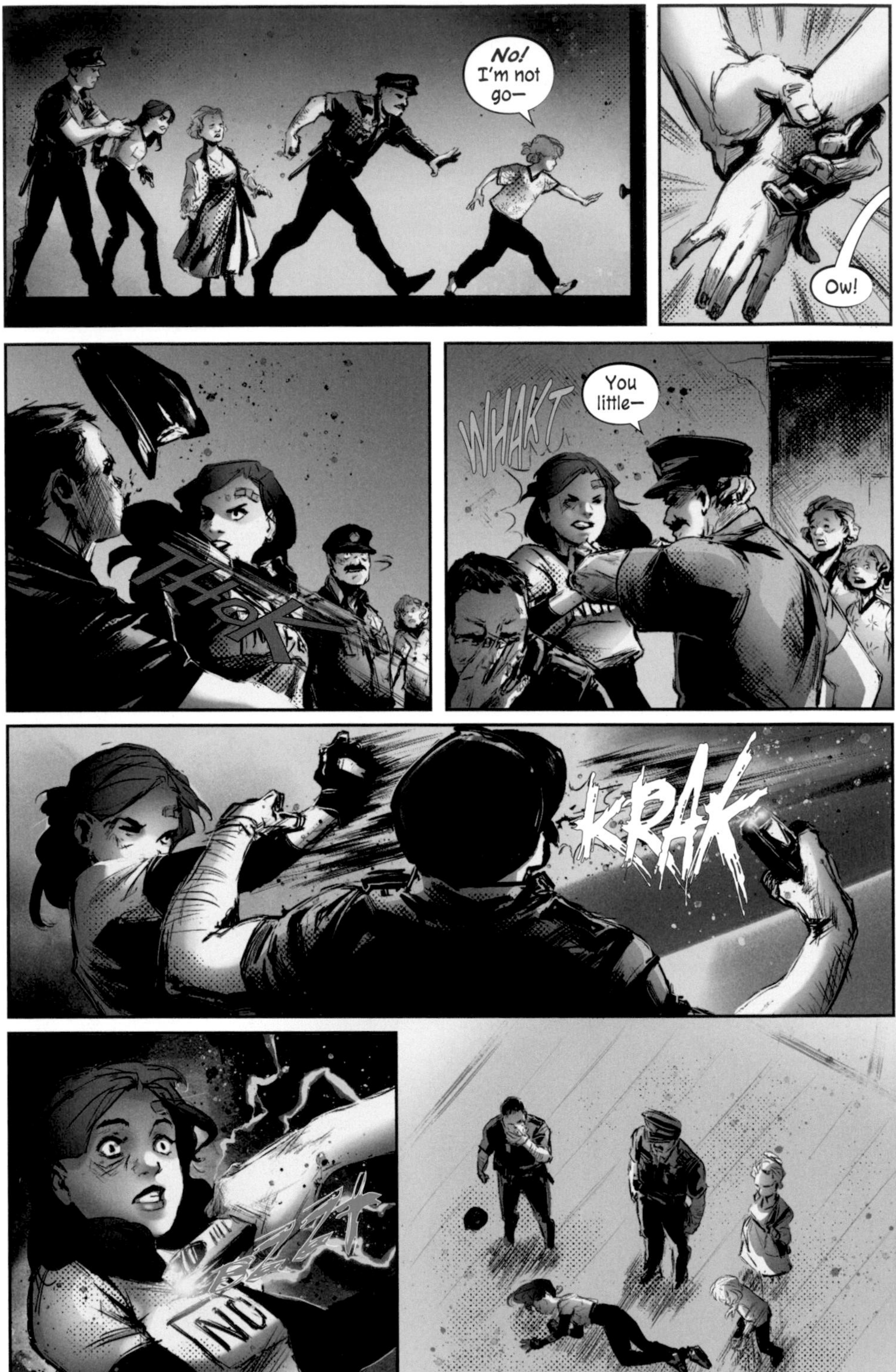
No! I'm not go—
Ow!
THOK
WHAKT
You little—
KRAK

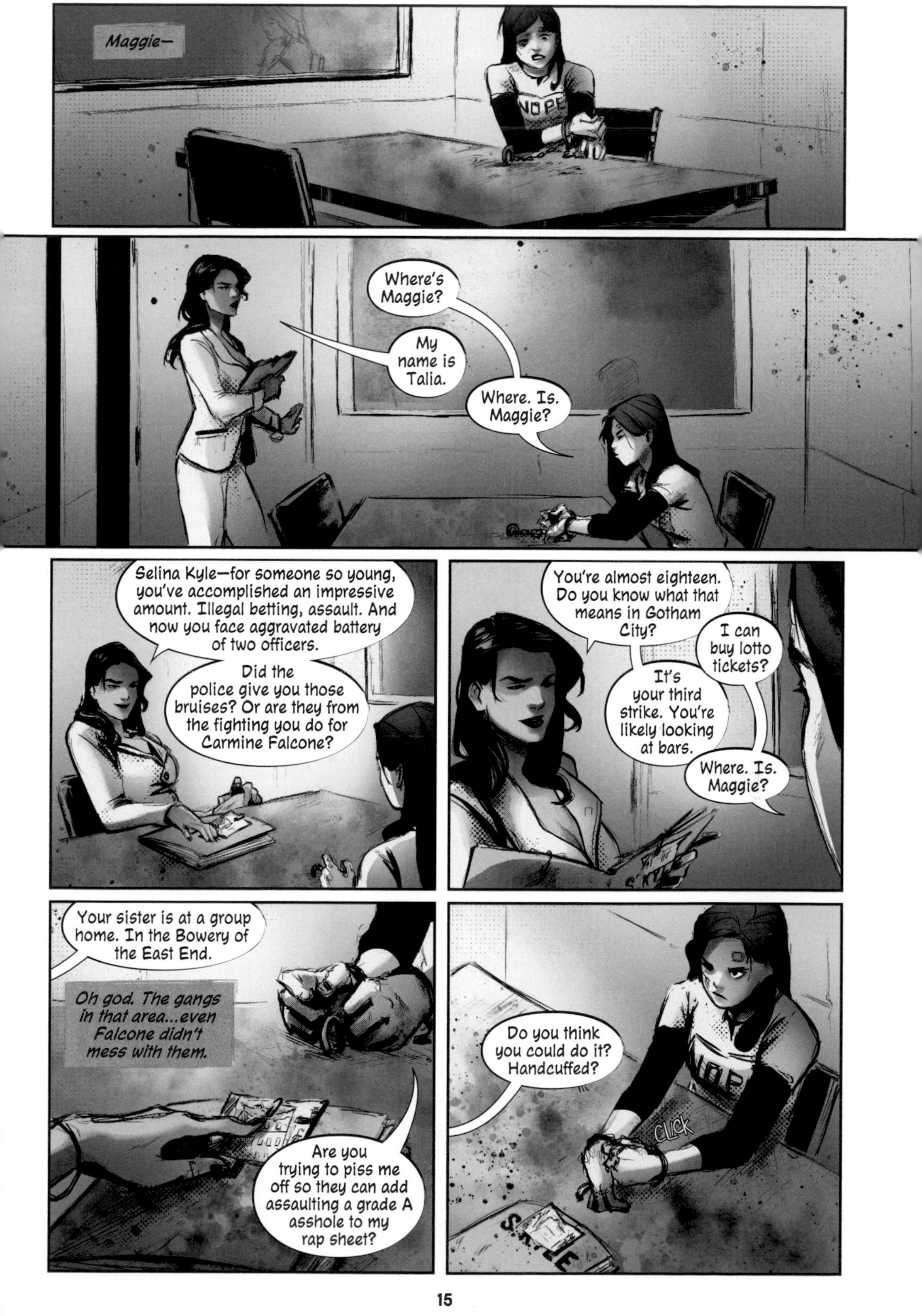
Maggie—
Where's Maggie?
My name is Talia.
Where. Is. Maggie?
Selina Kyle—for someone so young, you've accomplished an impressive amount. Illegal betting, assault. And now you face aggravated battery of two officers.
Did the police give you those bruises? Or are they from the fighting you do for Carmine Falcone?
You're almost eighteen. Do you know what that means in Gotham City?
I can buy lotto tickets?
It's your third strike. You're likely looking at bars.
Where. Is. Maggie?
Your sister is at a group home. In the Bowery of the East End.
Oh god. The gangs in that area...even Falcone didn't mess with them.
Are you trying to piss me off so they can add assaulting a grade A asshole to my rap sheet?
Do you think you could do it? Handcuffed?
CLICK

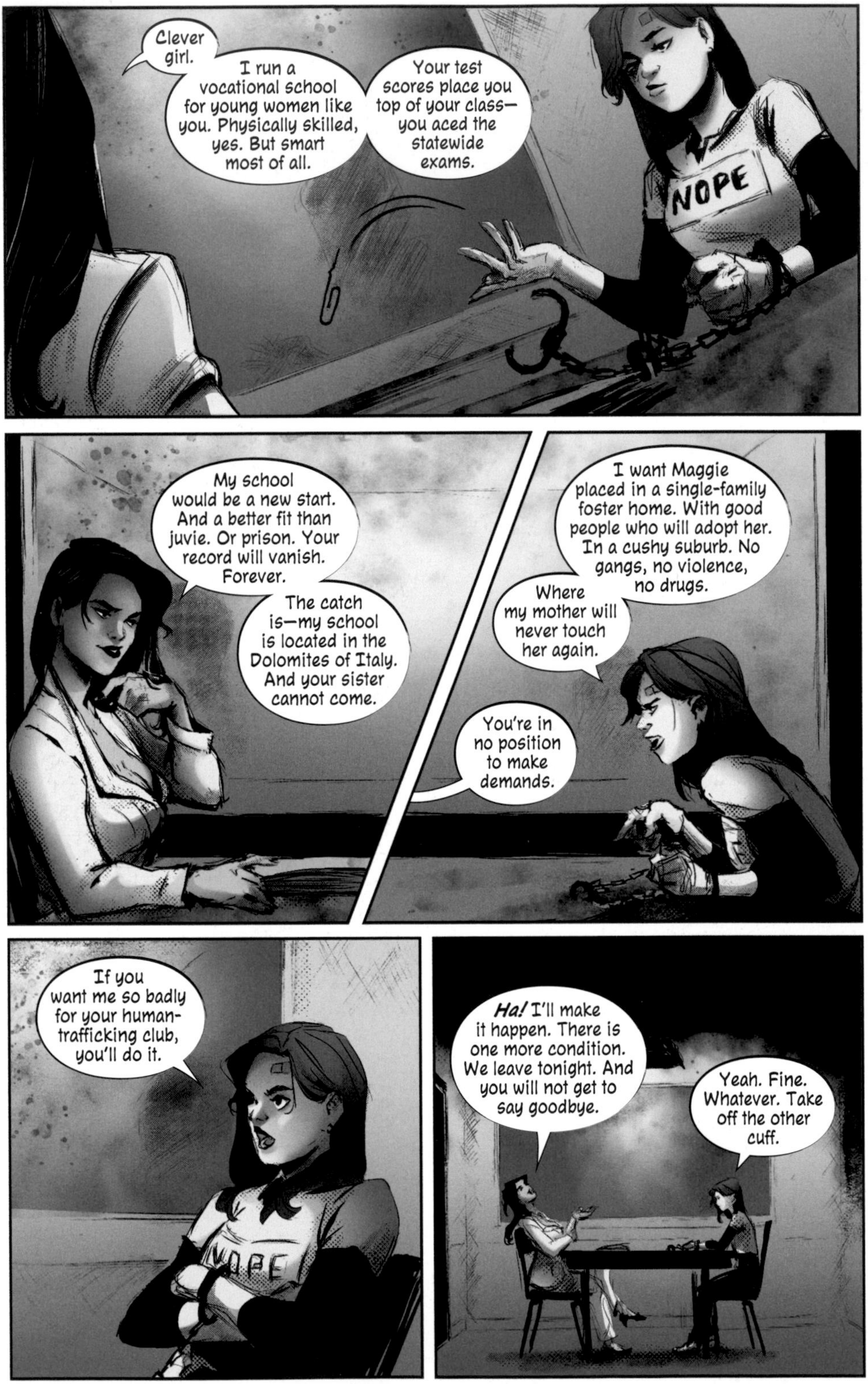
Clever girl.
I run a vocational school for young women like you. Physically skilled, yes. But smart most of all.
Your test scores place you top of your class—you aced the statewide exams.
NOPE
My school would be a new start. And a better fit than juvie. Or prison. Your record will vanish. Forever.
The catch is—my school is located in the Dolomites of Italy. And your sister cannot come.
I want Maggie placed in a single-family foster home. With good people who will adopt her. In a cushy suburb. No gangs, no violence, no drugs.
Where my mother will never touch her again.
You're in no position to make demands.
If you want me so badly for your human-trafficking club, you'll do it.
NOPE
Ha! I'll make it happen. There is one more condition. We leave tonight. And you will not get to say goodbye.
Yeah. Fine. Whatever. Take off the other cuff.

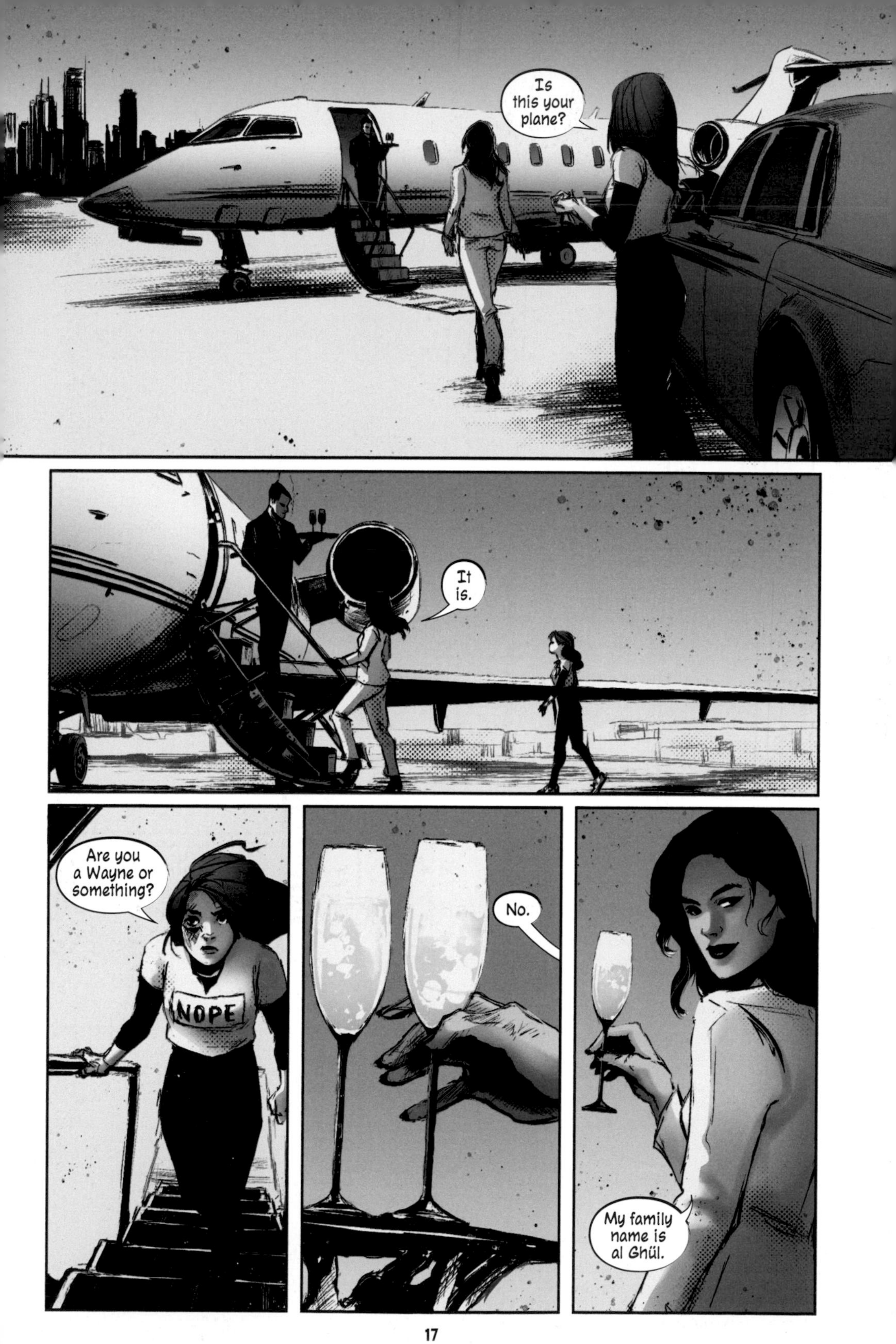

Is this your plane?
It is.
Are you a Wayne or something?
NOPE
No.
My family name is al Ghûl.

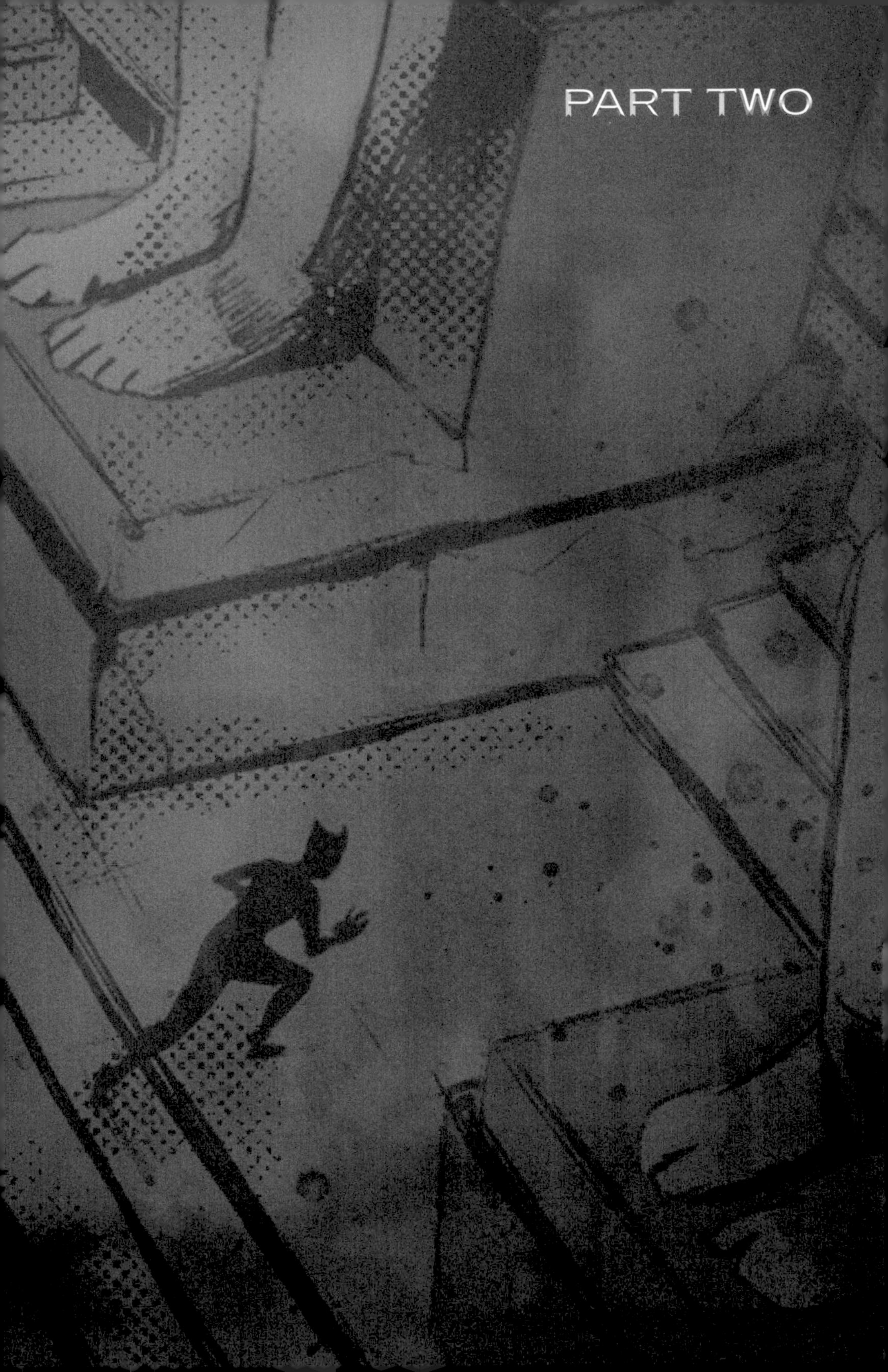
PART TWO

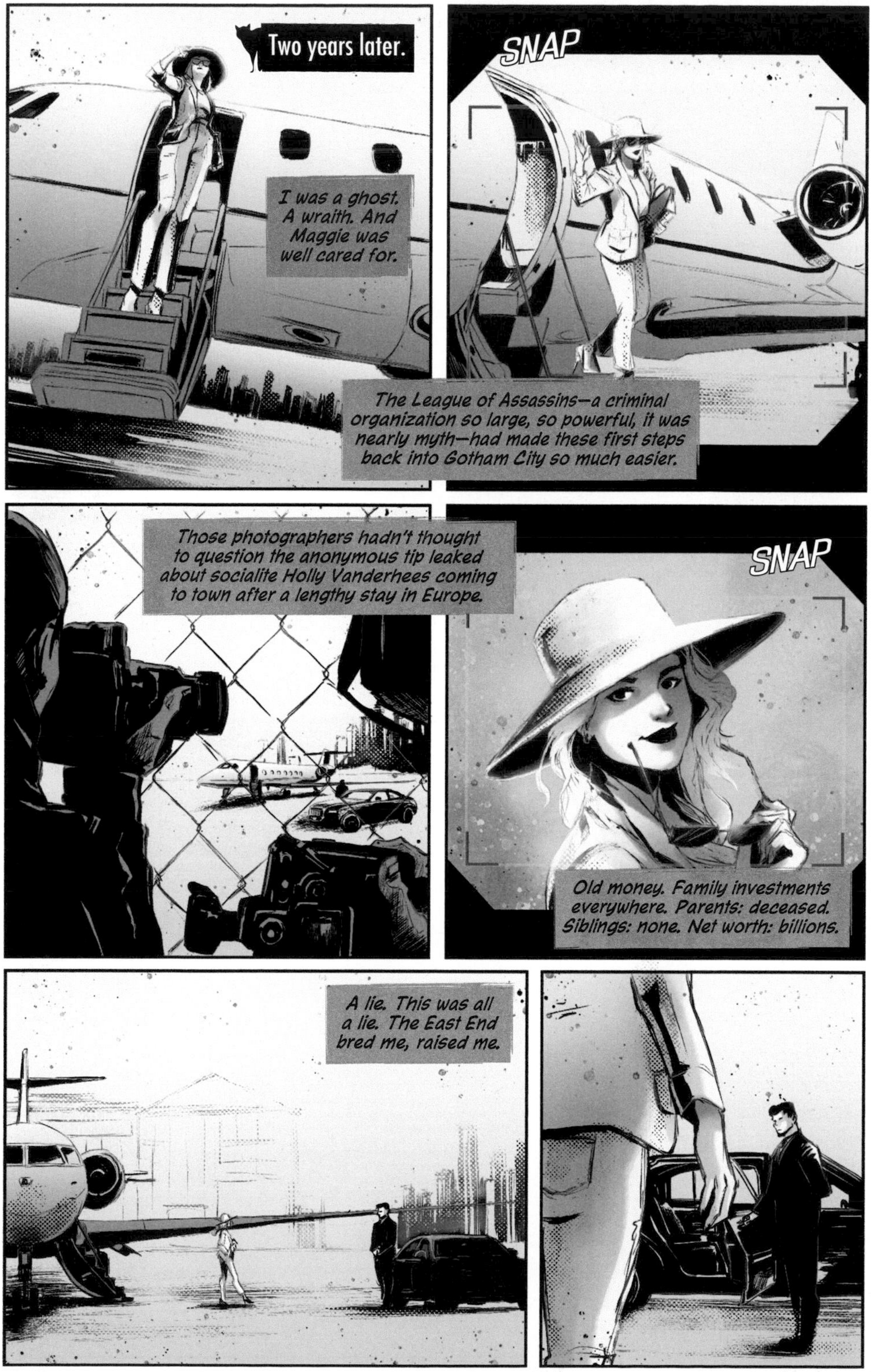
Two years later.
I was a ghost. A wraith. And Maggie was well cared for.
SNAP
The League of Assassins—a criminal organization so large, so powerful, it was nearly myth—had made these first steps back into Gotham City so much easier.
Those photographers hadn't thought to question the anonymous tip leaked about socialite Holly Vanderhees coming to town after a lengthy stay in Europe.
SNAP
Old money. Family investments everywhere. Parents: deceased. Siblings: none. Net worth: billions.
A lie. This was all a lie. The East End bred me, raised me.

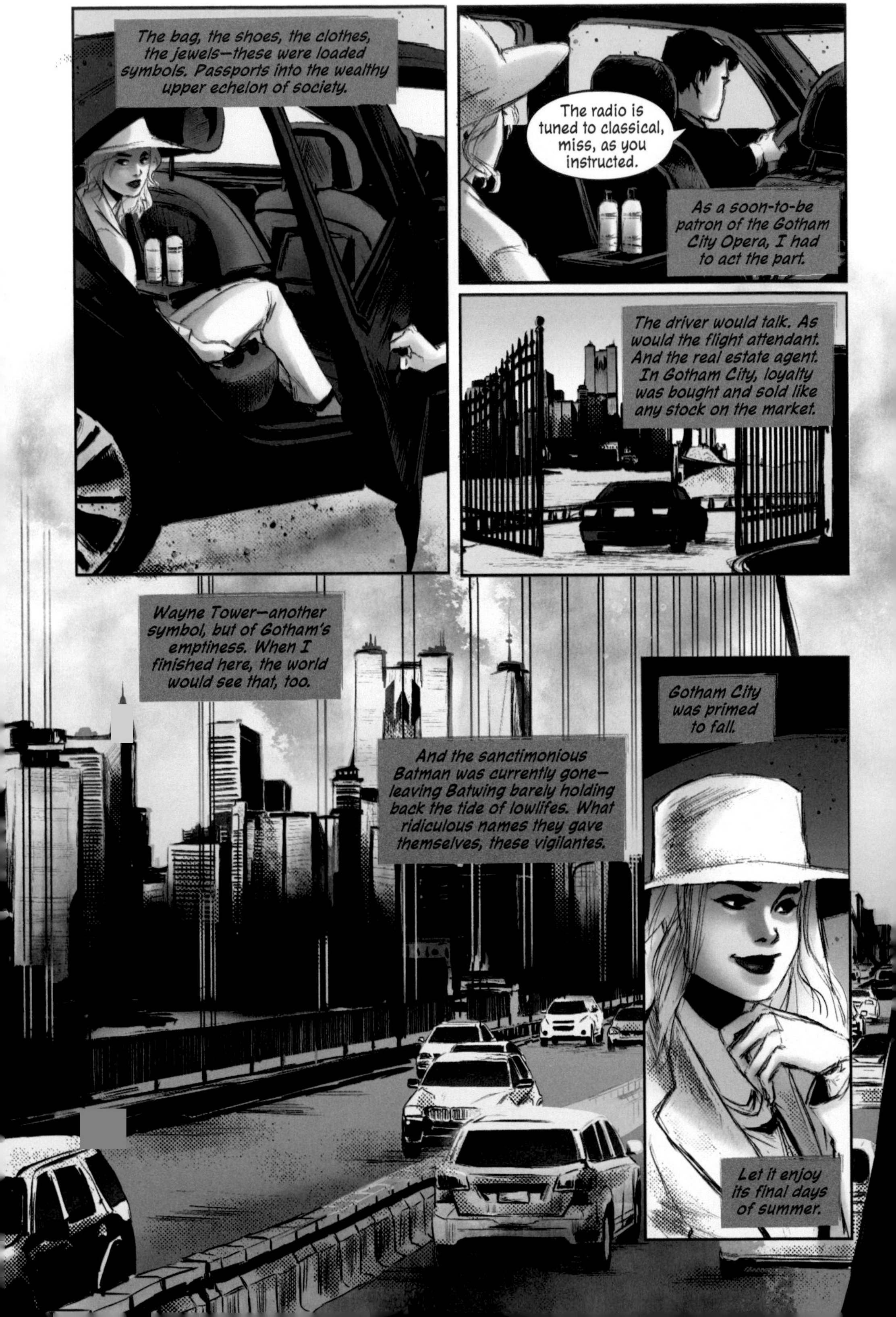
The bag, the shoes, the clothes, the jewels—these were loaded symbols. Passports into the wealthy upper echelon of society.
The radio is tuned to classical, miss, as you instructed.
As a soon-to-be patron of the Gotham City Opera, I had to act the part.
The driver would talk. As would the flight attendant. And the real estate agent. In Gotham City, loyalty was bought and sold like any stock on the market.
Wayne Tower—another symbol, but of Gotham's emptiness. When I finished here, the world would see that, too.
And the sanctimonious Batman was currently gone—leaving Batwing barely holding back the tide of lowlifes. What ridiculous names they gave themselves, these vigilantes.
Gotham City was primed to fall.
Let it enjoy its final days of summer.

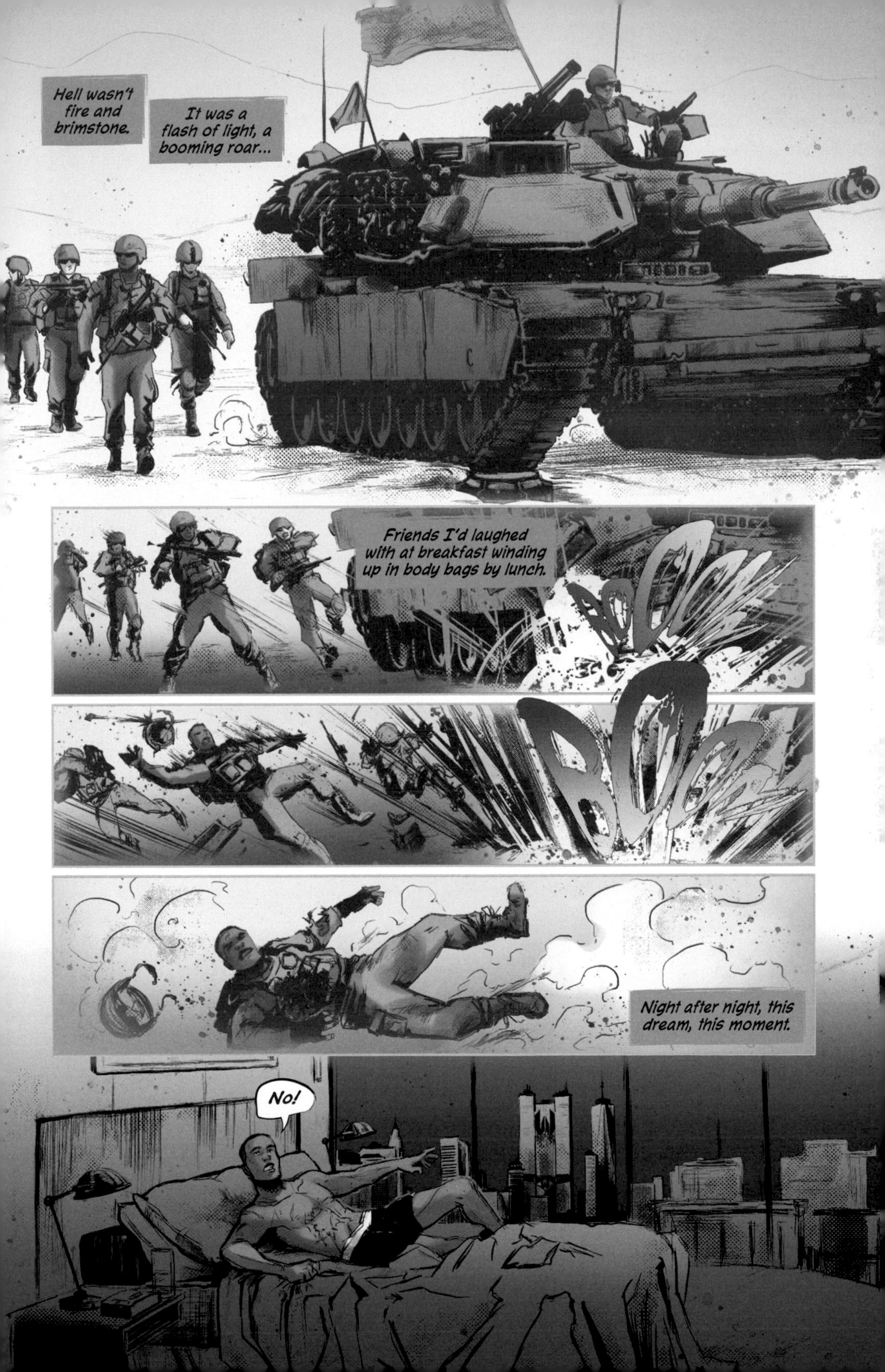
Hell wasn't fire and brimstone.
It was a flash of light, a booming roar...
Friends I'd laughed with at breakfast winding up in body bags by lunch.
BOOM
Night after night, this dream, this moment.
No!

A year had passed since I returned to Gotham City, and I was still crawling back toward who I'd been before. Whoever that person had been.

At least I still had my sense of humor. Sort of.

Bruce Wayne didn't have one. Or hadn't revealed one in the months I'd been training with him.

My dad's idea. After the incident.

My first full-blown panic attack.

In the middle of my family's annual party. As if I were again in that blood-soaked desert.

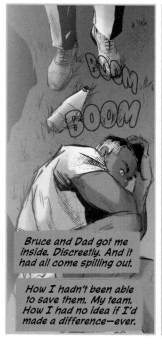

Bruce and Dad got me inside. Discreetly. And it had all come spilling out.

How I hadn't been able to save them. My team. How I had no idea if I'd made a difference—ever.

The subsequent diagnosis—post-traumatic stress disorder...

...triggered by the crack and boom of the fireworks, by the flashing lights. I'd gotten professional help...

...but Dad's suggested treatment had been just between us.

If you want to make a difference, perhaps there's something you can do about it.

A visit to Wayne Manor. To a secret chamber beneath it.

We bonded over the tech. I'm good at tech.

22

No bat-shaped signal lit up the night. No sirens. Nothing to call me out of bed.

Nothing to do when sleep would no longer...

Someone was there.

Then I remembered the other penthouse had been leased by some socialite—Holly Vanderhees. I should have bought it just to keep it empty.

A stupid mistake. A rookie mistake. I'd have to be careful now.

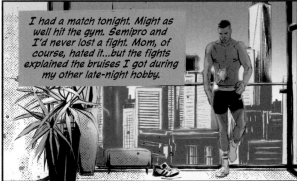

I had a match tonight. Might as well hit the gym. Semipro and I'd never lost a fight. Mom, of course, hated it...but the fights explained the bruises I got during my other late-night hobby.

The TV blared a constant barrage of horrors from Gotham's East End. The despair, the crime, the ugliness of it.

Reminding me the battle hadn't ended.

My body was a tool. A weapon. The same as any I wielded overseas.

Another day. I'd make it count. For the friends who hadn't made it home, for the people living in this city...I'd make it count. As Batwing.

GOTHAM MUSEUM ANTIQUITIES

My helmet's scanner gave me a constant stream of information, tailored to my specifics.

I'd modified the standard Death Mask helmet the League gave their acolytes.

It seemed...necessary. It began with the taunts inspired by my Leopard's spots.

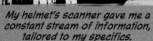

Little kitten! Kitty-cat! Where's your balance? Where's your nine lives now?

One of my earliest lessons. Control is vital. Control is everything. So I took control. Of the narrative.

After that, the taunting stopped.

Of the hated nickname.

Especially when I settled things—most effectively—with Tigress, one of the League's most valued assassins.

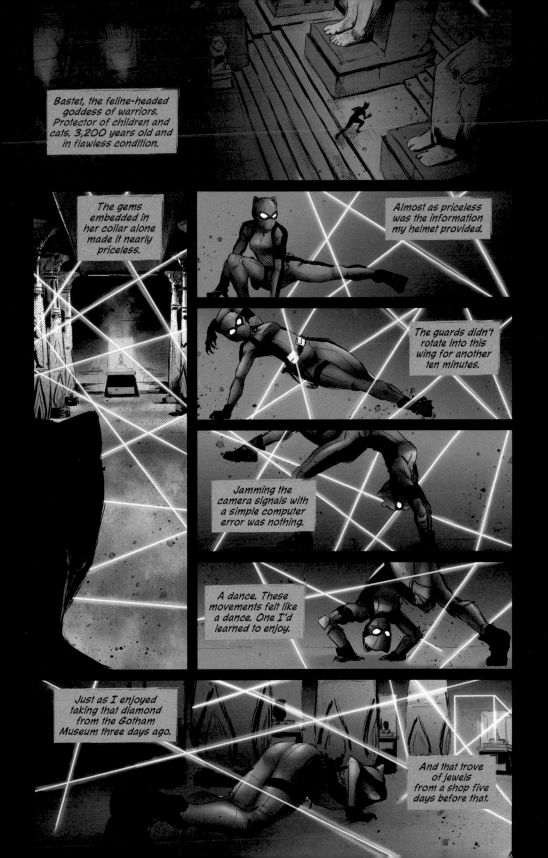

Bastet, the feline-headed goddess of warriors. Protector of children and cats. 3,200 years old and in flawless condition.

The gems embedded in her collar alone made it nearly priceless.

Almost as priceless was the information my helmet provided.

The guards didn't rotate into this wing for another ten minutes.

Jamming the camera signals with a simple computer error was nothing.

A dance. These movements felt like a dance. One I'd learned to enjoy.

Just as I enjoyed taking that diamond from the Gotham Museum three days ago.

And that trove of jewels from a shop five days before that.

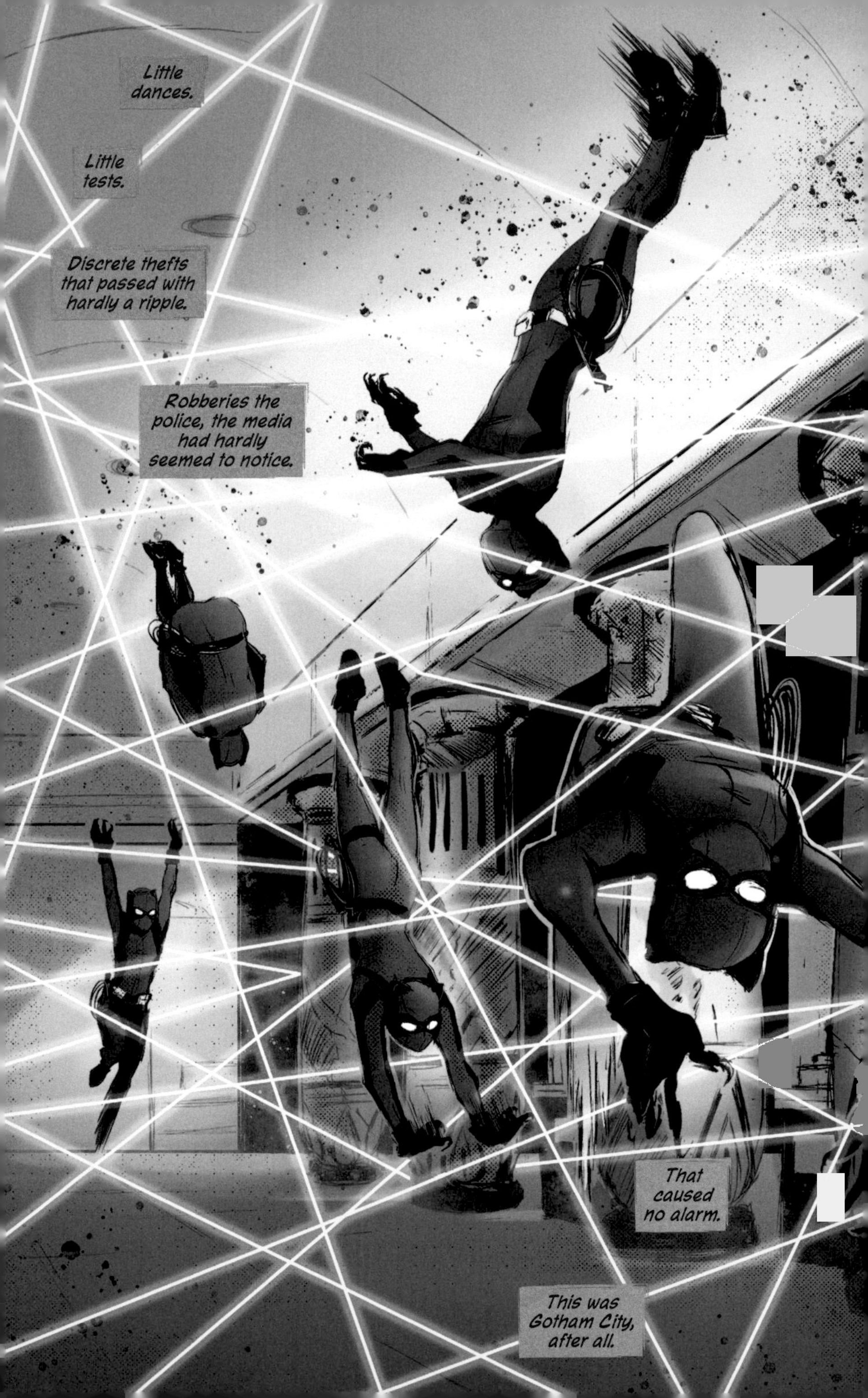
Little dances.
Little tests.
Discrete thefts that passed with hardly a ripple.
Robberies the police, the media had hardly seemed to notice.
That caused no alarm.
This was Gotham City, after all.

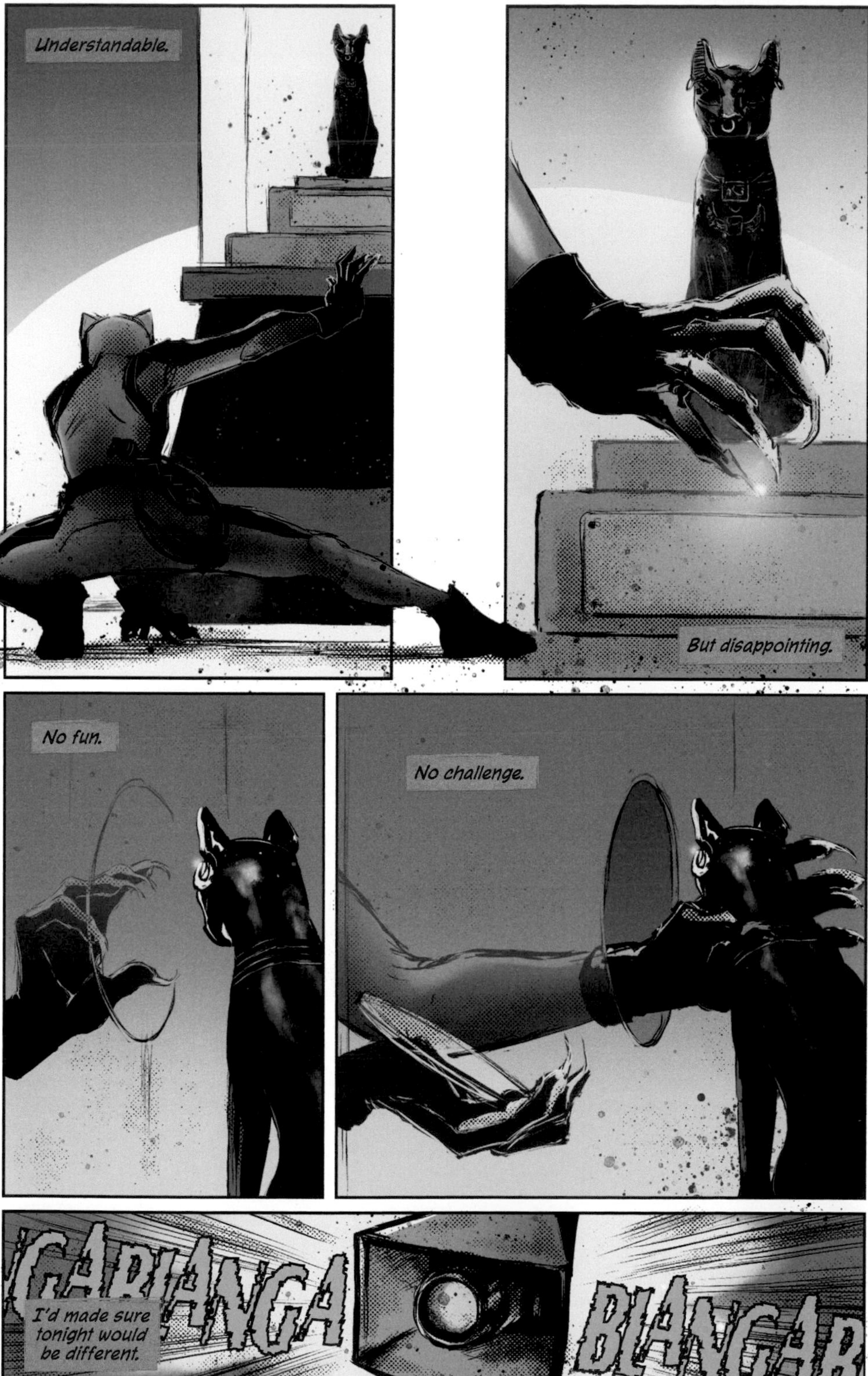
Understandable.
But disappointing.
No fun.
No challenge.
GARLANGA
I'd made sure tonight would be different.
BLANGAR

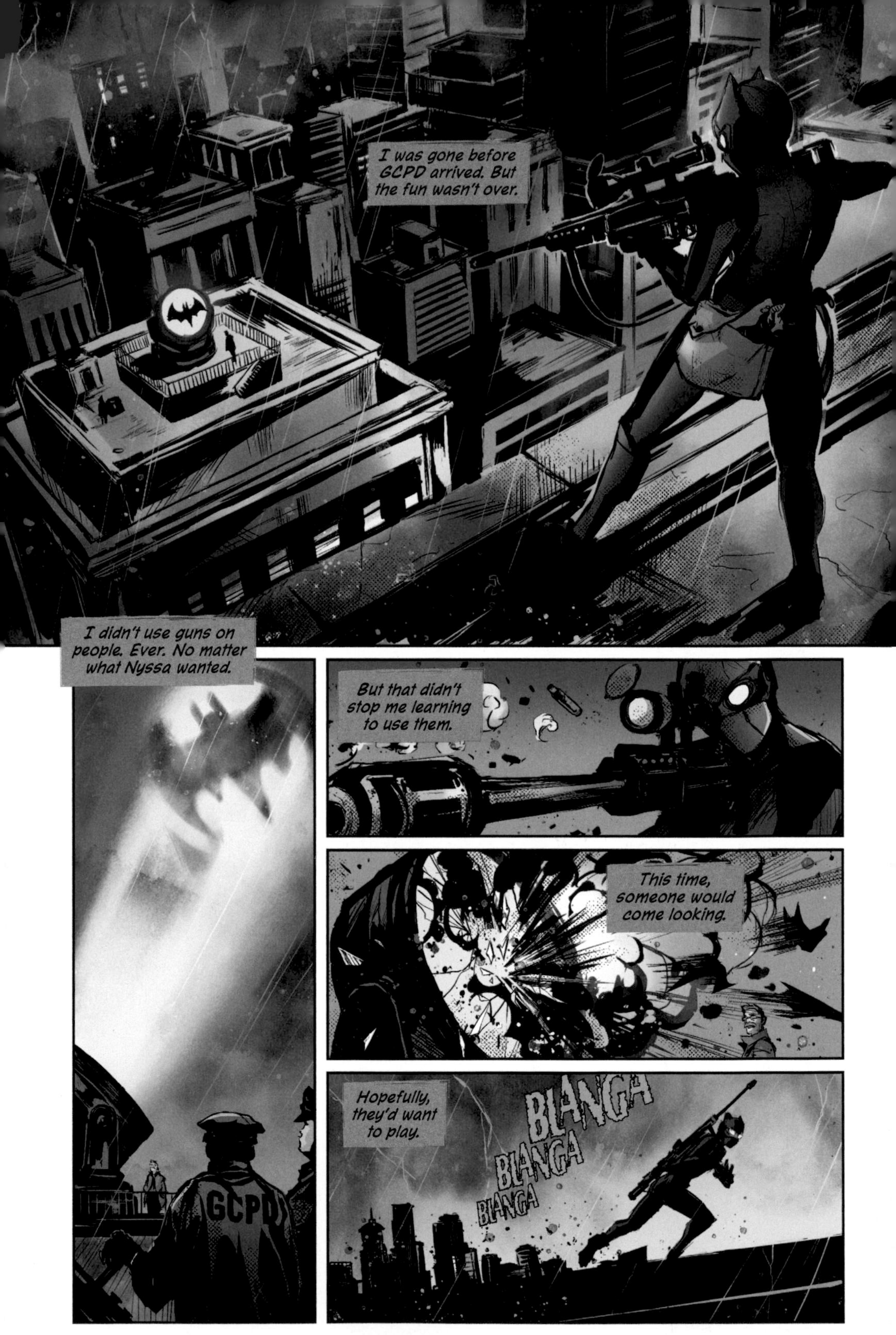

I was gone before GCPD arrived. But the fun wasn't over.
I didn't use guns on people. Ever. No matter what Nyssa wanted.
GCPD
But that didn't stop me learning to use them.
This time, someone would come looking.
Hopefully, they'd want to play.
BLANGA
BLANGA
BLANGA

Hey, Alfred. What's up? Is Bruce all right?

Yes. His mission is going well.

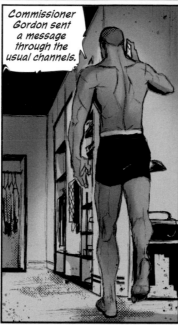

Commissioner Gordon sent a message through the usual channels.

He says he needs to speak to one of the Bats flapping around this city. He claimed it's urgent.

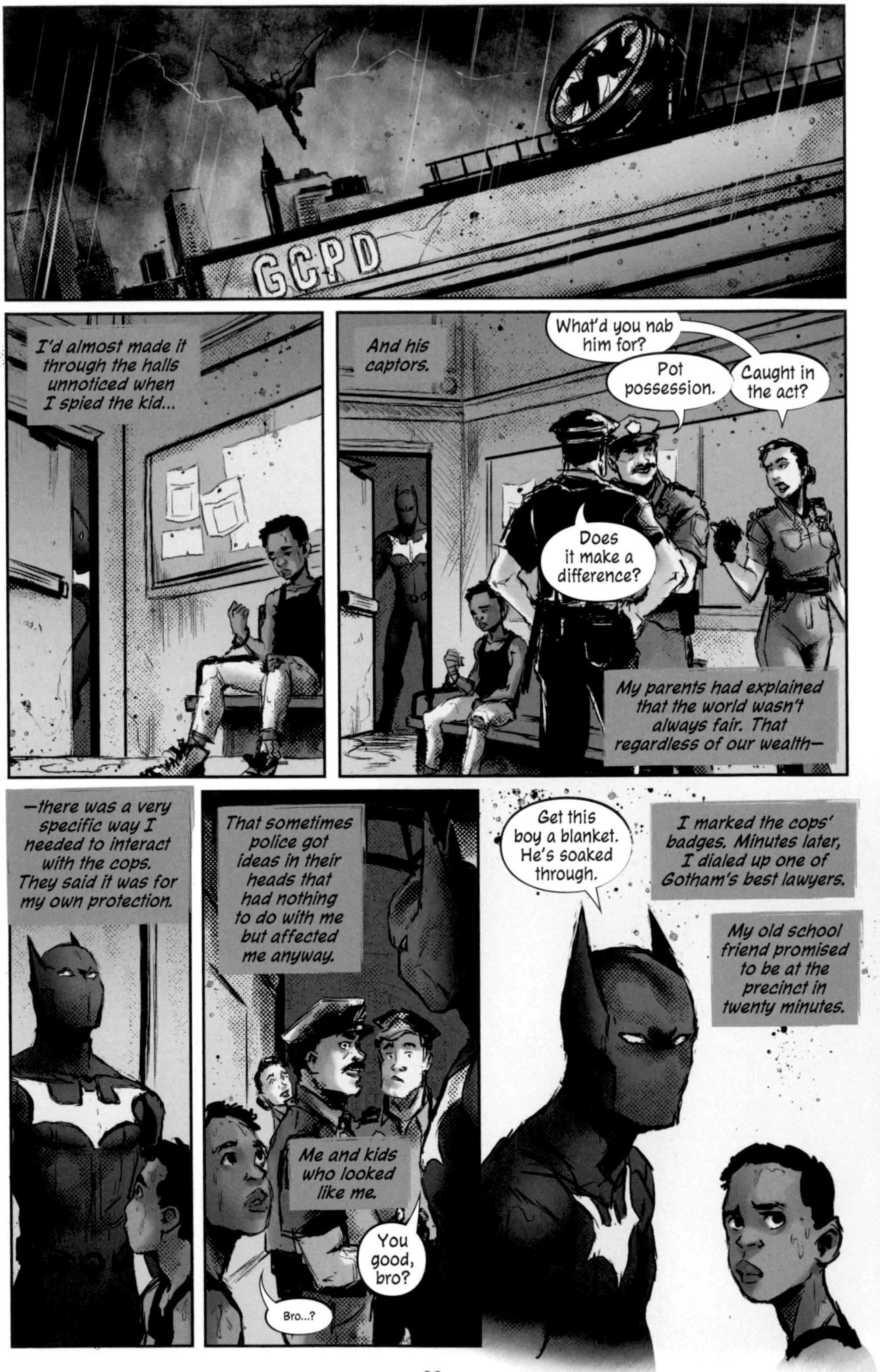
GCPD
I'd almost made it through the halls unnoticed when I spied the kid...
And his captors.
What'd you nab him for?
Pot possession.
Caught in the act?
Does it make a difference?
My parents had explained that the world wasn't always fair. That regardless of our wealth—
—there was a very specific way I needed to interact with the cops. They said it was for my own protection.
That sometimes police got ideas in their heads that had nothing to do with me but affected me anyway.
Me and kids who looked like me.
You good, bro?
Bro...?
Get this boy a blanket. He's soaked through.
I marked the cops' badges. Minutes later, I dialed up one of Gotham's best lawyers.
My old school friend promised to be at the precinct in twenty minutes.

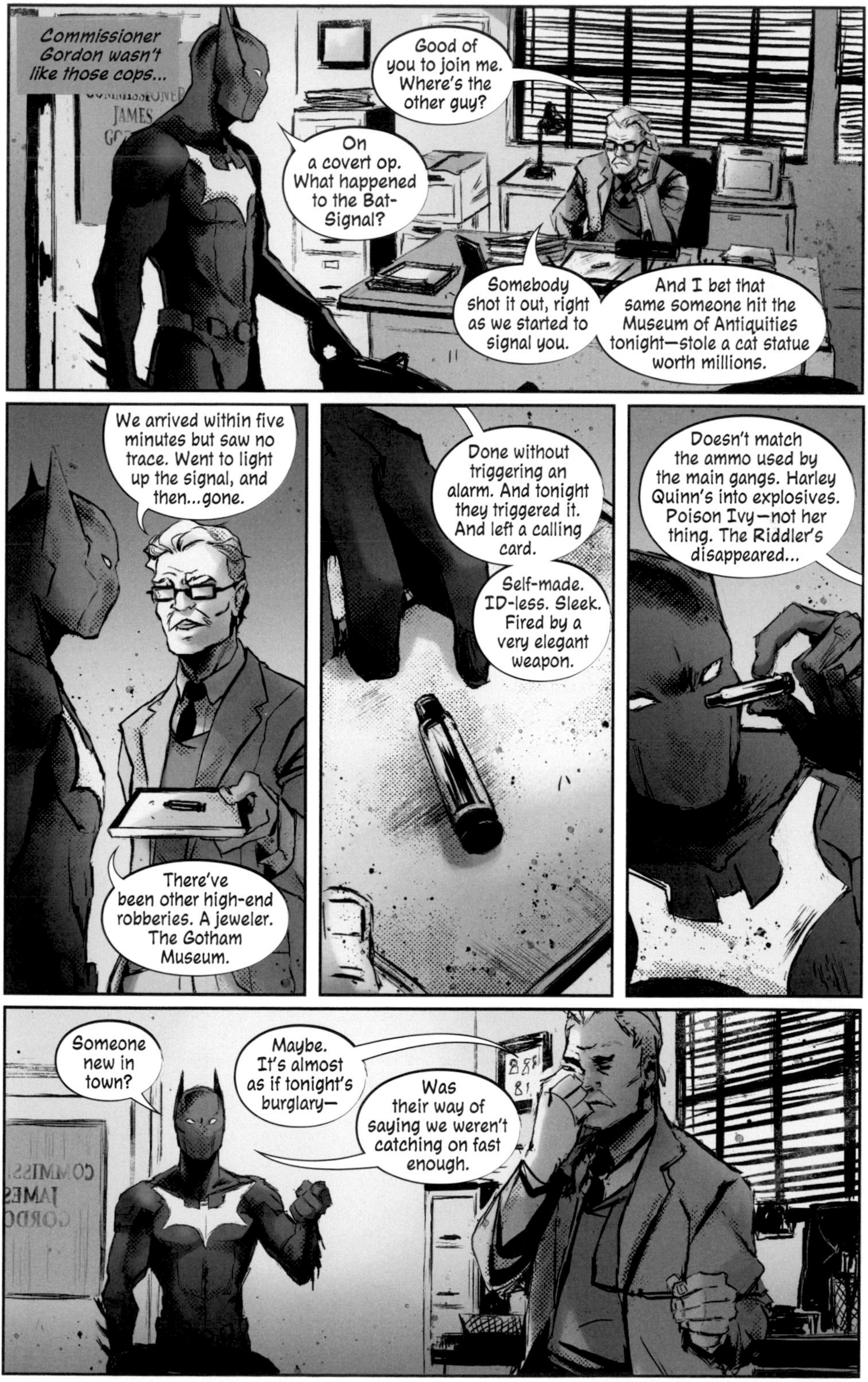
Commissioner Gordon wasn't like those cops...
COMMISSIONER JAMES GO
Good of you to join me. Where's the other guy?
On a covert op. What happened to the Bat-Signal?
Somebody shot it out, right as we started to signal you.
And I bet that same someone hit the Museum of Antiquities tonight—stole a cat statue worth millions.
We arrived within five minutes but saw no trace. Went to light up the signal, and then...gone.
There've been other high-end robberies. A jeweler. The Gotham Museum.
Done without triggering an alarm. And tonight they triggered it. And left a calling card.
Self-made. ID-less. Sleek. Fired by a very elegant weapon.
Doesn't match the ammo used by the main gangs. Harley Quinn's into explosives. Poison Ivy—not her thing. The Riddler's disappeared...
Someone new in town?
Maybe. It's almost as if tonight's burglary—
Was their way of saying we weren't catching on fast enough.

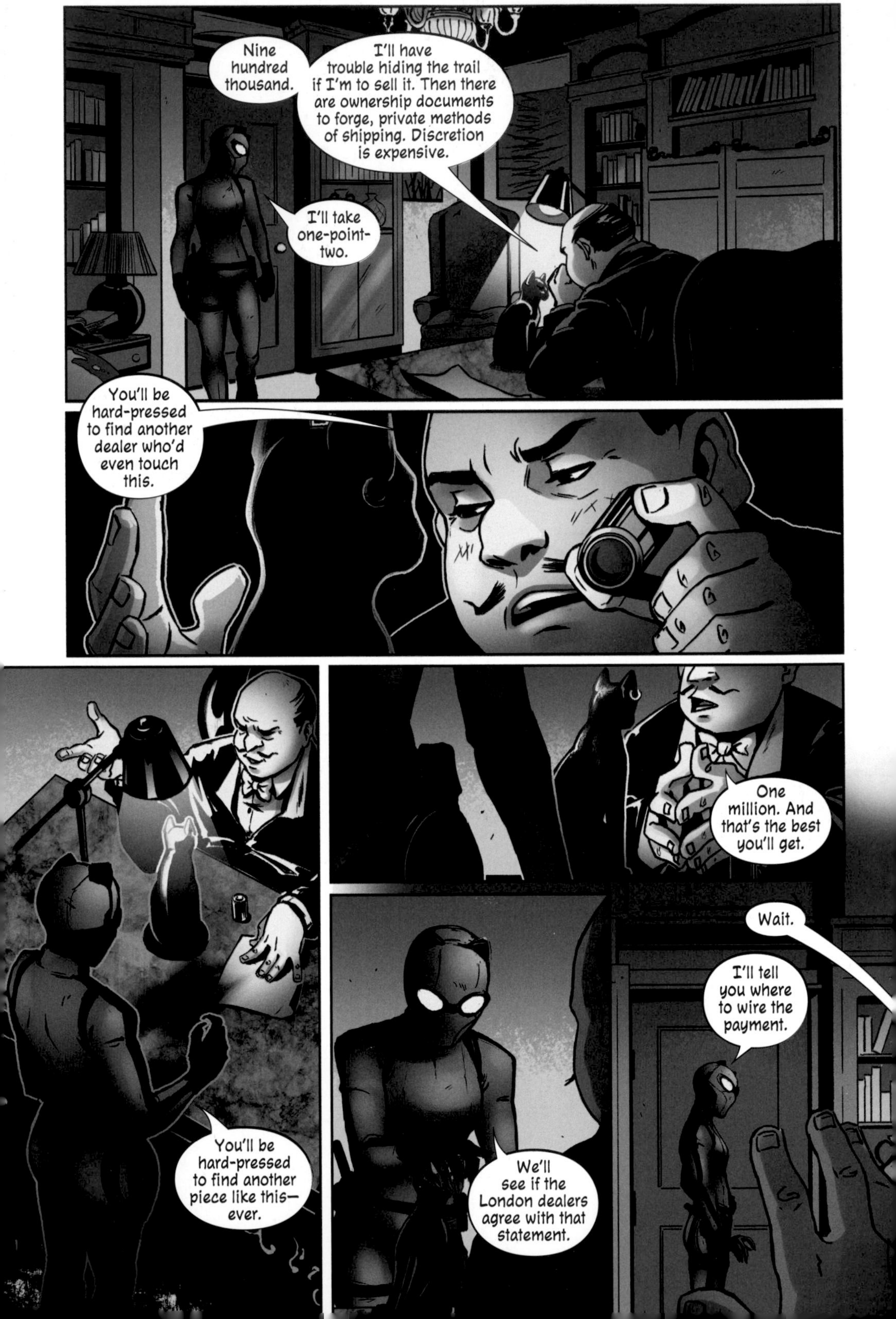
Nine hundred thousand.
I'll have trouble hiding the trail if I'm to sell it. Then there are ownership documents to forge, private methods of shipping. Discretion is expensive.
I'll take one-point-two.
You'll be hard-pressed to find another dealer who'd even touch this.
You'll be hard-pressed to find another piece like this—ever.
One million. And that's the best you'll get.
We'll see if the London dealers agree with that statement.
Wait.
I'll tell you where to wire the payment.

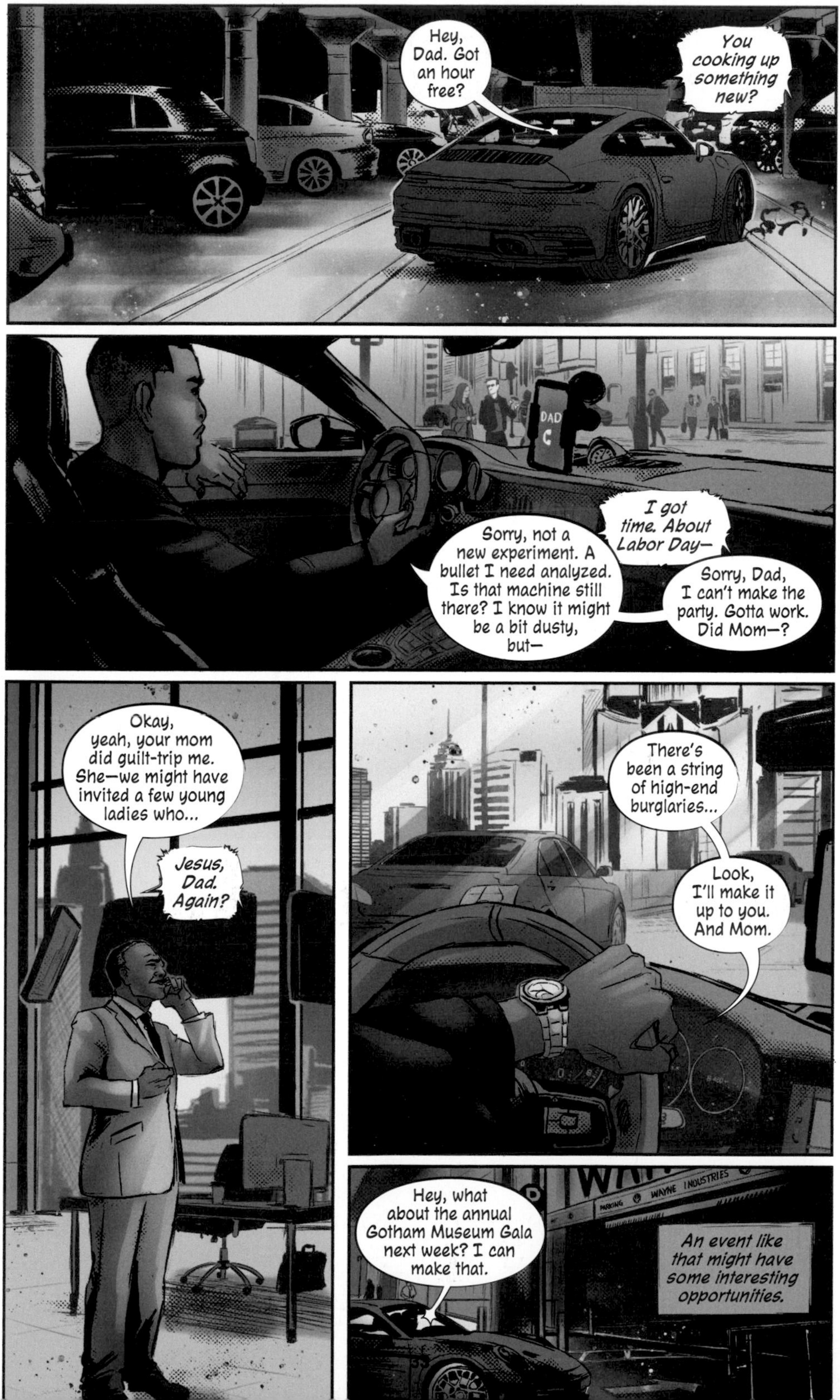
Hey, Dad. Got an hour free?
You cooking up something new?
DAD
Sorry, not a new experiment. A bullet I need analyzed. Is that machine still there? I know it might be a bit dusty, but—
I got time. About Labor Day—
Sorry, Dad, I can't make the party. Gotta work. Did Mom—?
Okay, yeah, your mom did guilt-trip me. She—we might have invited a few young ladies who...
Jesus, Dad. Again?
There's been a string of high-end burglaries...
Look, I'll make it up to you. And Mom.
WAYNE INDUSTRIES
PARKING
Hey, what about the annual Gotham Museum Gala next week? I can make that.
An event like that might have some interesting opportunities.

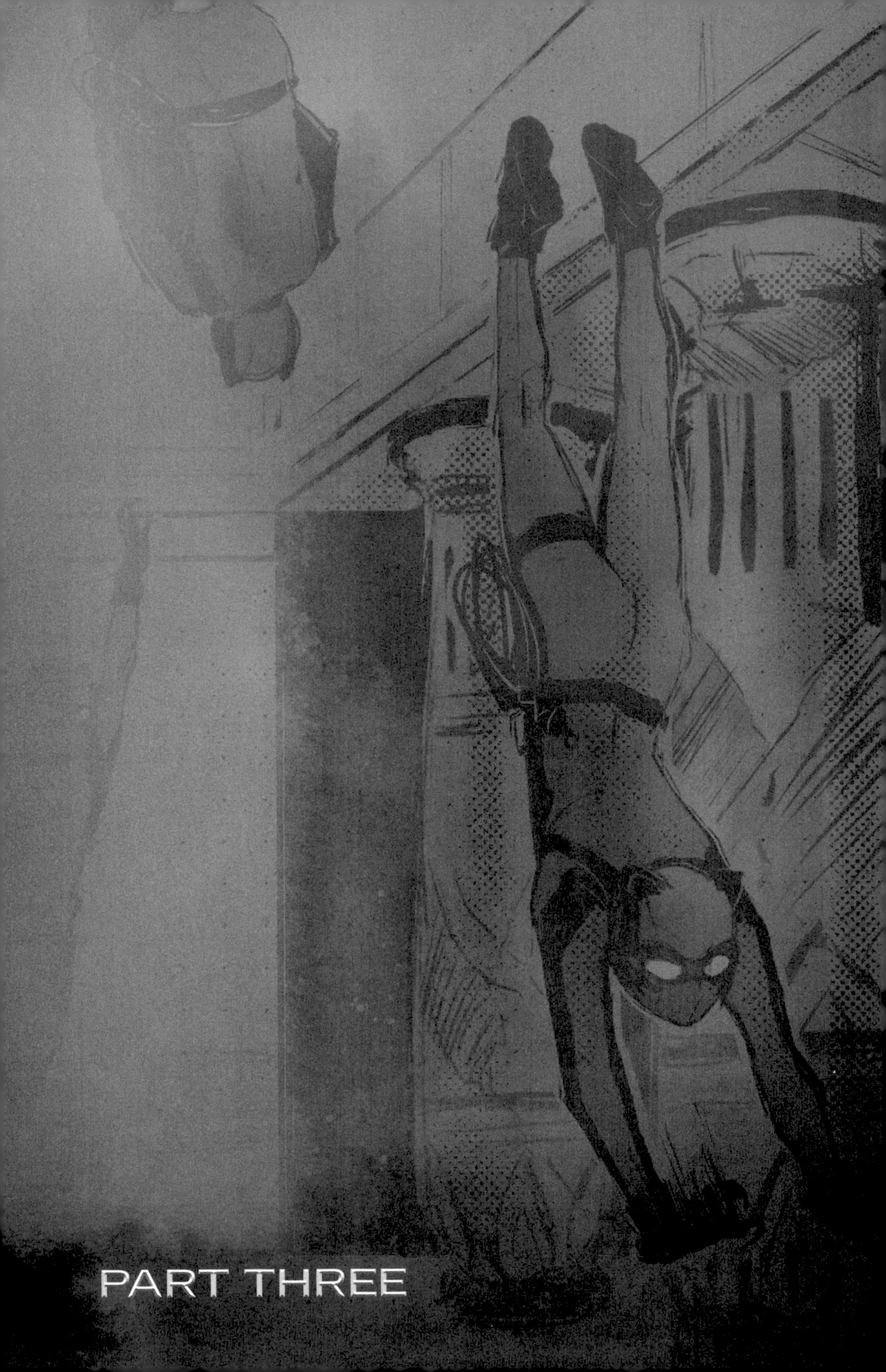

PART THREE

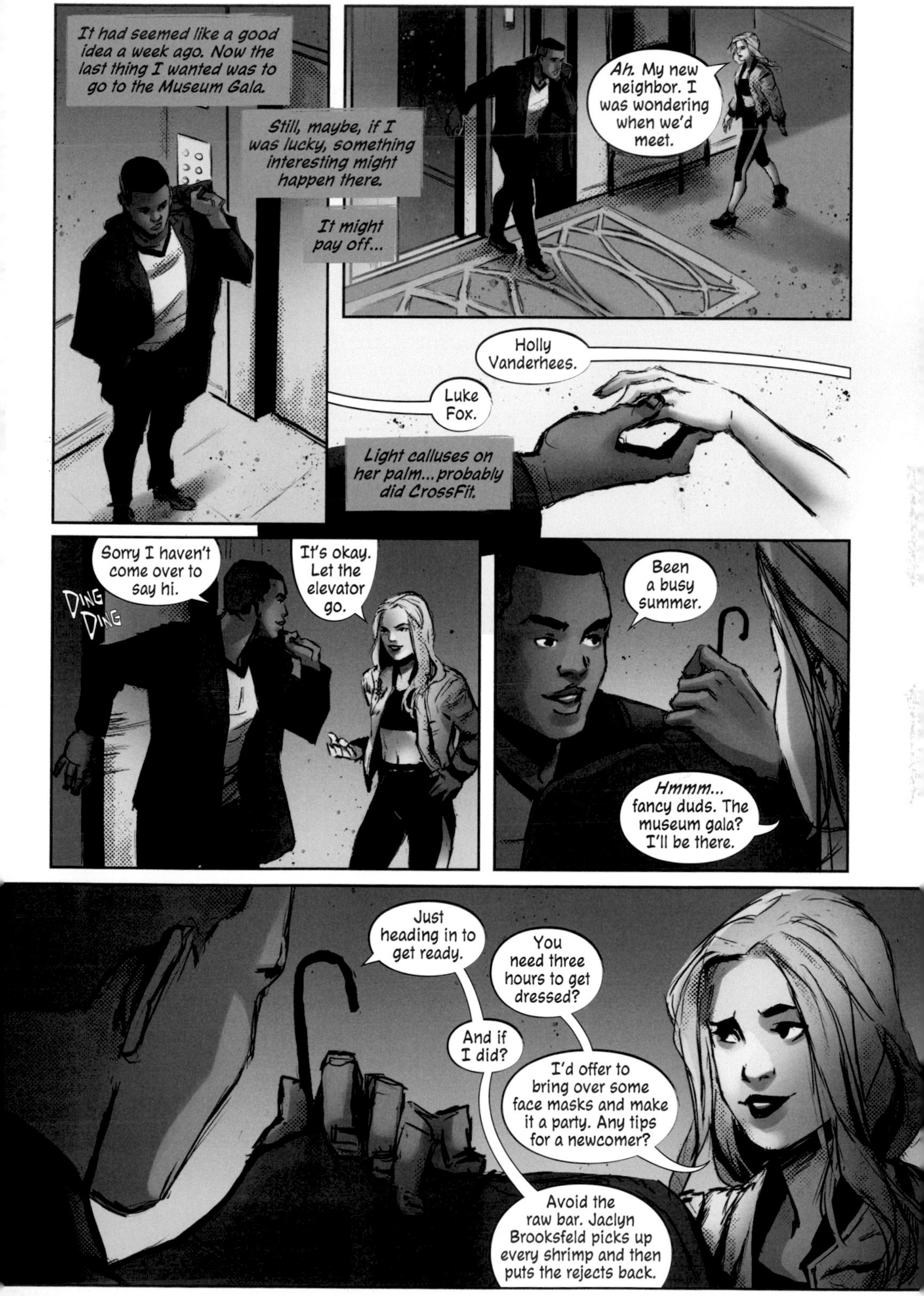
It had seemed like a good idea a week ago. Now the last thing I wanted was to go to the Museum Gala.
Still, maybe, if I was lucky, something interesting might happen there.
It might pay off...
Ah. My new neighbor. I was wondering when we'd meet.
Holly Vanderhees.
Luke Fox.
Light calluses on her palm...probably did CrossFit.
DING DING
Sorry I haven't come over to say hi.
It's okay. Let the elevator go.
Been a busy summer.
Hmmm... fancy duds. The museum gala? I'll be there.
Just heading in to get ready.
You need three hours to get dressed?
And if I did?
I'd offer to bring over some face masks and make it a party. Any tips for a newcomer?
Avoid the raw bar. Jaclyn Brooksfeld picks up every shrimp and then puts the rejects back.

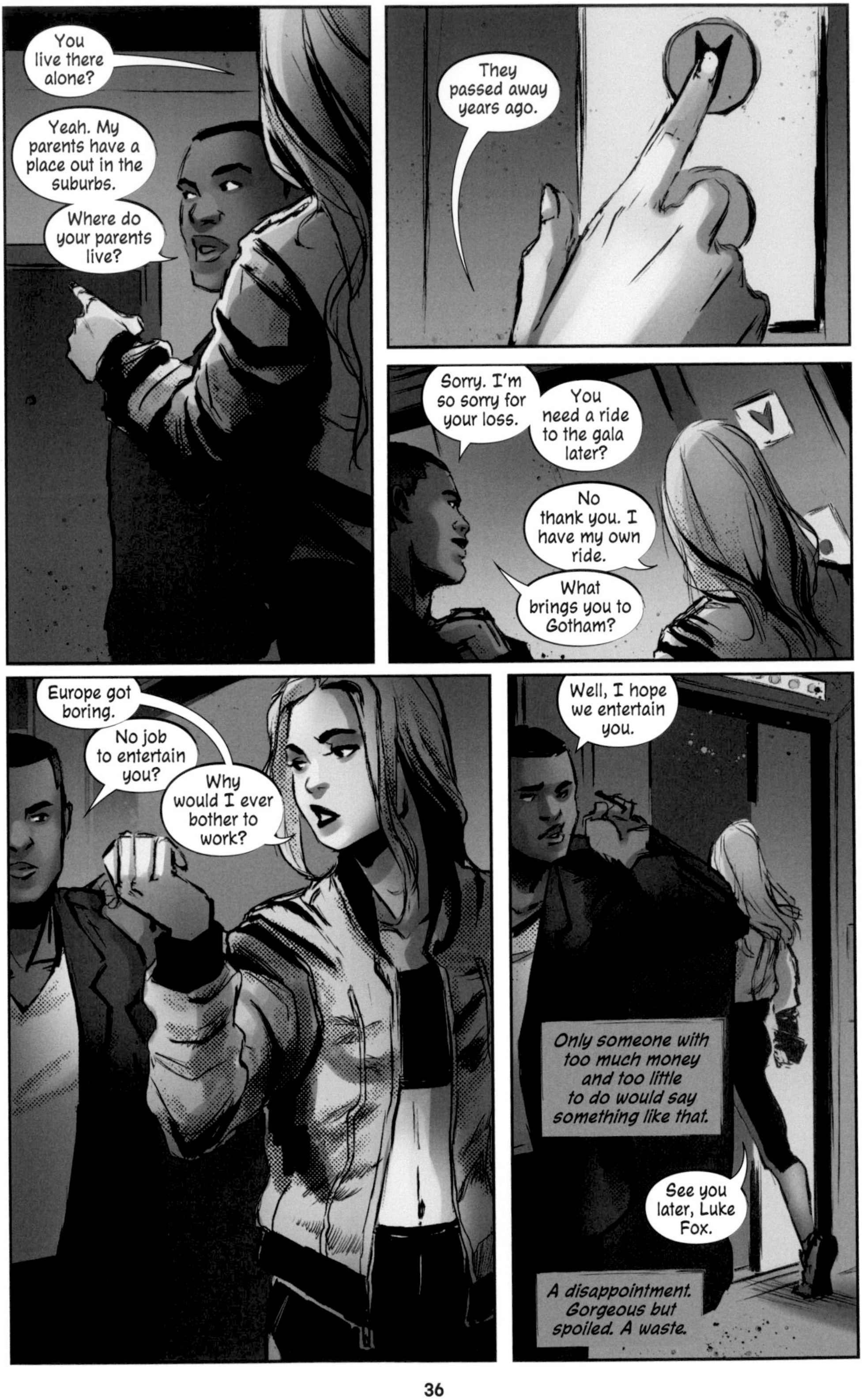
You live there alone?
Yeah. My parents have a place out in the suburbs.
Where do your parents live?
They passed away years ago.
Sorry. I'm so sorry for your loss.
You need a ride to the gala later?
No thank you. I have my own ride.
What brings you to Gotham?
Europe got boring.
No job to entertain you?
Why would I ever bother to work?
Well, I hope we entertain you.
Only someone with too much money and too little to do would say something like that.
See you later, Luke Fox.
A disappointment. Gorgeous but spoiled. A waste.

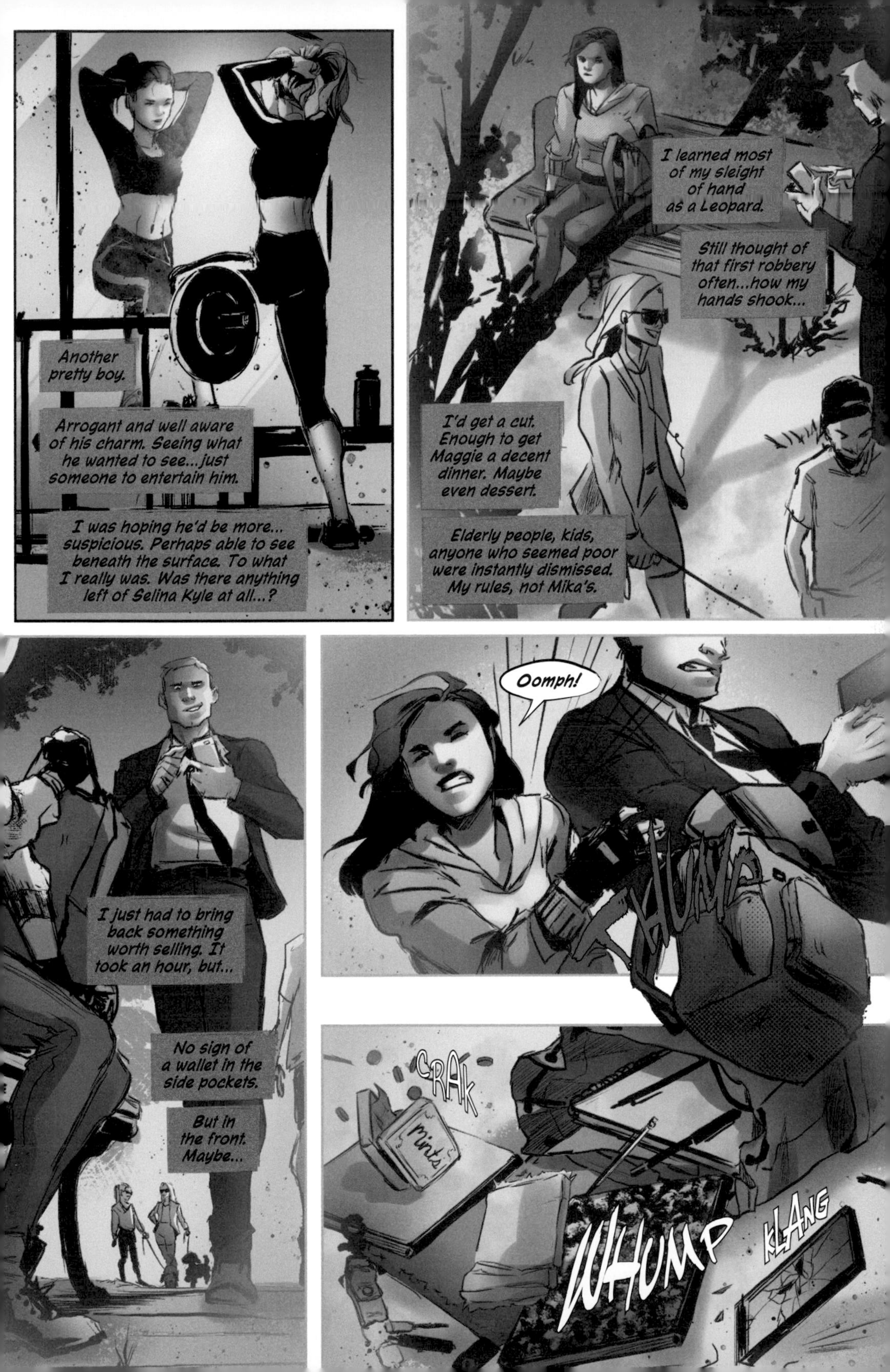

Another pretty boy.
Arrogant and well aware of his charm. Seeing what he wanted to see...just someone to entertain him.
I was hoping he'd be more... suspicious. Perhaps able to see beneath the surface. To what I really was. Was there anything left of Selina Kyle at all...?
I learned most of my sleight of hand as a Leopard.
Still thought of that first robbery often...how my hands shook...
I'd get a cut. Enough to get Maggie a decent dinner. Maybe even dessert.
Elderly people, kids, anyone who seemed poor were instantly dismissed. My rules, not Mika's.
I just had to bring back something worth selling. It took an hour, but...
No sign of a wallet in the side pockets.
But in the front. Maybe...
Oomph!
THUMP
CRAK
mints
WHUMP
KLANG

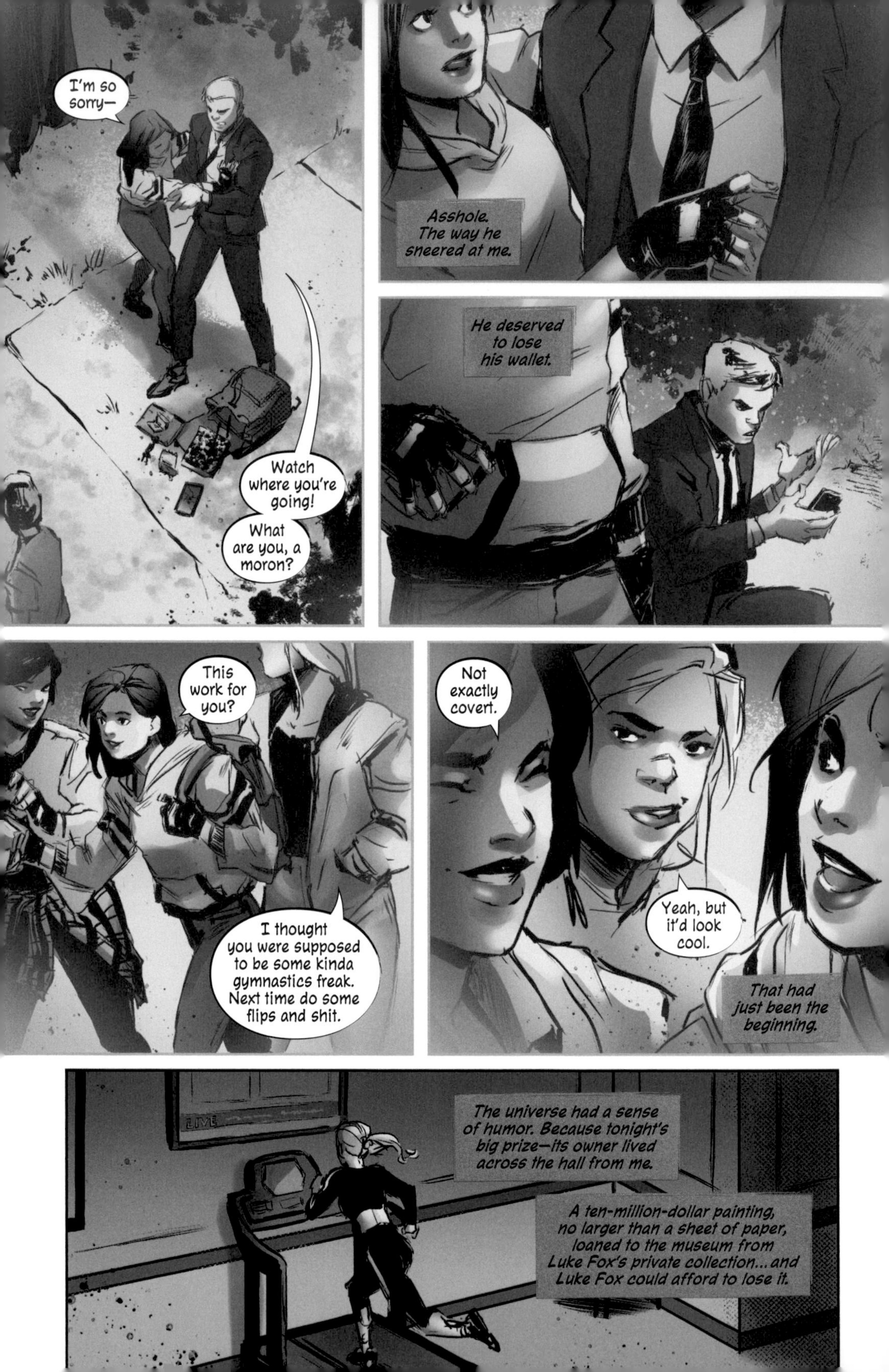
I'm so sorry—
Watch where you're going!
What are you, a moron?
Asshole. The way he sneered at me.
He deserved to lose his wallet.
This work for you?
I thought you were supposed to be some kinda gymnastics freak. Next time do some flips and shit.
Not exactly covert.
Yeah, but it'd look cool.
That had just been the beginning.
The universe had a sense of humor. Because tonight's big prize—its owner lived across the hall from me.
A ten-million-dollar painting, no larger than a sheet of paper, loaned to the museum from Luke Fox's private collection...and Luke Fox could afford to lose it.

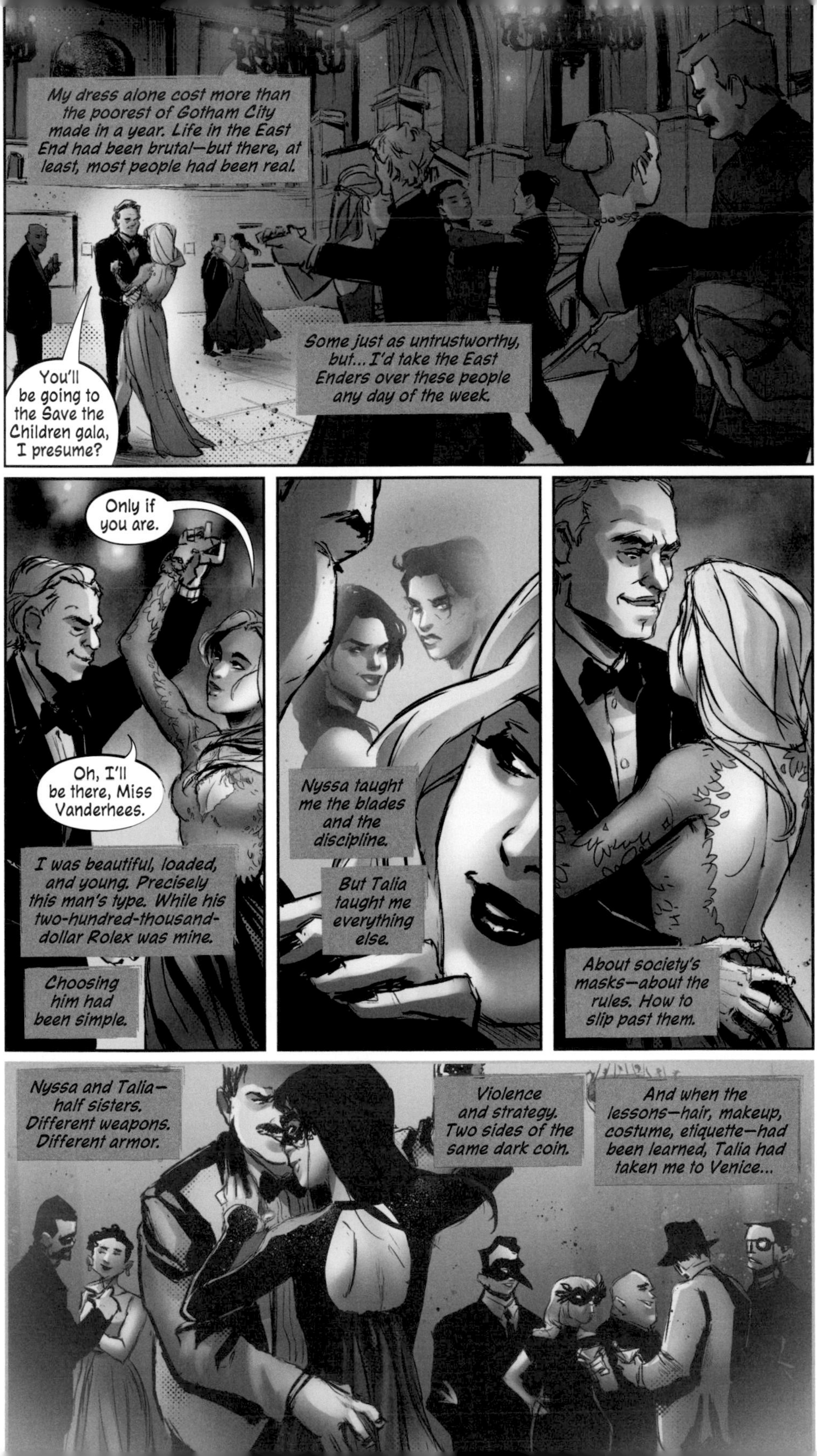
My dress alone cost more than the poorest of Gotham City made in a year. Life in the East End had been brutal—but there, at least, most people had been real.
Some just as untrustworthy, but... I'd take the East Enders over these people any day of the week.
You'll be going to the Save the Children gala, I presume?
Only if you are.
Oh, I'll be there, Miss Vanderhees.
I was beautiful, loaded, and young. Precisely this man's type. While his two-hundred-thousand-dollar Rolex was mine.
Choosing him had been simple.
Nyssa taught me the blades and the discipline.
But Talia taught me everything else.
About society's masks—about the rules. How to slip past them.
Nyssa and Talia—half sisters. Different weapons. Different armor.
Violence and strategy. Two sides of the same dark coin.
And when the lessons—hair, makeup, costume, etiquette—had been learned, Talia had taken me to Venice...

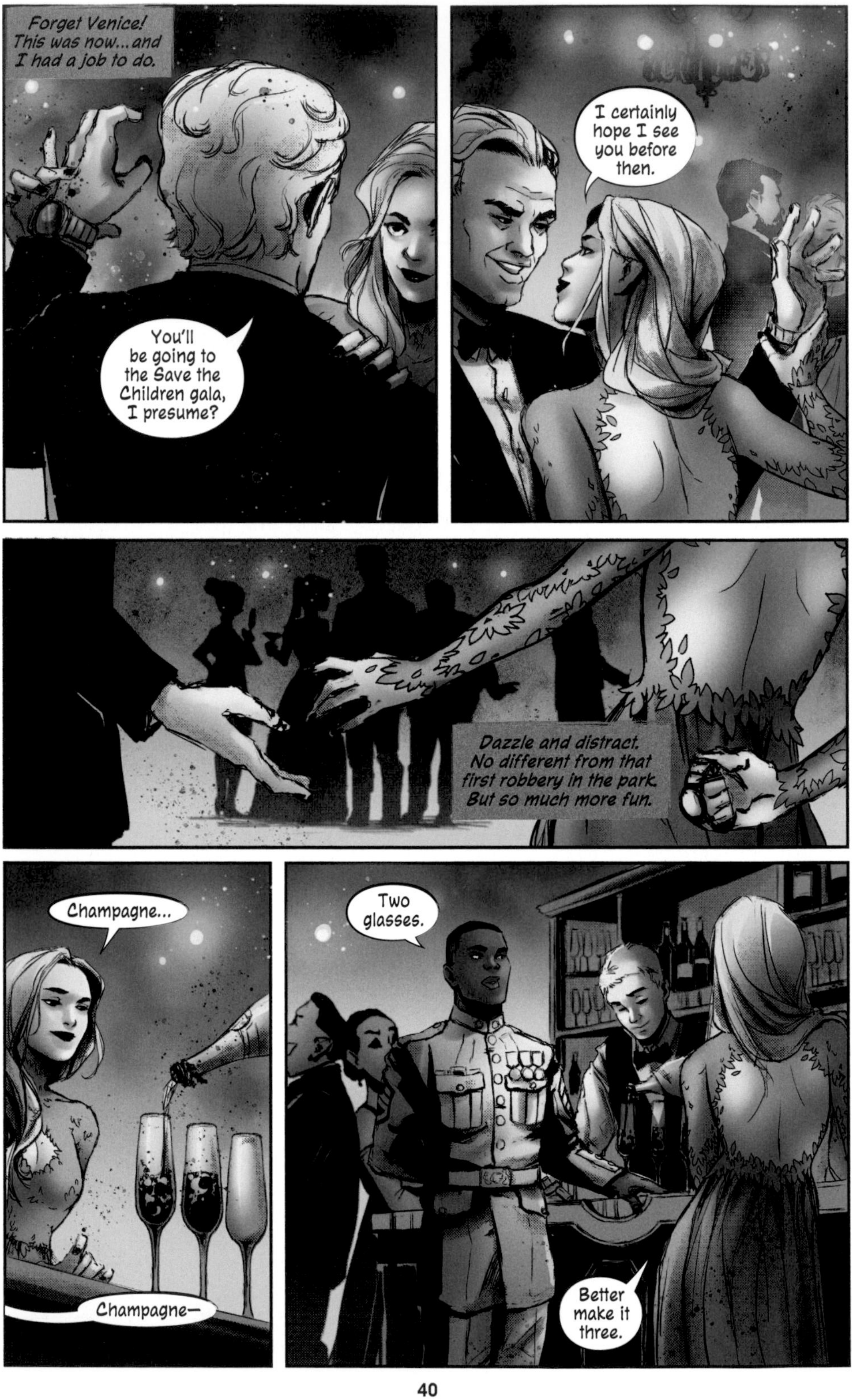
Forget Venice! This was now...and I had a job to do.
You'll be going to the Save the Children gala, I presume?
I certainly hope I see you before then.
Dazzle and distract. No different from that first robbery in the park. But so much more fun.
Champagne...
Champagne—
Two glasses.
Better make it three.

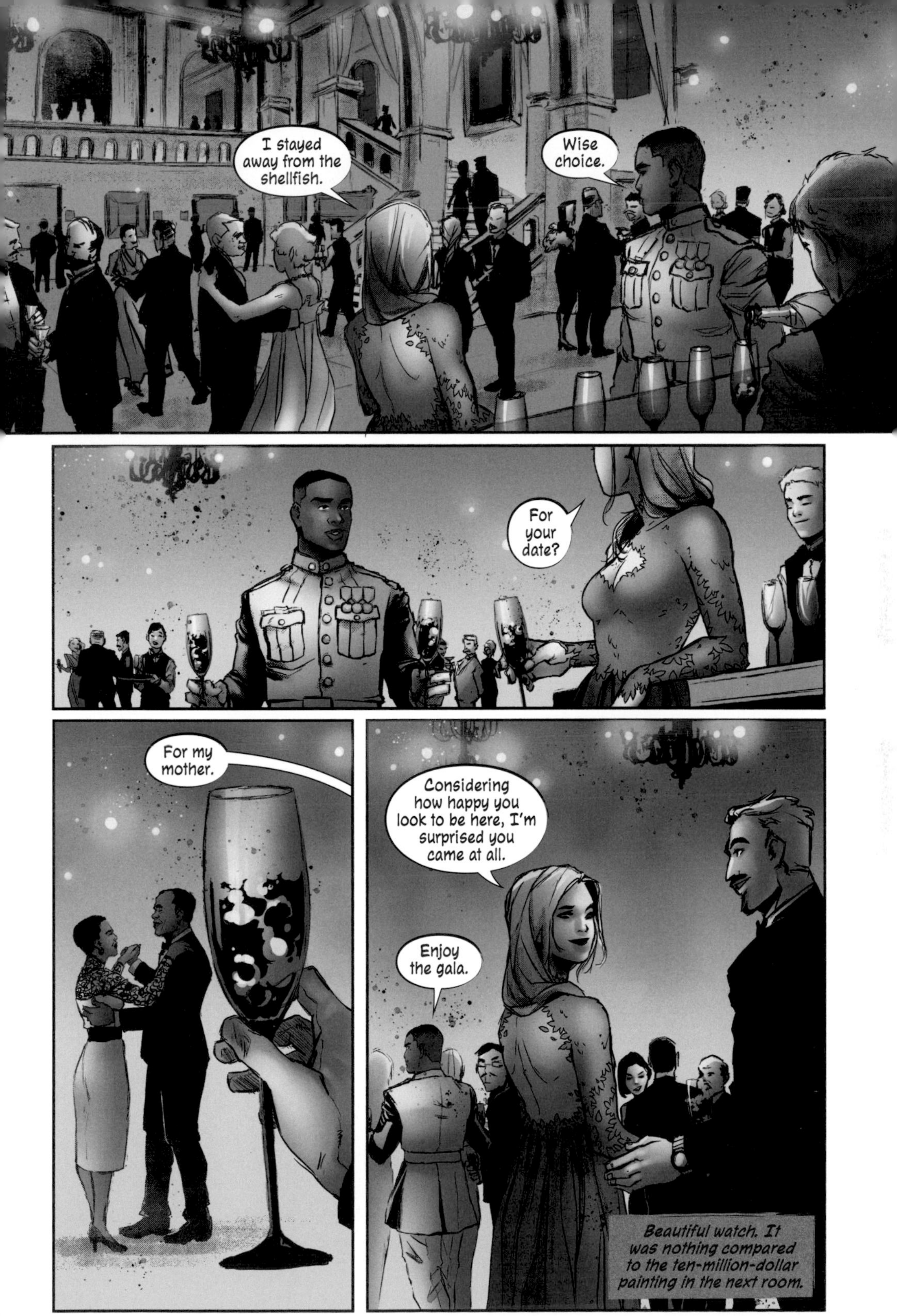

I stayed away from the shellfish.
Wise choice.
For your date?
For my mother.
Considering how happy you look to be here, I'm surprised you came at all.
Enjoy the gala.
Beautiful watch. It was nothing compared to the ten-million-dollar painting in the next room.

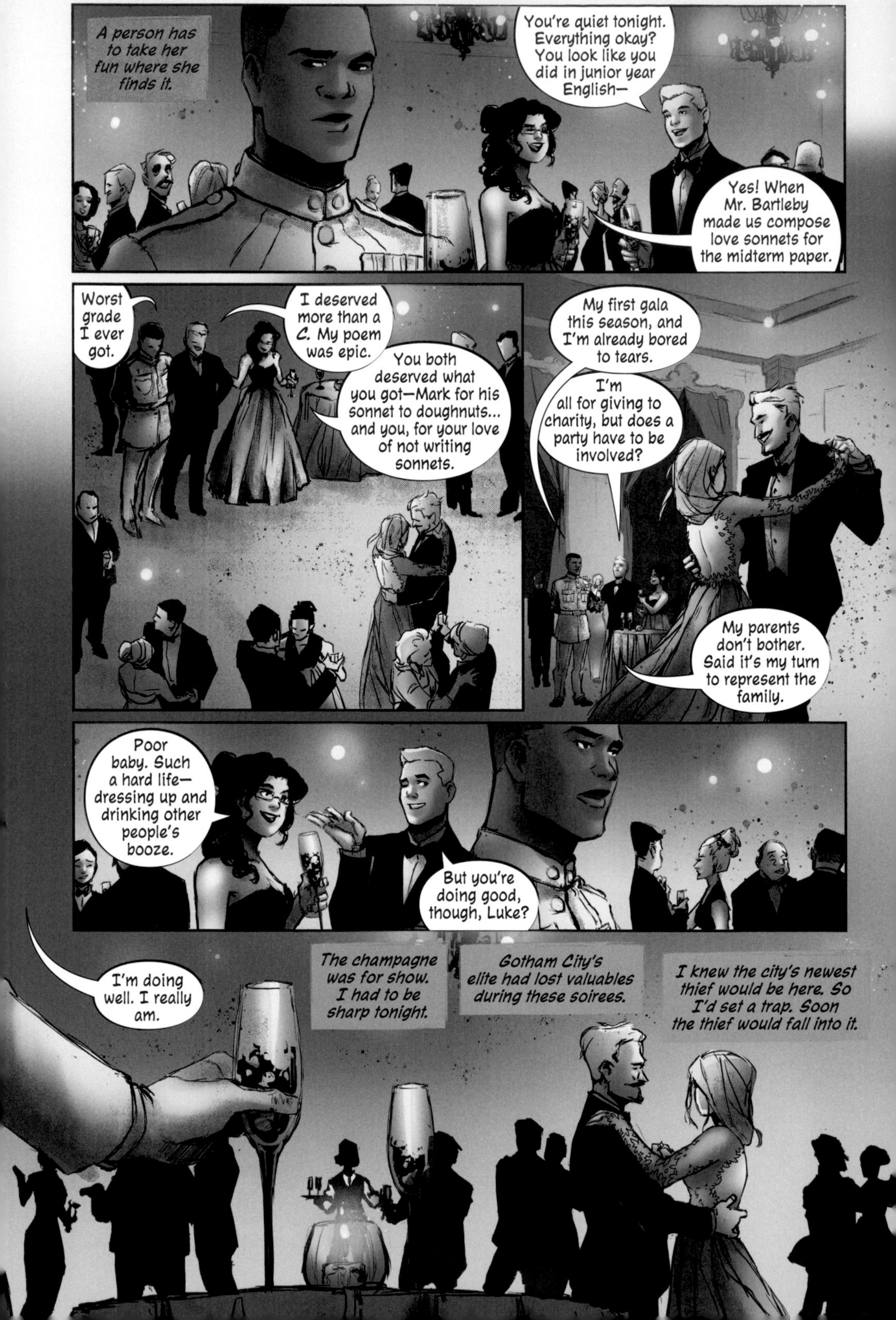
A person has to take her fun where she finds it.
You're quiet tonight. Everything okay? You look like you did in junior year English—
Yes! When Mr. Bartleby made us compose love sonnets for the midterm paper.
Worst grade I ever got.
I deserved more than a C. My poem was epic.
You both deserved what you got—Mark for his sonnet to doughnuts... and you, for your love of not writing sonnets.
My first gala this season, and I'm already bored to tears.
I'm all for giving to charity, but does a party have to be involved?
My parents don't bother. Said it's my turn to represent the family.
Poor baby. Such a hard life—dressing up and drinking other people's booze.
But you're doing good, though, Luke?
I'm doing well. I really am.
The champagne was for show. I had to be sharp tonight.
Gotham City's elite had lost valuables during these soirees.
I knew the city's newest thief would be here. So I'd set a trap. Soon the thief would fall into it.

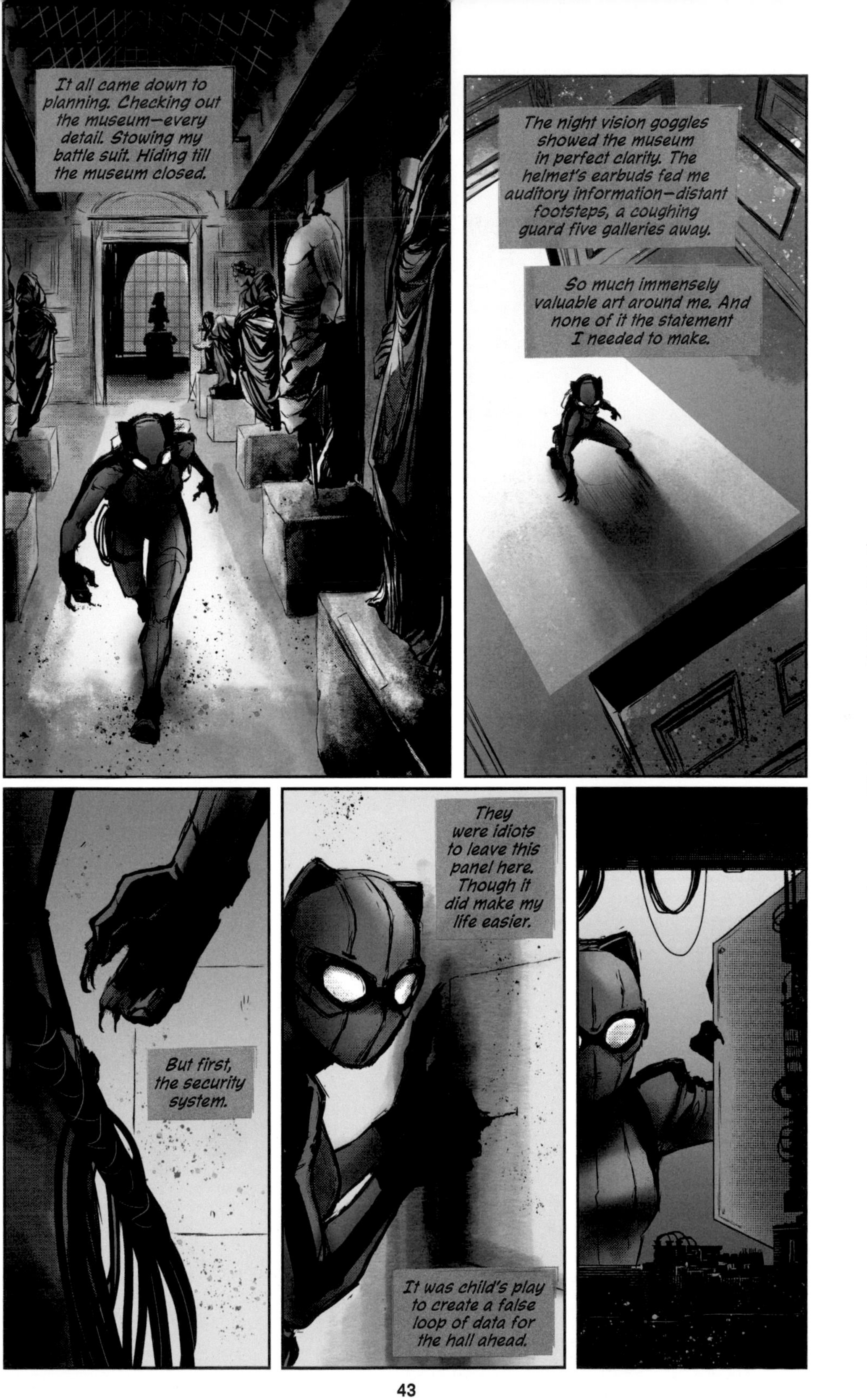
It all came down to planning. Checking out the museum—every detail. Stowing my battle suit. Hiding till the museum closed.
The night vision goggles showed the museum in perfect clarity. The helmet's earbuds fed me auditory information—distant footsteps, a coughing guard five galleries away.
So much immensely valuable art around me. And none of it the statement I needed to make.
But first, the security system.
They were idiots to leave this panel here. Though it did make my life easier.
It was child's play to create a false loop of data for the hall ahead.

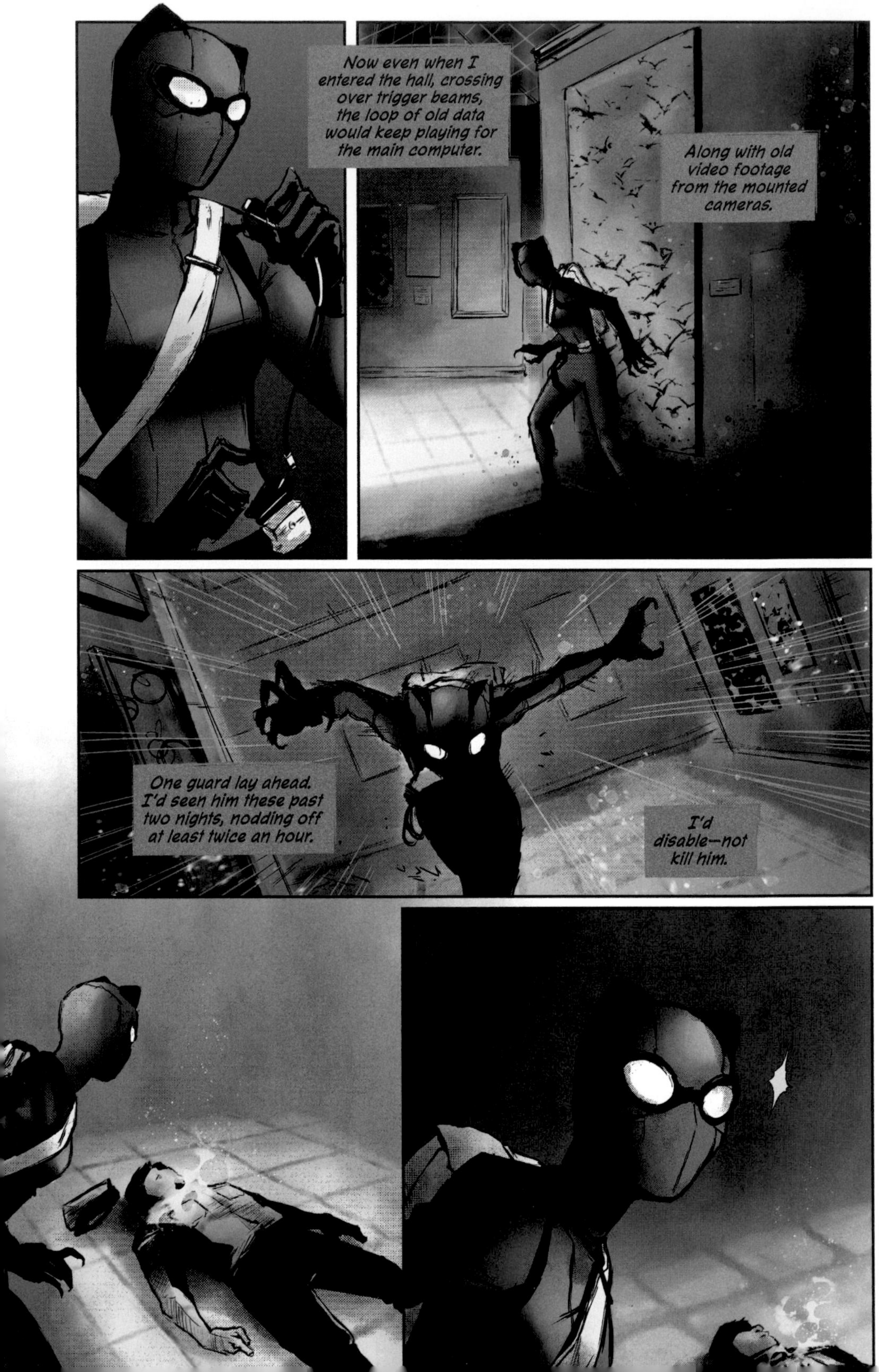
Now even when I entered the hall, crossing over trigger beams, the loop of old data would keep playing for the main computer.
Along with old video footage from the mounted cameras.
One guard lay ahead. I'd seen him these past two nights, nodding off at least twice an hour.
I'd disable—not kill him.

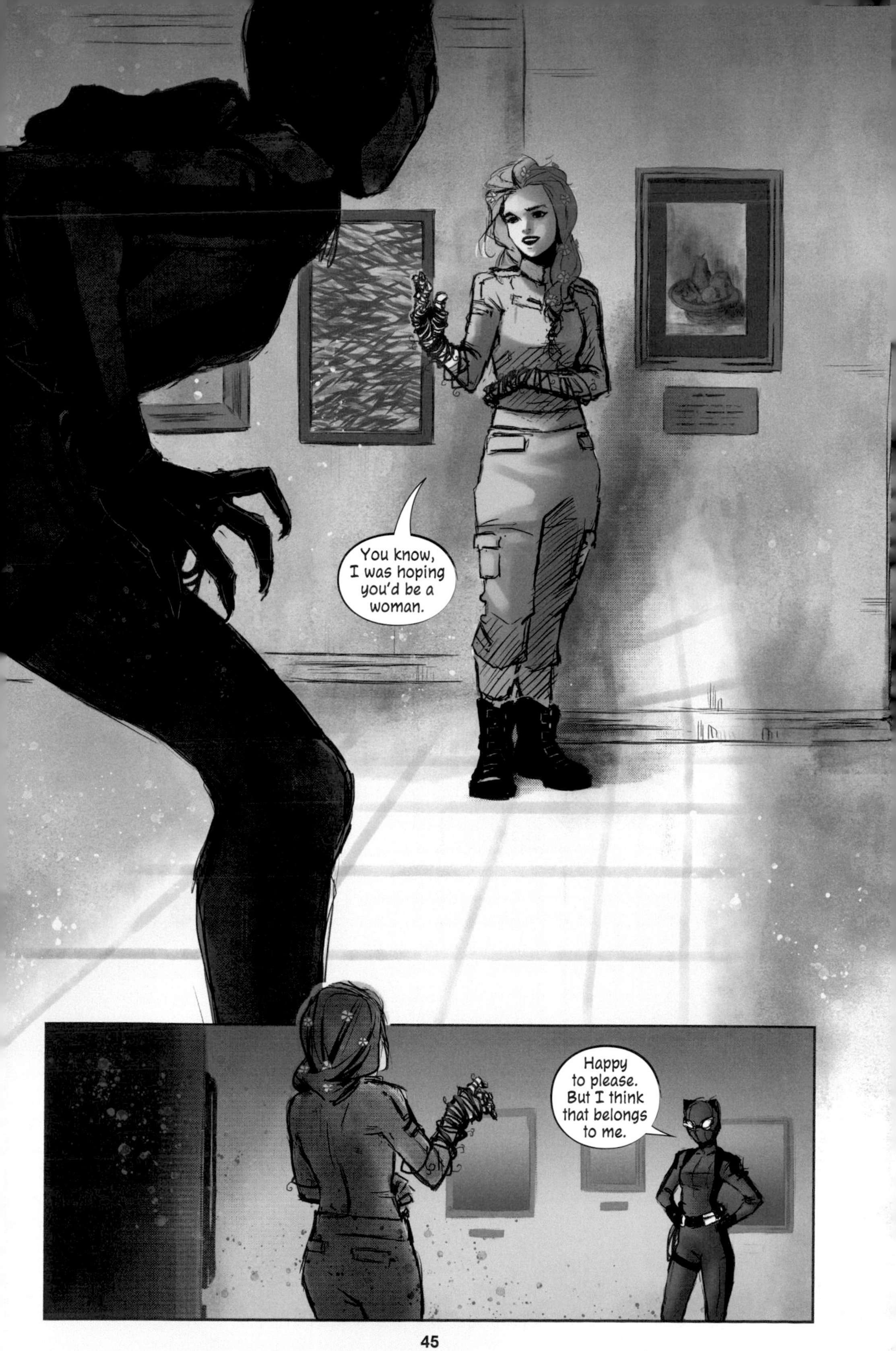
You know, I was hoping you'd be a woman.
Happy to please. But I think that belongs to me.

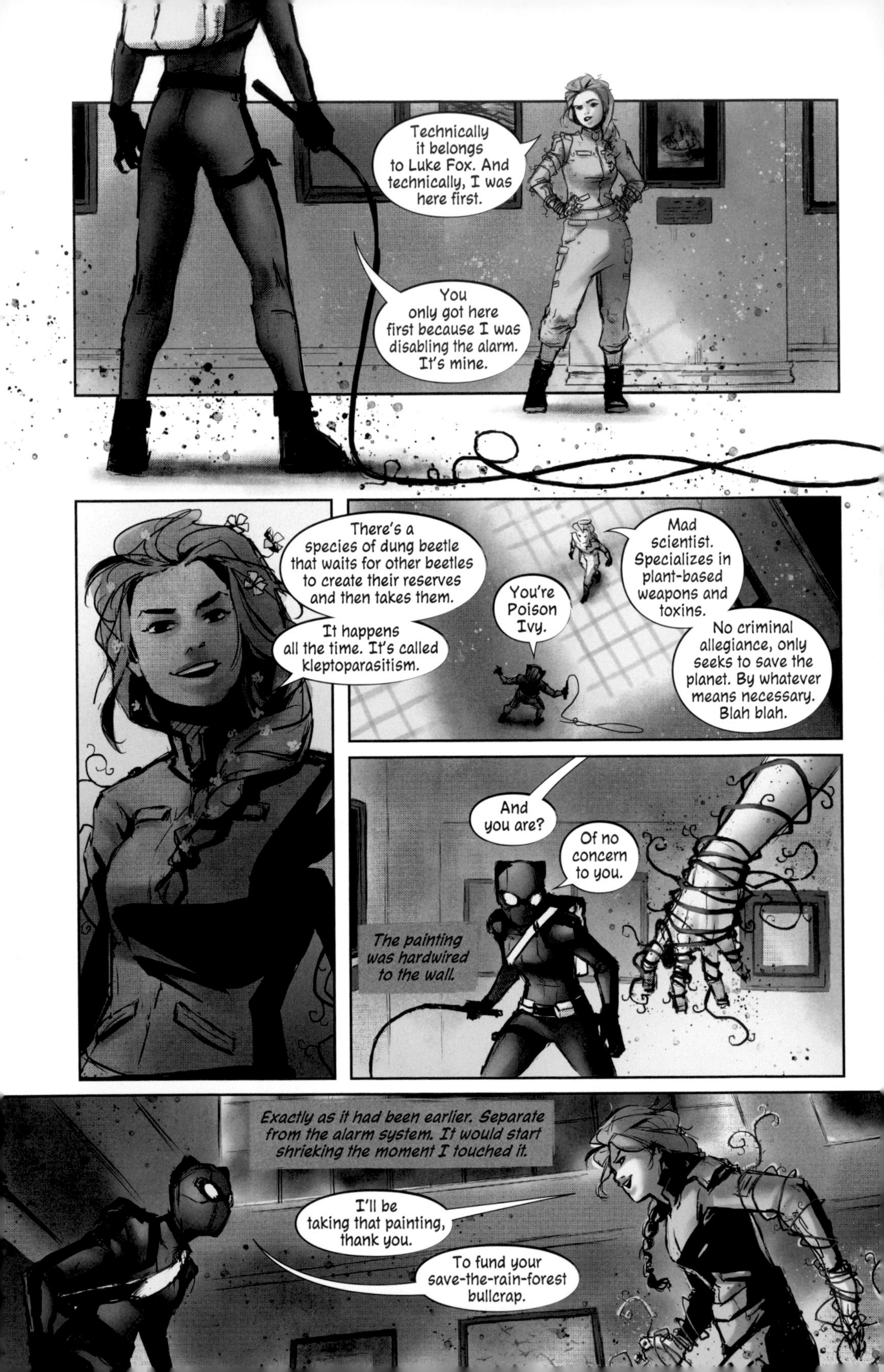
Technically it belongs to Luke Fox. And technically, I was here first.
You only got here first because I was disabling the alarm. It's mine.
There's a species of dung beetle that waits for other beetles to create their reserves and then takes them.
It happens all the time. It's called kleptoparasitism.
You're Poison Ivy.
Mad scientist. Specializes in plant-based weapons and toxins.
No criminal allegiance, only seeks to save the planet. By whatever means necessary. Blah blah.
And you are?
Of no concern to you.
The painting was hardwired to the wall.
Exactly as it had been earlier. Separate from the alarm system. It would start shrieking the moment I touched it.
I'll be taking that painting, thank you.
To fund your save-the-rain-forest bullcrap.

You know how much money was at that gala tonight? For what? This museum? These dead, lifeless things?

So sad. Just awful.

You buy that exterminator-at-the-ball getup at the Halloween store?

Yeah, but now I wish I hadn't passed up the sexy cat costume.

First rule of disorder—find some interesting company.

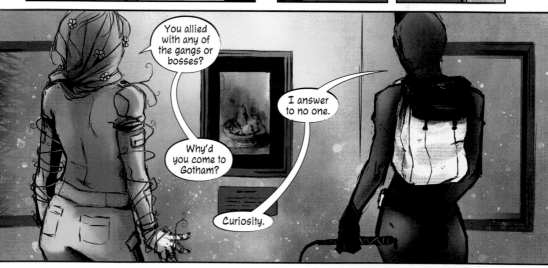

You allied with any of the gangs or bosses?

I answer to no one.

Why'd you come to Gotham?

Curiosity.

Doesn't that sort of thing usually not end well for your kind?

Things have been quiet—and the money is easy pickings.

You sound like a cyborg with that helmet. Here's the deal. We split it fifty/fifty.

Ninety/ten. Be grateful you get a million out of capitalizing on my hard work.

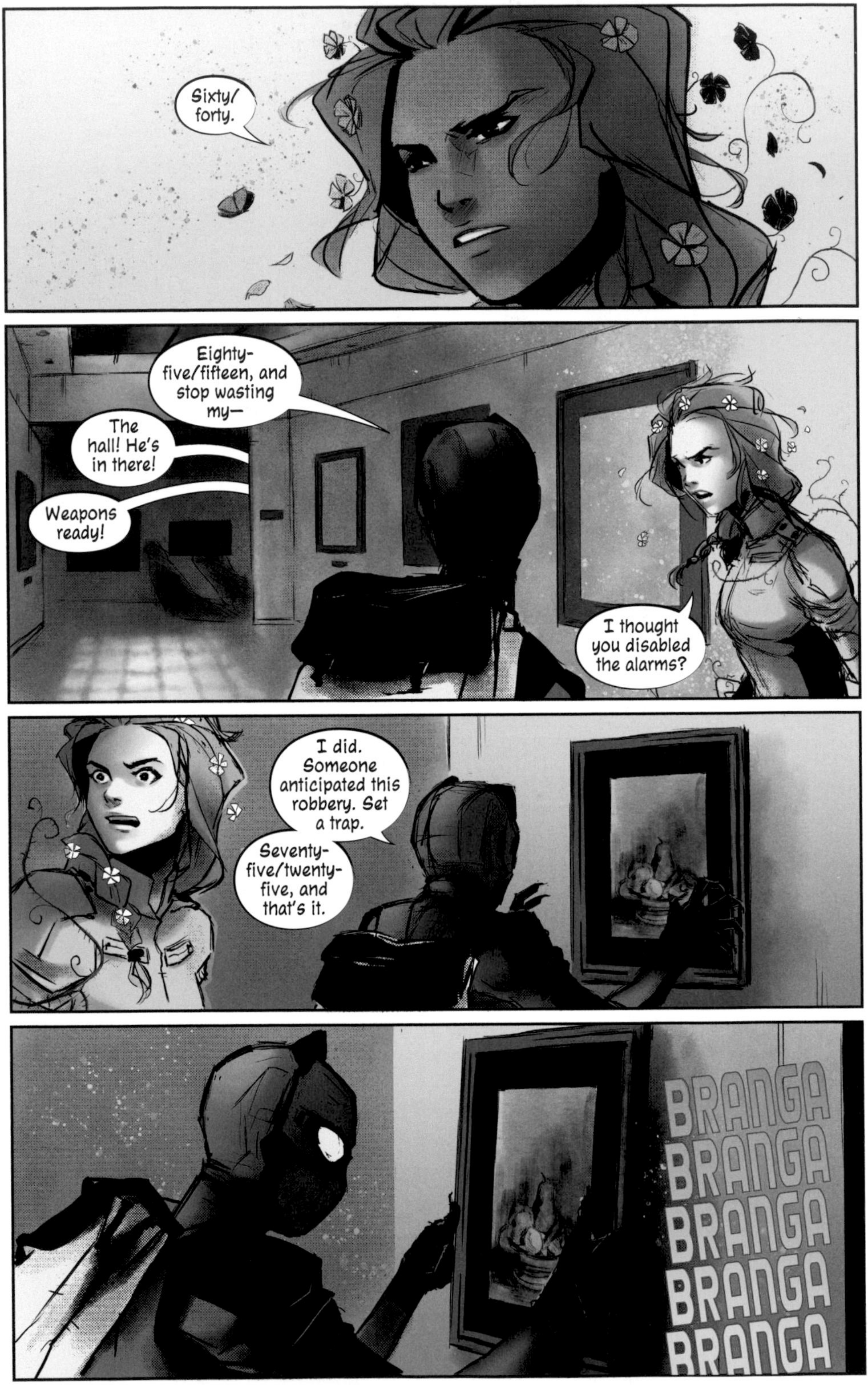

Sixty/ forty.
Eighty-five/fifteen, and stop wasting my—
The hall! He's in there!
Weapons ready!
I thought you disabled the alarms?
I did. Someone anticipated this robbery. Set a trap.
Seventy-five/twenty-five, and that's it.
BRANGA BRANGA BRANGA BRANGA BRANGA

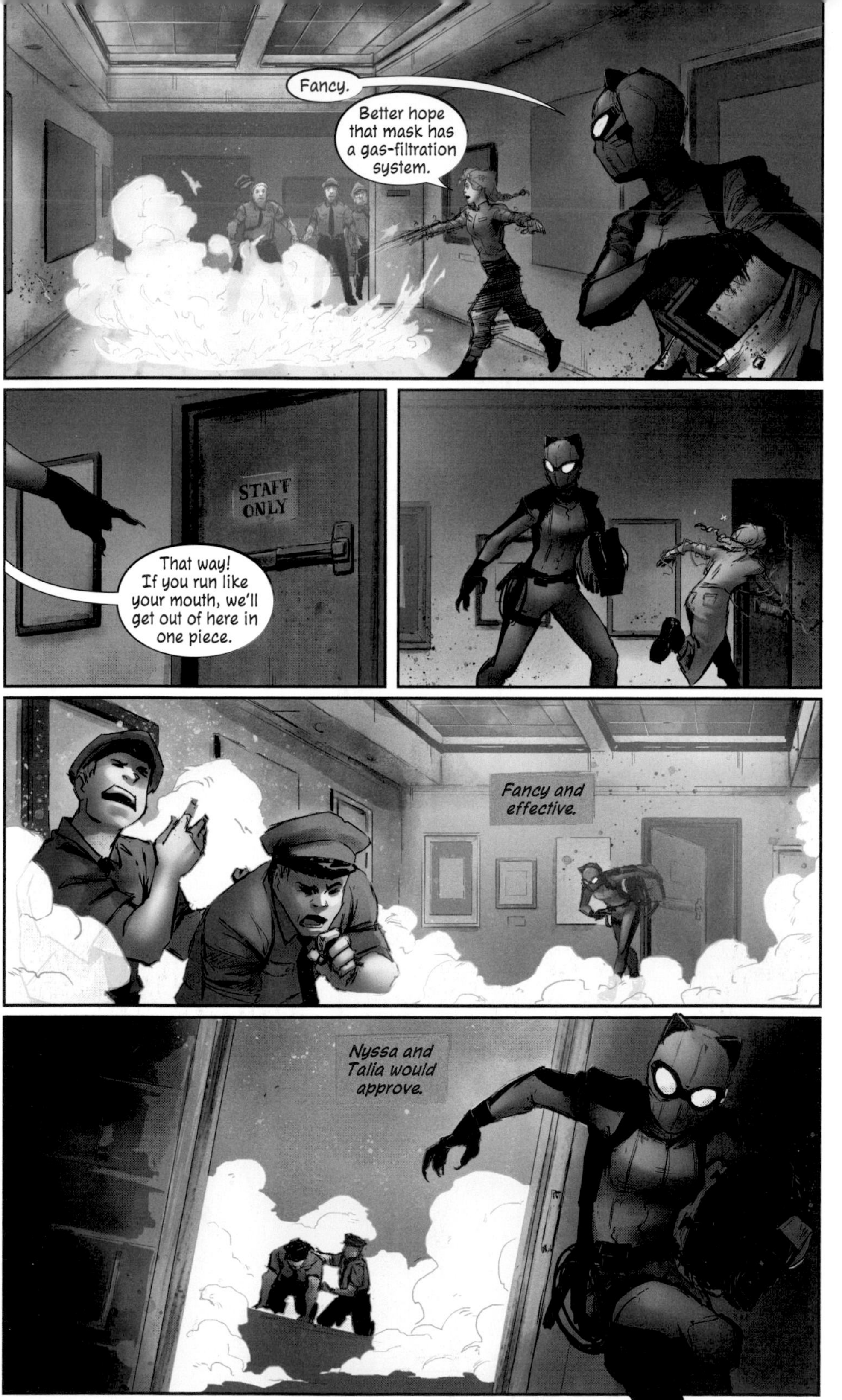
Fancy.
Better hope that mask has a gas-filtration system.
STAFF ONLY
That way! If you run like your mouth, we'll get out of here in one piece.
Fancy and effective.
Nyssa and Talia would approve.

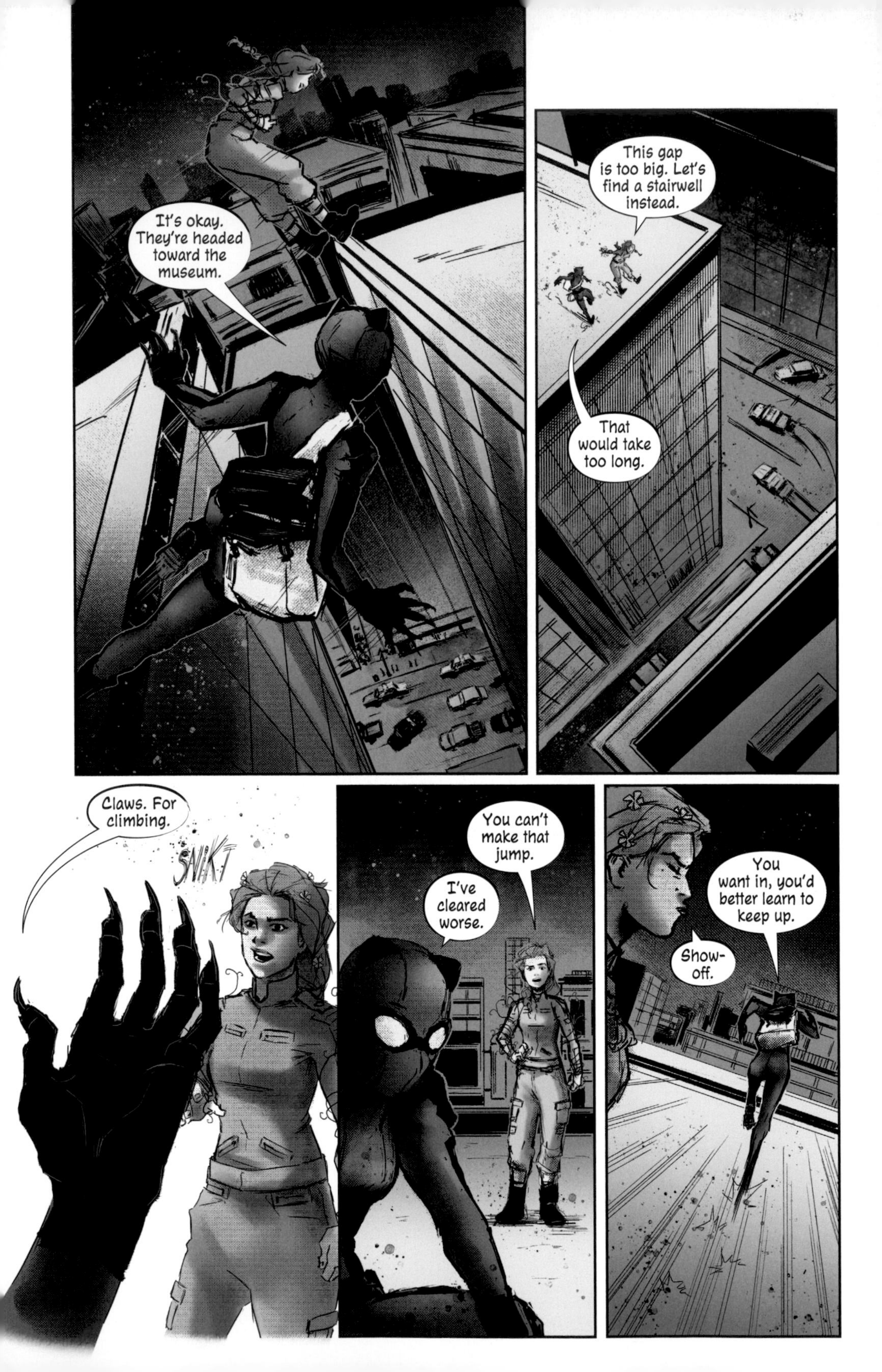
It's okay. They're headed toward the museum.
This gap is too big. Let's find a stairwell instead.
That would take too long.
Claws. For climbing.
SNIKT
You can't make that jump.
I've cleared worse.
You want in, you'd better learn to keep up.
Show-off.

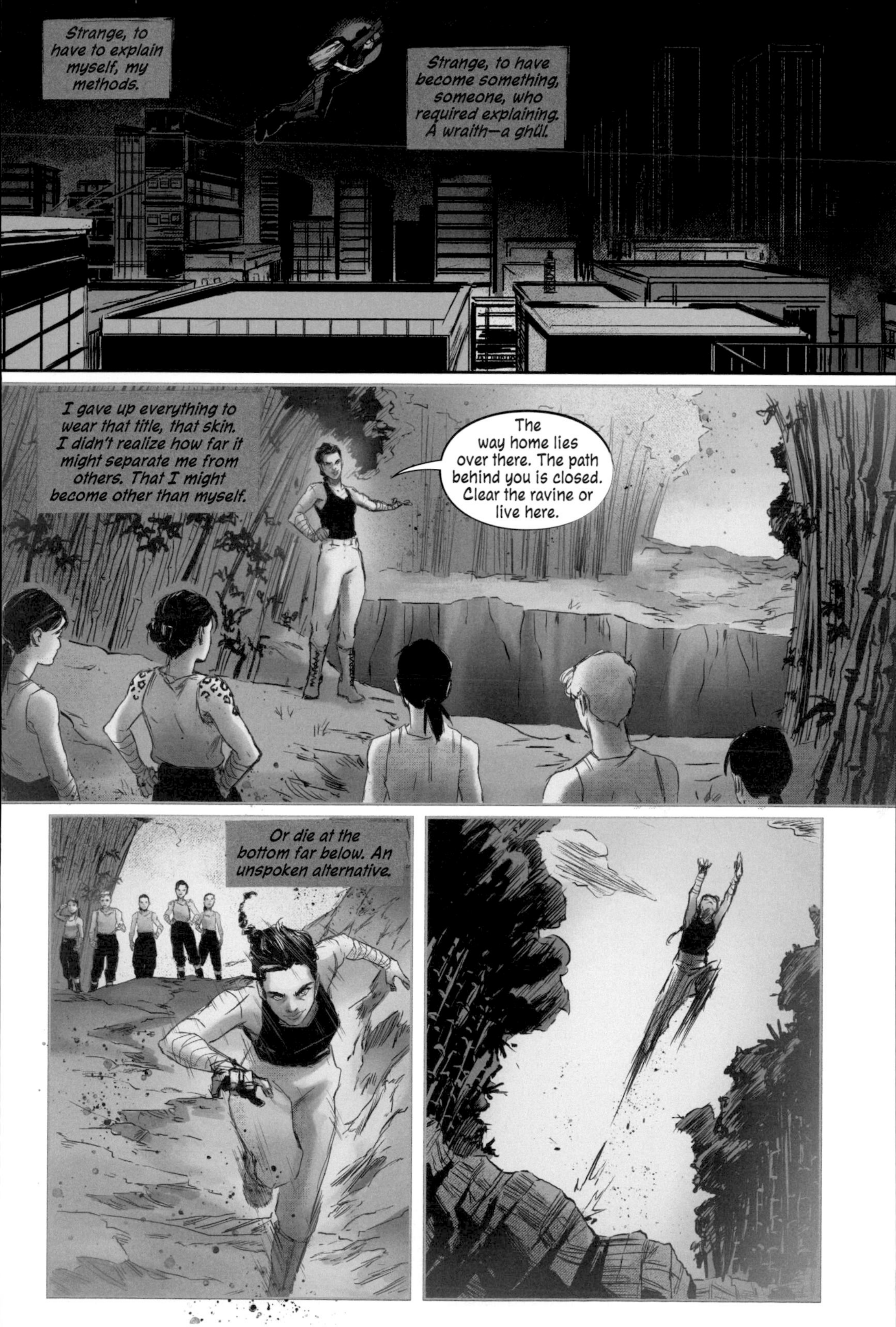
Strange, to have to explain myself, my methods.
Strange, to have become something, someone, who required explaining. A wraith—a ghūl.
I gave up everything to wear that title, that skin. I didn't realize how far it might separate me from others. That I might become other than myself.
The way home lies over there. The path behind you is closed. Clear the ravine or live here.
Or die at the bottom far below. An unspoken alternative.

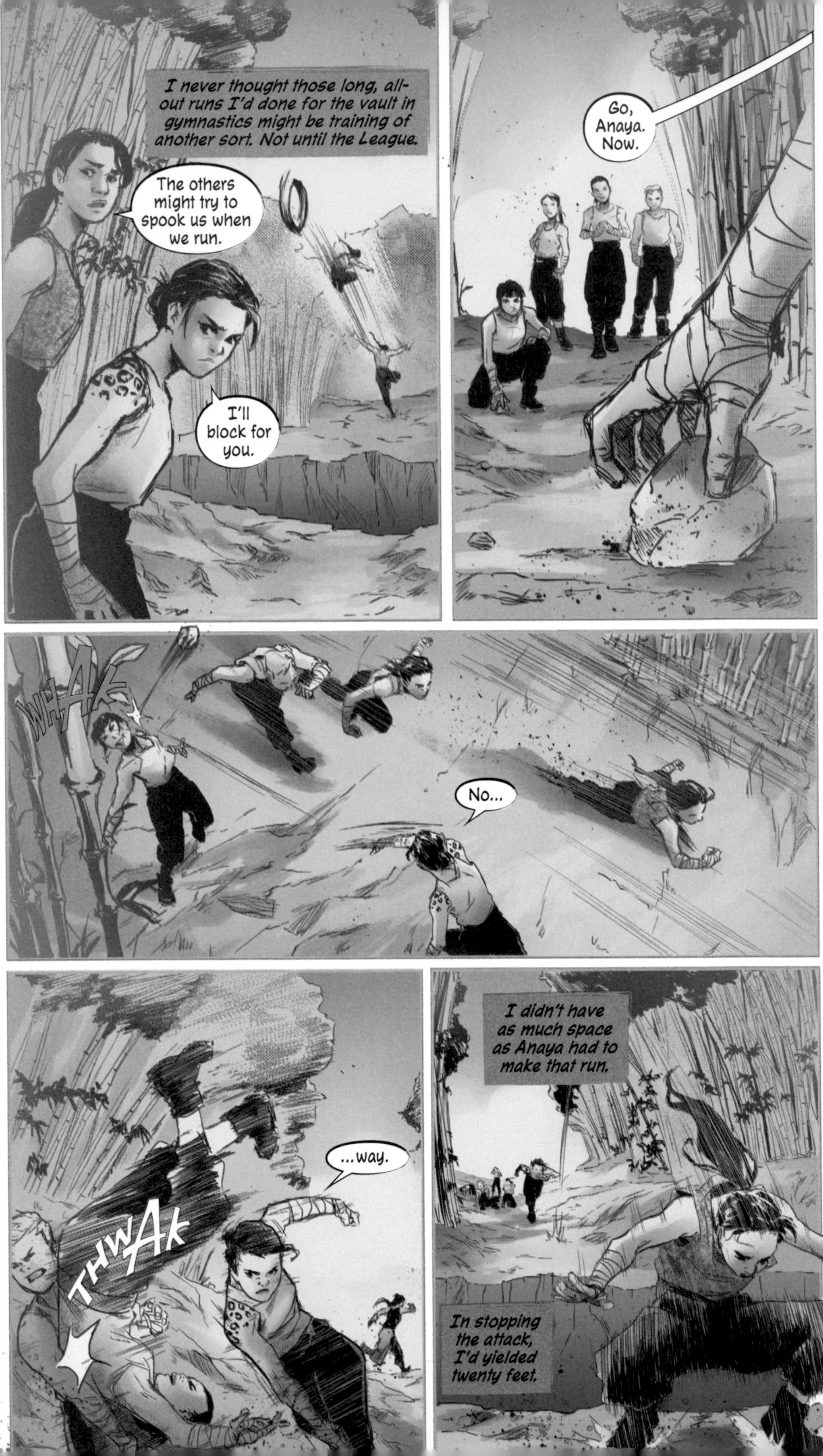

I never thought those long, all-out runs I'd done for the vault in gymnastics might be training of another sort. Not until the League.
The others might try to spook us when we run.
I'll block for you.
Go, Anaya. Now.
WHAK
No...
...way.
THWAK
I didn't have as much space as Anaya had to make that run.
In stopping the attack, I'd yielded twenty feet.

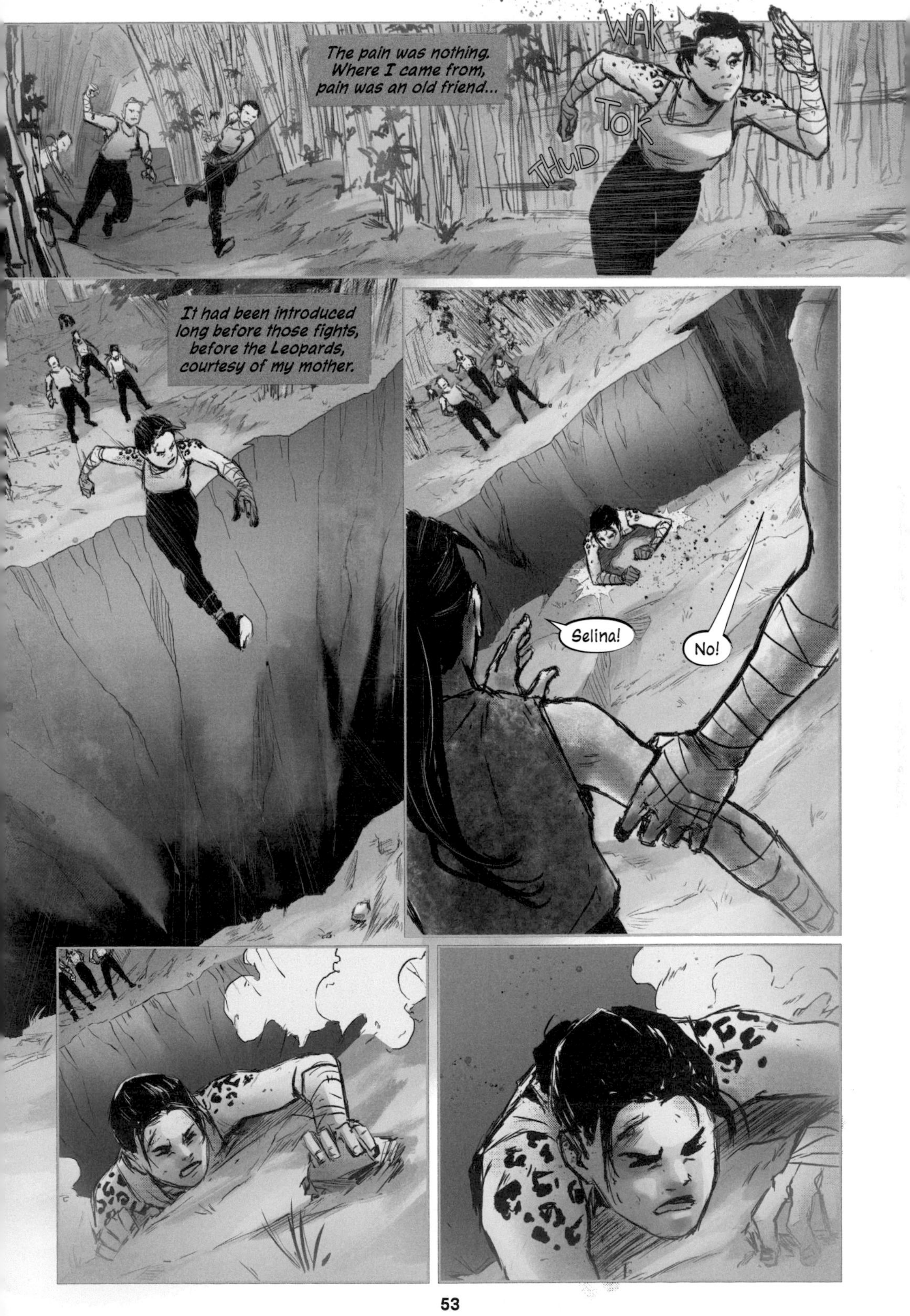

The pain was nothing. Where I came from, pain was an old friend...
WAK
TOK
THUD
It had been introduced long before those fights, before the Leopards, courtesy of my mother.
Selina!
No!

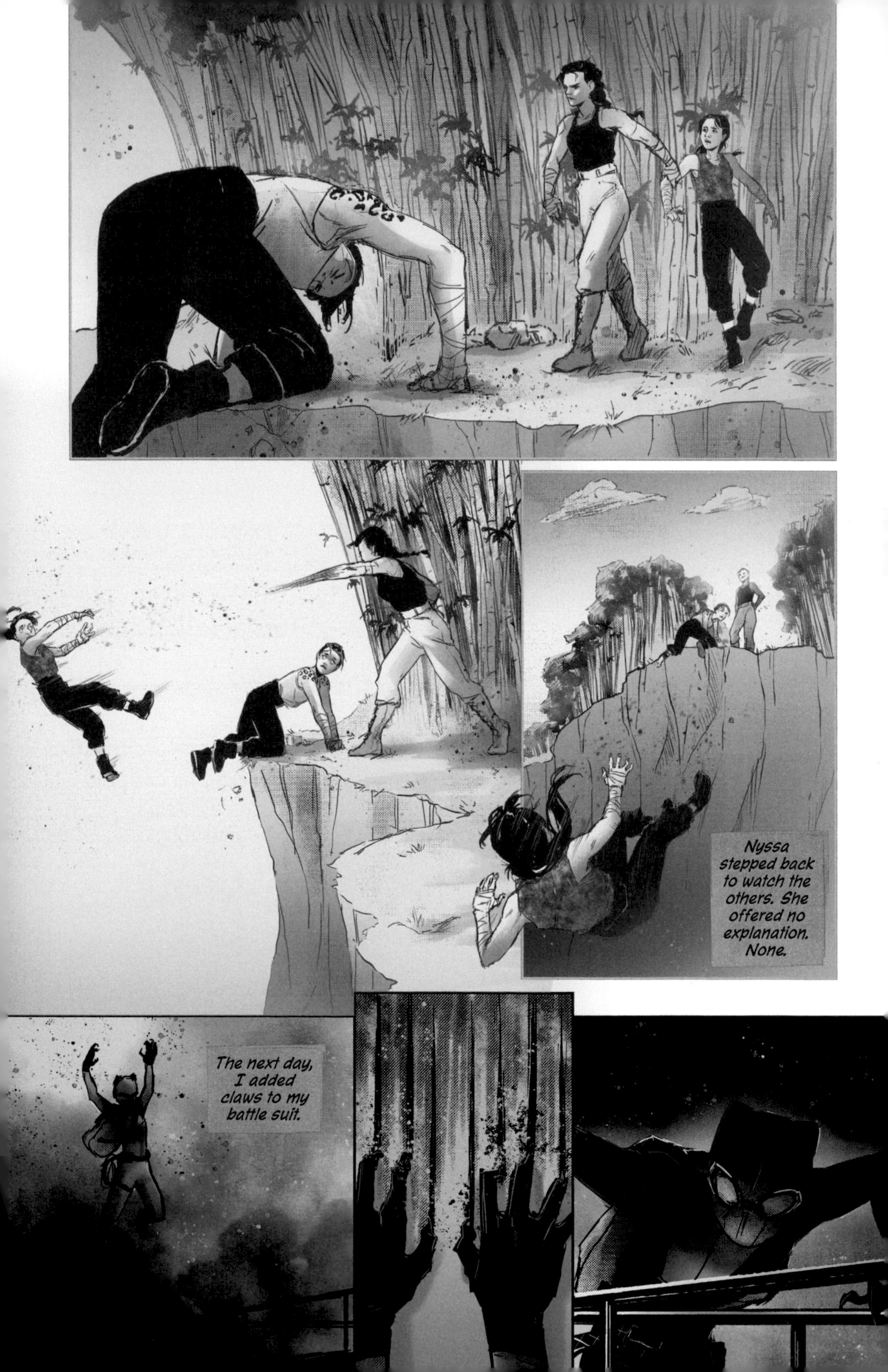
Nyssa stepped back to watch the others. She offered no explanation. None.
The next day, I added claws to my battle suit.

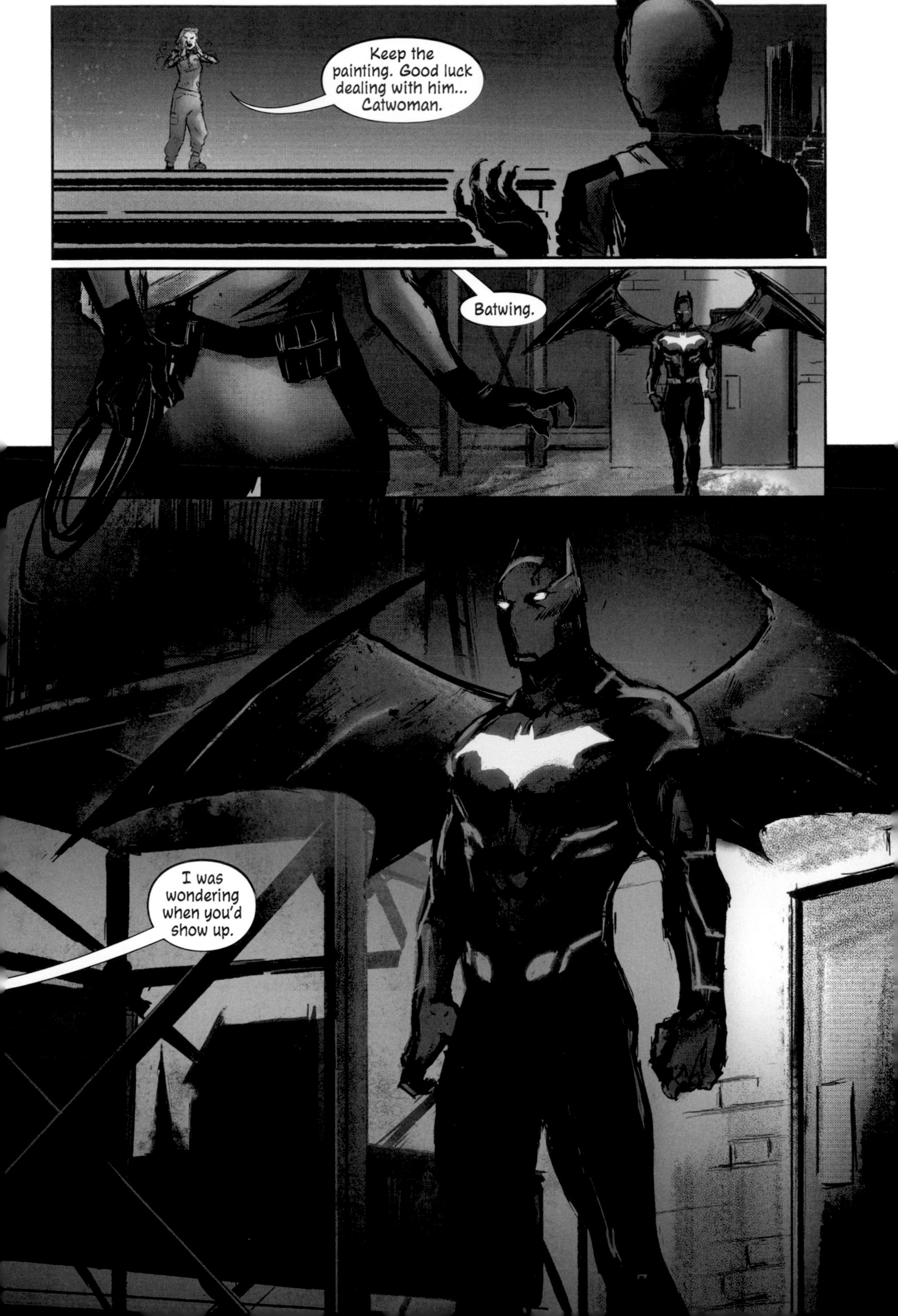
Keep the painting. Good luck dealing with him... Catwoman.
Batwing.
I was wondering when you'd show up.

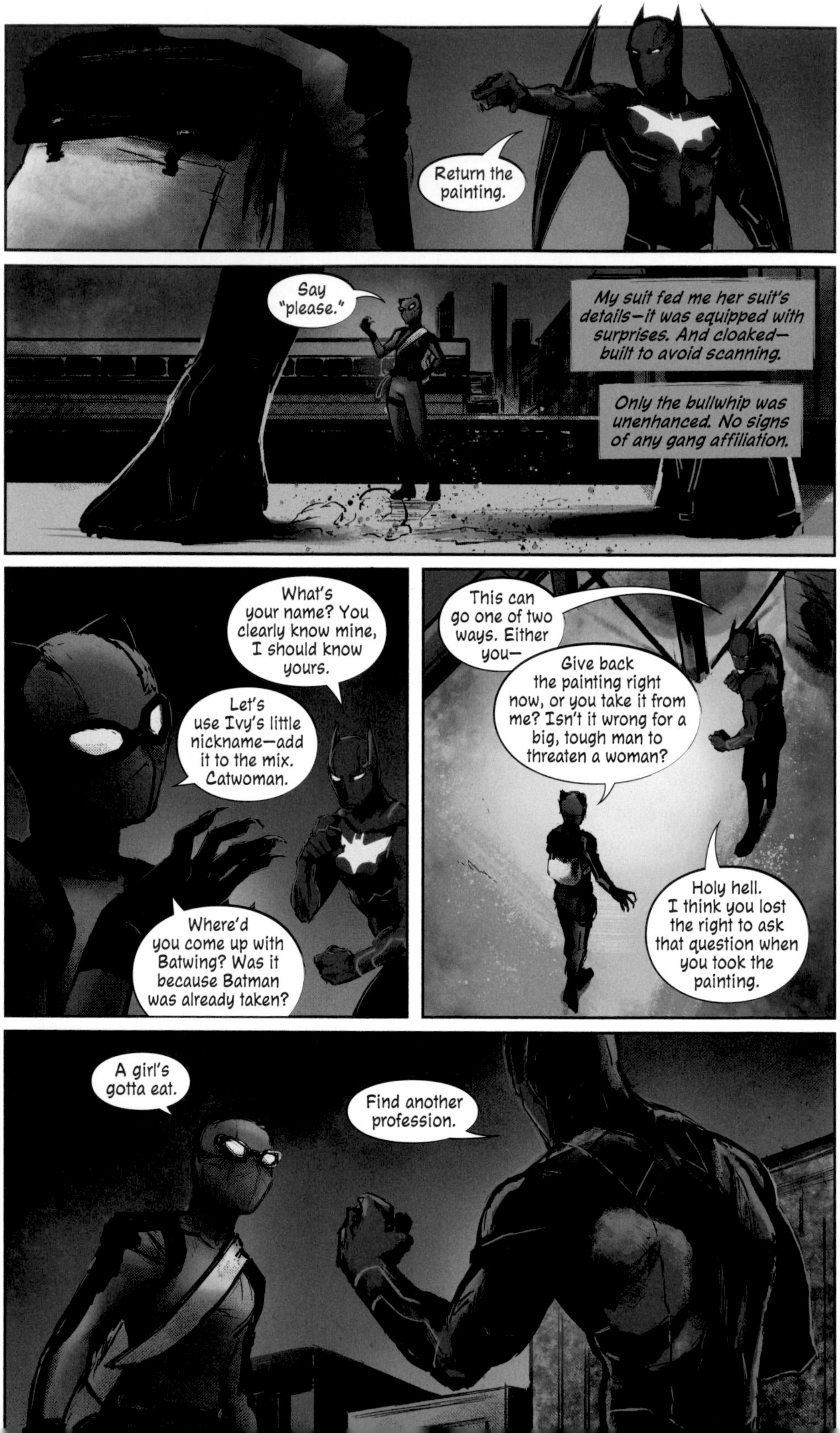
Return the painting.
Say "please."
My suit fed me her suit's details—it was equipped with surprises. And cloaked—built to avoid scanning.
Only the bullwhip was unenhanced. No signs of any gang affiliation.
What's your name? You clearly know mine, I should know yours.
Let's use Ivy's little nickname—add it to the mix. Catwoman.
Where'd you come up with Batwing? Was it because Batman was already taken?
This can go one of two ways. Either you—
Give back the painting right now, or you take it from me? Isn't it wrong for a big, tough man to threaten a woman?
Holy hell. I think you lost the right to ask that question when you took the painting.
A girl's gotta eat.
Find another profession.

If you want stealth, that night-light on your chest isn't very helpful.

It's a symbol.

And symbols have power.

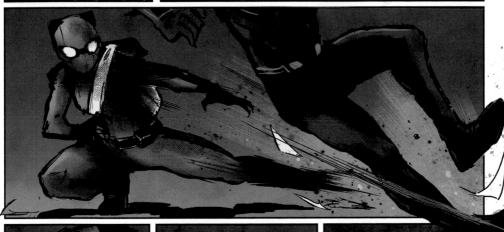

I forgot how boring you self-righteous do-gooders can be.

Knocked on my ass.

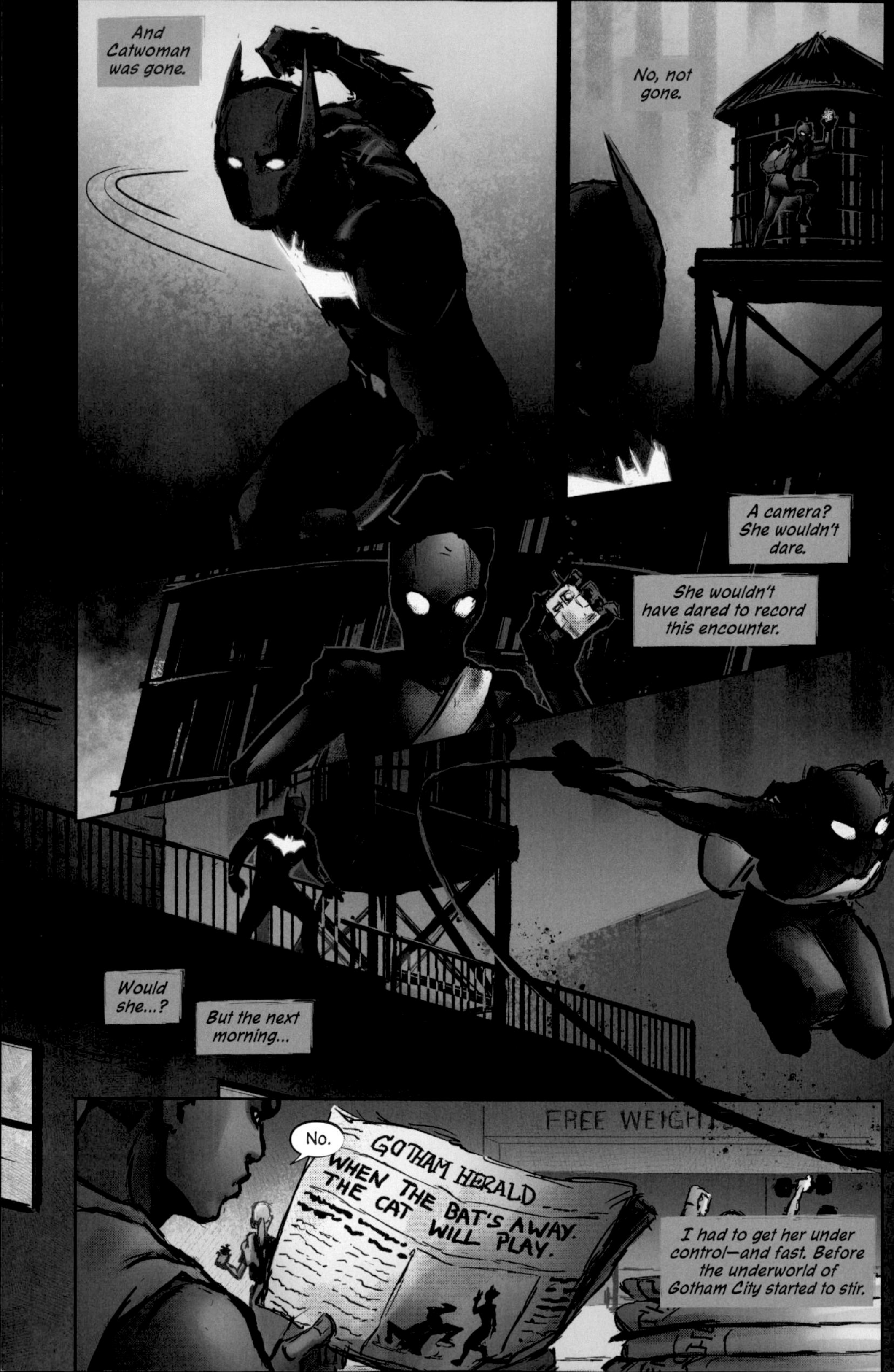

And Catwoman was gone.
No, not gone.
A camera? She wouldn't dare.
She wouldn't have dared to record this encounter.
Would she...?
But the next morning...
FREE WEIGH
No.
GOTHAM HERALD
WHEN THE BAT'S AWAY. THE CAT WILL PLAY.
I had to get her under control—and fast. Before the underworld of Gotham City started to stir.

PART FOUR

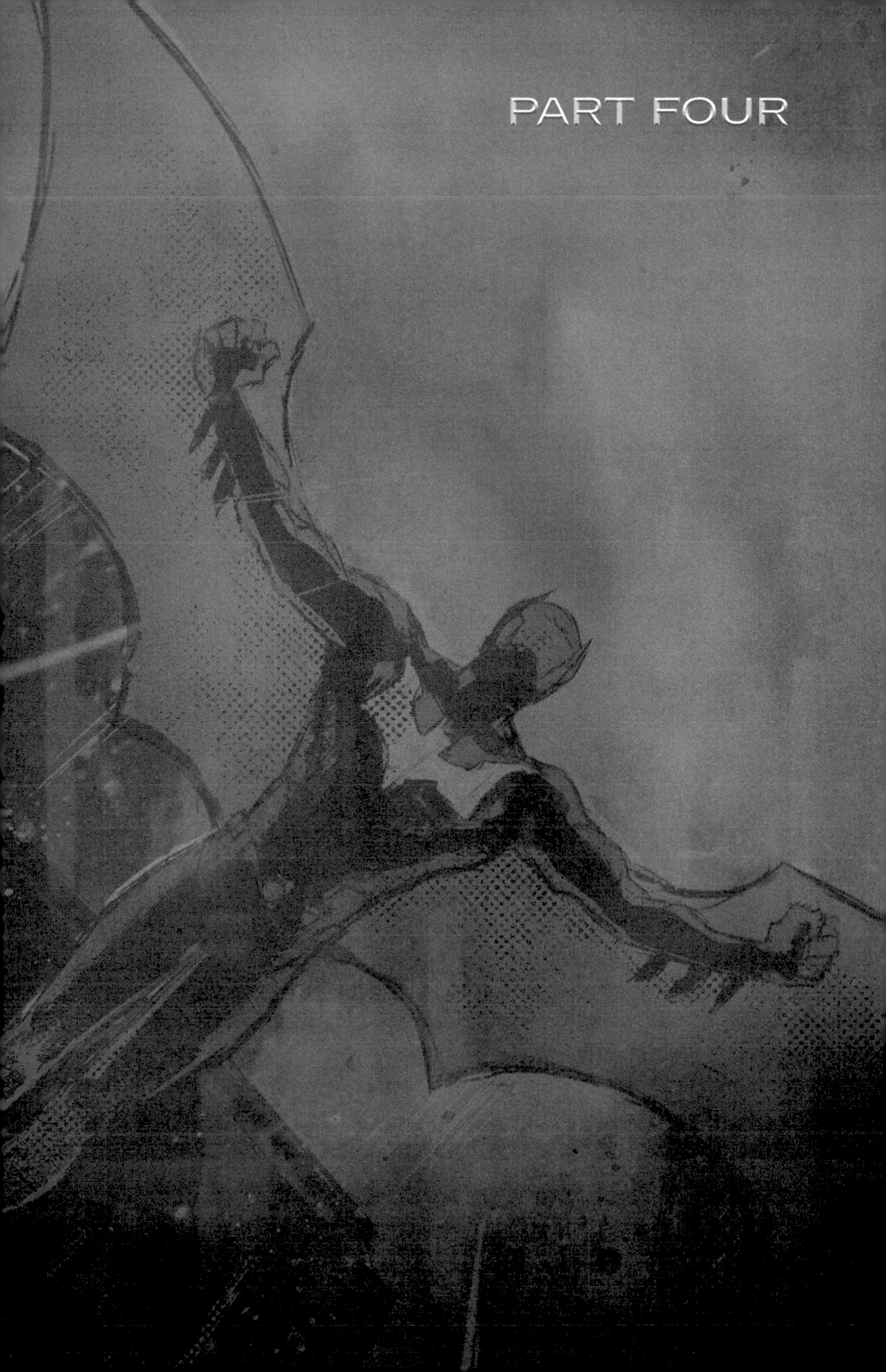

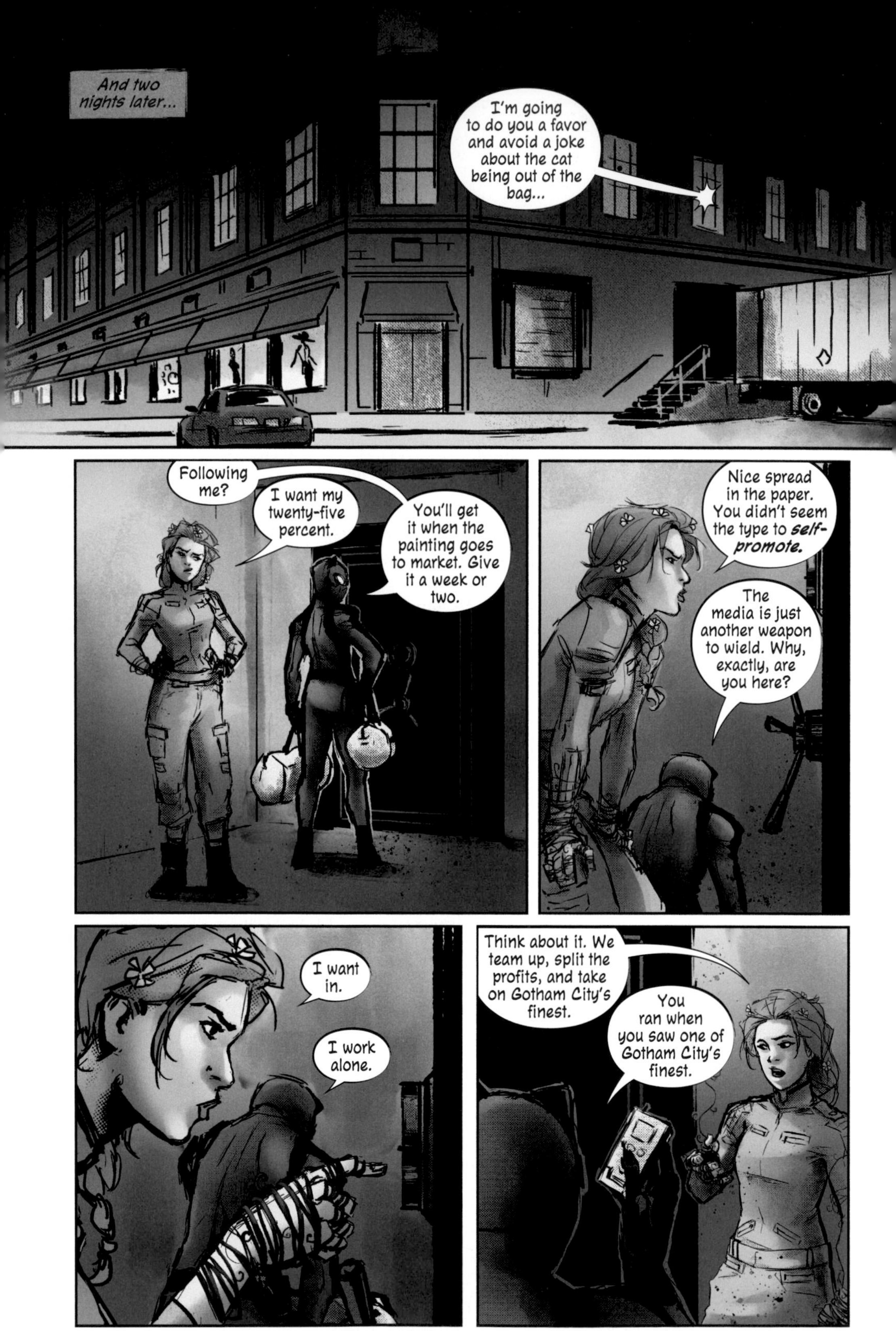
And two nights later...
I'm going to do you a favor and avoid a joke about the cat being out of the bag...
Following me?
I want my twenty-five percent.
You'll get it when the painting goes to market. Give it a week or two.
Nice spread in the paper. You didn't seem the type to *self-promote.*
The media is just another weapon to wield. Why, exactly, are you here?
I want in.
I work alone.
Think about it. We team up, split the profits, and take on Gotham City's finest.
You ran when you saw one of Gotham City's finest.

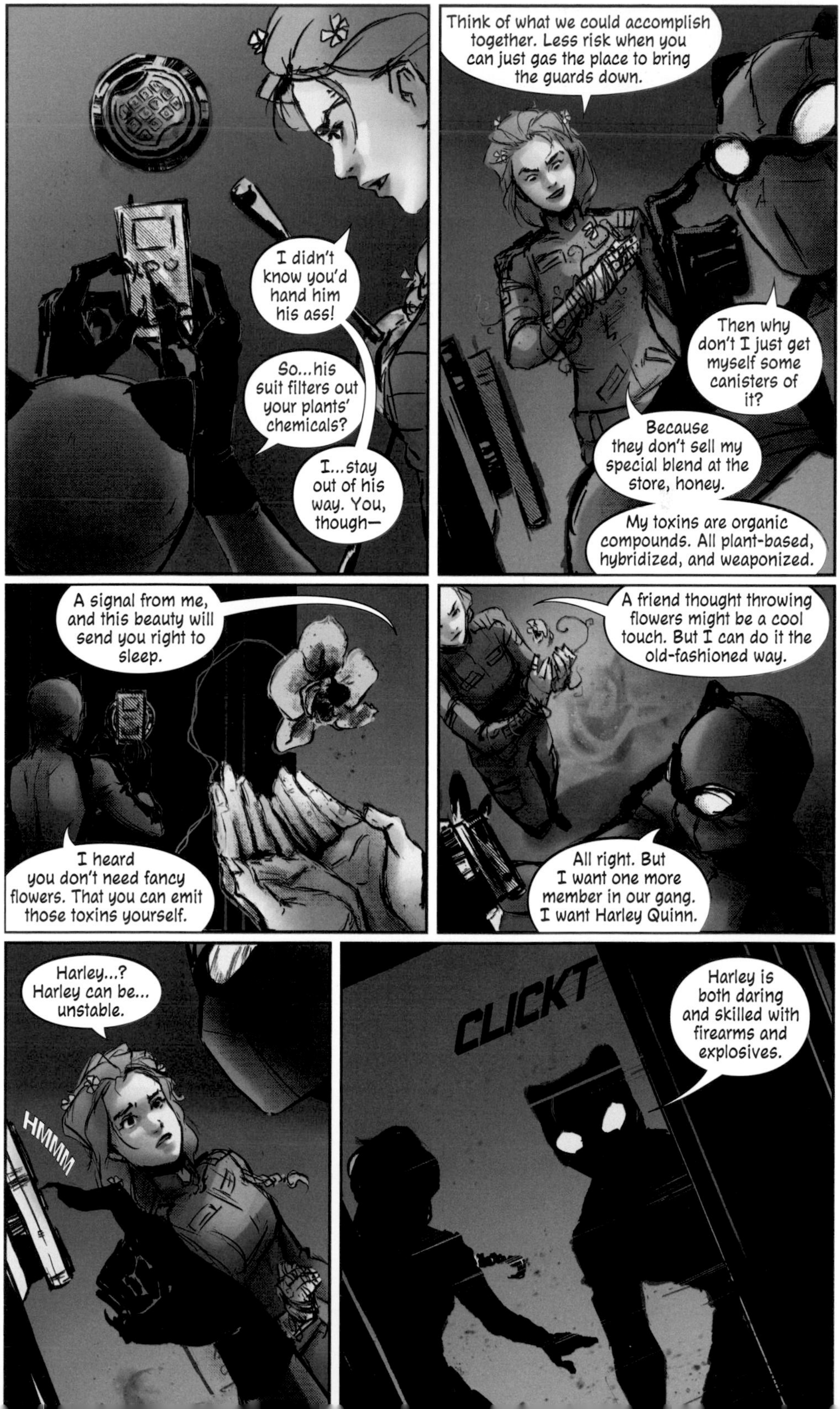
I didn't know you'd hand him his ass!
So...his suit filters out your plants' chemicals?
I...stay out of his way. You, though—
Think of what we could accomplish together. Less risk when you can just gas the place to bring the guards down.
Then why don't I just get myself some canisters of it?
Because they don't sell my special blend at the store, honey.
My toxins are organic compounds. All plant-based, hybridized, and weaponized.
A signal from me, and this beauty will send you right to sleep.
I heard you don't need fancy flowers. That you can emit those toxins yourself.
A friend thought throwing flowers might be a cool touch. But I can do it the old-fashioned way.
All right. But I want one more member in our gang. I want Harley Quinn.
Harley...? Harley can be... unstable.
HMMM
CLICKT
Harley is both daring and skilled with firearms and explosives.

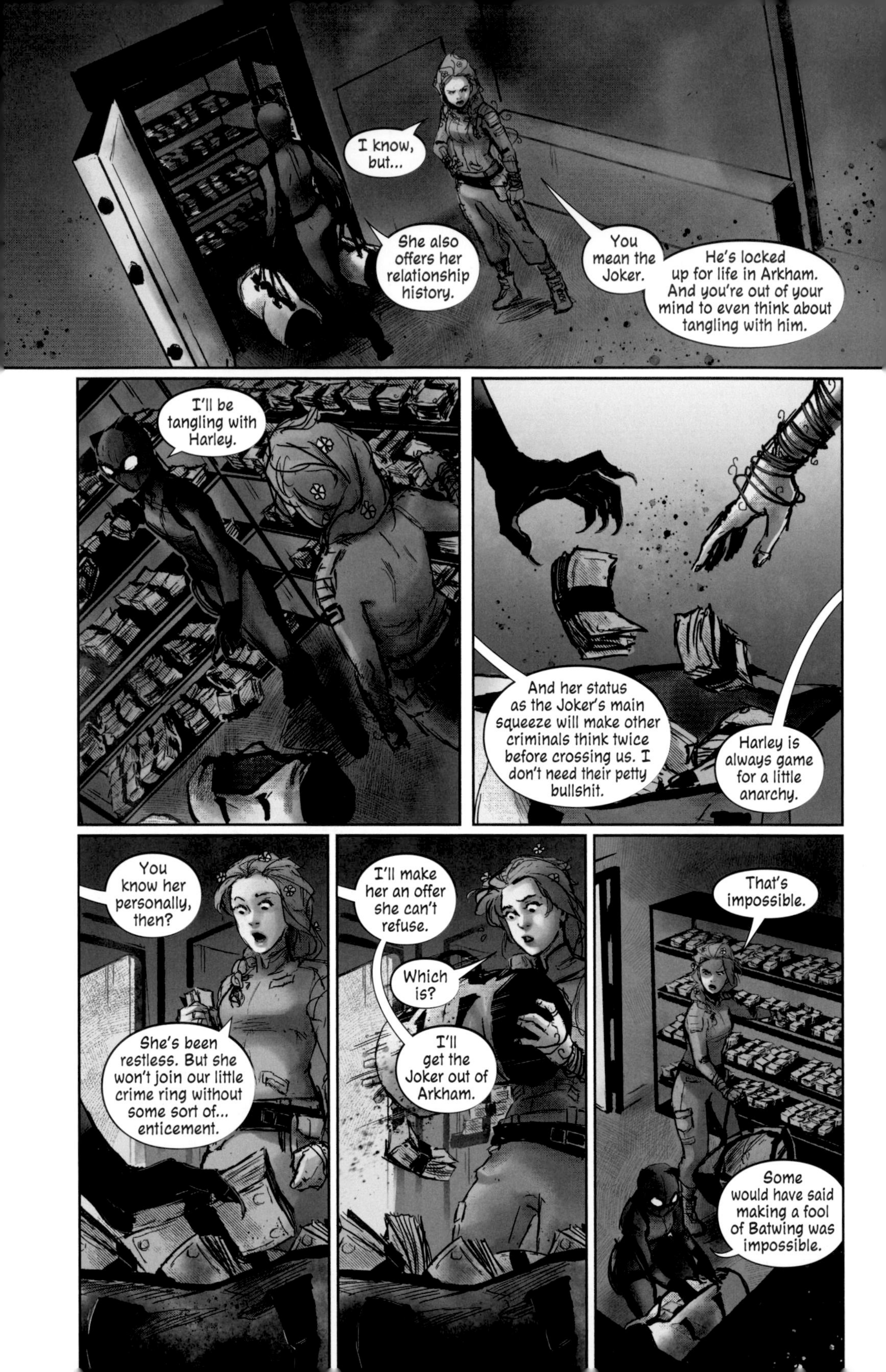
I know, but...
She also offers her relationship history.
You mean the Joker.
He's locked up for life in Arkham. And you're out of your mind to even think about tangling with him.
I'll be tangling with Harley.
And her status as the Joker's main squeeze will make other criminals think twice before crossing us. I don't need their petty bullshit.
Harley is always game for a little anarchy.
You know her personally, then?
She's been restless. But she won't join our little crime ring without some sort of... enticement.
I'll make her an offer she can't refuse.
Which is?
I'll get the Joker out of Arkham.
That's impossible.
Some would have said making a fool of Batwing was impossible.

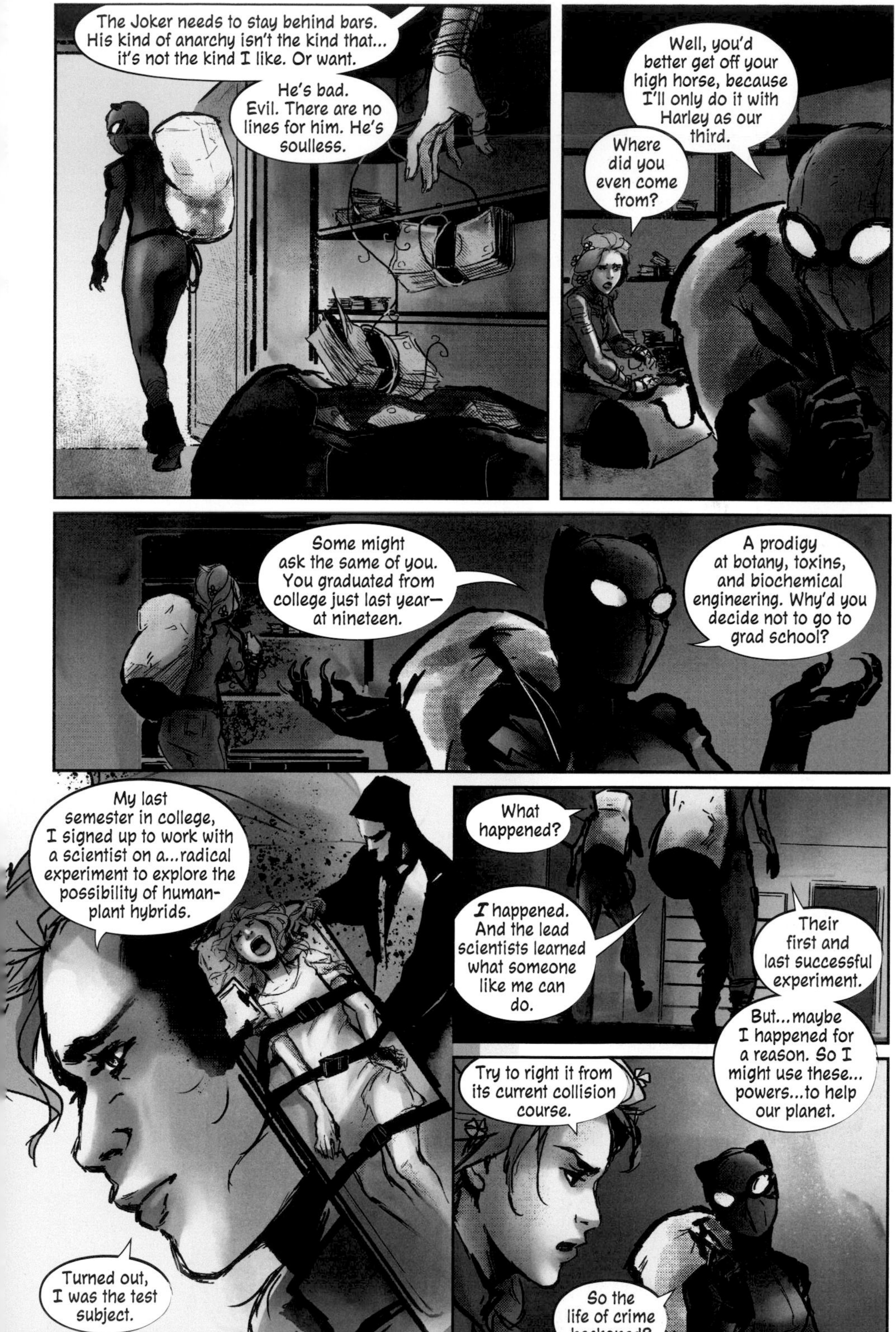
The Joker needs to stay behind bars. His kind of anarchy isn't the kind that... it's not the kind I like. Or want.
He's bad. Evil. There are no lines for him. He's soulless.
Well, you'd better get off your high horse, because I'll only do it with Harley as our third.
Where did you even come from?
Some might ask the same of you. You graduated from college just last year—at nineteen.
A prodigy at botany, toxins, and biochemical engineering. Why'd you decide not to go to grad school?
My last semester in college, I signed up to work with a scientist on a...radical experiment to explore the possibility of human-plant hybrids.
Turned out, I was the test subject.
What happened?
I happened. And the lead scientists learned what someone like me can do.
Their first and last successful experiment.
But...maybe I happened for a reason. So I might use these... powers...to help our planet.
Try to right it from its current collision course.
So the life of crime beckoned?

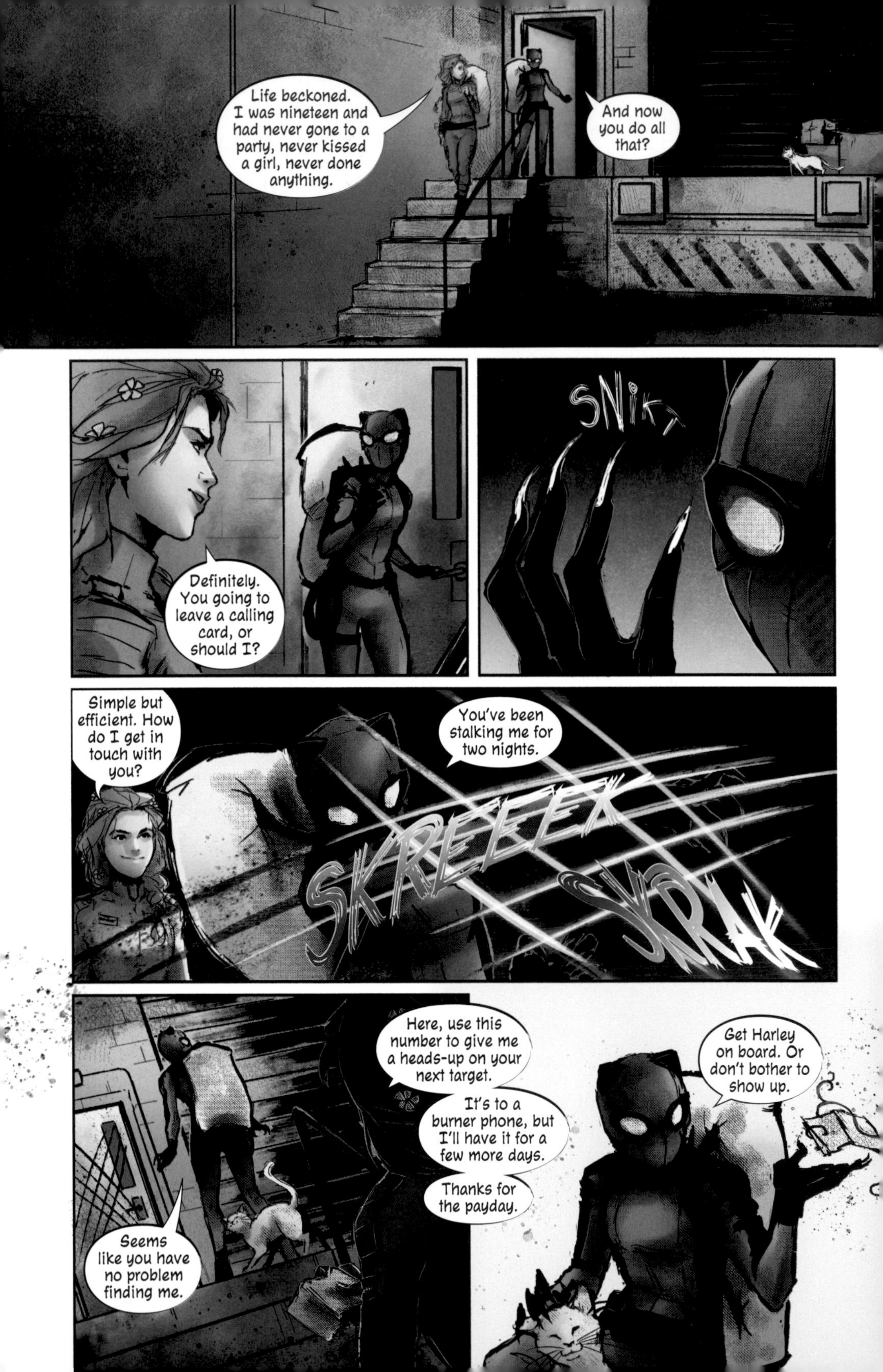
Life beckoned. I was nineteen and had never gone to a party, never kissed a girl, never done anything.
And now you do all that?
Definitely. You going to leave a calling card, or should I?
SNIKT
Simple but efficient. How do I get in touch with you?
You've been stalking me for two nights.
SKREEEK
SKRAK
Seems like you have no problem finding me.
Here, use this number to give me a heads-up on your next target.
It's to a burner phone, but I'll have it for a few more days.
Thanks for the payday.
Get Harley on board. Or don't bother to show up.

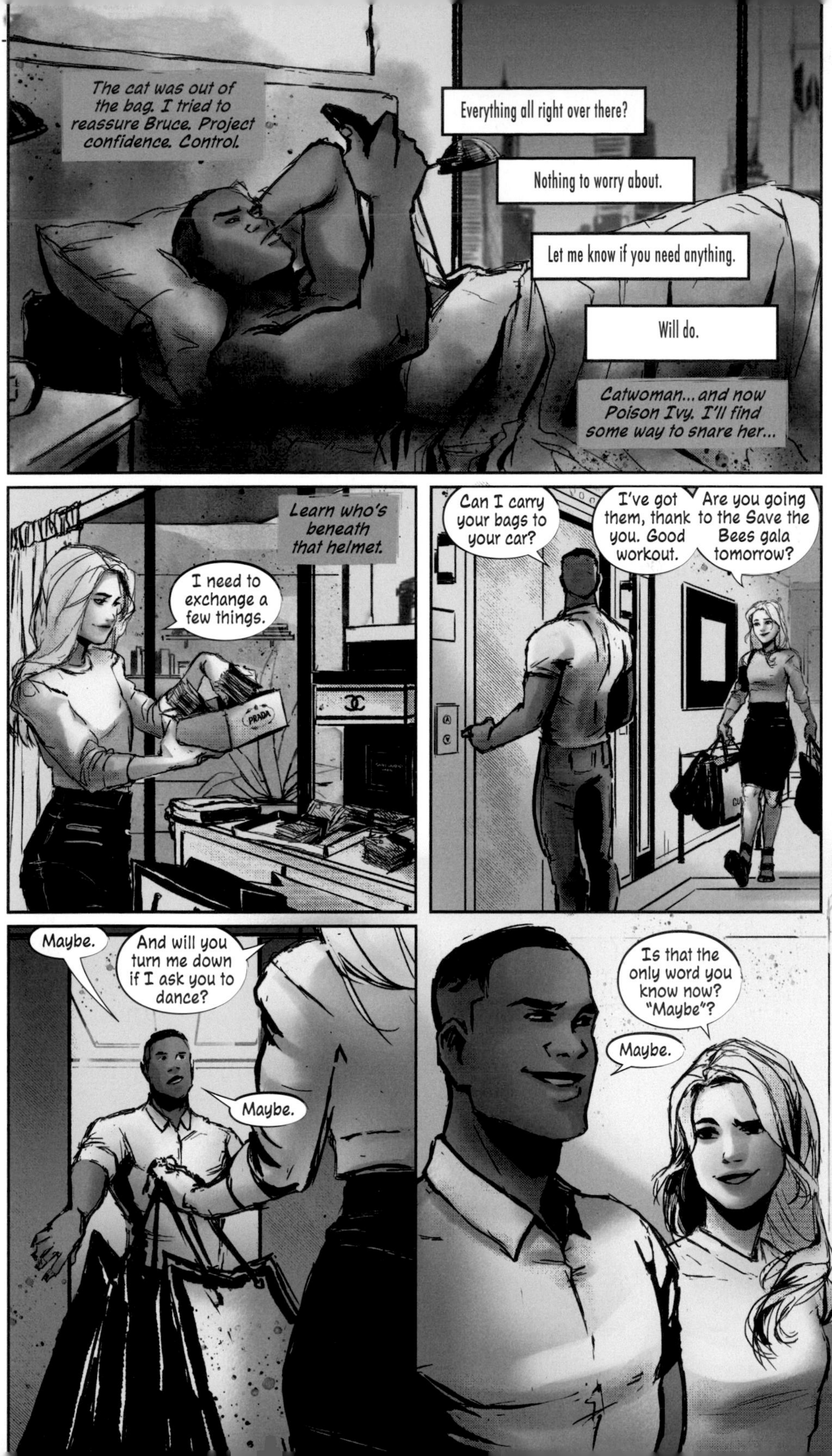
The cat was out of the bag. I tried to reassure Bruce. Project confidence. Control.
Everything all right over there?
Nothing to worry about.
Let me know if you need anything.
Will do.
Catwoman...and now Poison Ivy. I'll find some way to snare her...
Learn who's beneath that helmet.
I need to exchange a few things.
PRADA
Can I carry your bags to your car?
I've got them, thank you. Good workout.
Are you going to the Save the Bees gala tomorrow?
Maybe.
And will you turn me down if I ask you to dance?
Maybe.
Is that the only word you know now? "Maybe"?
Maybe.

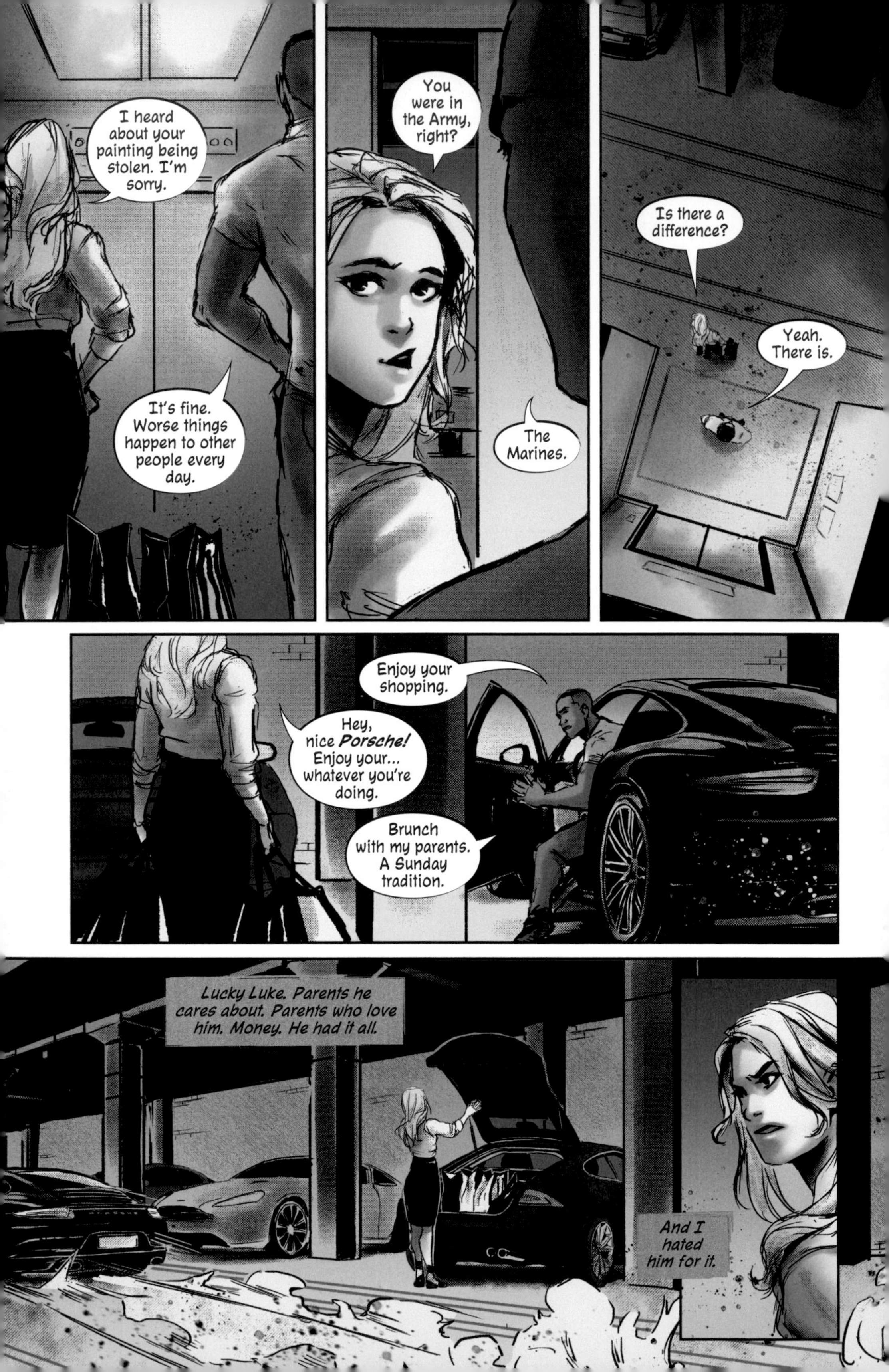
I heard about your painting being stolen. I'm sorry.
It's fine. Worse things happen to other people every day.
You were in the Army, right?
The Marines.
Is there a difference?
Yeah. There is.
Enjoy your shopping.
Hey, nice *Porsche!* Enjoy your... whatever you're doing.
Brunch with my parents. A Sunday tradition.
Lucky Luke. Parents he cares about. Parents who love him. Money. He had it all.
And I hated him for it.

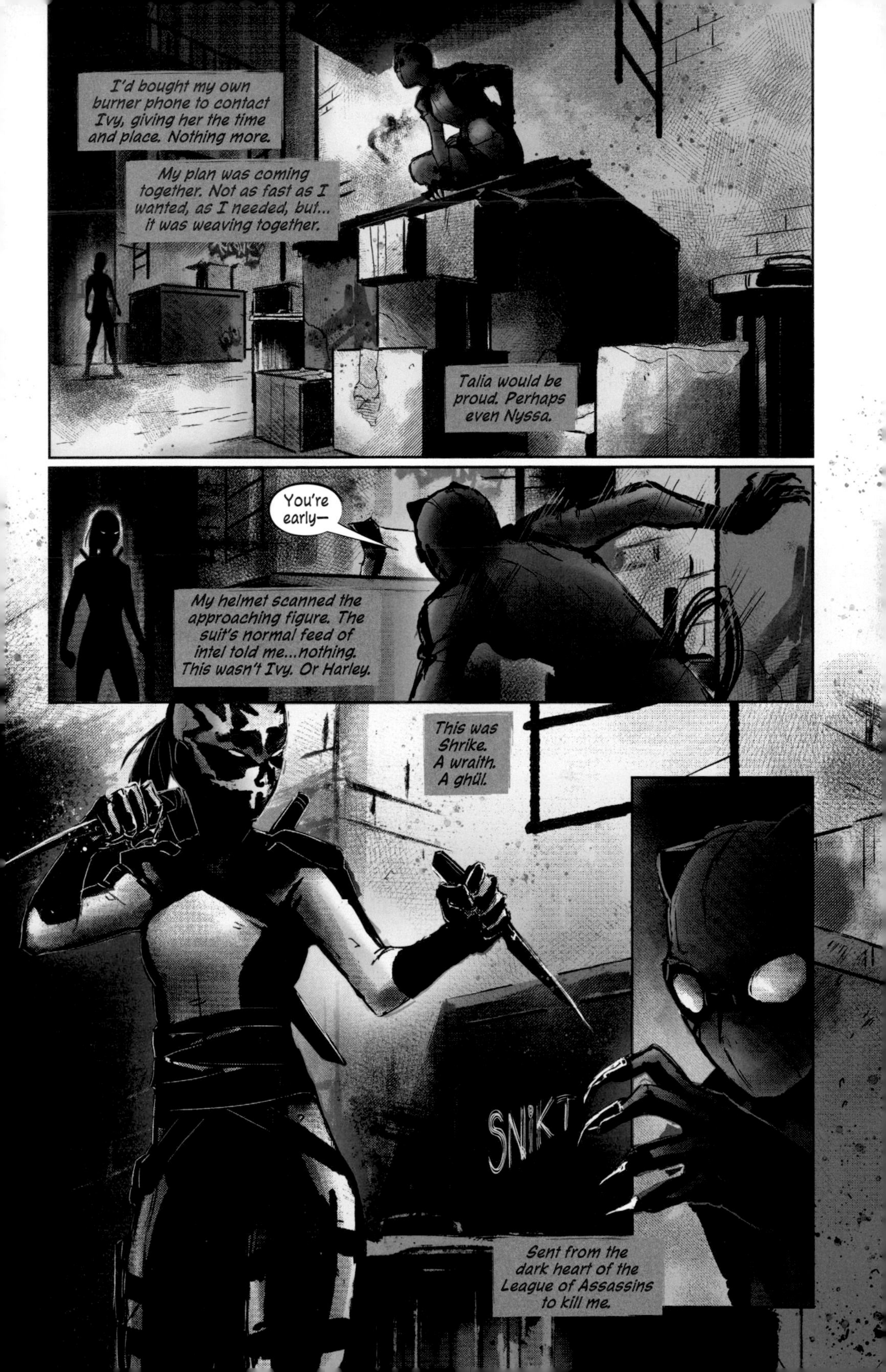
I'd bought my own burner phone to contact Ivy, giving her the time and place. Nothing more.
My plan was coming together. Not as fast as I wanted, as I needed, but... it was weaving together.
Talia would be proud. Perhaps even Nyssa.
You're early—
My helmet scanned the approaching figure. The suit's normal feed of intel told me...nothing. This wasn't Ivy. Or Harley.
This was Shrike. A wraith. A ghūl.
SNIKT
Sent from the dark heart of the League of Assassins to kill me.

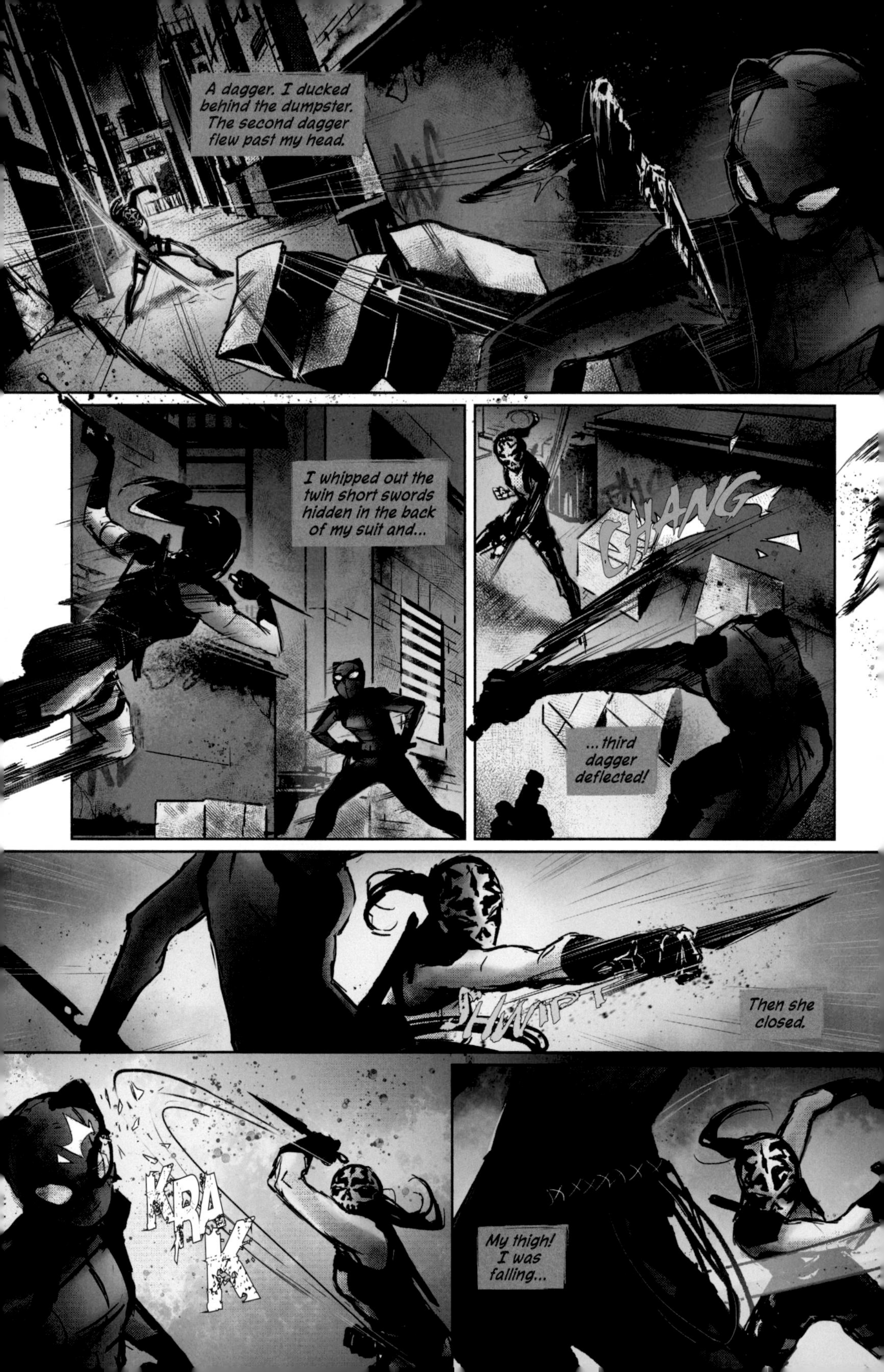
A dagger. I ducked behind the dumpster. The second dagger flew past my head.
I whipped out the twin short swords hidden in the back of my suit and...
CHANG
...third dagger deflected!
SHWIPT
Then she closed.
KRAK
My thigh! I was falling...

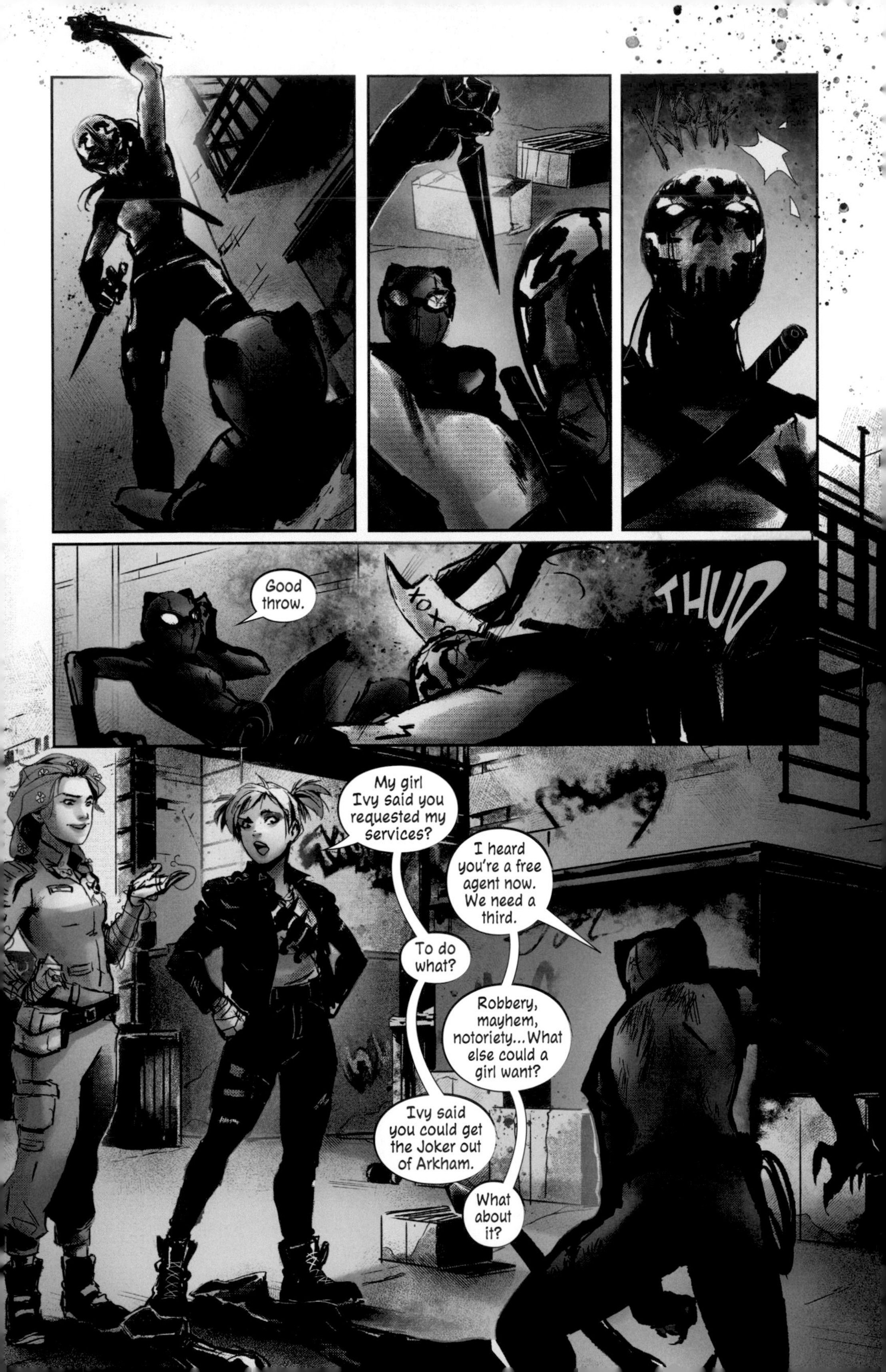
KRAK
Good throw.
XOXO
THUD
My girl Ivy said you requested my services?
I heard you're a free agent now. We need a third.
To do what?
Robbery, mayhem, notoriety... What else could a girl want?
Ivy said you could get the Joker out of Arkham.
What about it?

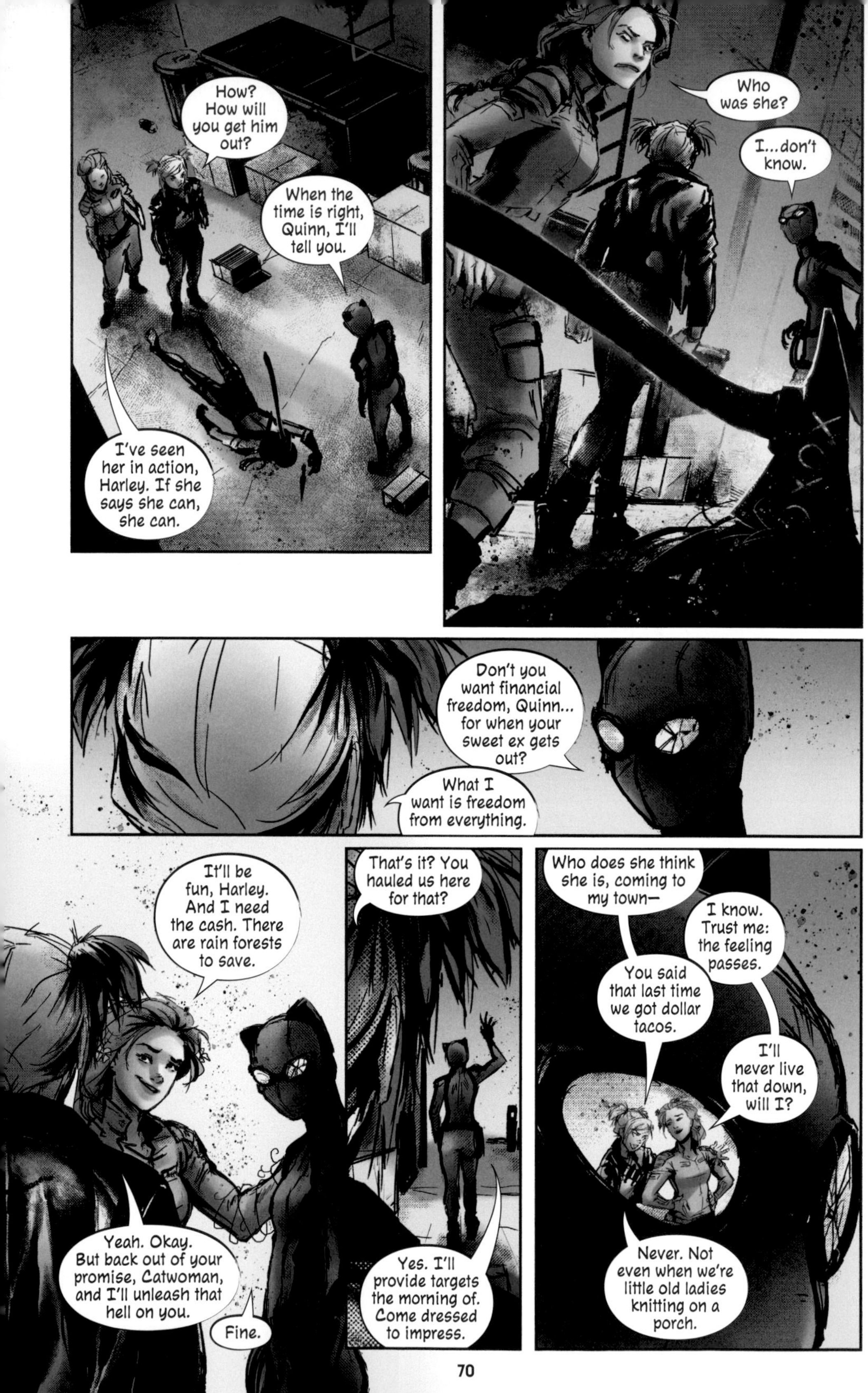
How? How will you get him out?
When the time is right, Quinn, I'll tell you.
I've seen her in action, Harley. If she says she can, she can.
Who was she?
I...don't know.
Don't you want financial freedom, Quinn... for when your sweet ex gets out?
What I want is freedom from everything.
It'll be fun, Harley. And I need the cash. There are rain forests to save.
Yeah. Okay. But back out of your promise, Catwoman, and I'll unleash that hell on you.
Fine.
That's it? You hauled us here for that?
Yes. I'll provide targets the morning of. Come dressed to impress.
Who does she think she is, coming to my town—
I know. Trust me: the feeling passes.
You said that last time we got dollar tacos.
I'll never live that down, will I?
Never. Not even when we're little old ladies knitting on a porch.

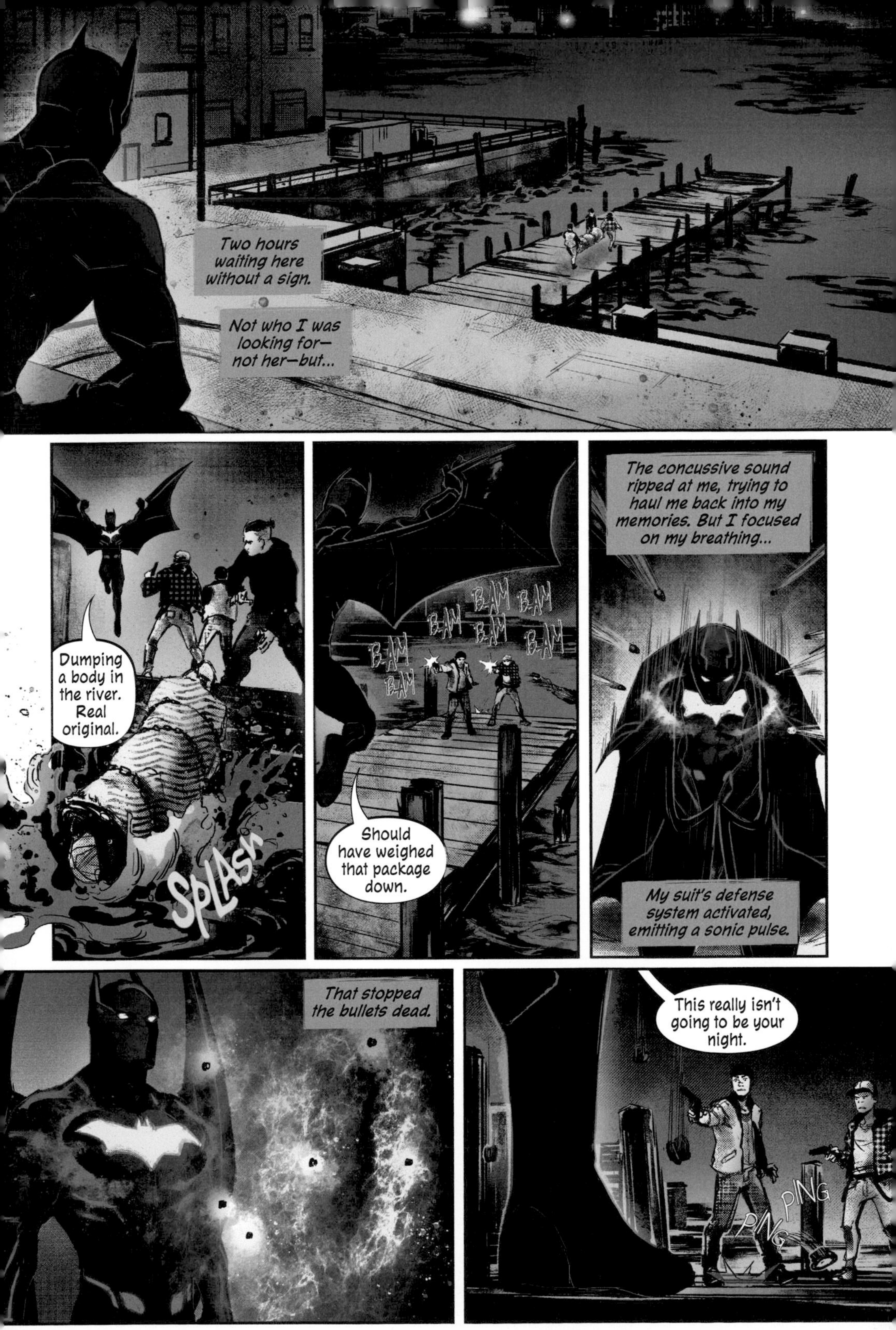

Two hours waiting here without a sign.
Not who I was looking for—not her—but...
Dumping a body in the river. Real original.
SPLASH
BAM BAM BAM BAM BAM BAM BAM BAM
Should have weighed that package down.
The concussive sound ripped at me, trying to haul me back into my memories. But I focused on my breathing...
My suit's defense system activated, emitting a sonic pulse.
That stopped the bullets dead.
This really isn't going to be your night.
PING PING

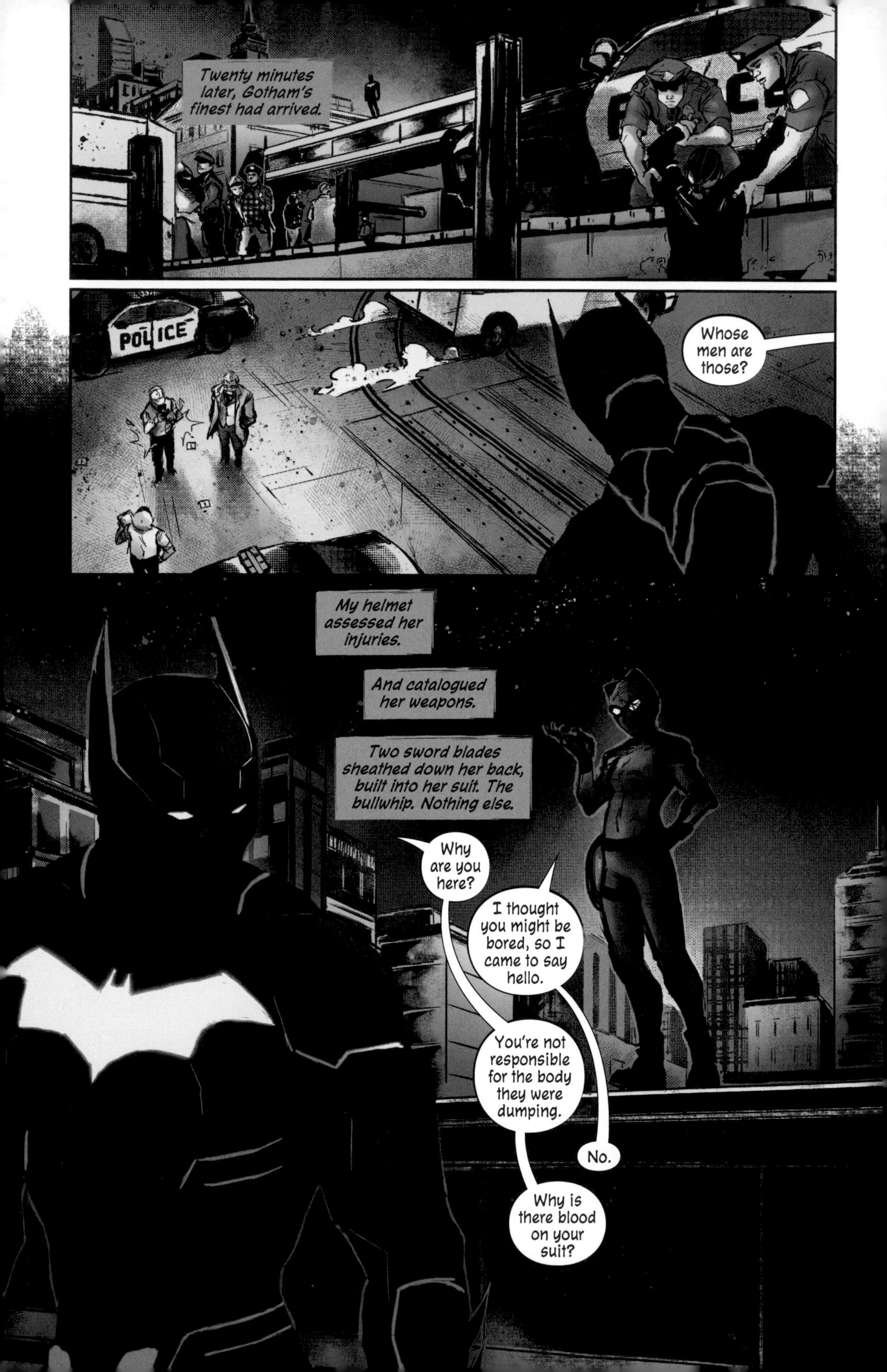

Twenty minutes later, Gotham's finest had arrived.
POLICE
POLICE
Whose men are those?
My helmet assessed her injuries.
And catalogued her weapons.
Two sword blades sheathed down her back, built into her suit. The bullwhip. Nothing else.
Why are you here?
I thought you might be bored, so I came to say hello.
You're not responsible for the body they were dumping.
No.
Why is there blood on your suit?

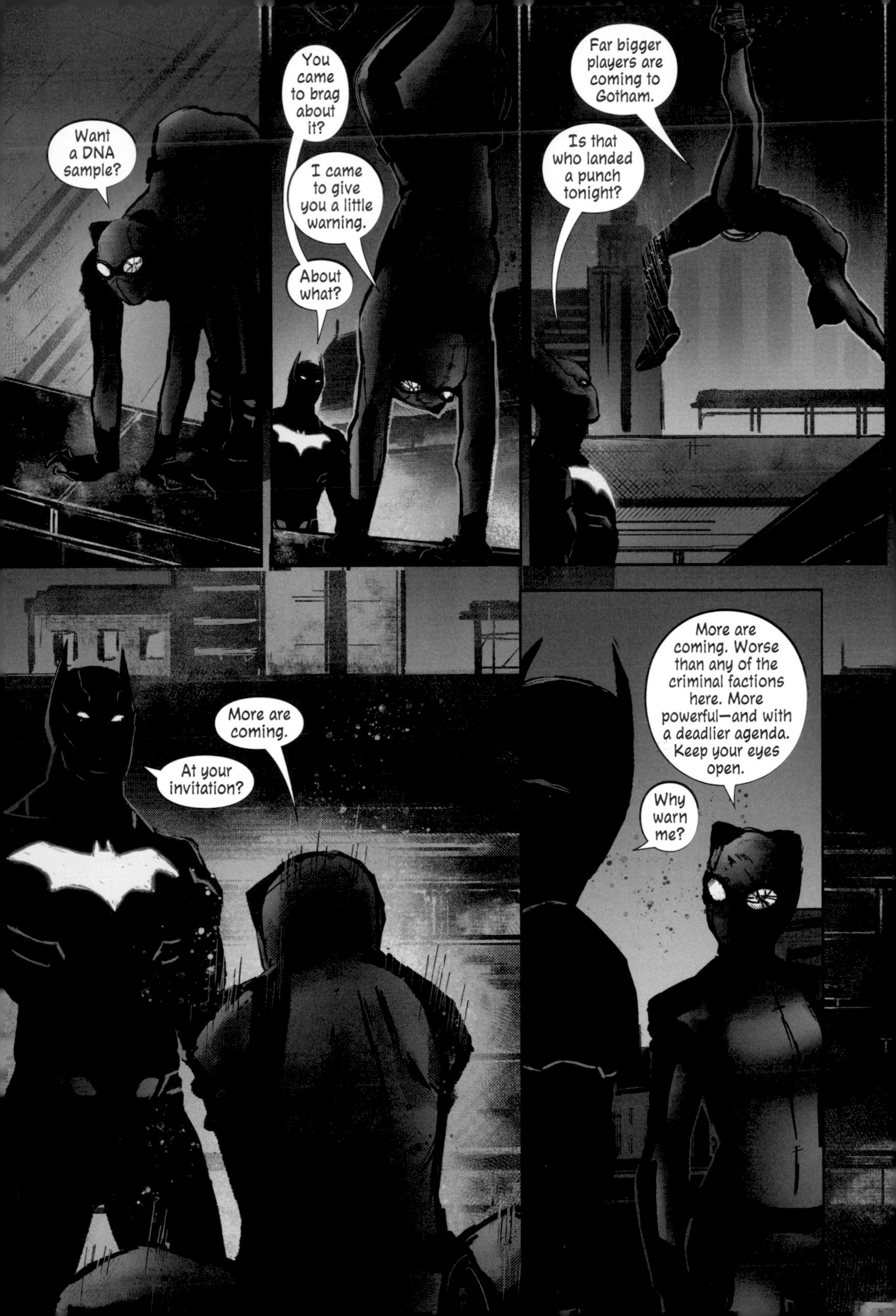
Want a DNA sample?
You came to brag about it?
I came to give you a little warning.
About what?
Far bigger players are coming to Gotham.
Is that who landed a punch tonight?
More are coming.
At your invitation?
More are coming. Worse than any of the criminal factions here. More powerful—and with a deadlier agenda. Keep your eyes open.
Why warn me?

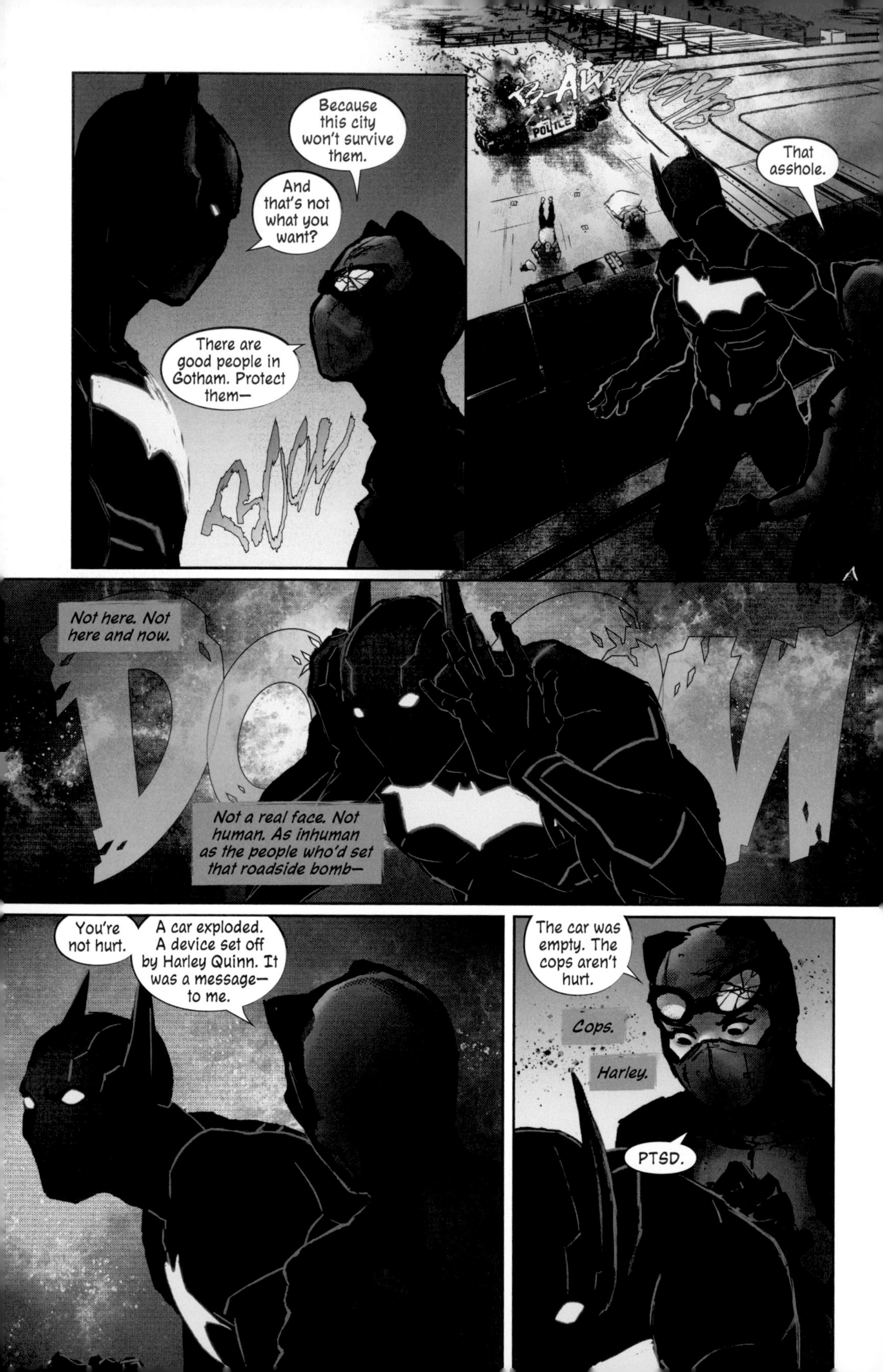
Because this city won't survive them.
And that's not what you want?
There are good people in Gotham. Protect them—
BOOM
BAWHOOMP
That asshole.
Not here. Not here and now.
DOOM
Not a real face. Not human. As inhuman as the people who'd set that roadside bomb—
You're not hurt.
A car exploded. A device set off by Harley Quinn. It was a message— to me.
The car was empty. The cops aren't hurt.
Cops.
Harley.
PTSD.

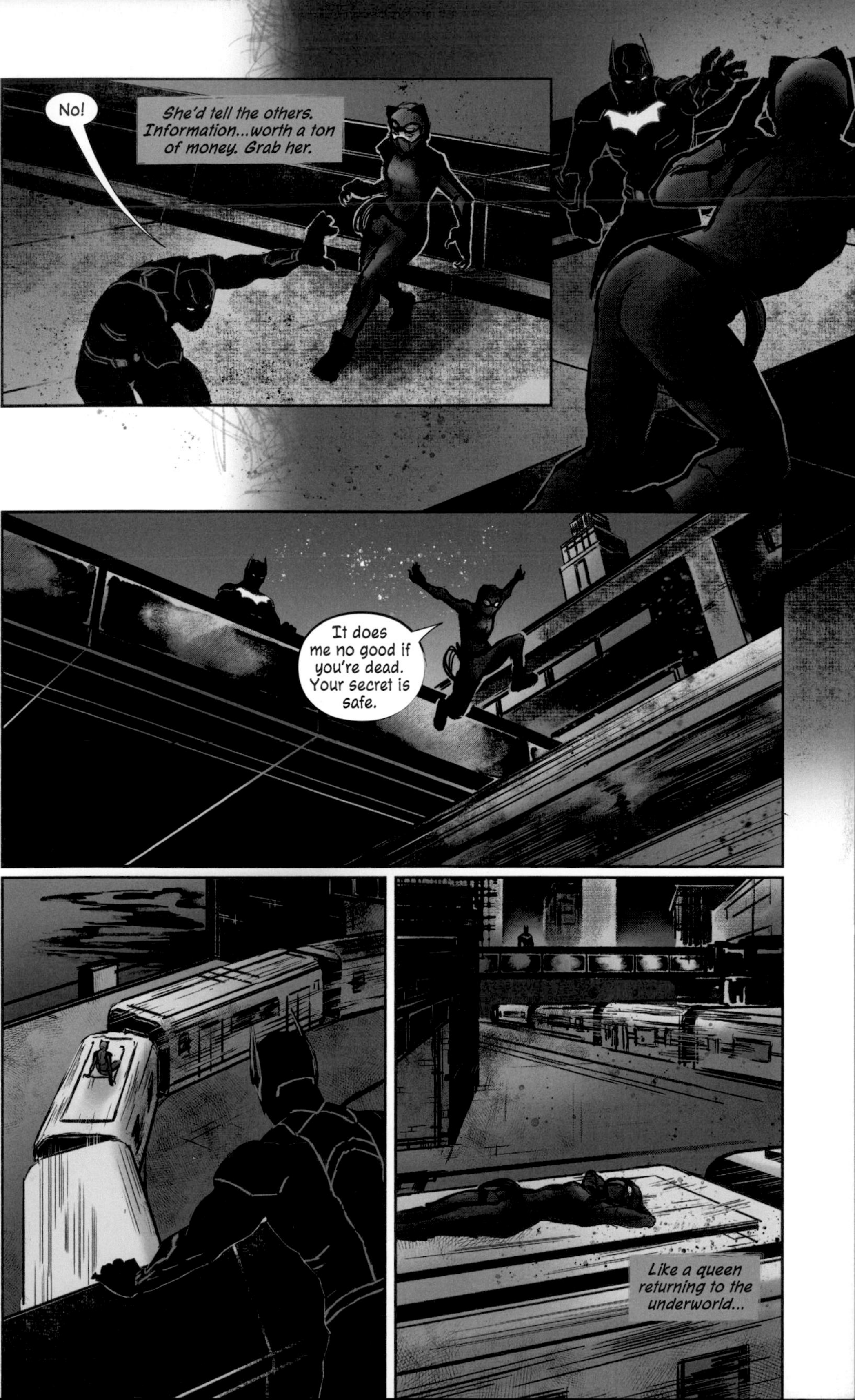
No!
She'd tell the others. Information...worth a ton of money. Grab her.
It does me no good if you're dead. Your secret is safe.
Like a queen returning to the underworld...

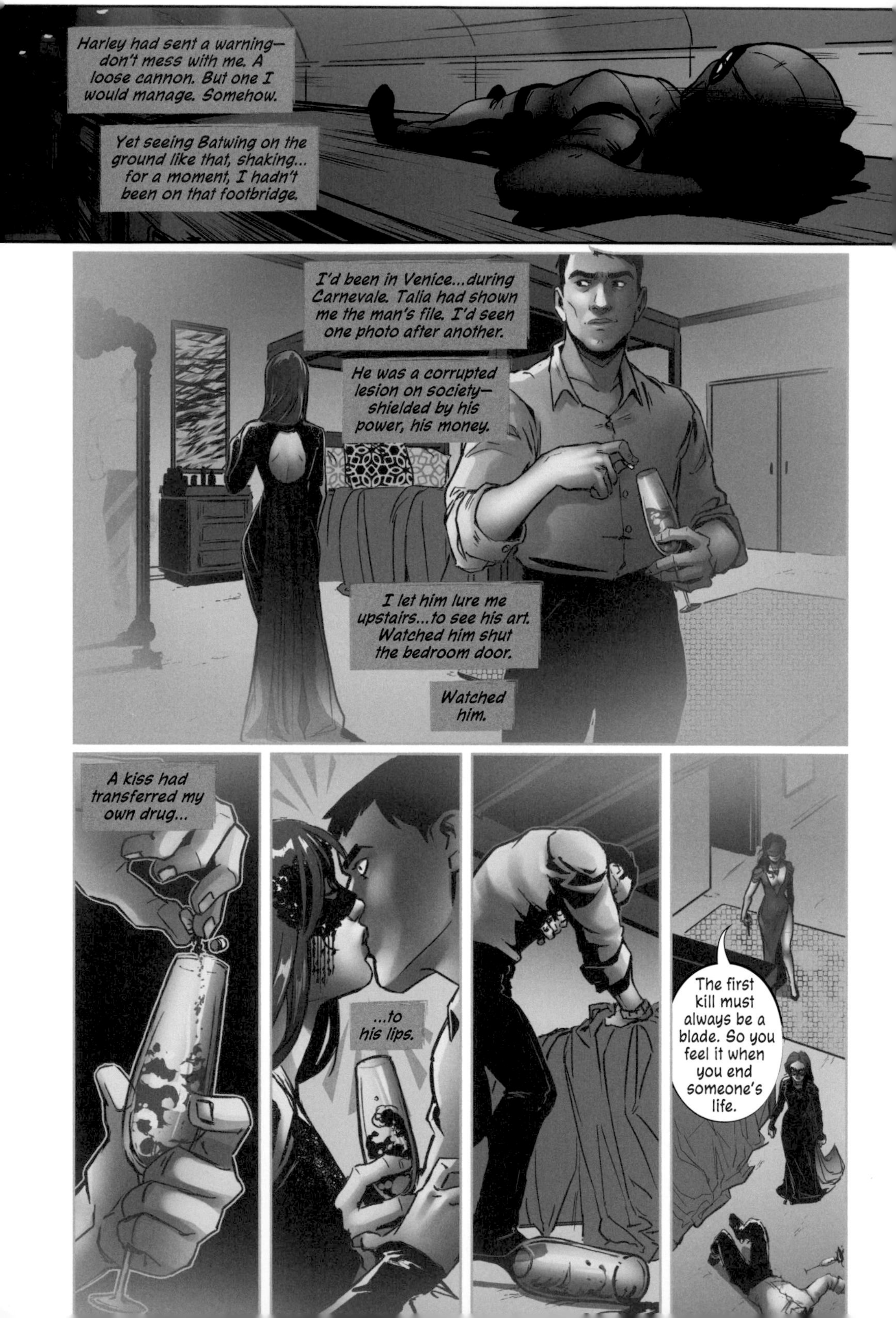
Harley had sent a warning—don't mess with me. A loose cannon. But one I would manage. Somehow.
Yet seeing Batwing on the ground like that, shaking... for a moment, I hadn't been on that footbridge.
I'd been in Venice...during Carnevale. Talia had shown me the man's file. I'd seen one photo after another.
He was a corrupted lesion on society—shielded by his power, his money.
I let him lure me upstairs...to see his art. Watched him shut the bedroom door.
Watched him.
A kiss had transferred my own drug...
...to his lips.
The first kill must always be a blade. So you feel it when you end someone's life.

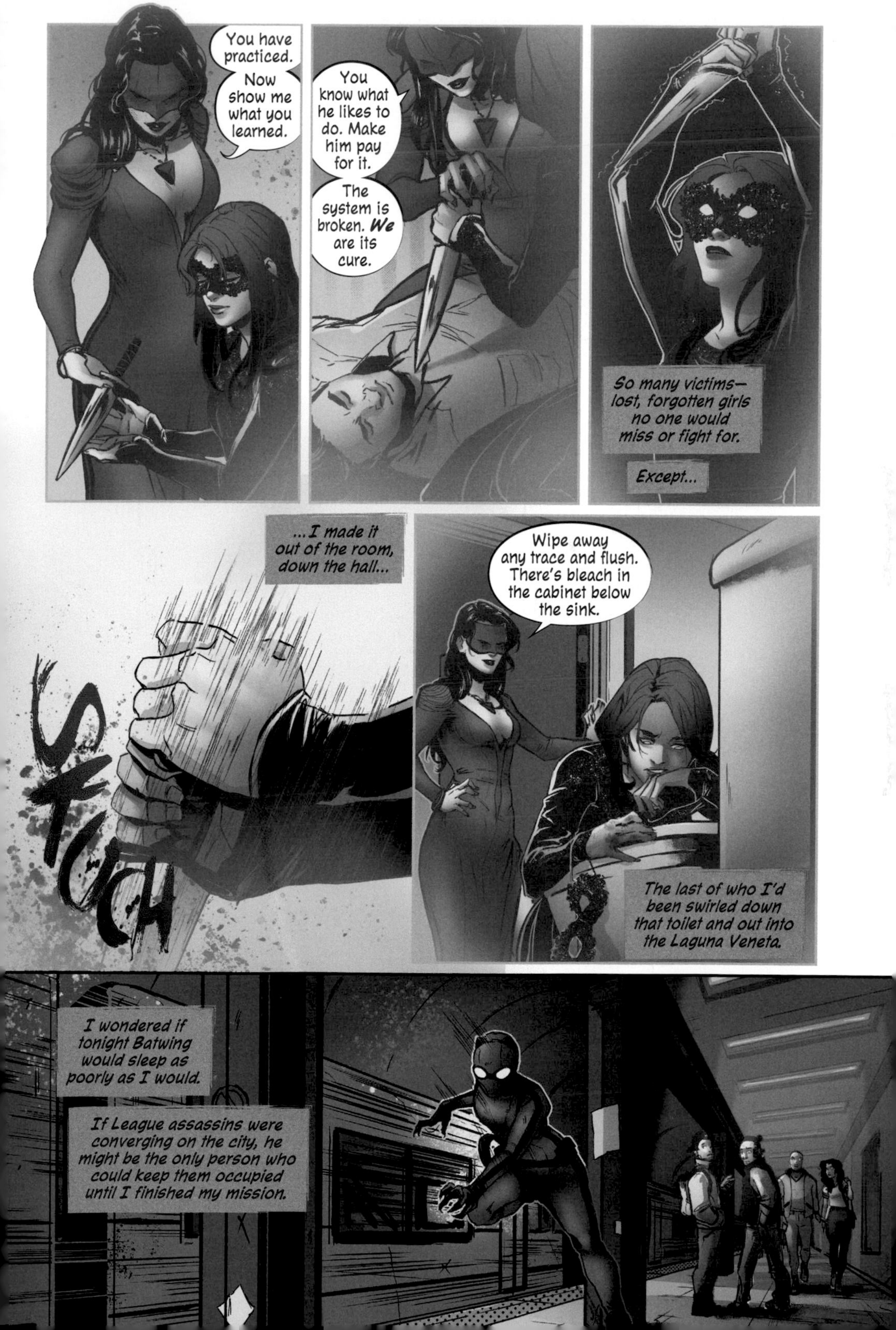

You have practiced.
Now show me what you learned.
You know what he likes to do. Make him pay for it.
The system is broken. We are its cure.
So many victims— lost, forgotten girls no one would miss or fight for.
Except...
...I made it out of the room, down the hall...
SHLUCH
Wipe away any trace and flush. There's bleach in the cabinet below the sink.
The last of who I'd been swirled down that toilet and out into the Laguna Veneta.
I wondered if tonight Batwing would sleep as poorly as I would.
If League assassins were converging on the city, he might be the only person who could keep them occupied until I finished my mission.

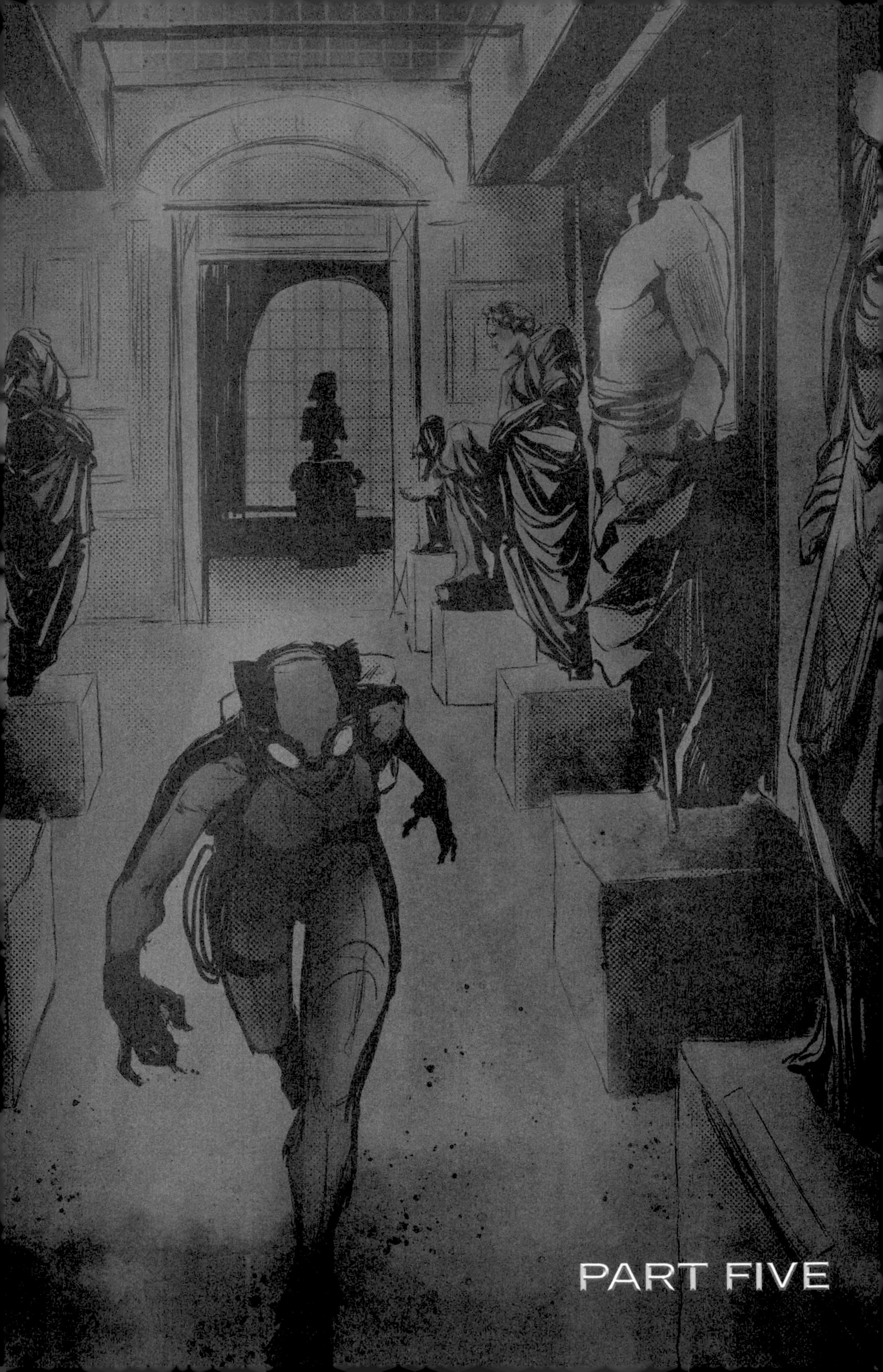
PART FIVE

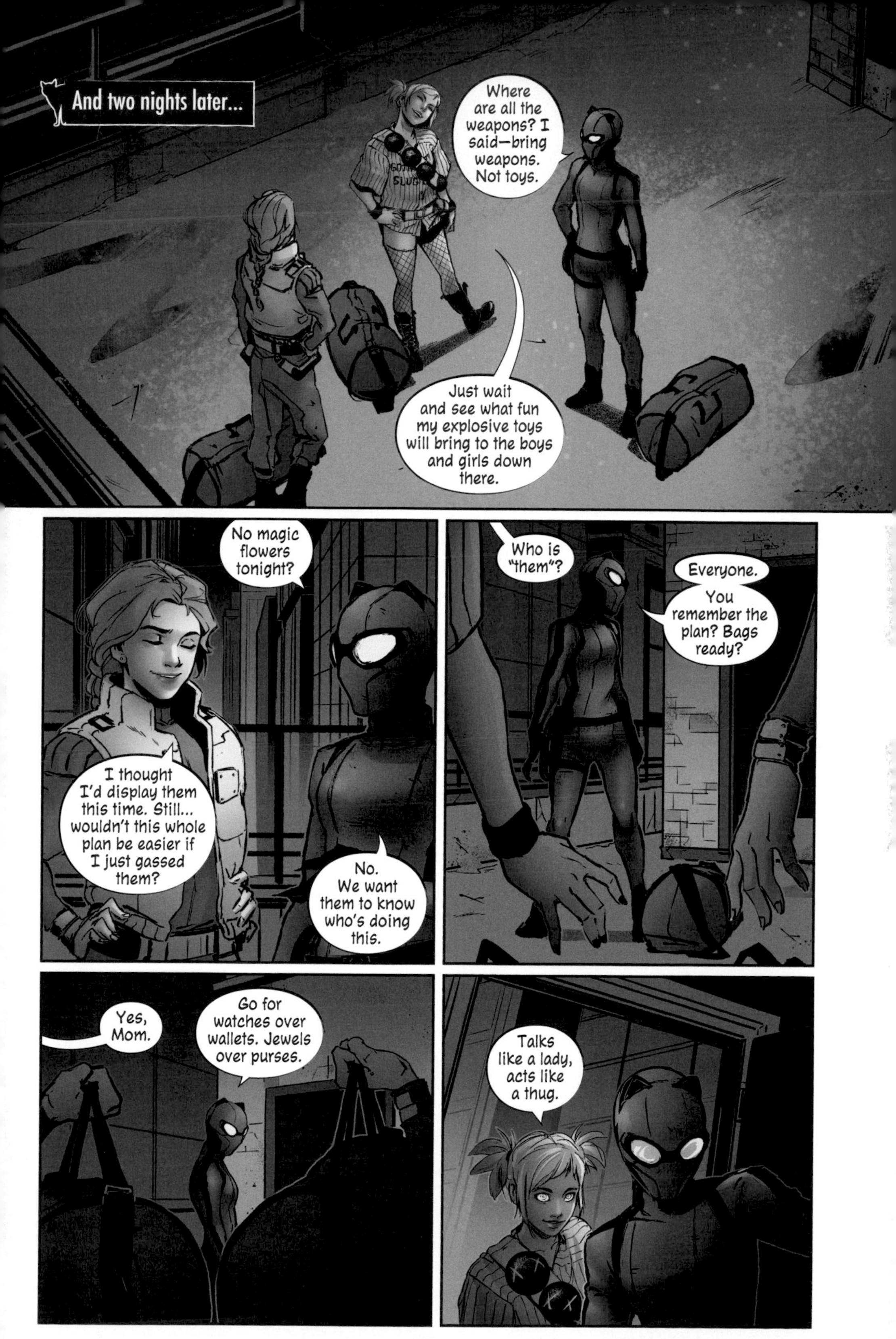
And two nights later...
Where are all the weapons? I said—bring weapons. Not toys.
Just wait and see what fun my explosive toys will bring to the boys and girls down there.
No magic flowers tonight?
I thought I'd display them this time. Still... wouldn't this whole plan be easier if I just gassed them?
No. We want them to know who's doing this.
Who is "them"?
Everyone.
You remember the plan? Bags ready?
Go for watches over wallets. Jewels over purses.
Yes, Mom.
Talks like a lady, acts like a thug.

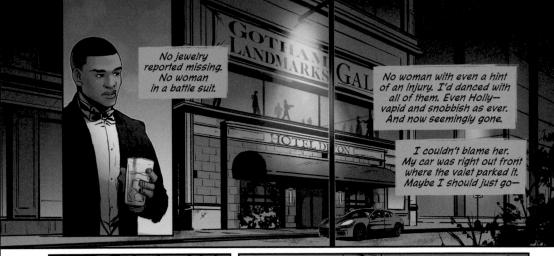

No jewelry reported missing. No woman in a battle suit.

No woman with even a hint of an injury. I'd danced with all of them. Even Holly—vapid and snobbish as ever. And now seemingly gone.

I couldn't blame her. My car was right out front where the valet parked it. Maybe I should just go—

Catwoman!

WHRA—

But Poison Ivy and Harley Quinn, too?! Shit. Shit. Shit.

I'd read their files. Never dealt with them. Either of them. But Bruce had warned me.

Who's ready to party?

I needed my suit. It would take five minutes to slip out and return as Batwing.

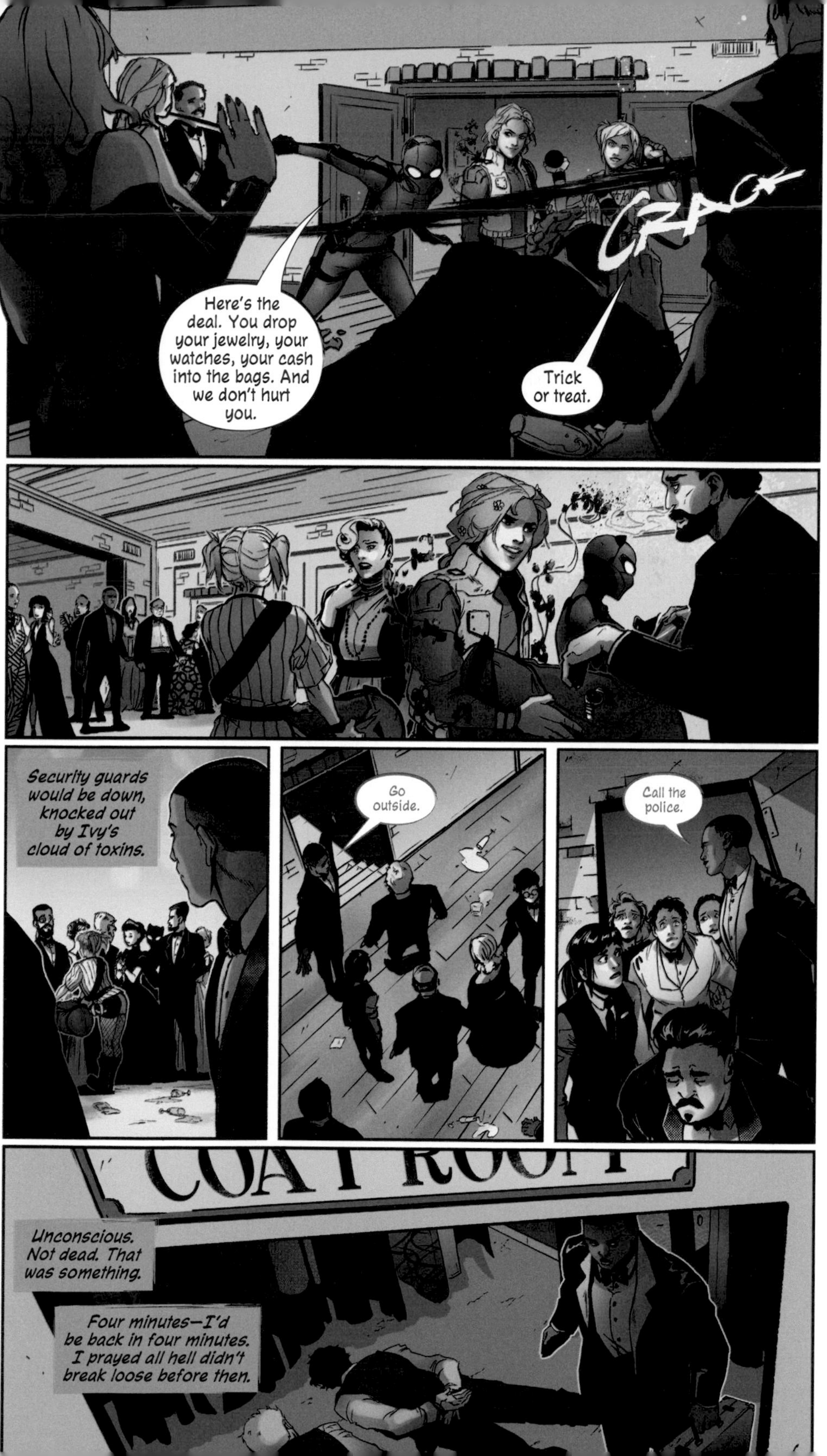
Here's the deal. You drop your jewelry, your watches, your cash into the bags. And we don't hurt you.
CRACK
Trick or treat.
Security guards would be down, knocked out by Ivy's cloud of toxins.
Go outside.
Call the police.
COAT ROOM
Unconscious. Not dead. That was something.
Four minutes—I'd be back in four minutes. I prayed all hell didn't break loose before then.

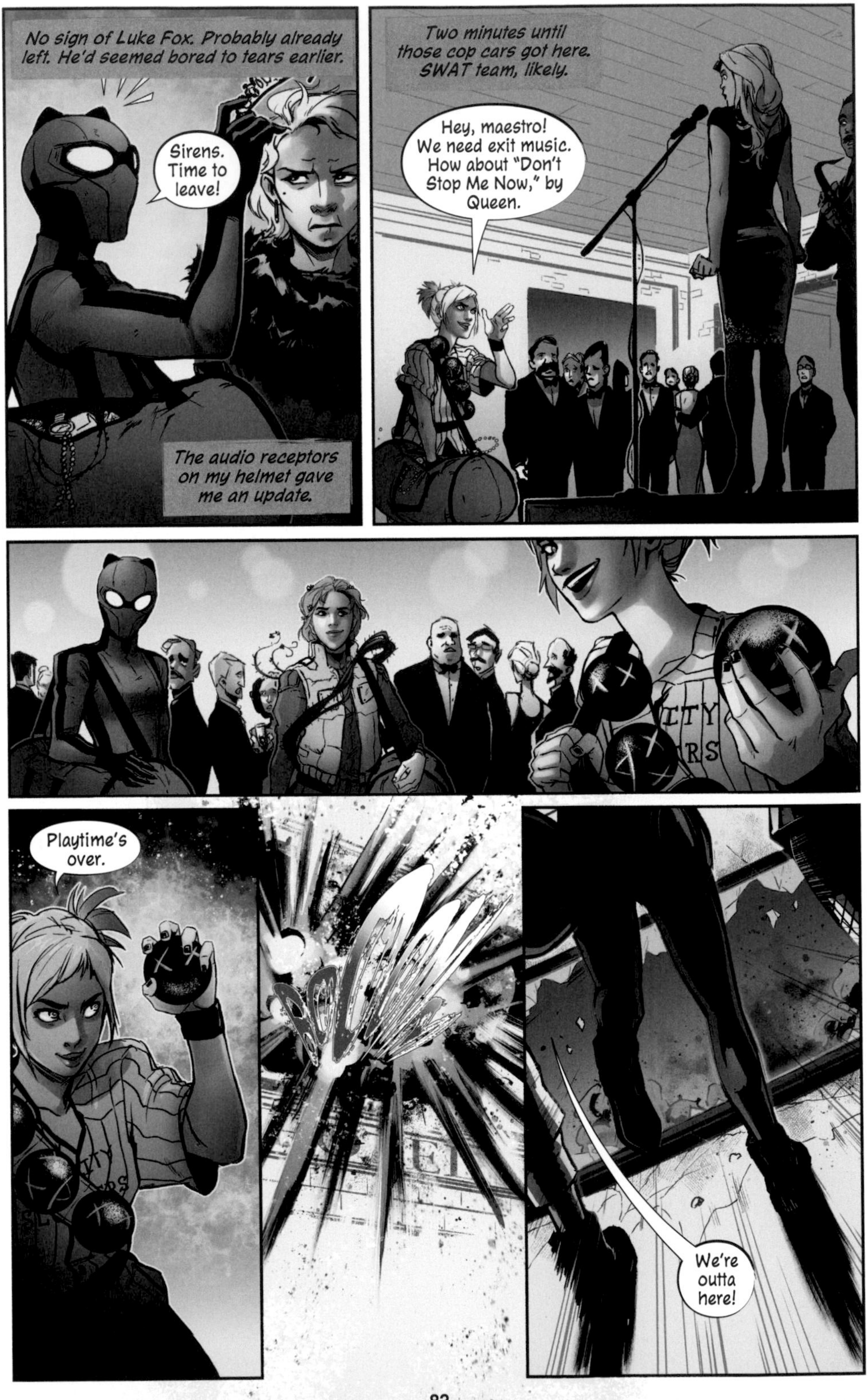
No sign of Luke Fox. Probably already left. He'd seemed bored to tears earlier.
Sirens. Time to leave!
The audio receptors on my helmet gave me an update.
Two minutes until those cop cars got here. SWAT team, likely.
Hey, maestro! We need exit music. How about "Don't Stop Me Now," by Queen.
Playtime's over.
We're outta here!

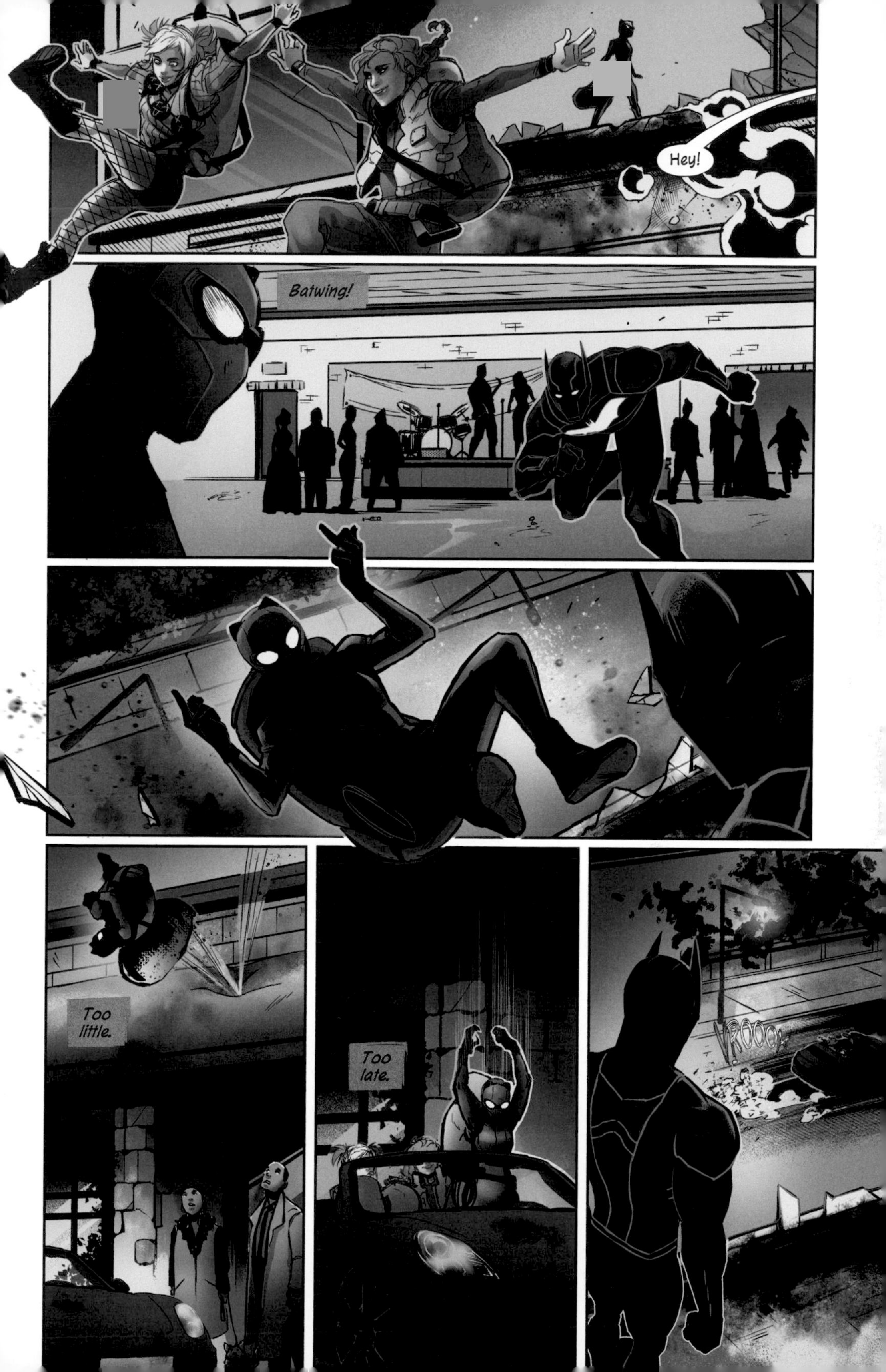
Hey!
Batwing!
Too little.
Too late.
VROOO

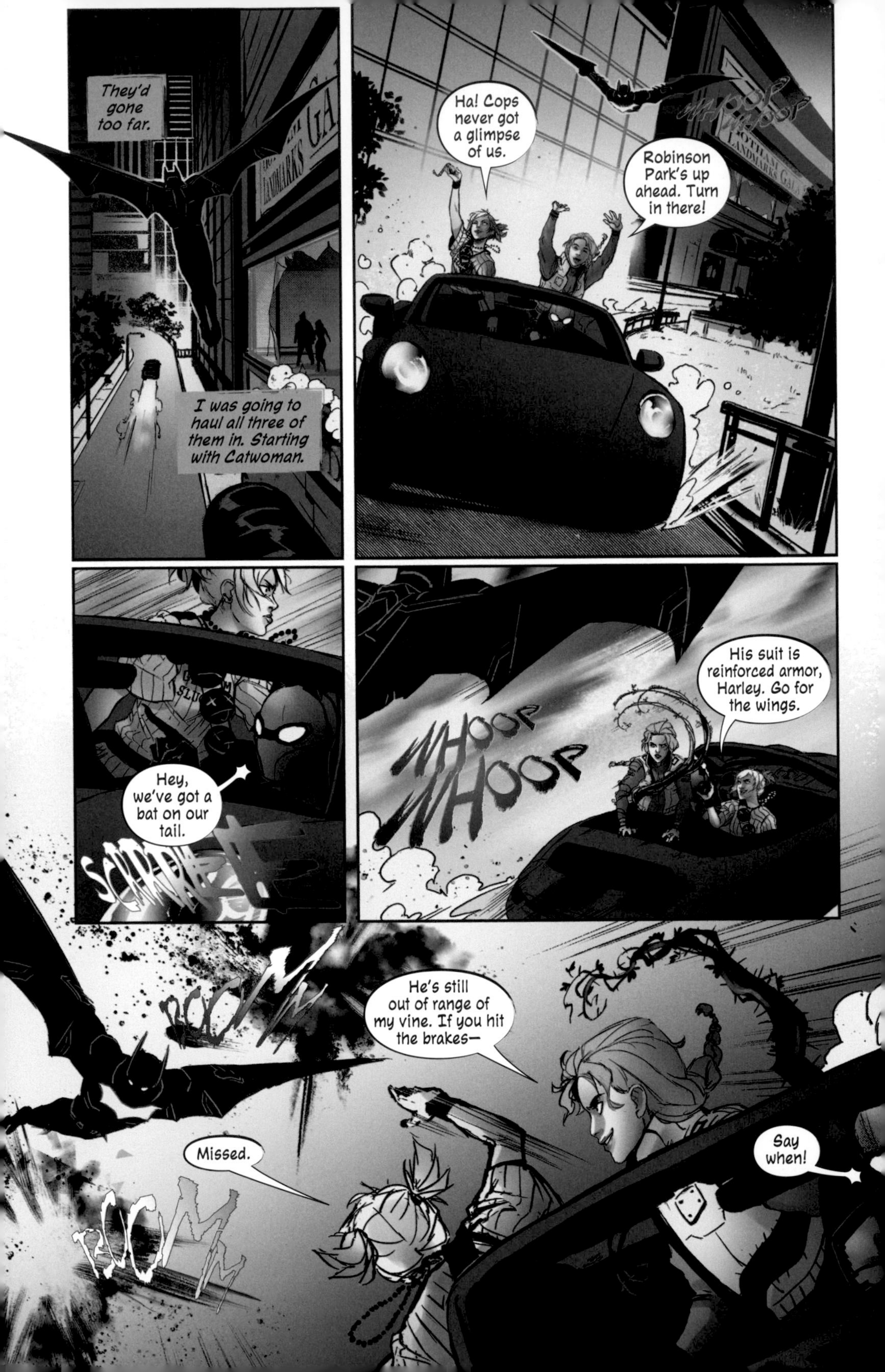
They'd gone too far.
I was going to haul all three of them in. Starting with Catwoman.
Ha! Cops never got a glimpse of us.
Robinson Park's up ahead. Turn in there!
Hey, we've got a bat on our tail.
His suit is reinforced armor, Harley. Go for the wings.
WHOOP WHOOP
He's still out of range of my vine. If you hit the brakes—
Missed.
Say when!

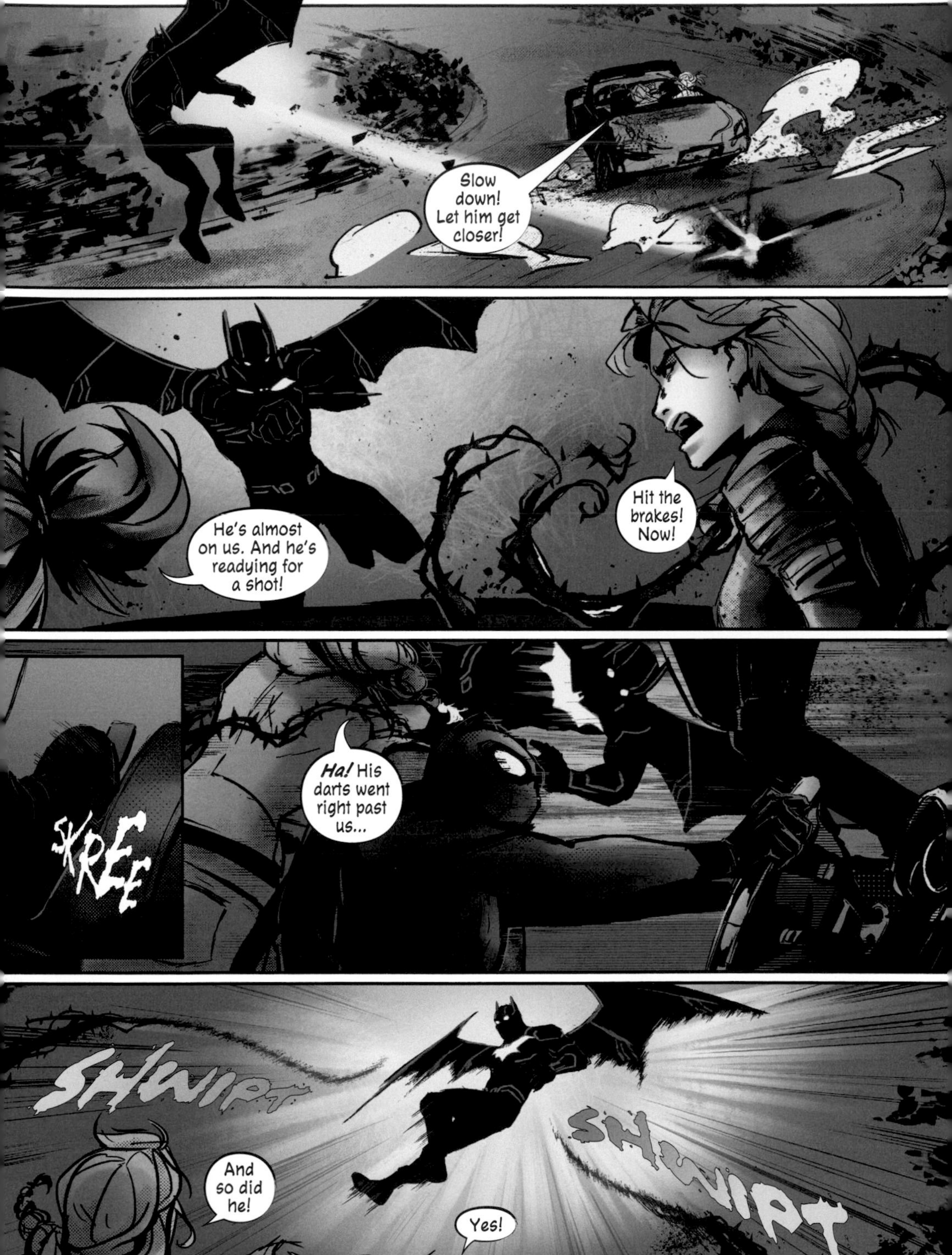
Slow down! Let him get closer!
Hit the brakes! Now!
He's almost on us. And he's readying for a shot!
SKREE
Ha! His darts went right past us...
SHWIPT
SHWIPT
And so did he!
Yes!

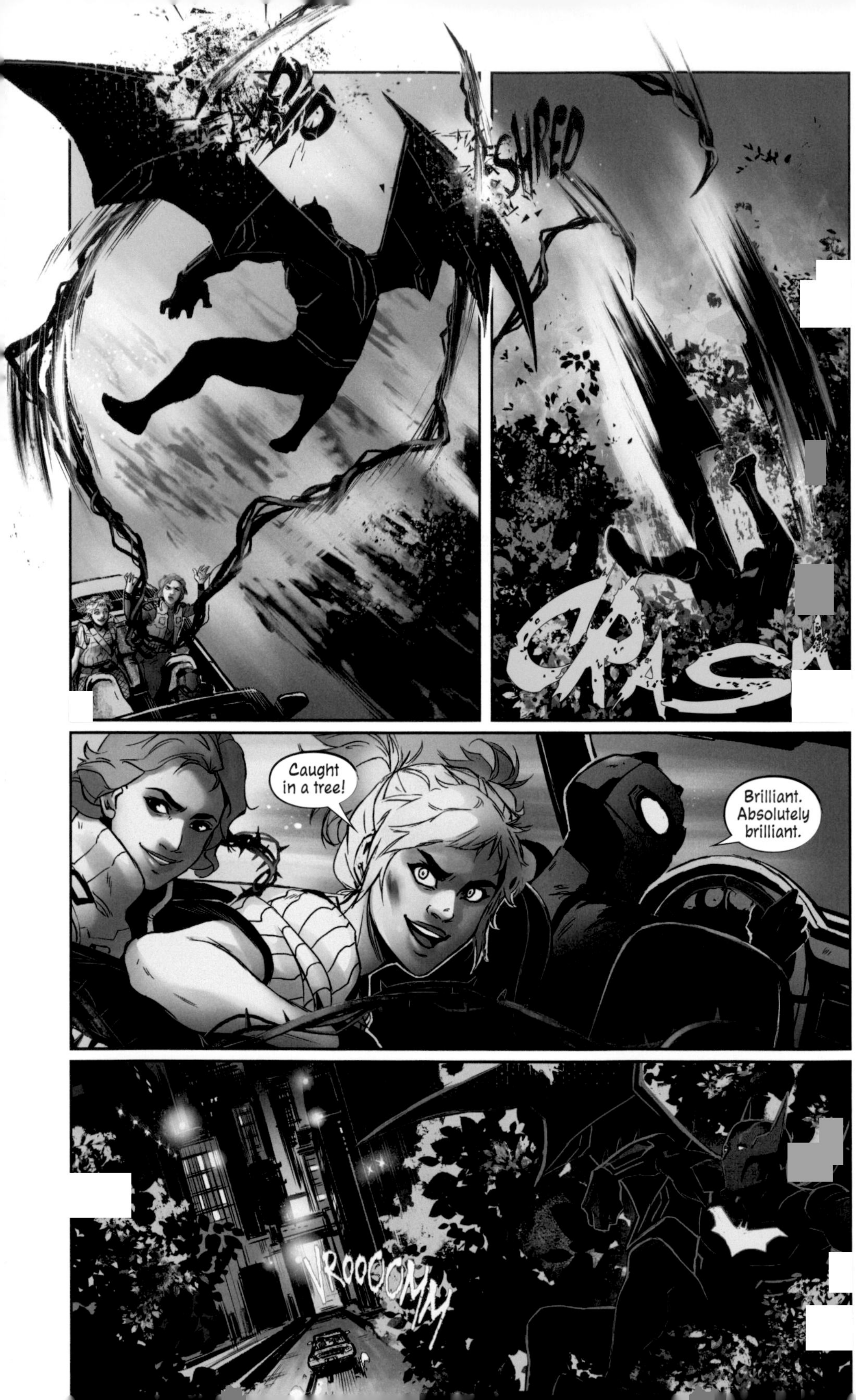
SHRED
CRASH
Caught in a tree!
Brilliant. Absolutely brilliant.
VROOOOMM

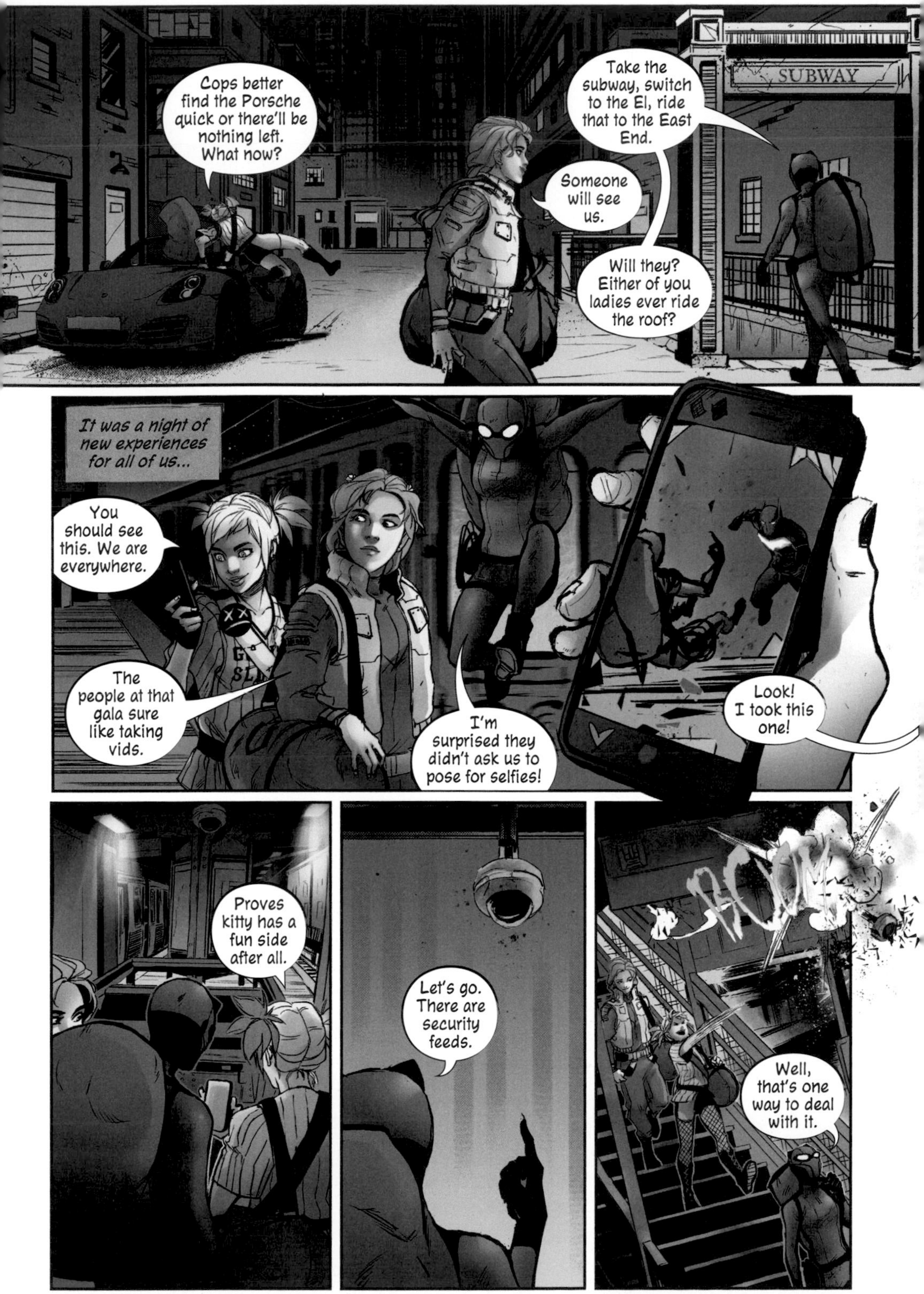
Cops better find the Porsche quick or there'll be nothing left. What now?
Take the subway, switch to the El, ride that to the East End.
SUBWAY
Someone will see us.
Will they? Either of you ladies ever ride the roof?
It was a night of new experiences for all of us...
You should see this. We are everywhere.
The people at that gala sure like taking vids.
I'm surprised they didn't ask us to pose for selfies!
Look! I took this one!
Proves kitty has a fun side after all.
Let's go. There are security feeds.
BOOM
Well, that's one way to deal with it.

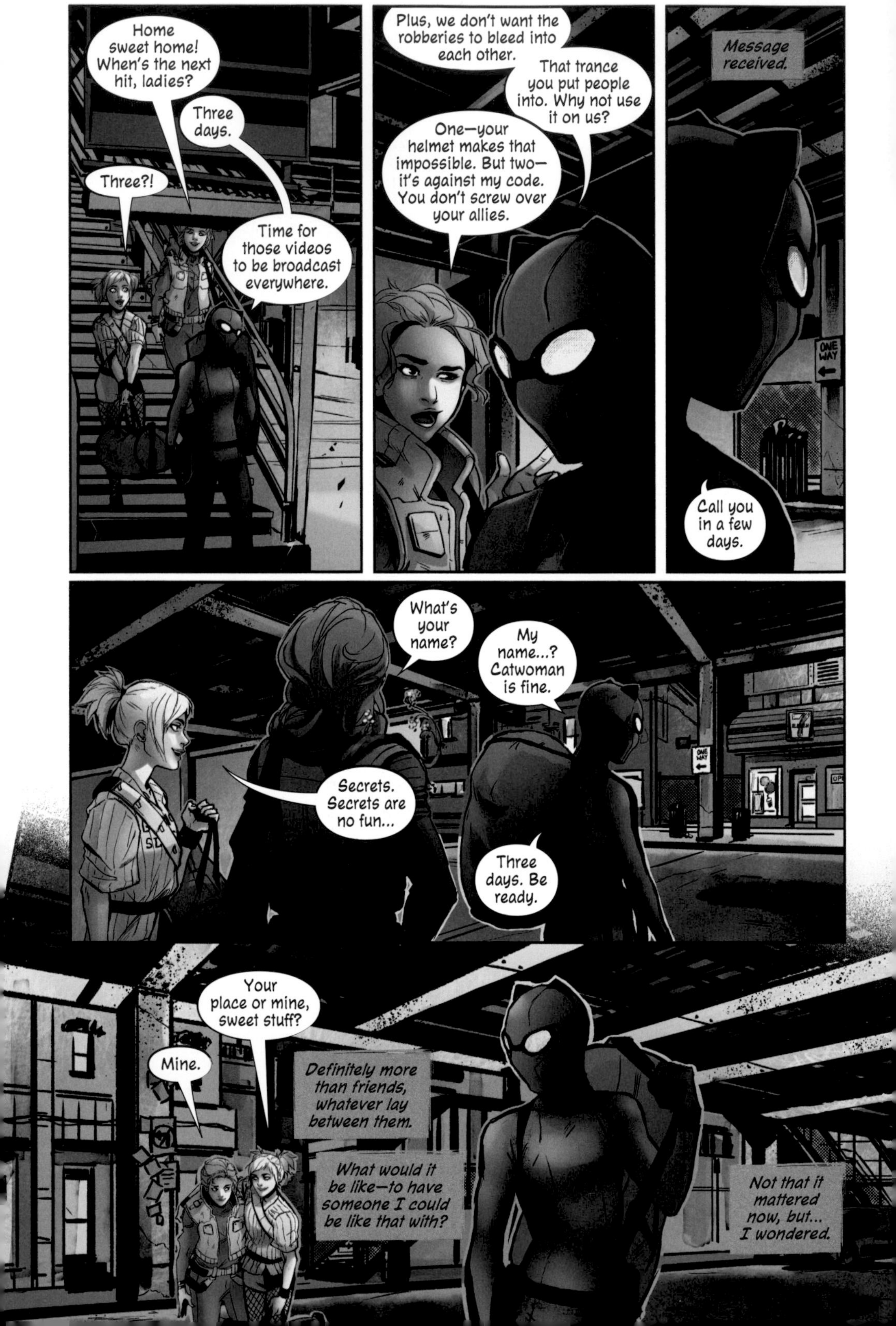
Home sweet home! When's the next hit, ladies?
Three days.
Three?!
Time for those videos to be broadcast everywhere.
Plus, we don't want the robberies to bleed into each other.
That trance you put people into. Why not use it on us?
One—your helmet makes that impossible. But two—it's against my code. You don't screw over your allies.
Message received.
Call you in a few days.
What's your name?
My name...? Catwoman is fine.
Secrets. Secrets are no fun...
Three days. Be ready.
Your place or mine, sweet stuff?
Mine.
Definitely more than friends, whatever lay between them.
What would it be like—to have someone I could be like that with?
Not that it mattered now, but... I wondered.

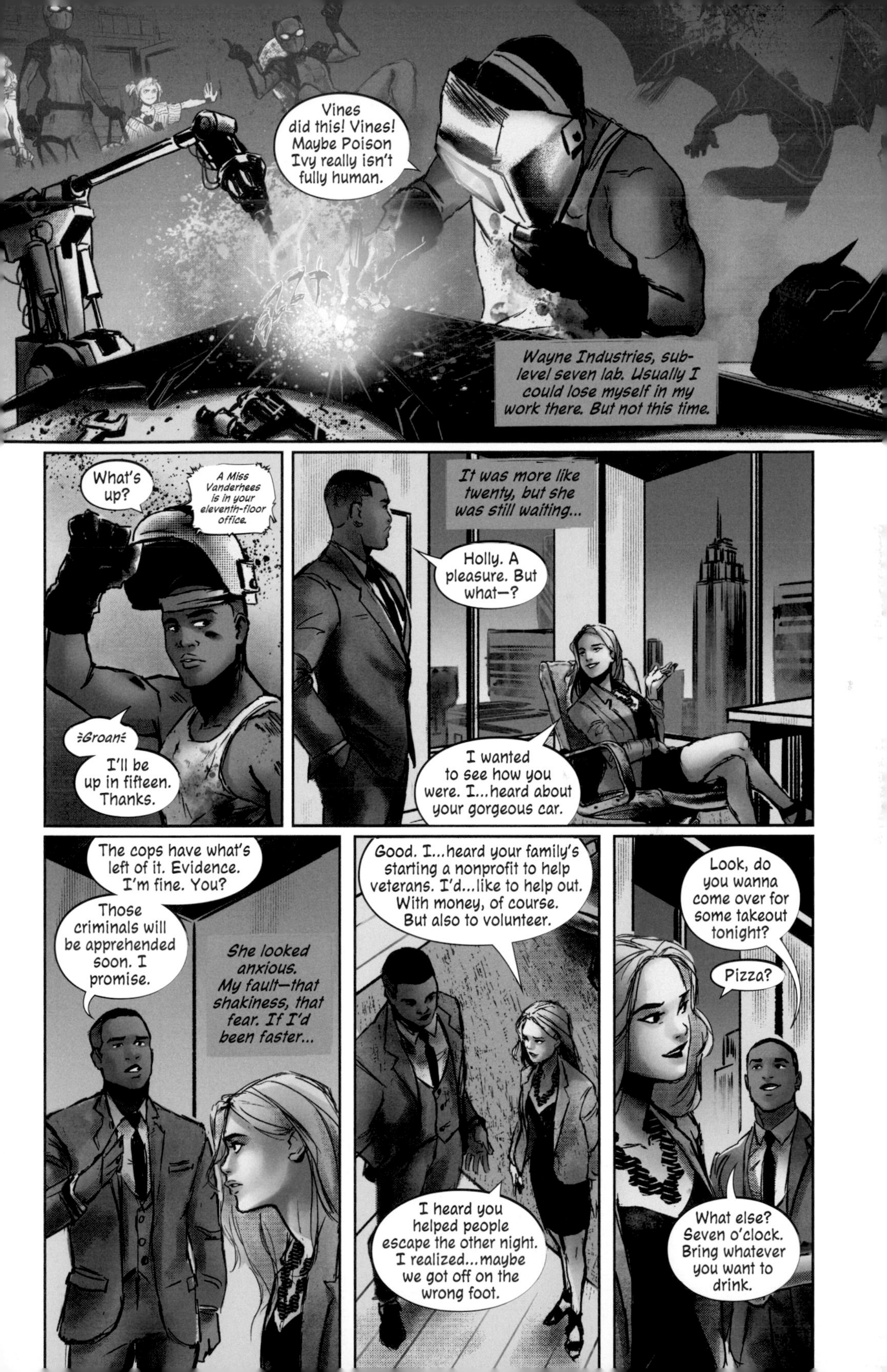
Vines did this! Vines! Maybe Poison Ivy really isn't fully human.
BZZT
Wayne Industries, sub-level seven lab. Usually I could lose myself in my work there. But not this time.
What's up?
A Miss Vanderhees is in your eleventh-floor office.
Groan
I'll be up in fifteen. Thanks.
It was more like twenty, but she was still waiting...
Holly. A pleasure. But what—?
I wanted to see how you were. I...heard about your gorgeous car.
The cops have what's left of it. Evidence. I'm fine. You?
Those criminals will be apprehended soon. I promise.
She looked anxious. My fault—that shakiness, that fear. If I'd been faster...
Good. I...heard your family's starting a nonprofit to help veterans. I'd...like to help out. With money, of course. But also to volunteer.
I heard you helped people escape the other night. I realized...maybe we got off on the wrong foot.
Look, do you wanna come over for some takeout tonight?
Pizza?
What else? Seven o'clock. Bring whatever you want to drink.

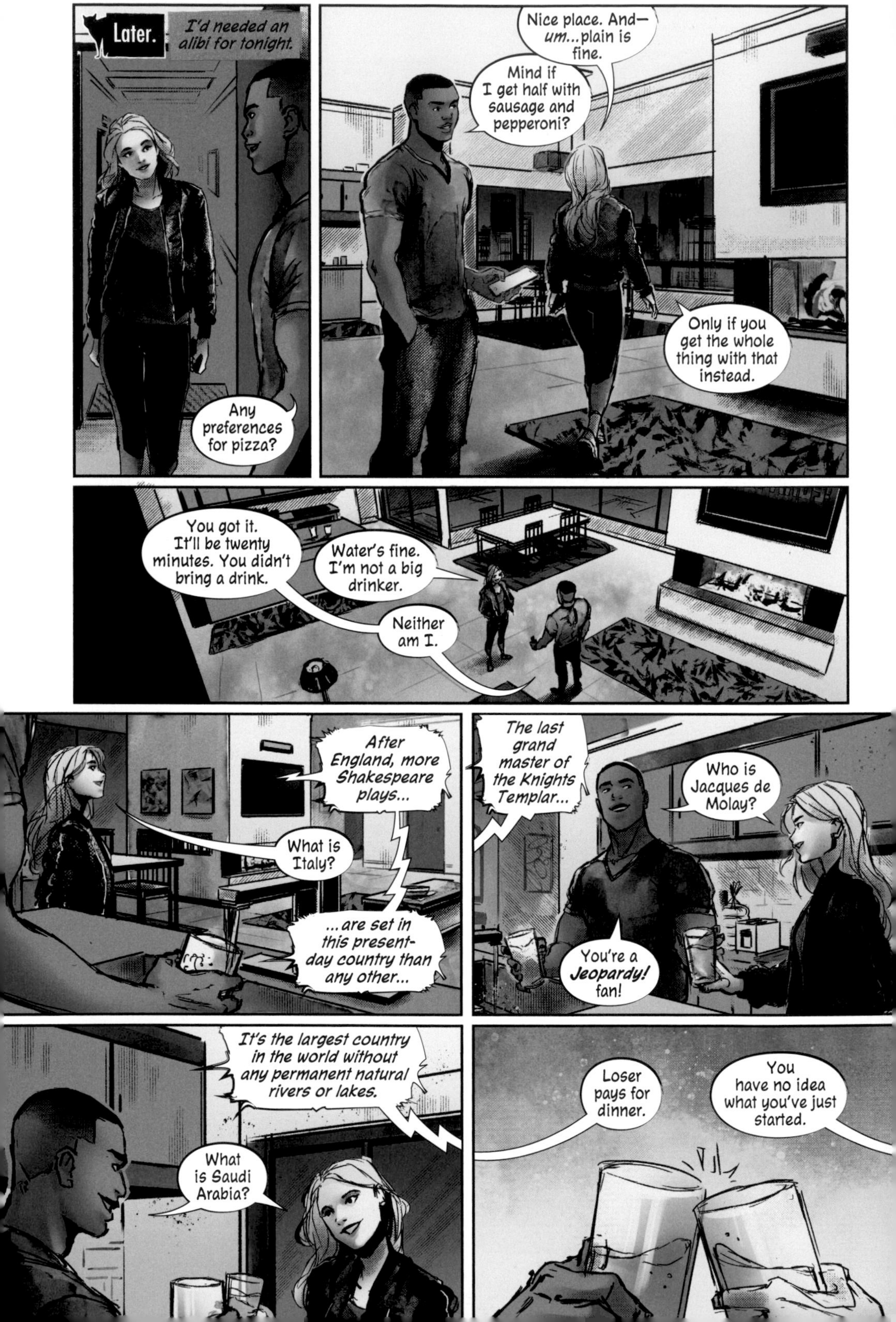
Later.
I'd needed an alibi for tonight.
Any preferences for pizza?
Nice place. And—um...plain is fine.
Mind if I get half with sausage and pepperoni?
Only if you get the whole thing with that instead.
You got it. It'll be twenty minutes. You didn't bring a drink.
Water's fine. I'm not a big drinker.
Neither am I.
After England, more Shakespeare plays...
What is Italy?
...are set in this present-day country than any other...
The last grand master of the Knights Templar...
Who is Jacques de Molay?
You're a Jeopardy! fan!
It's the largest country in the world without any permanent natural rivers or lakes.
What is Saudi Arabia?
Loser pays for dinner.
You have no idea what you've just started.

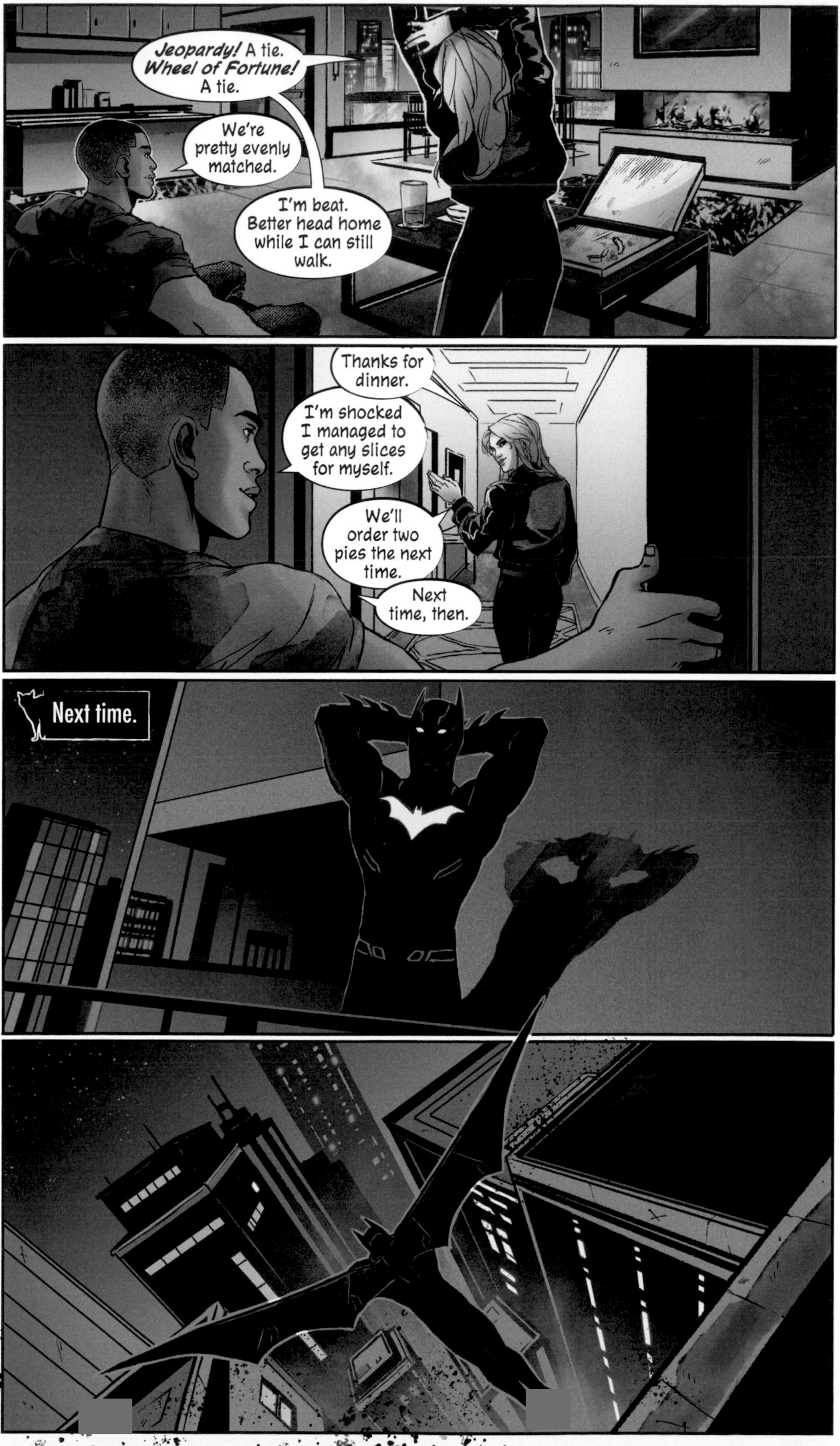
Jeopardy! A tie. Wheel of Fortune! A tie.
We're pretty evenly matched.
I'm beat. Better head home while I can still walk.
Thanks for dinner.
I'm shocked I managed to get any slices for myself.
We'll order two pies the next time.
Next time, then.
Next time.

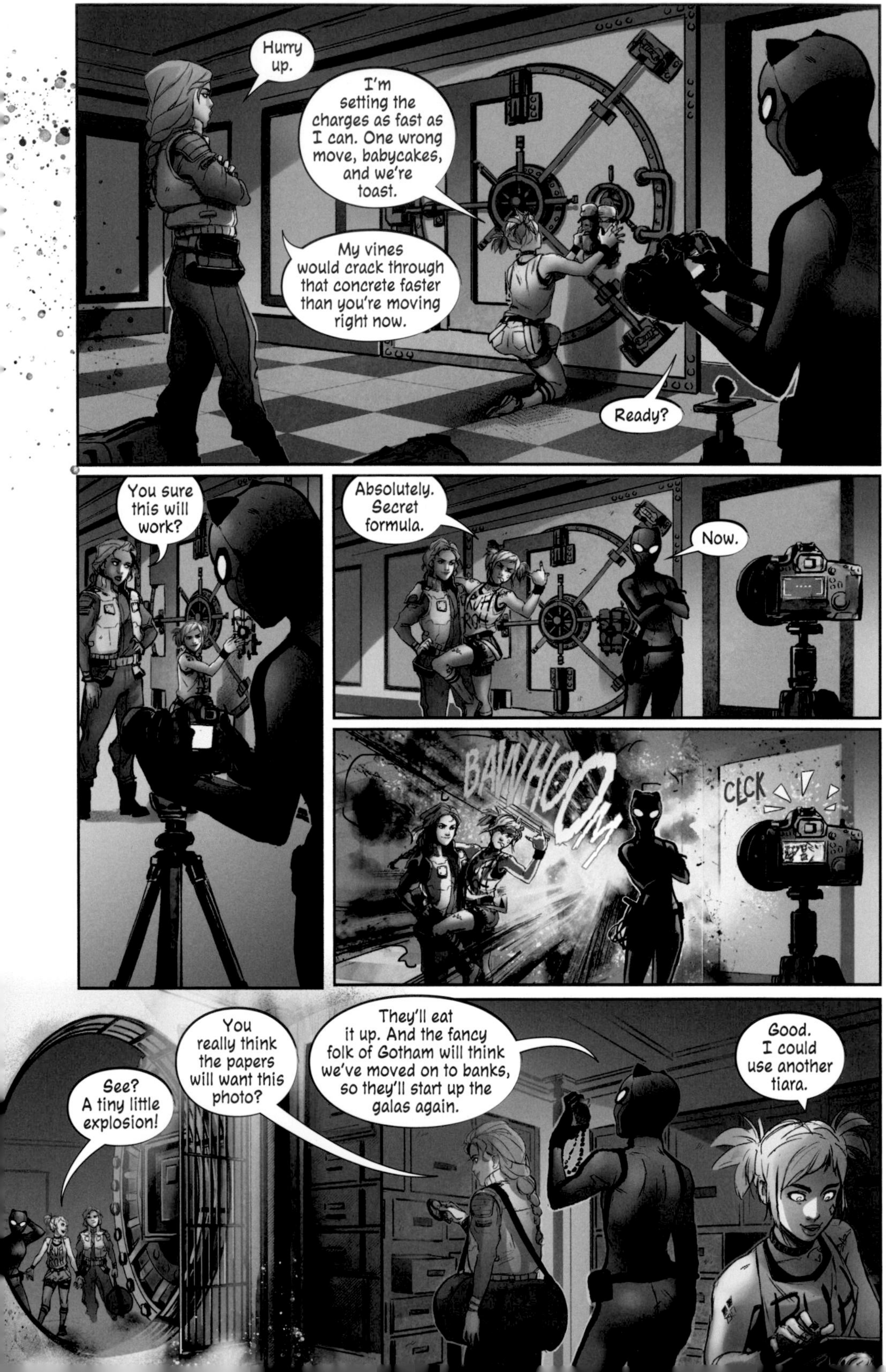
Hurry up.
I'm setting the charges as fast as I can. One wrong move, babycakes, and we're toast.
My vines would crack through that concrete faster than you're moving right now.
Ready?
You sure this will work?
Absolutely. Secret formula.
Now.
BAWHOOM
CLCK
See? A tiny little explosion!
You really think the papers will want this photo?
They'll eat it up. And the fancy folk of Gotham will think we've moved on to banks, so they'll start up the galas again.
Good. I could use another tiara.

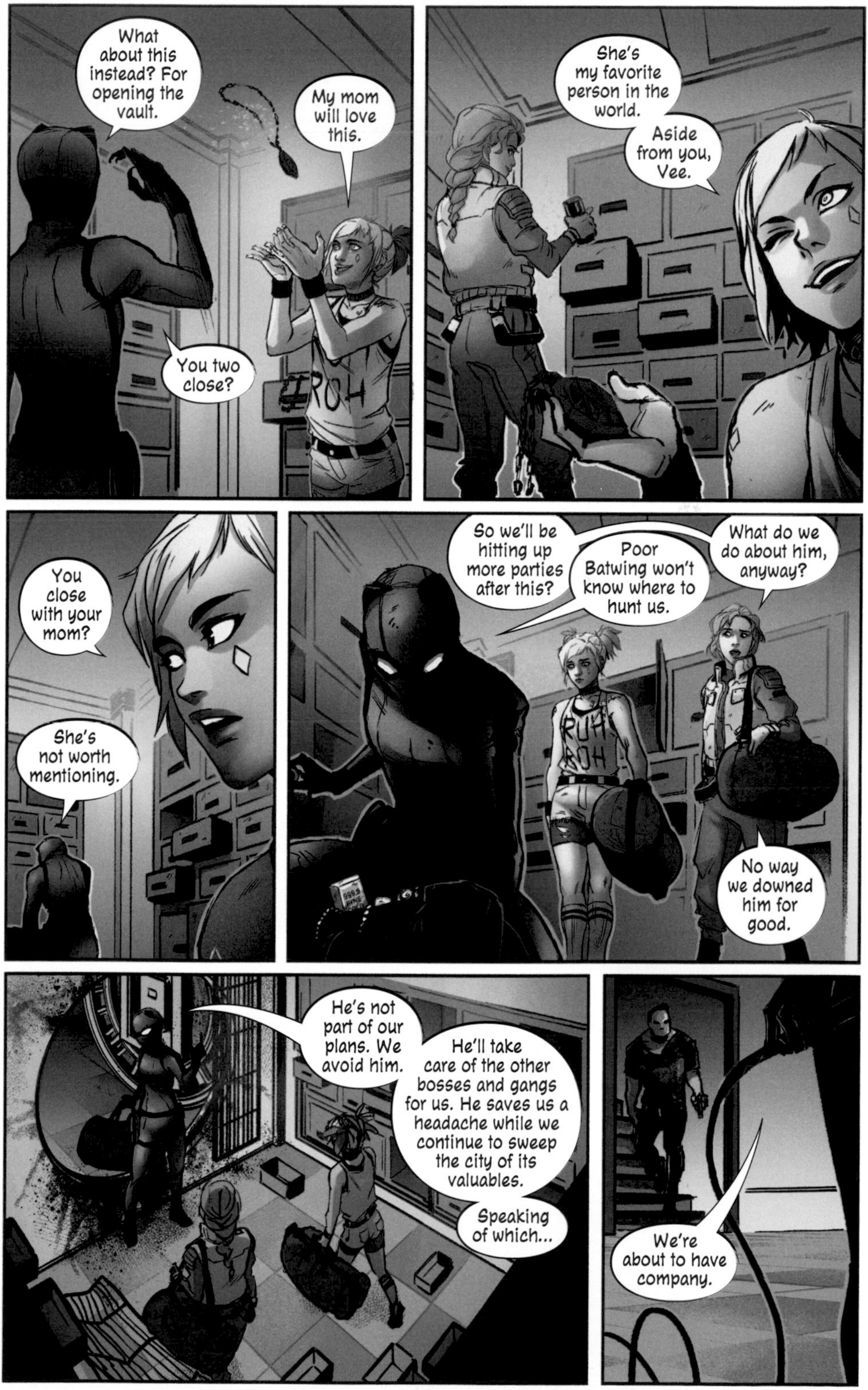
What about this instead? For opening the vault.
My mom will love this.
You two close?
She's my favorite person in the world.
Aside from you, Vee.
You close with your mom?
She's not worth mentioning.
So we'll be hitting up more parties after this?
Poor Batwing won't know where to hunt us.
What do we do about him, anyway?
No way we downed him for good.
He's not part of our plans. We avoid him.
He'll take care of the other bosses and gangs for us. He saves us a headache while we continue to sweep the city of its valuables.
Speaking of which...
We're about to have company.

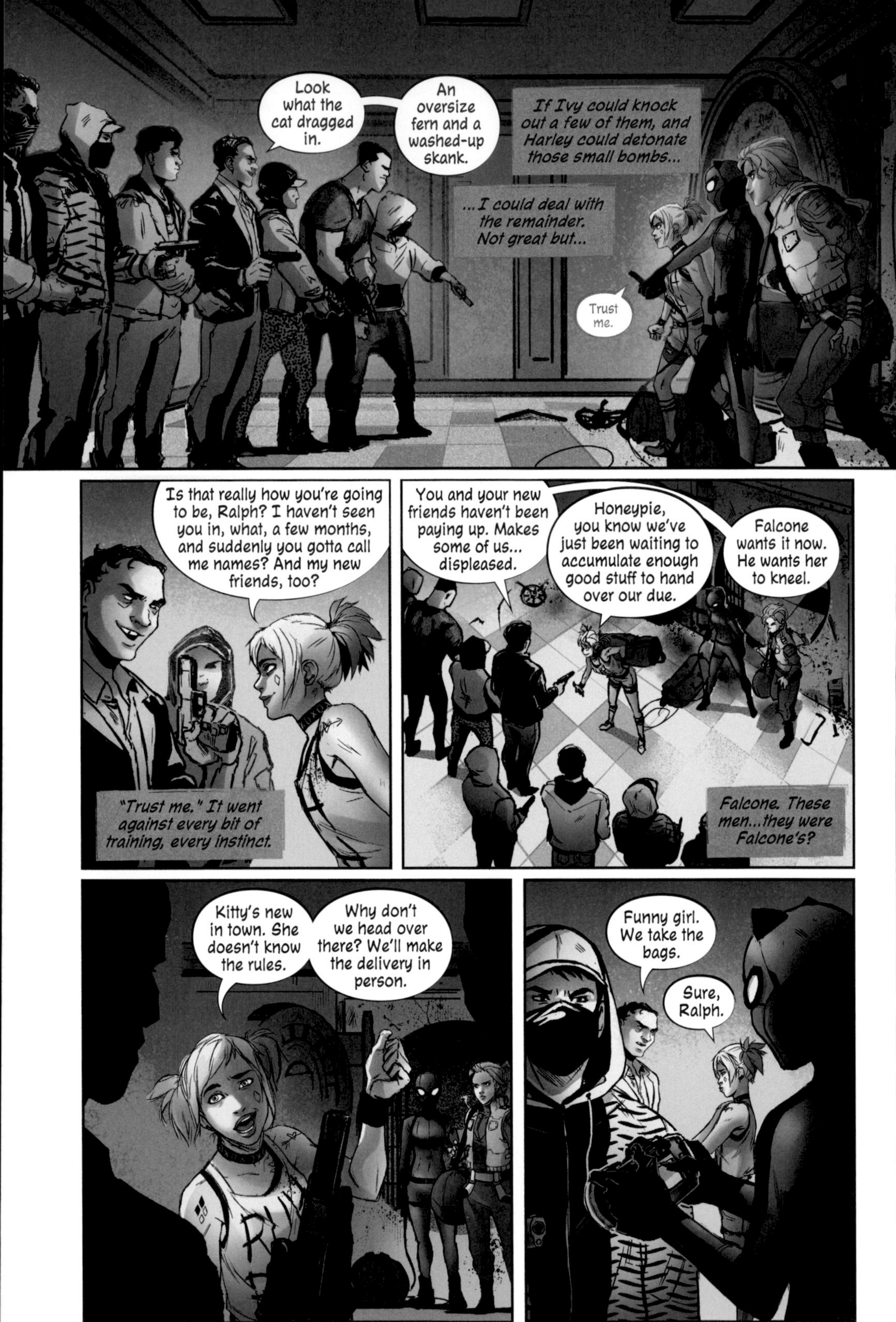
Look what the cat dragged in.
An oversize fern and a washed-up skank.
If Ivy could knock out a few of them, and Harley could detonate those small bombs...
...I could deal with the remainder. Not great but...
Trust me.
Is that really how you're going to be, Ralph? I haven't seen you in, what, a few months, and suddenly you gotta call me names? And my new friends, too?
"Trust me." It went against every bit of training, every instinct.
You and your new friends haven't been paying up. Makes some of us... displeased.
Honeypie, you know we've just been waiting to accumulate enough good stuff to hand over our due.
Falcone wants it now. He wants her to kneel.
Falcone. These men...they were Falcone's?
Kitty's new in town. She doesn't know the rules.
Why don't we head over there? We'll make the delivery in person.
Funny girl. We take the bags.
Sure, Ralph.

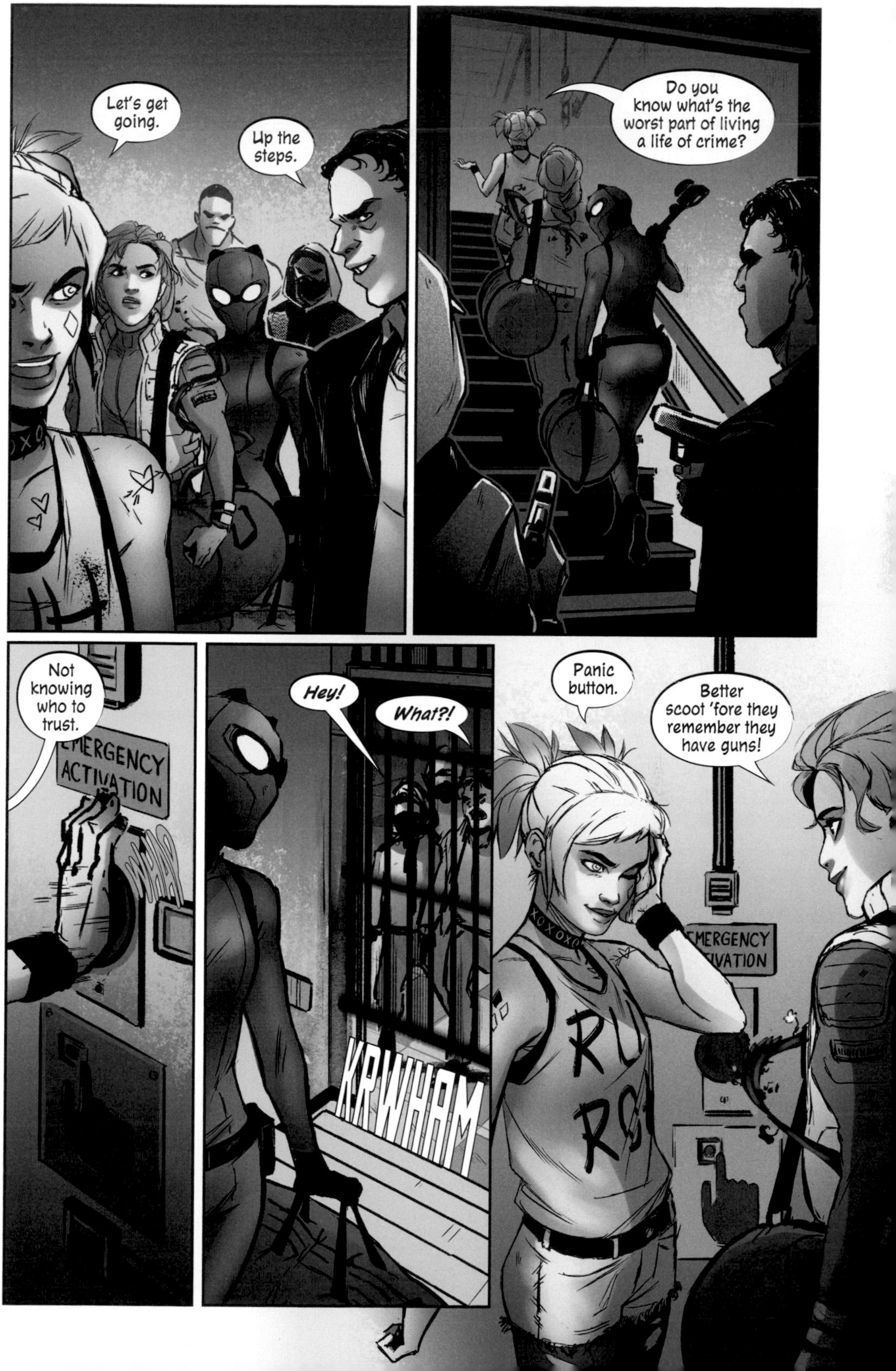
Let's get going.
Up the steps.
Do you know what's the worst part of living a life of crime?
Not knowing who to trust.
EMERGENCY ACTIVATION
WHAM
Hey!
What?!
KRWHAM
Panic button.
Better scoot 'fore they remember they have guns!
EMERGENCY ACTIVATION

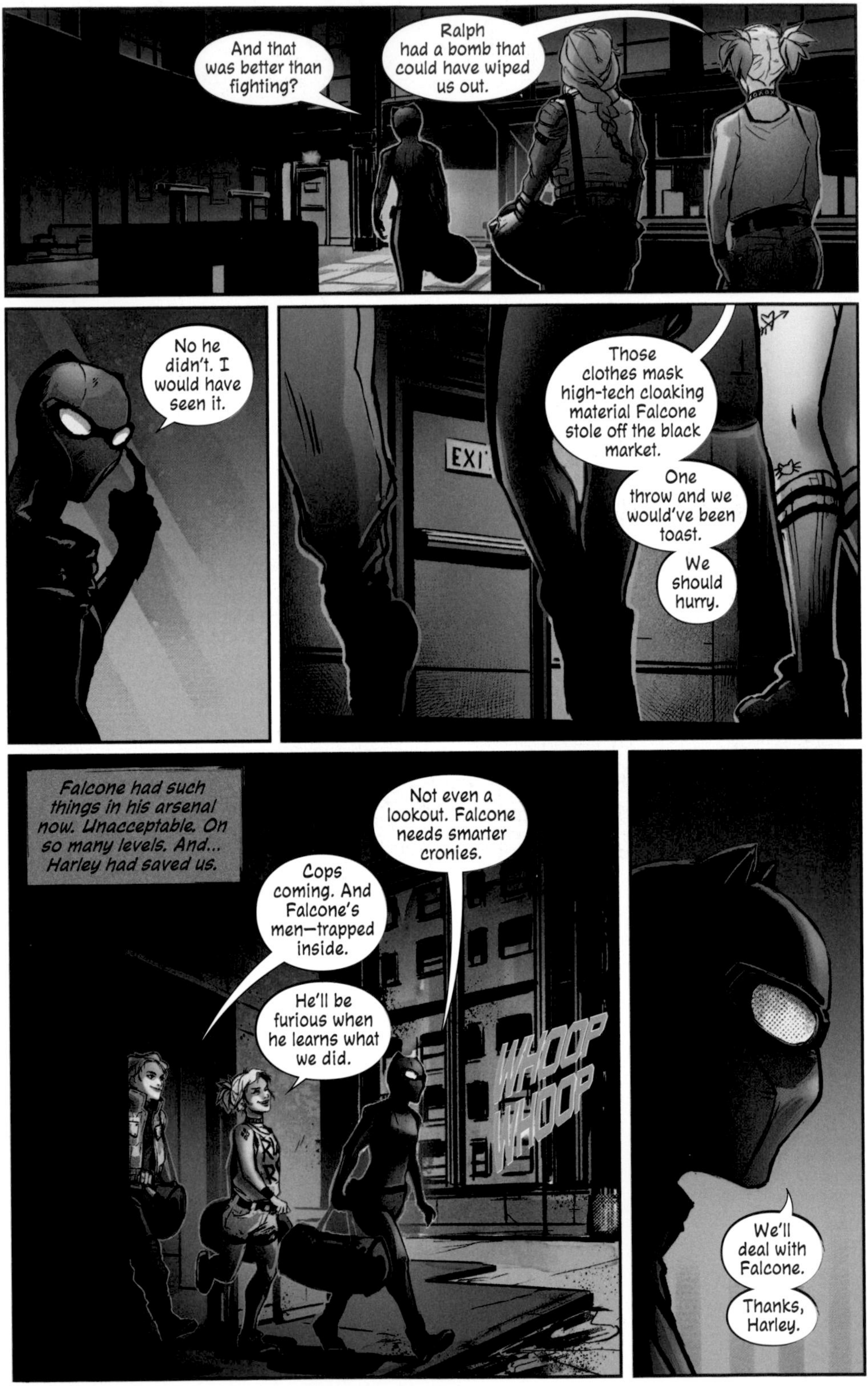
And that was better than fighting?
Ralph had a bomb that could have wiped us out.
No he didn't. I would have seen it.
EXIT
Those clothes mask high-tech cloaking material Falcone stole off the black market.
One throw and we would've been toast.
We should hurry.
Falcone had such things in his arsenal now. Unacceptable. On so many levels. And... Harley had saved us.
Not even a lookout. Falcone needs smarter cronies.
Cops coming. And Falcone's men—trapped inside.
He'll be furious when he learns what we did.
WHOOP WHOOP
We'll deal with Falcone.
Thanks, Harley.

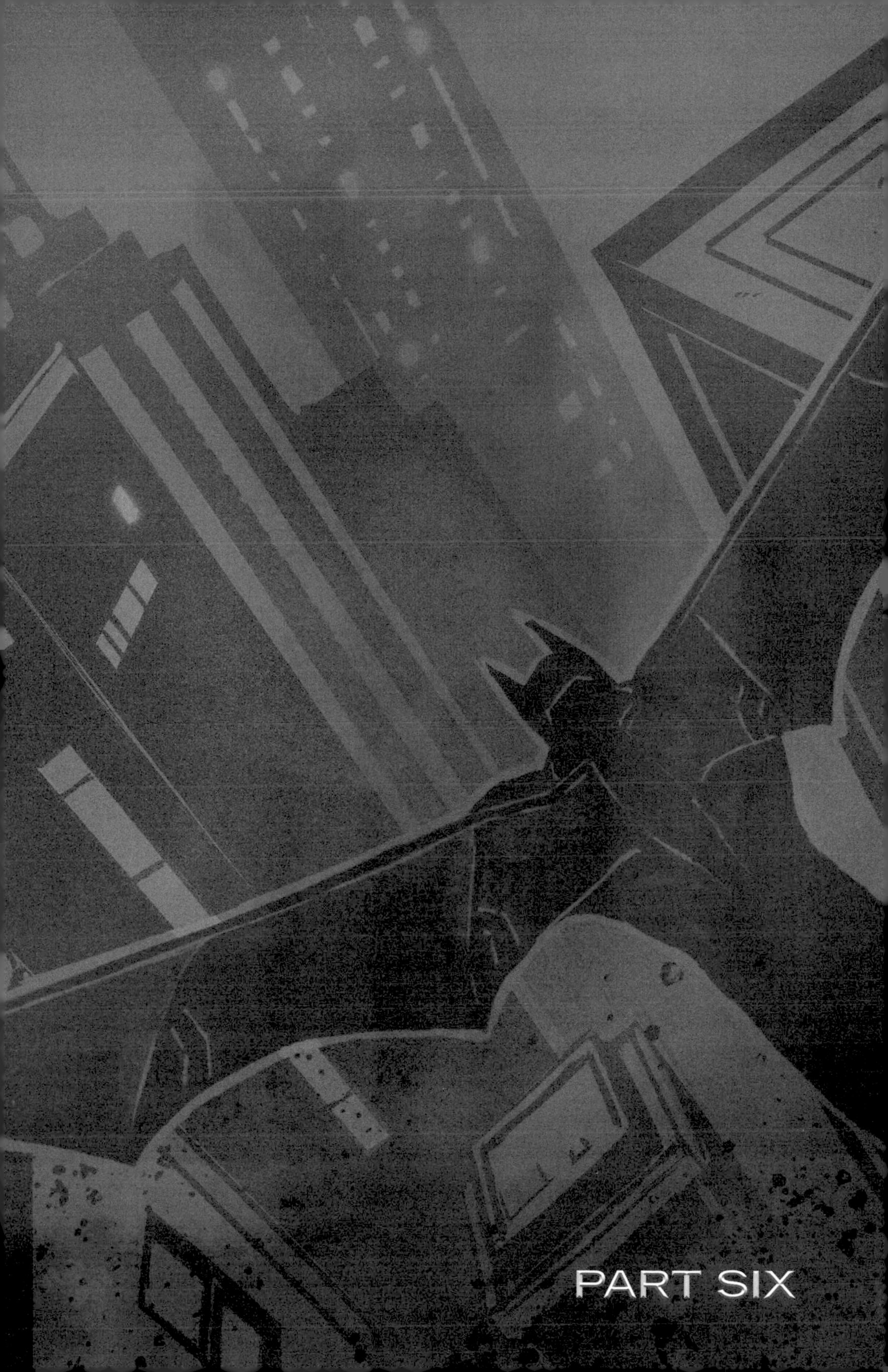
PART SIX

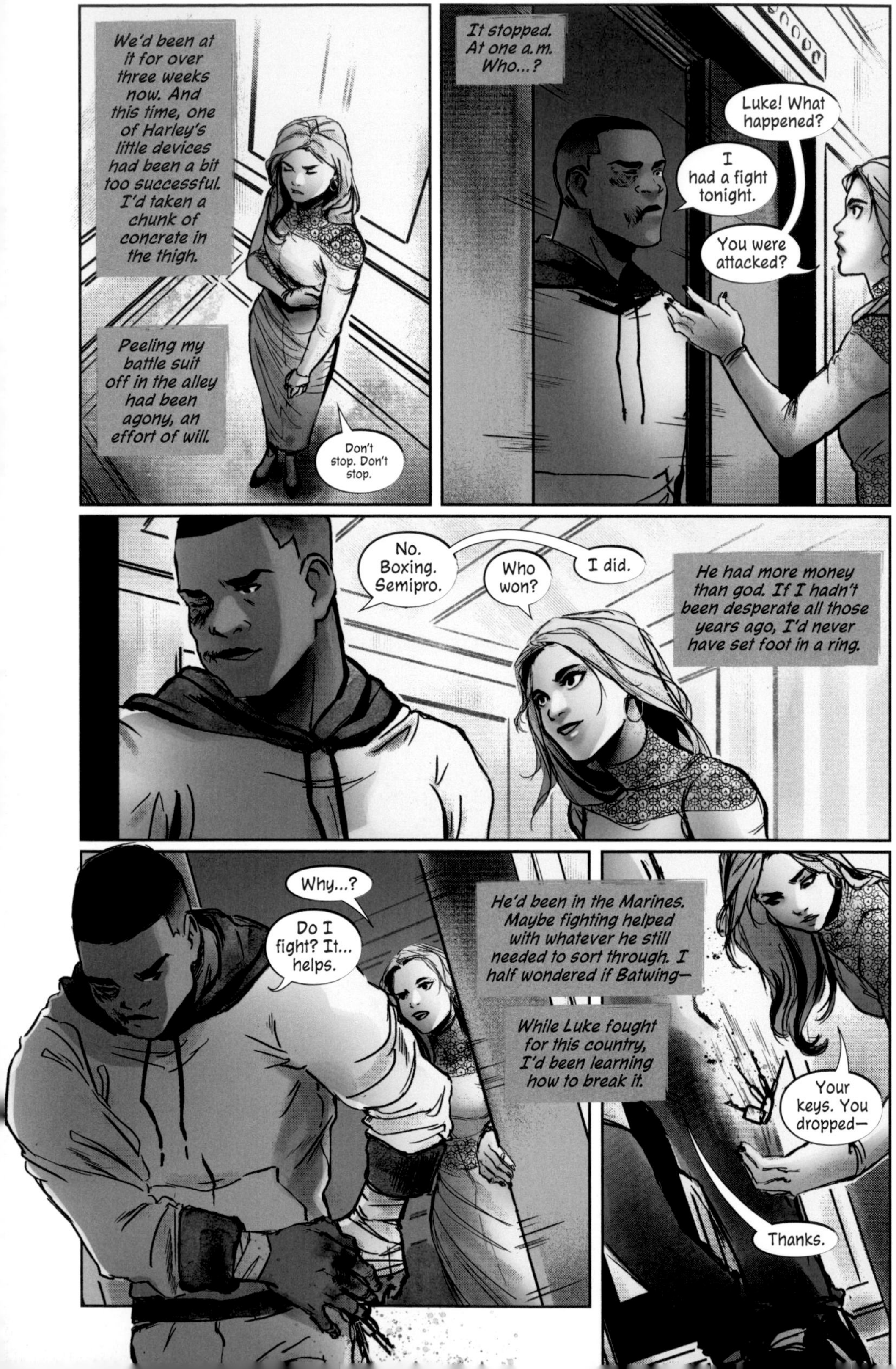
We'd been at it for over three weeks now. And this time, one of Harley's little devices had been a bit too successful. I'd taken a chunk of concrete in the thigh.
Peeling my battle suit off in the alley had been agony, an effort of will.
Don't stop. Don't stop.
It stopped. At one a.m. Who...?
Luke! What happened?
I had a fight tonight.
You were attacked?
No. Boxing. Semipro.
Who won?
I did.
He had more money than god. If I hadn't been desperate all those years ago, I'd never have set foot in a ring.
Why...?
Do I fight? It... helps.
He'd been in the Marines. Maybe fighting helped with whatever he still needed to sort through. I half wondered if Batwing—
While Luke fought for this country, I'd been learning how to break it.
Your keys. You dropped—
Thanks.

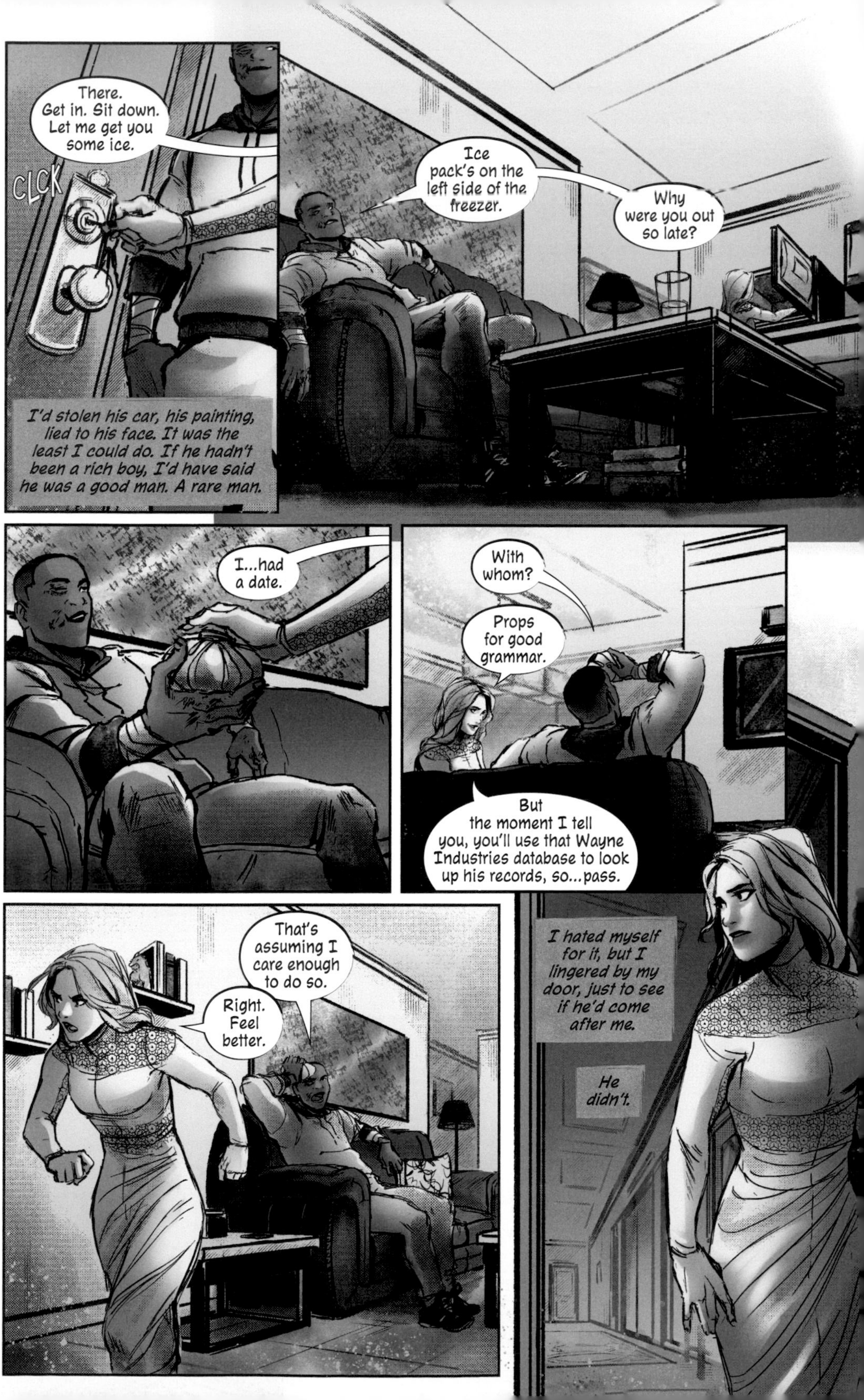

There. Get in. Sit down. Let me get you some ice.
CLCK
I'd stolen his car, his painting, lied to his face. It was the least I could do. If he hadn't been a rich boy, I'd have said he was a good man. A rare man.
Ice pack's on the left side of the freezer.
Why were you out so late?
I...had a date.
With whom?
Props for good grammar.
But the moment I tell you, you'll use that Wayne Industries database to look up his records, so...pass.
That's assuming I care enough to do so.
Right. Feel better.
I hated myself for it, but I lingered by my door, just to see if he'd come after me.
He didn't.

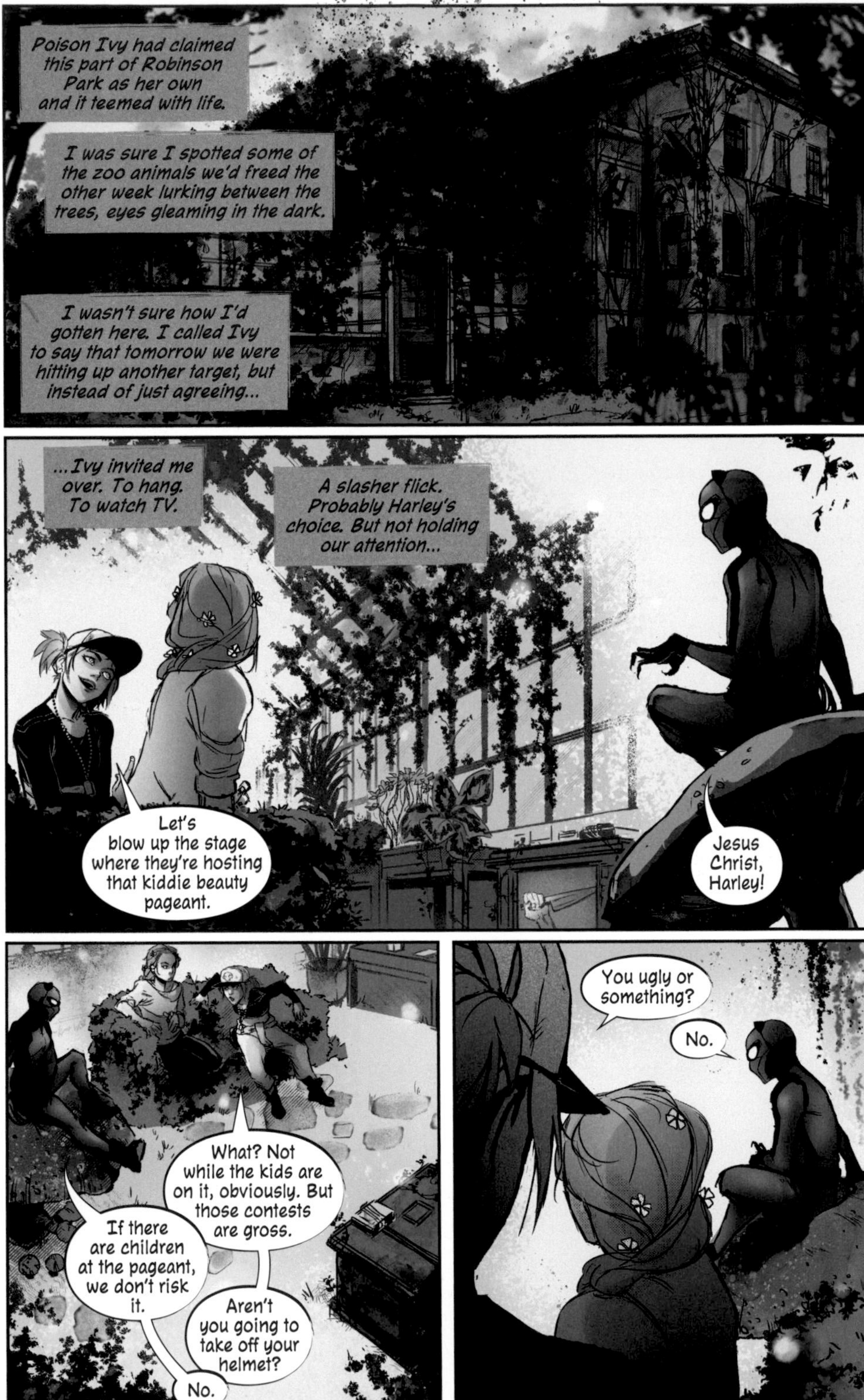
Poison Ivy had claimed this part of Robinson Park as her own and it teemed with life.
I was sure I spotted some of the zoo animals we'd freed the other week lurking between the trees, eyes gleaming in the dark.
I wasn't sure how I'd gotten here. I called Ivy to say that tomorrow we were hitting up another target, but instead of just agreeing...
...Ivy invited me over. To hang. To watch TV.
A slasher flick. Probably Harley's choice. But not holding our attention...
Let's blow up the stage where they're hosting that kiddie beauty pageant.
Jesus Christ, Harley!
What? Not while the kids are on it, obviously. But those contests are gross.
If there are children at the pageant, we don't risk it.
Aren't you going to take off your helmet?
No.
You ugly or something?
No.

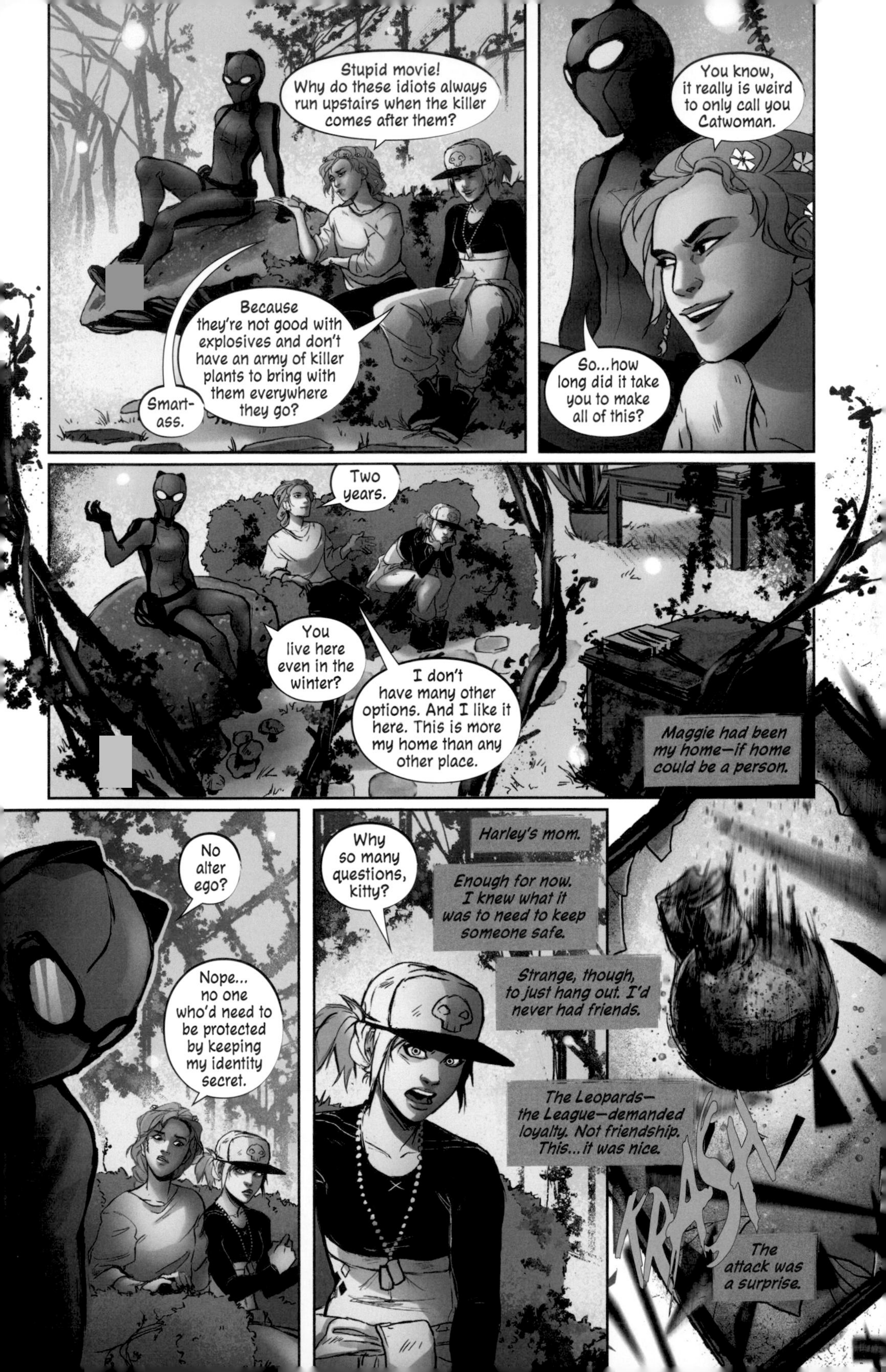

Stupid movie! Why do these idiots always run upstairs when the killer comes after them?
Because they're not good with explosives and don't have an army of killer plants to bring with them everywhere they go?
Smart-ass.
You know, it really is weird to only call you Catwoman.
So...how long did it take you to make all of this?
Two years.
You live here even in the winter?
I don't have many other options. And I like it here. This is more my home than any other place.
Maggie had been my home—if home could be a person.
No alter ego?
Nope... no one who'd need to be protected by keeping my identity secret.
Why so many questions, kitty?
Harley's mom.
Enough for now. I knew what it was to need to keep someone safe.
Strange, though, to just hang out. I'd never had friends.
The Leopards—the League—demanded loyalty. Not friendship. This...it was nice.
KRASH
The attack was a surprise.

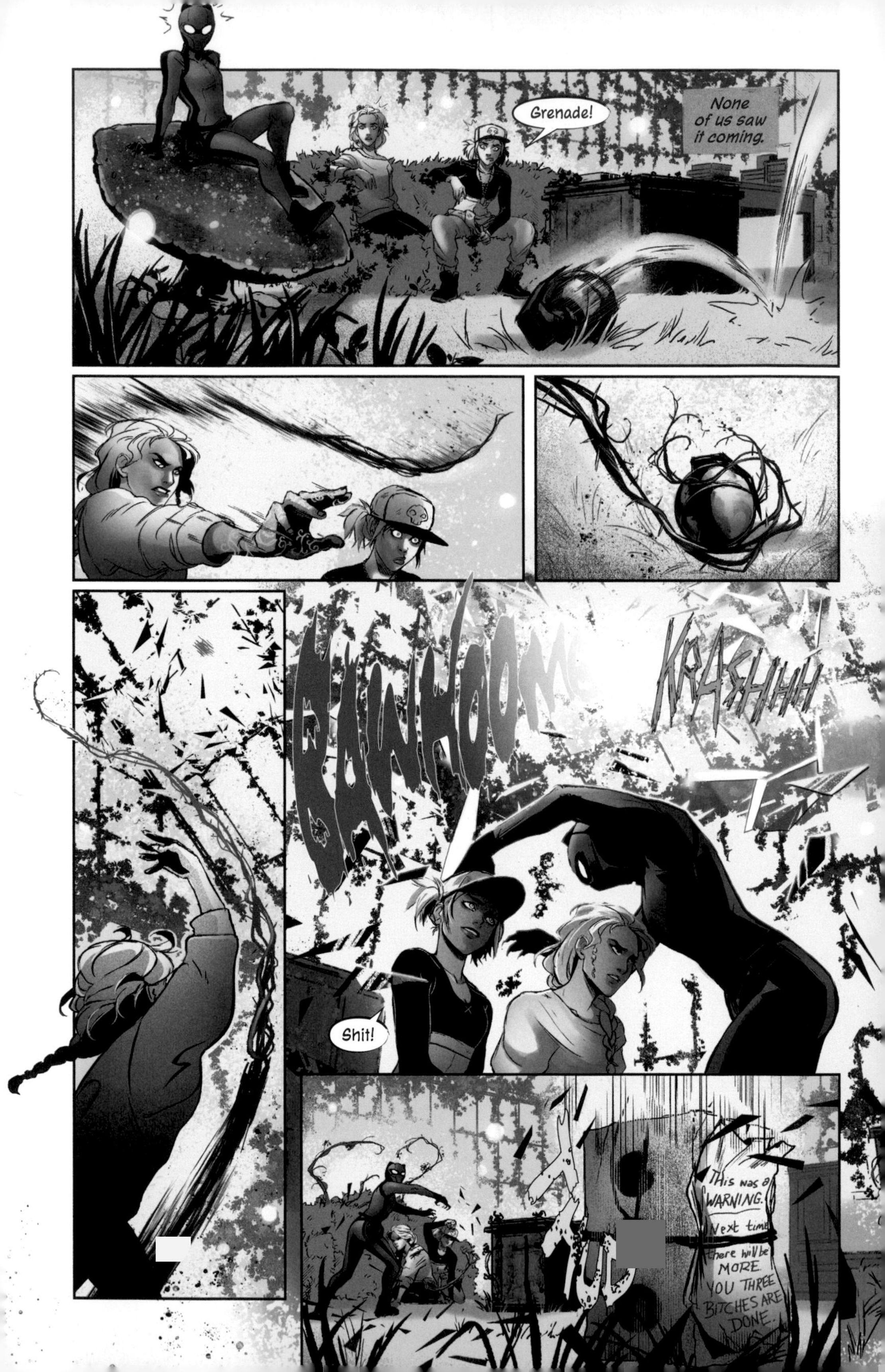
None of us saw it coming.
Grenade!
KRASHHH
Shit!
This was a WARNING. Next time there will be MORE. YOU THREE BITCHES ARE DONE.

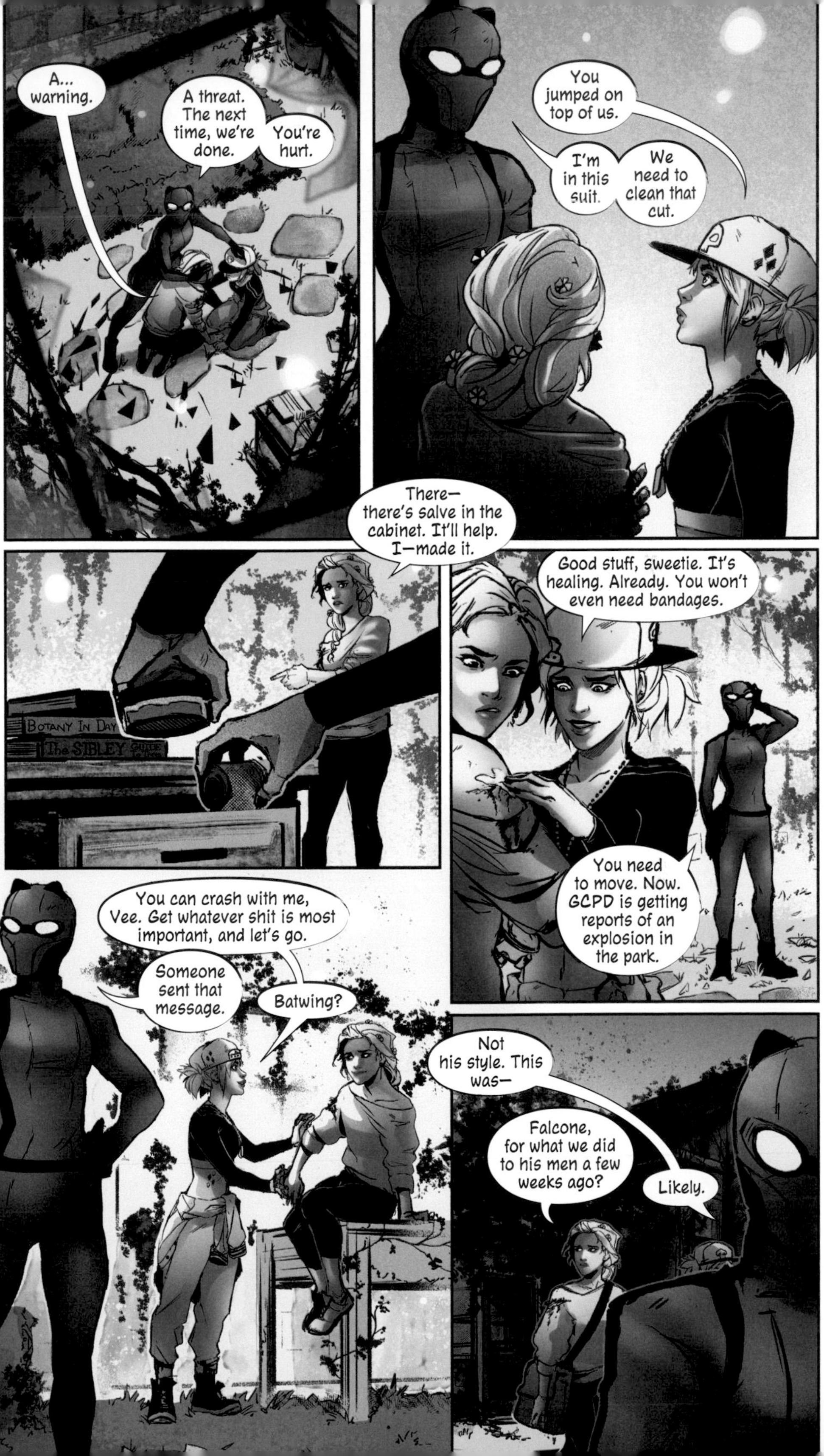
A... warning.
A threat. The next time, we're done.
You're hurt.
You jumped on top of us.
I'm in this suit.
We need to clean that cut.
There— there's salve in the cabinet. It'll help. I—made it.
BOTANY IN DAY
The SIBLEY GUIDE
Good stuff, sweetie. It's healing. Already. You won't even need bandages.
You need to move. Now. GCPD is getting reports of an explosion in the park.
You can crash with me, Vee. Get whatever shit is most important, and let's go.
Someone sent that message.
Batwing?
Not his style. This was—
Falcone, for what we did to his men a few weeks ago?
Likely.

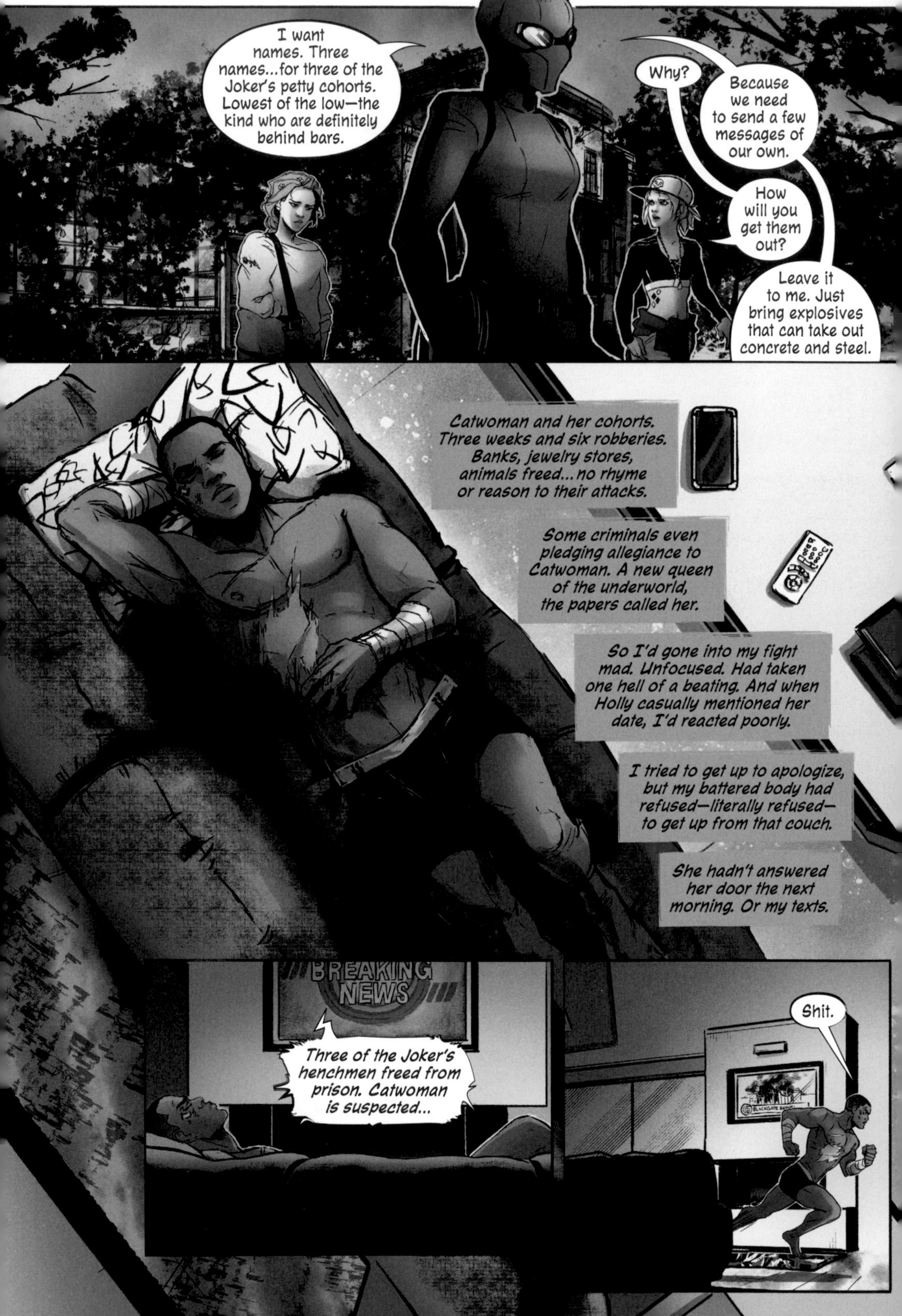

I want names. Three names...for three of the Joker's petty cohorts. Lowest of the low—the kind who are definitely behind bars.
Why?
Because we need to send a few messages of our own.
How will you get them out?
Leave it to me. Just bring explosives that can take out concrete and steel.
Catwoman and her cohorts. Three weeks and six robberies. Banks, jewelry stores, animals freed...no rhyme or reason to their attacks.
Some criminals even pledging allegiance to Catwoman. A new queen of the underworld, the papers called her.
So I'd gone into my fight mad. Unfocused. Had taken one hell of a beating. And when Holly casually mentioned her date, I'd reacted poorly.
I tried to get up to apologize, but my battered body had refused—literally refused—to get up from that couch.
She hadn't answered her door the next morning. Or my texts.
BREAKING NEWS
Three of the Joker's henchmen freed from prison. Catwoman is suspected...
Shit.

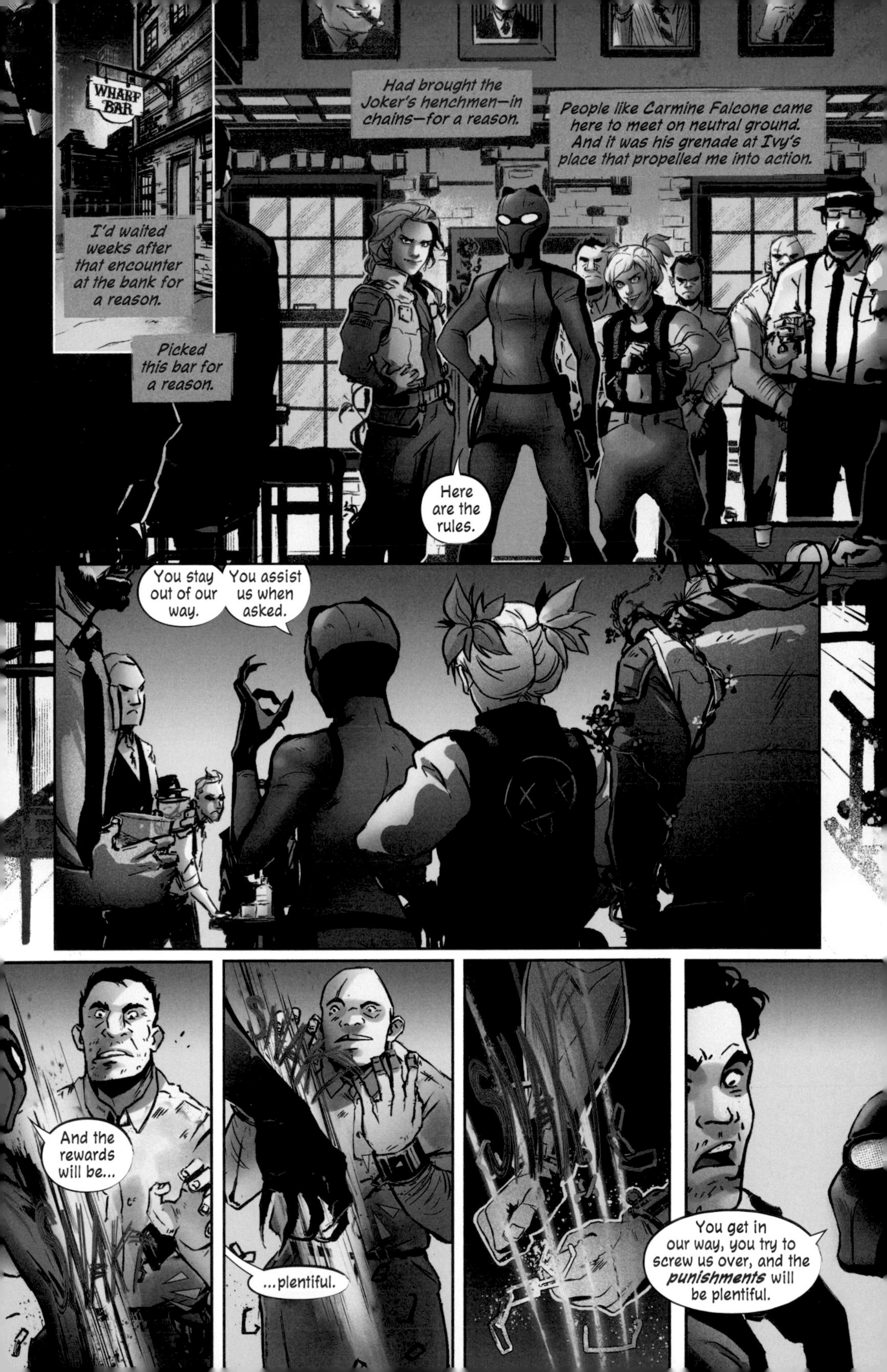
WHARF BAR
I'd waited weeks after that encounter at the bank for a reason.
Picked this bar for a reason.
Had brought the Joker's henchmen—in chains—for a reason.
People like Carmine Falcone came here to meet on neutral ground. And it was his grenade at Ivy's place that propelled me into action.
Here are the rules.
You stay out of our way.
You assist us when asked.
And the rewards will be...
...plentiful.
You get in our way, you try to screw us over, and the *punishments* will be plentiful.

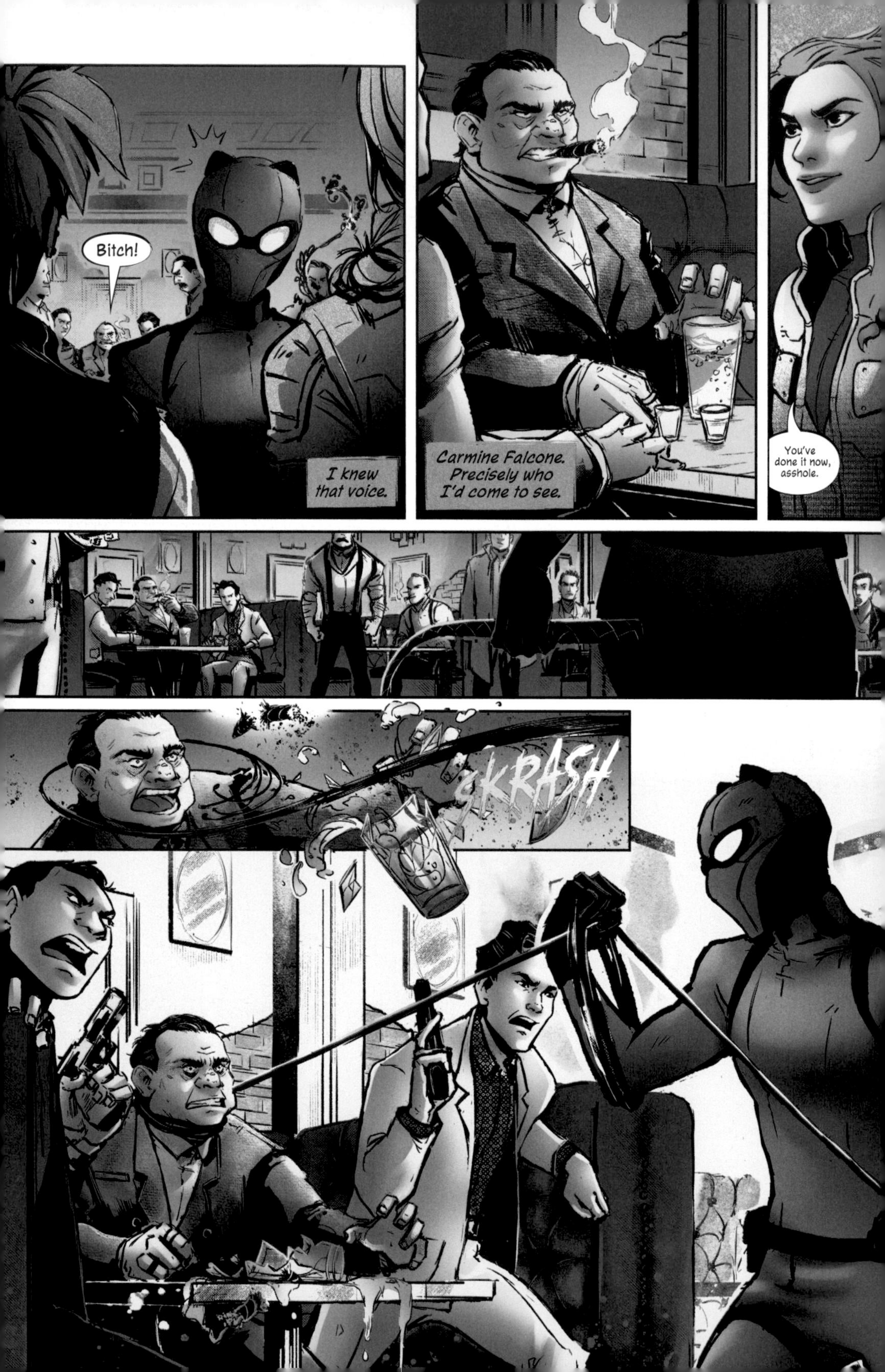
Bitch!
I knew that voice.
Carmine Falcone. Precisely who I'd come to see.
You've done it now, asshole.
SKRASH

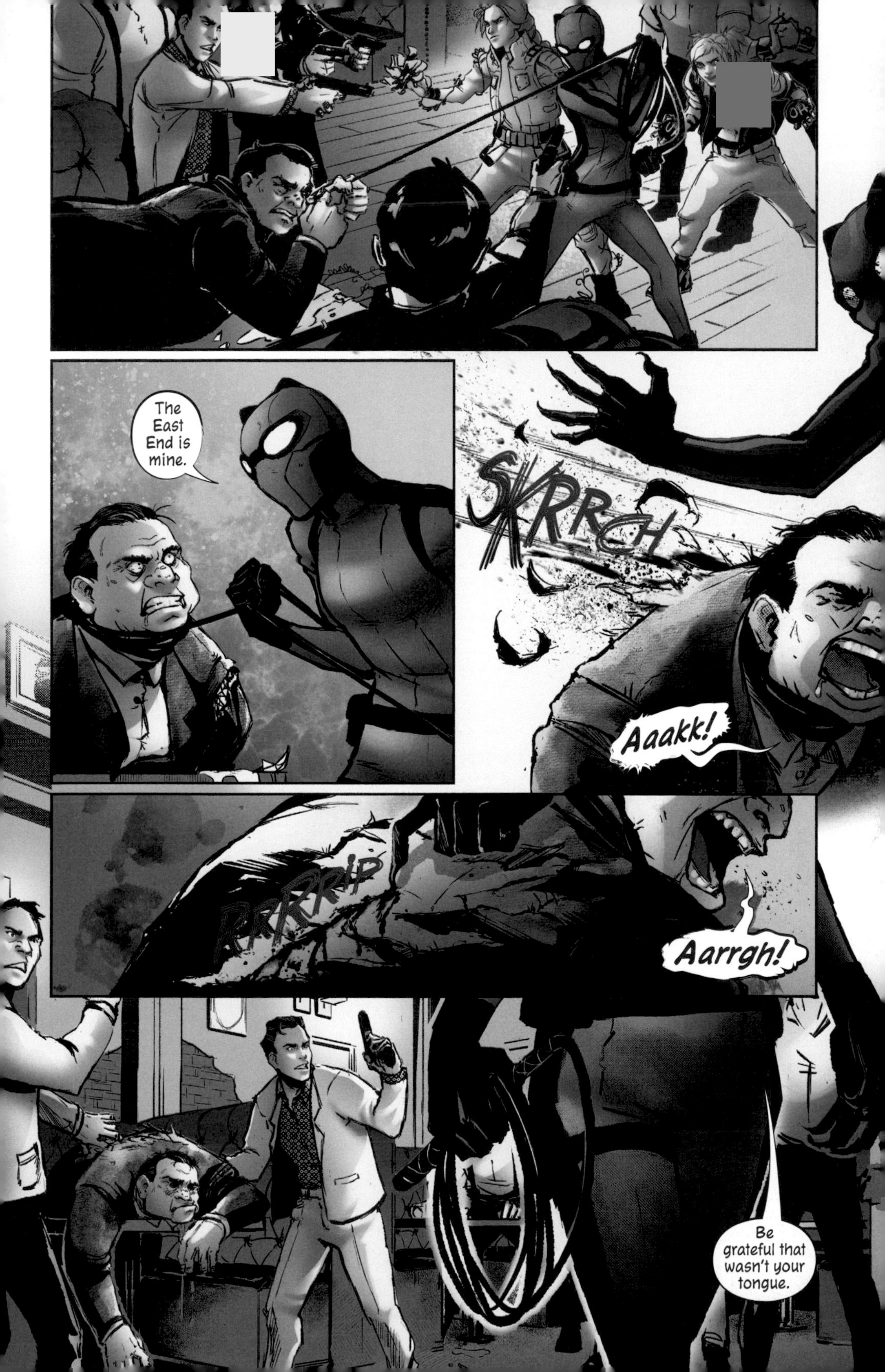
The East End is mine.
SKRRCH
Aaakk!
RRRRRIP
Aarrgh!
Be grateful that wasn't your tongue.

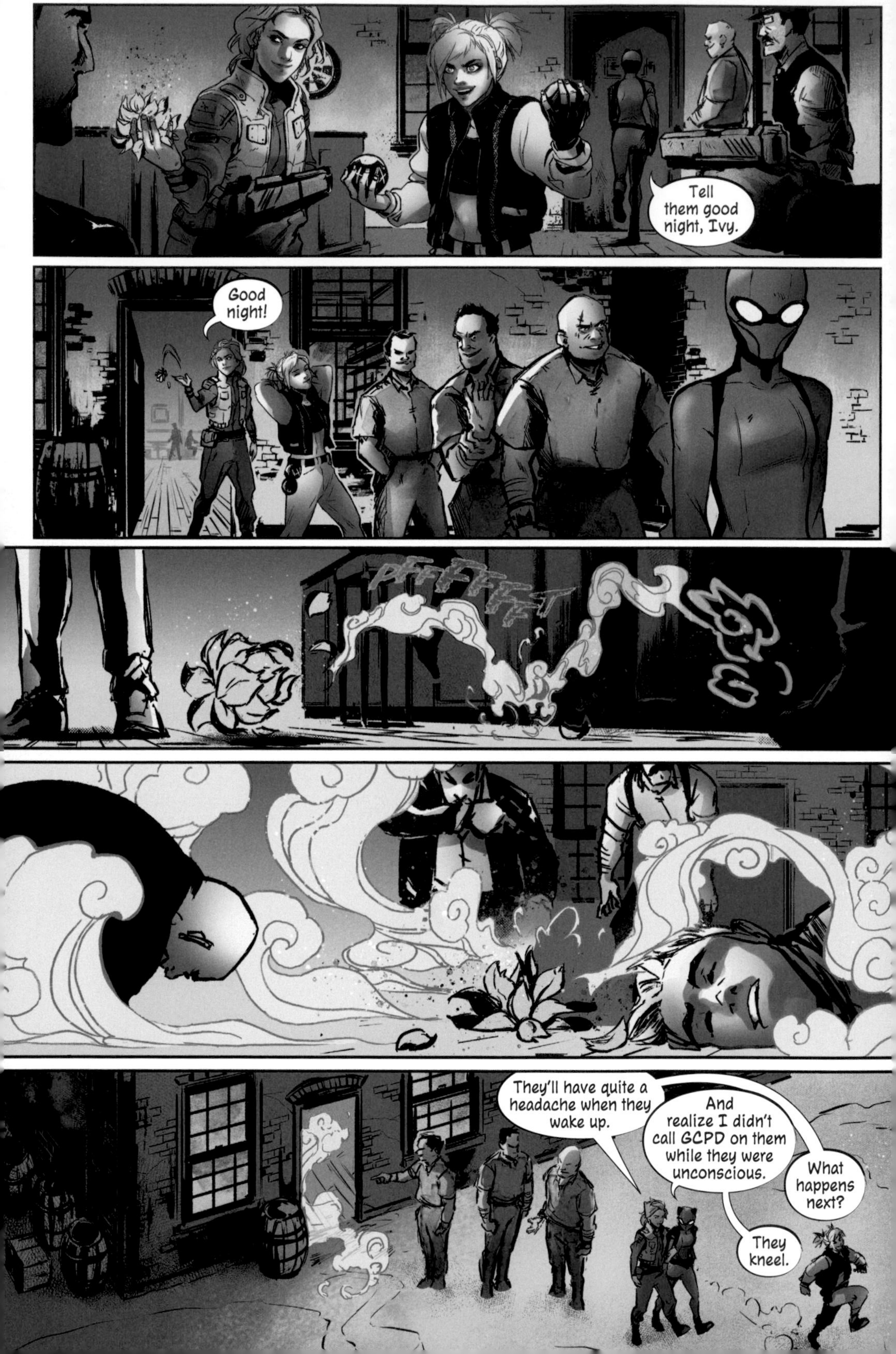
Tell them good night, Ivy.
Good night!
PFFFFFFT
They'll have quite a headache when they wake up.
And realize I didn't call GCPD on them while they were unconscious.
What happens next?
They kneel.

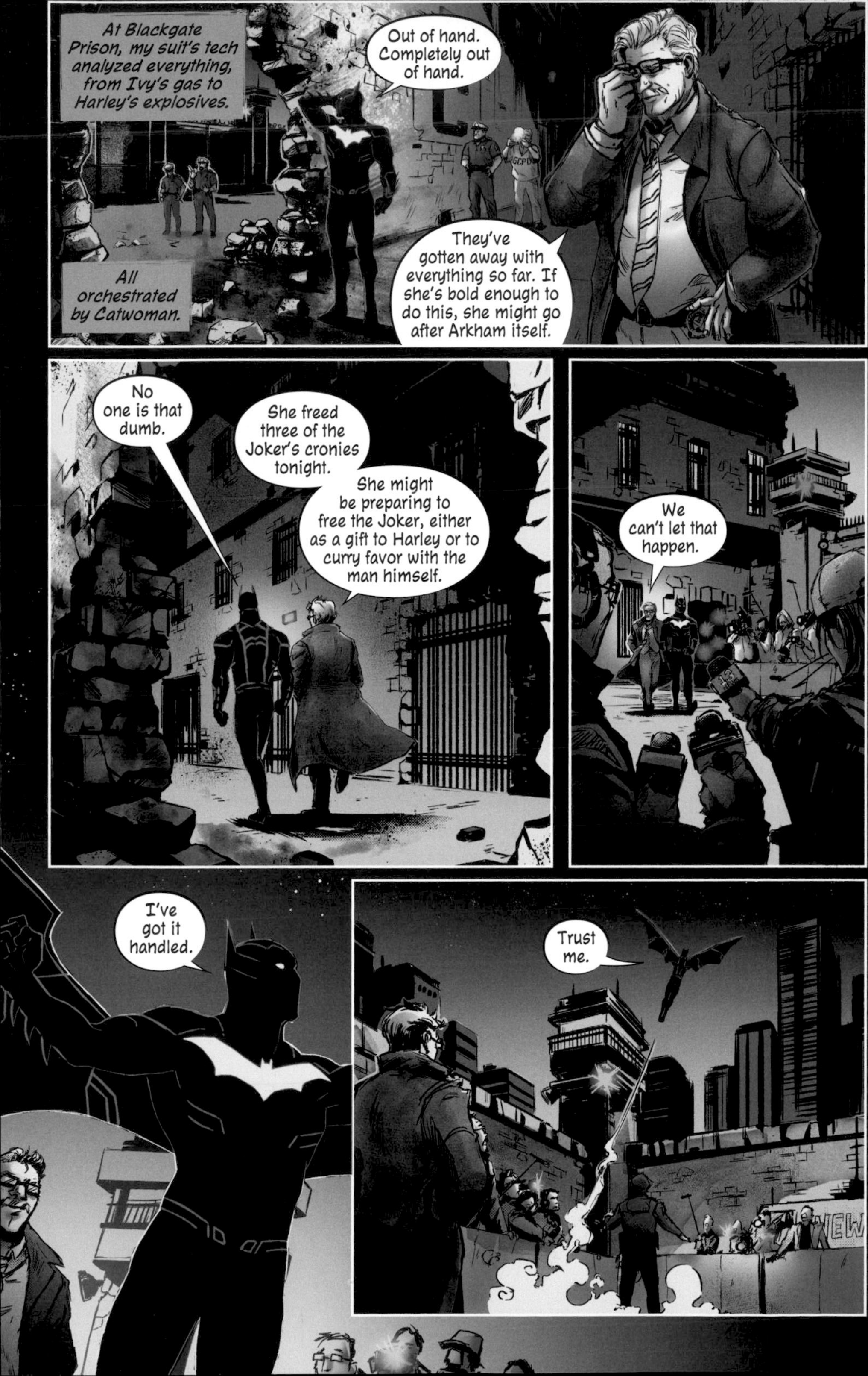
At Blackgate Prison, my suit's tech analyzed everything, from Ivy's gas to Harley's explosives.
Out of hand. Completely out of hand.
All orchestrated by Catwoman.
They've gotten away with everything so far. If she's bold enough to do this, she might go after Arkham itself.
No one is that dumb.
She freed three of the Joker's cronies tonight.
She might be preparing to free the Joker, either as a gift to Harley or to curry favor with the man himself.
We can't let that happen.
I've got it handled.
Trust me.

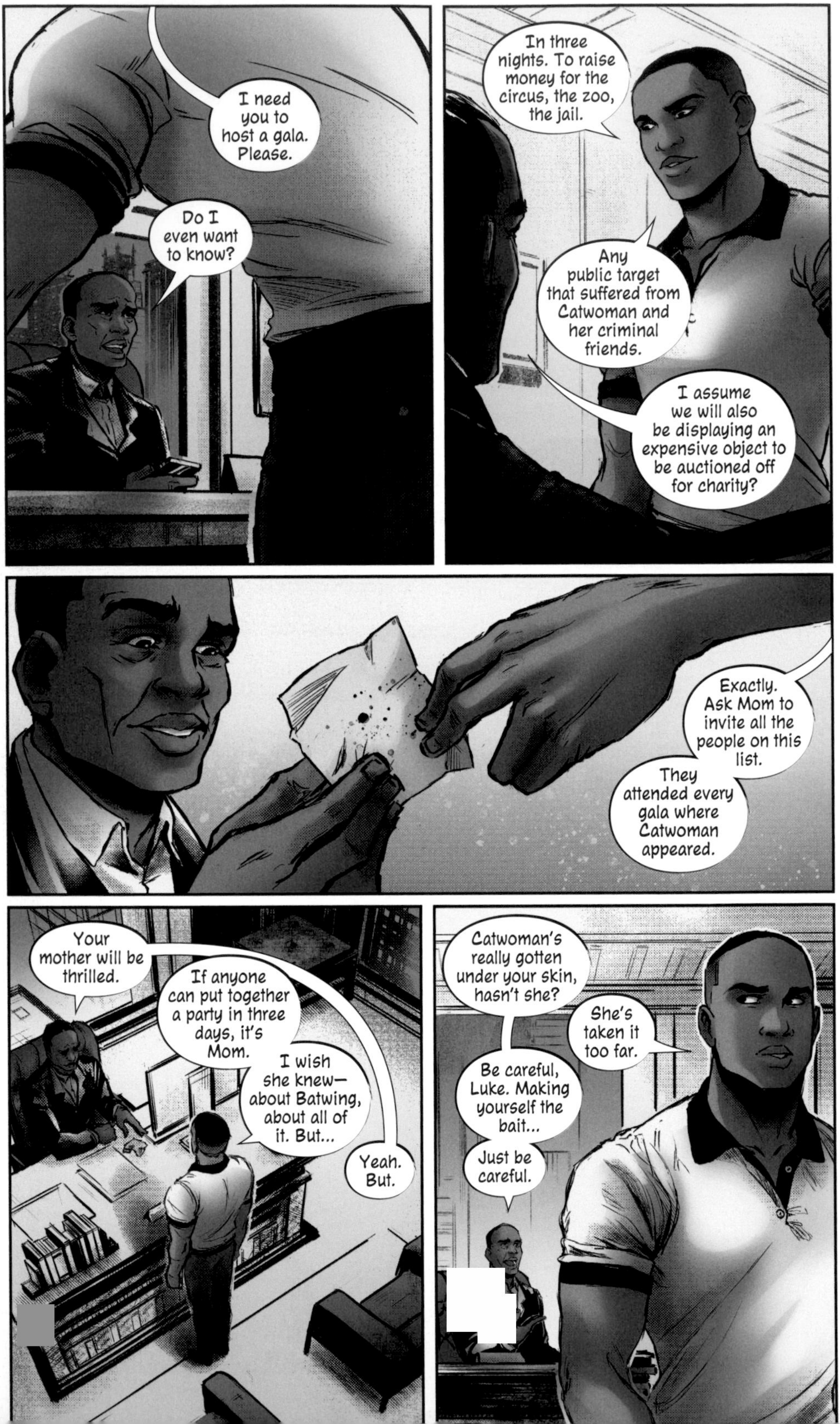
I need you to host a gala. Please.
Do I even want to know?
In three nights. To raise money for the circus, the zoo, the jail.
Any public target that suffered from Catwoman and her criminal friends.
I assume we will also be displaying an expensive object to be auctioned off for charity?
Exactly. Ask Mom to invite all the people on this list.
They attended every gala where Catwoman appeared.
Your mother will be thrilled.
If anyone can put together a party in three days, it's Mom.
I wish she knew— about Batwing, about all of it. But...
Yeah. But.
Catwoman's really gotten under your skin, hasn't she?
She's taken it too far.
Be careful, Luke. Making yourself the bait...
Just be careful.

PART SEVEN

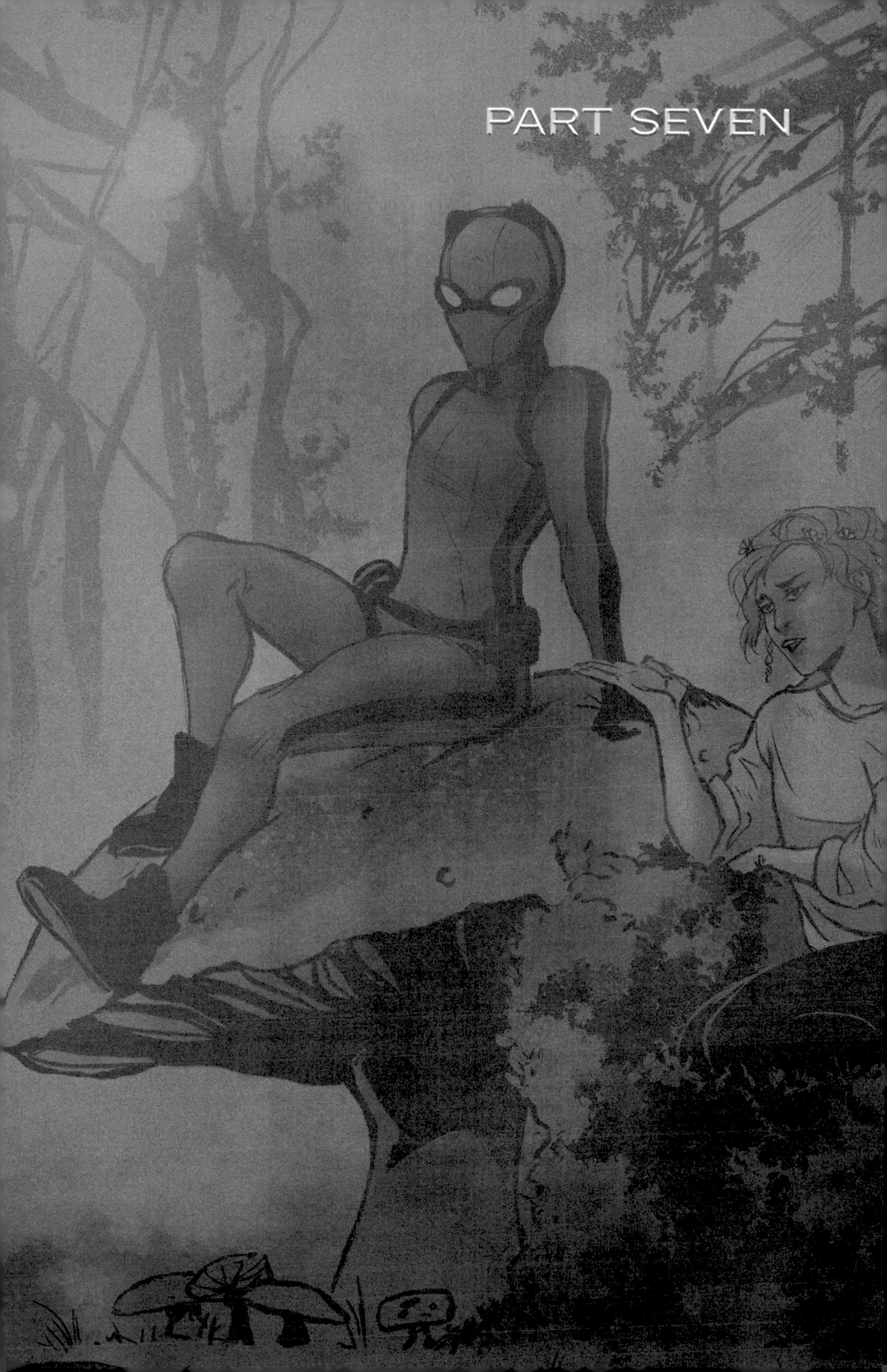

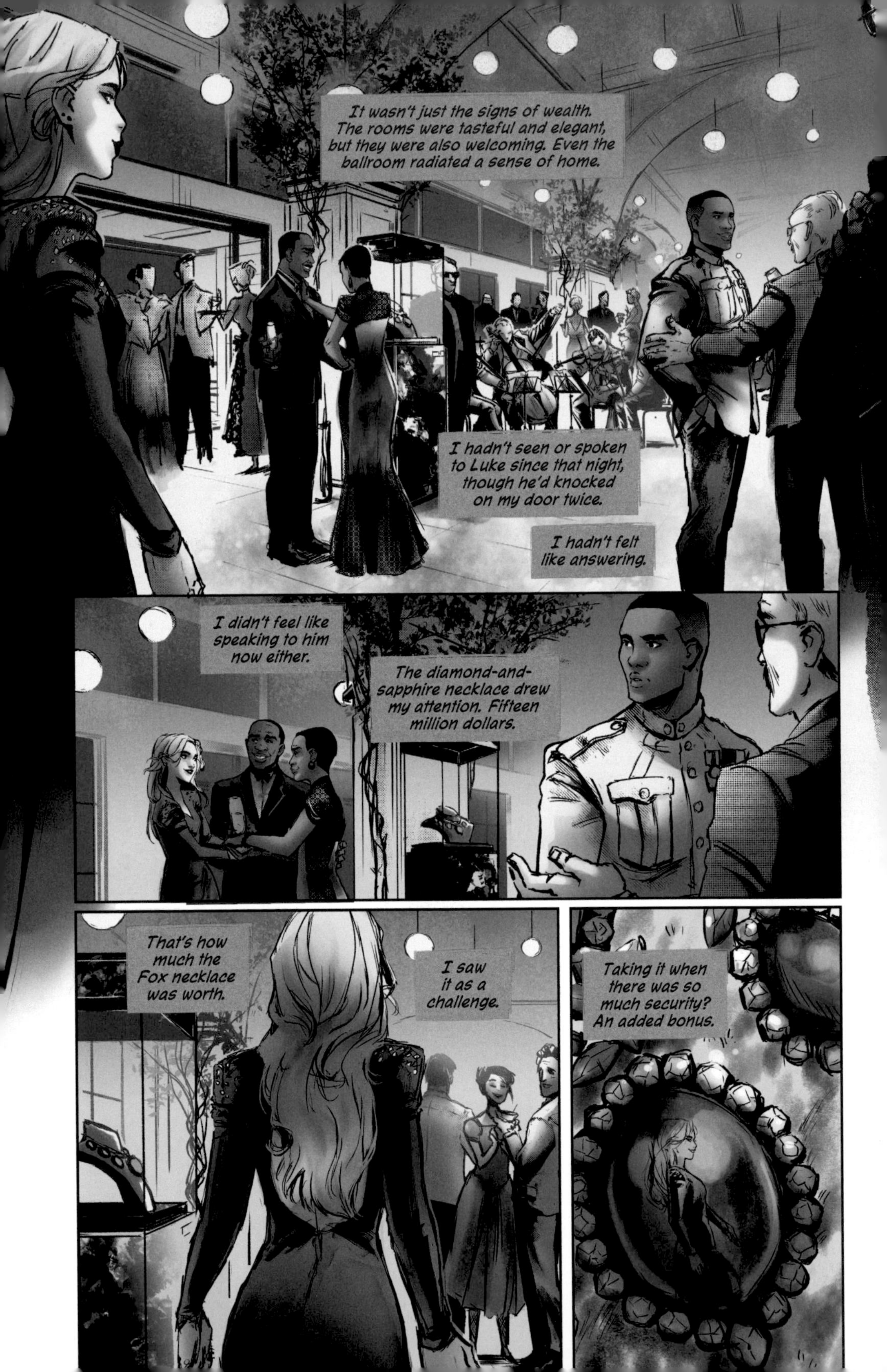
It wasn't just the signs of wealth. The rooms were tasteful and elegant, but they were also welcoming. Even the ballroom radiated a sense of home.
I hadn't seen or spoken to Luke since that night, though he'd knocked on my door twice.
I hadn't felt like answering.
I didn't feel like speaking to him now either.
The diamond-and-sapphire necklace drew my attention. Fifteen million dollars.
That's how much the Fox necklace was worth.
I saw it as a challenge.
Taking it when there was so much security? An added bonus.

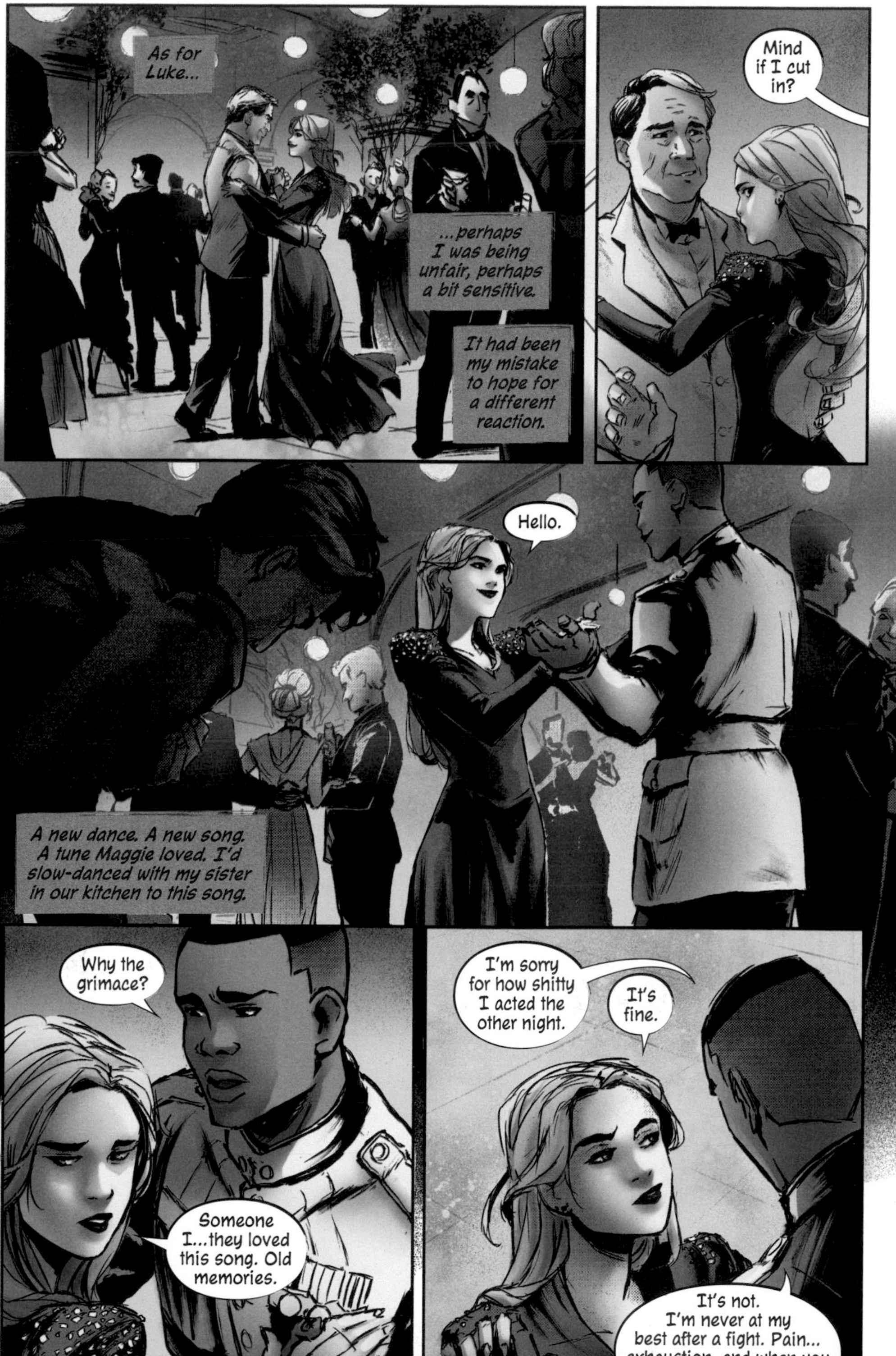
As for Luke...
...perhaps I was being unfair, perhaps a bit sensitive.
It had been my mistake to hope for a different reaction.
Mind if I cut in?
Hello.
A new dance. A new song. A tune Maggie loved. I'd slow-danced with my sister in our kitchen to this song.
Why the grimace?
Someone I...they loved this song. Old memories.
I'm sorry for how shitty I acted the other night.
It's fine.
It's not. I'm never at my best after a fight. Pain... exhaustion, and when you mentioned your date...

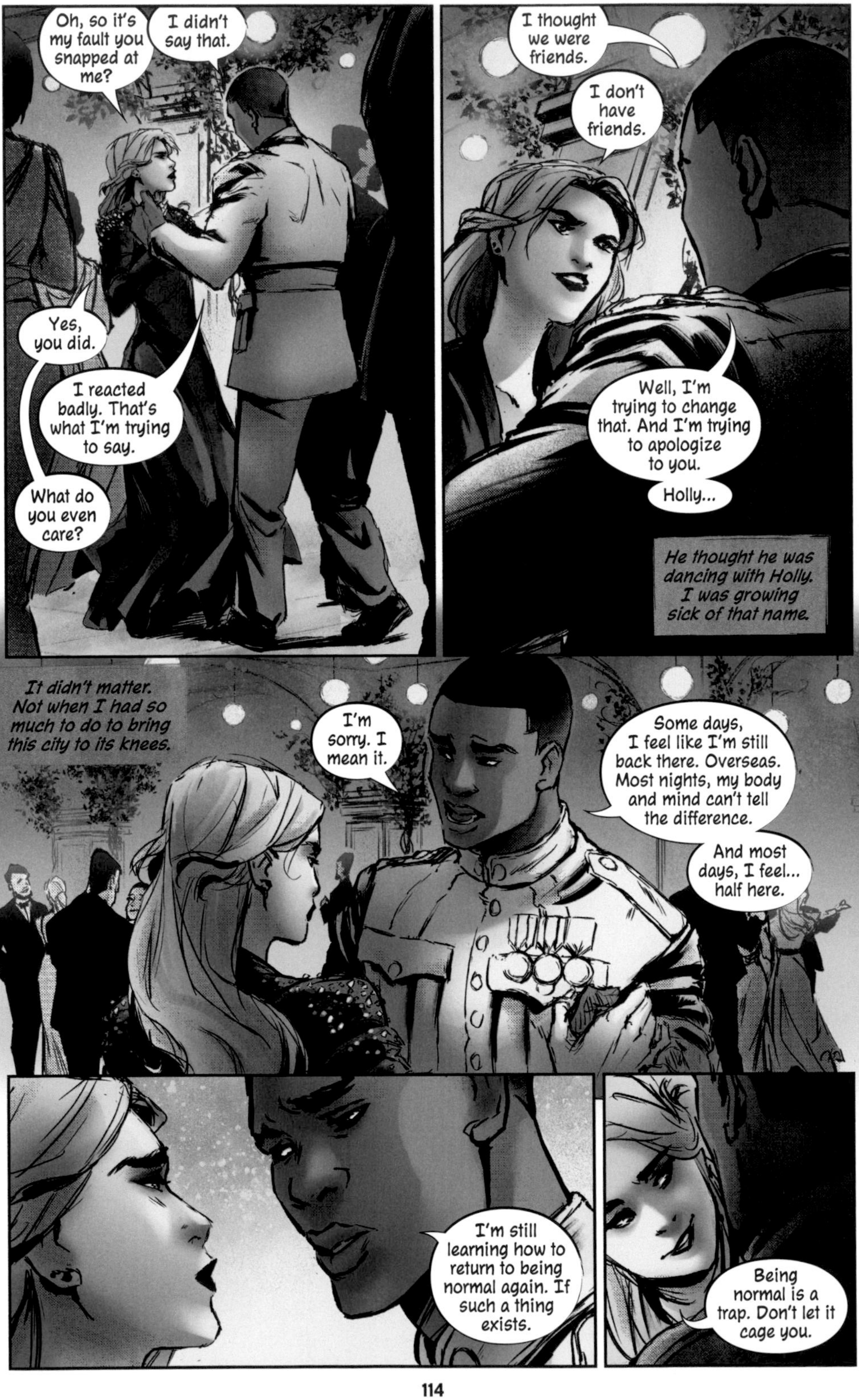

Oh, so it's my fault you snapped at me?
I didn't say that.
Yes, you did.
I reacted badly. That's what I'm trying to say.
What do you even care?
I thought we were friends.
I don't have friends.
Well, I'm trying to change that. And I'm trying to apologize to you.
Holly...
He thought he was dancing with Holly. I was growing sick of that name.
It didn't matter. Not when I had so much to do to bring this city to its knees.
I'm sorry. I mean it.
Some days, I feel like I'm still back there. Overseas. Most nights, my body and mind can't tell the difference.
And most days, I feel... half here.
I'm still learning how to return to being normal again. If such a thing exists.
Being normal is a trap. Don't let it cage you.

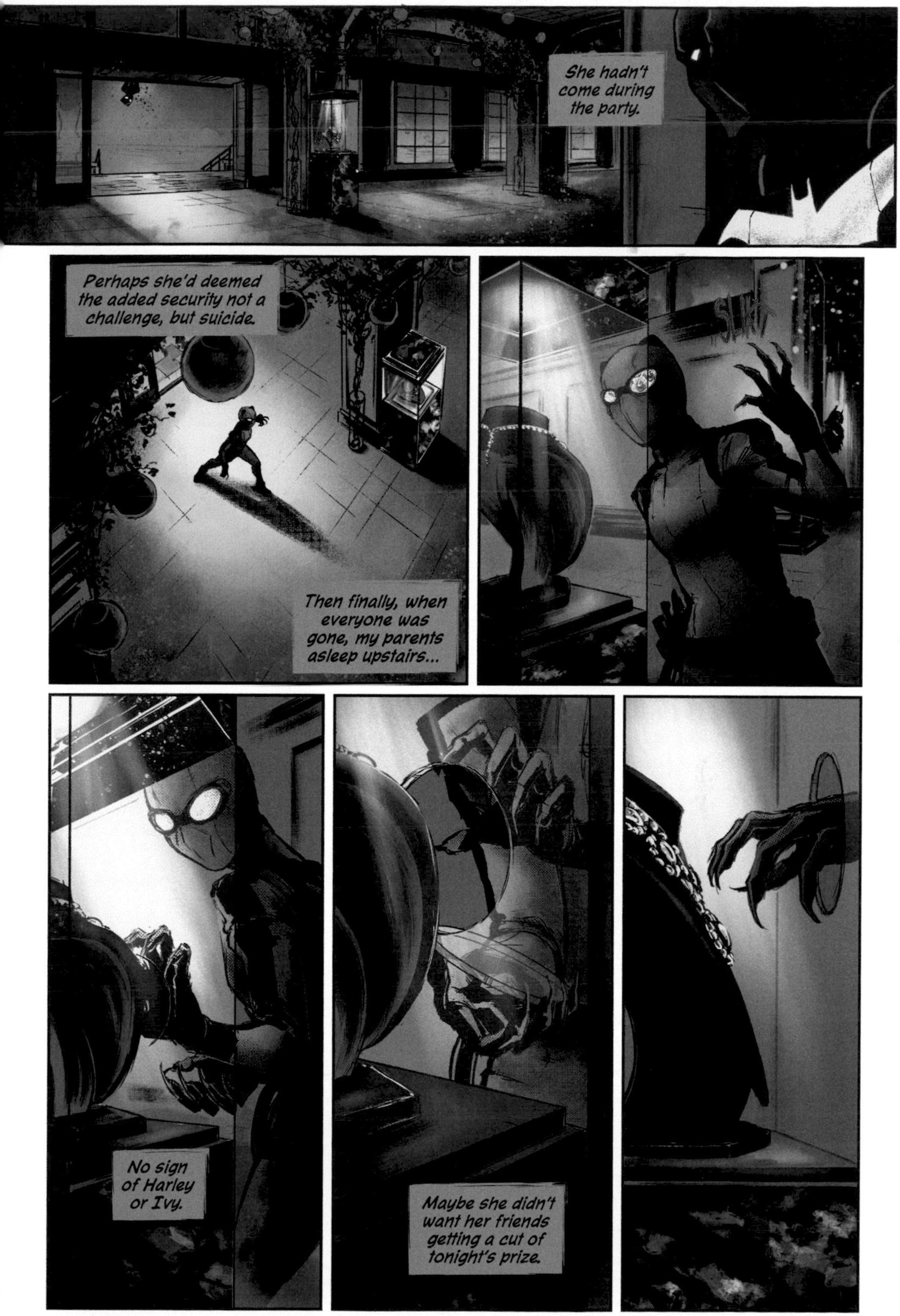
She hadn't come during the party.
Perhaps she'd deemed the added security not a challenge, but suicide.
Then finally, when everyone was gone, my parents asleep upstairs...
No sign of Harley or Ivy.
Maybe she didn't want her friends getting a cut of tonight's prize.

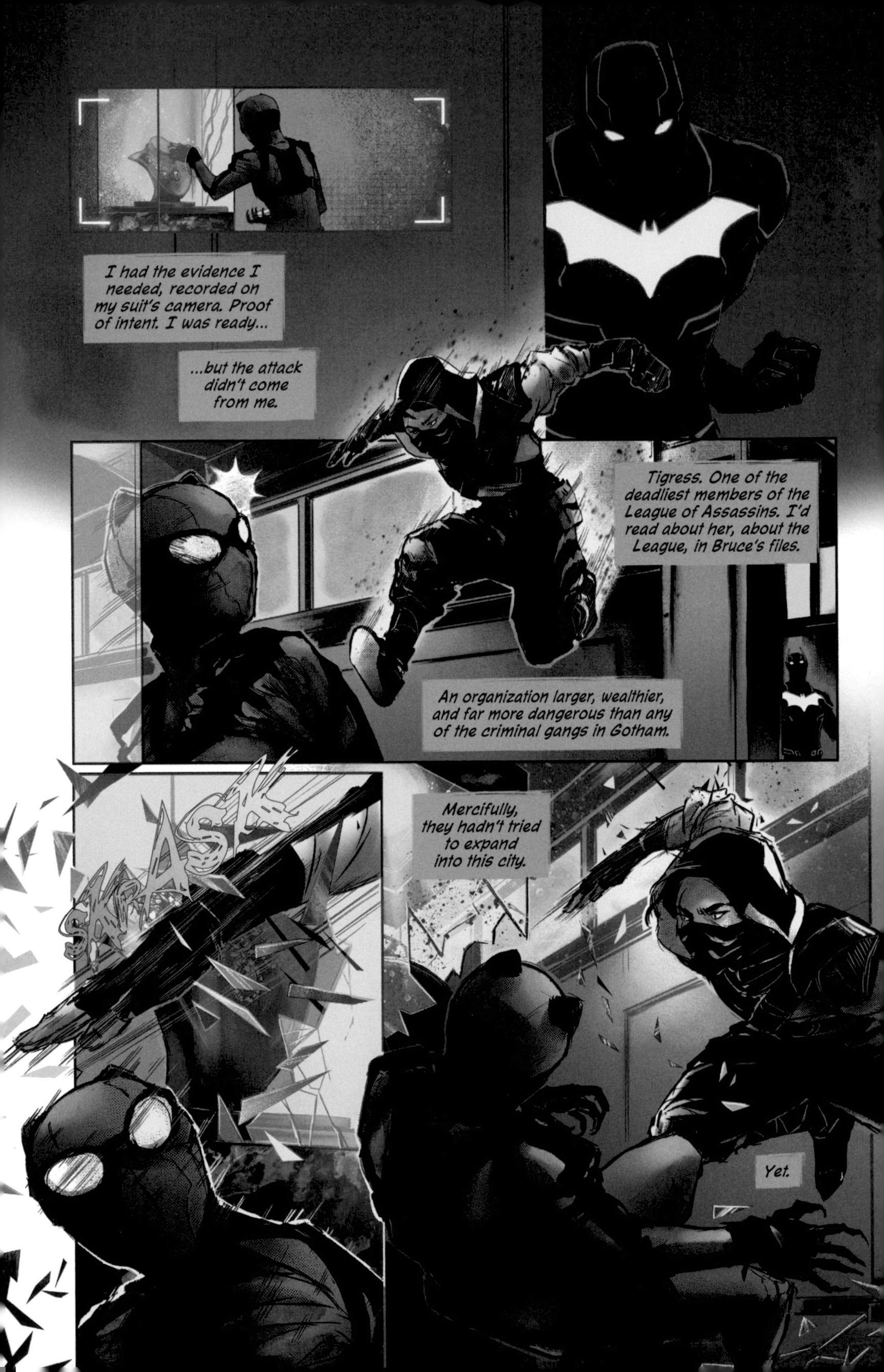
I had the evidence I needed, recorded on my suit's camera. Proof of intent. I was ready...
...but the attack didn't come from me.
Tigress. One of the deadliest members of the League of Assassins. I'd read about her, about the League, in Bruce's files.
An organization larger, wealthier, and far more dangerous than any of the criminal gangs in Gotham.
SKRASK
Mercifully, they hadn't tried to expand into this city.
Yet.

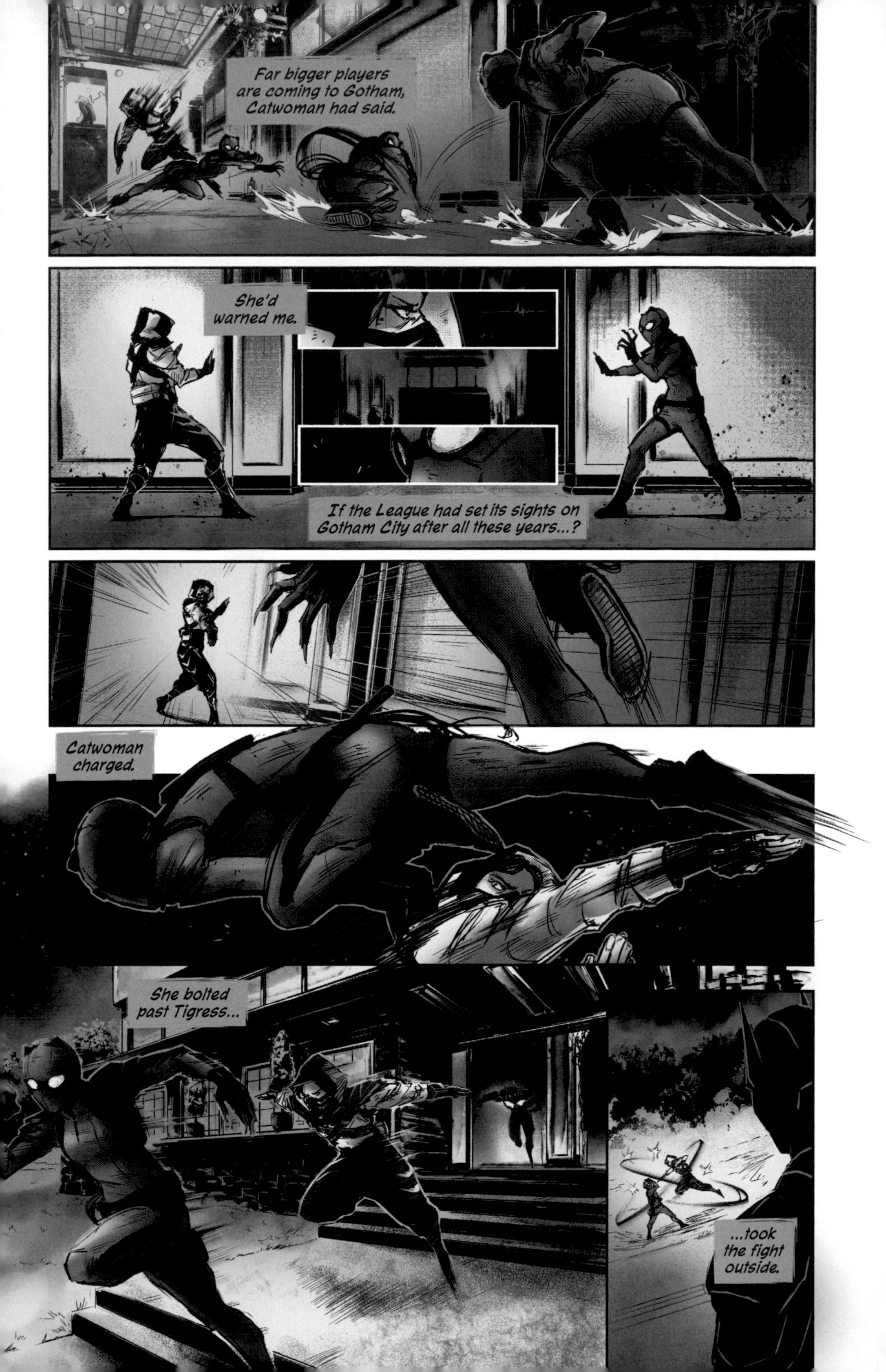
Far bigger players are coming to Gotham, Catwoman had said.
She'd warned me.
If the League had set its sights on Gotham City after all these years...?
Catwoman charged.
She bolted past Tigress...
...took the fight outside.

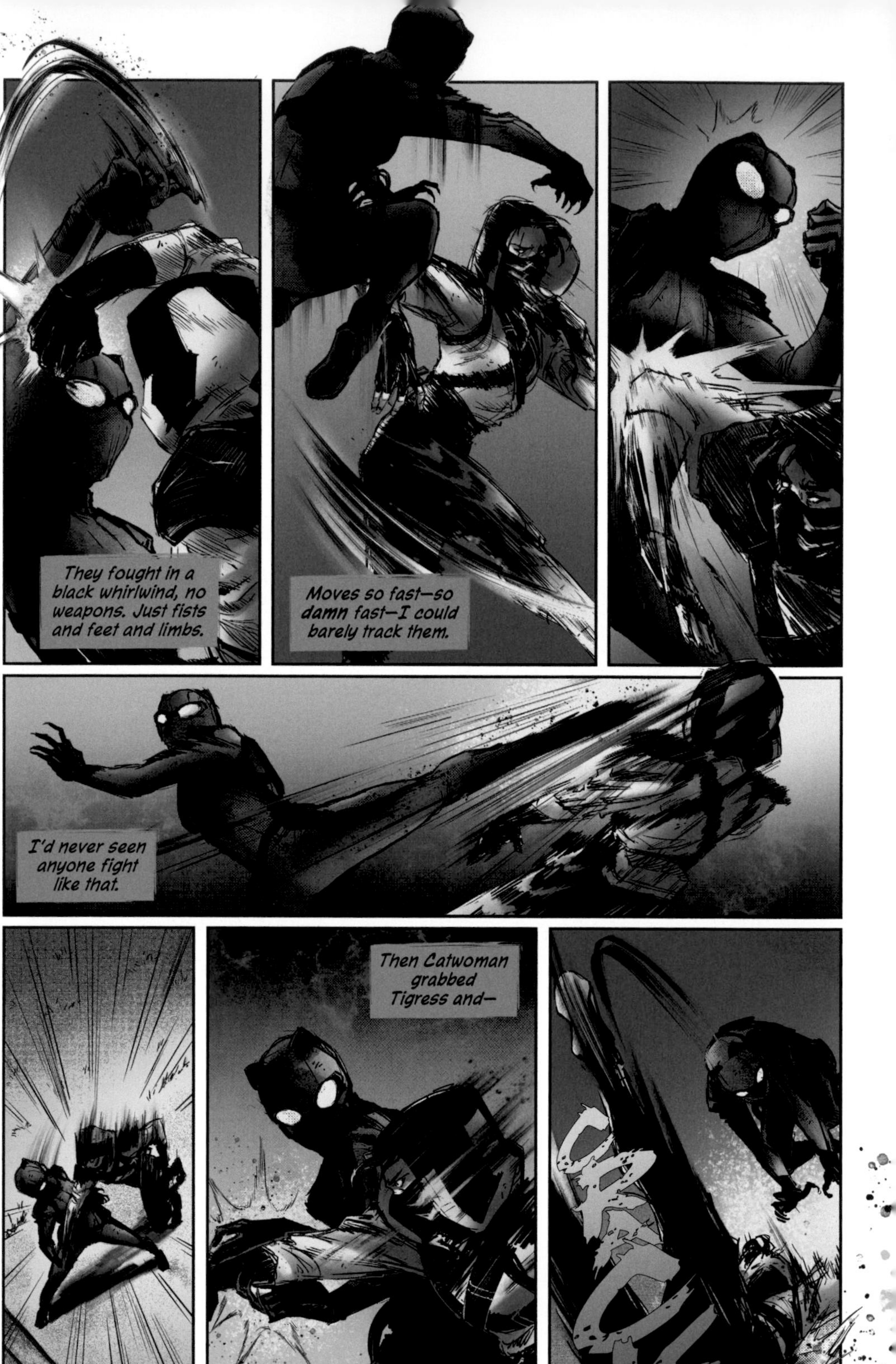
They fought in a black whirlwind, no weapons. Just fists and feet and limbs.
Moves so fast—so damn fast—I could barely track them.
I'd never seen anyone fight like that.
Then Catwoman grabbed Tigress and—

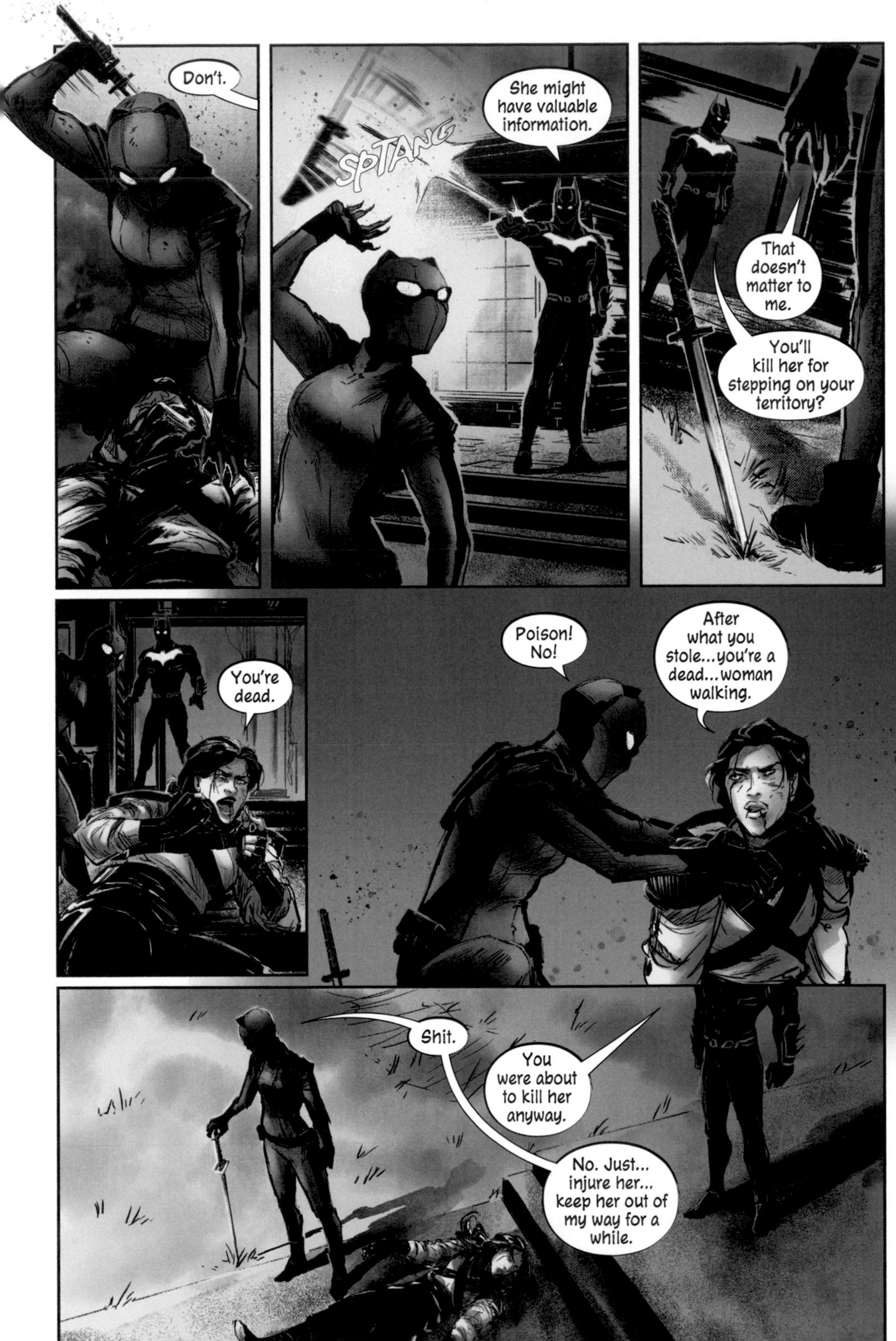
Don't.
SPTANG
She might have valuable information.
That doesn't matter to me.
You'll kill her for stepping on your territory?
You're dead.
Poison! No!
After what you stole...you're a dead...woman walking.
Shit.
You were about to kill her anyway.
No. Just... injure her... keep her out of my way for a while.

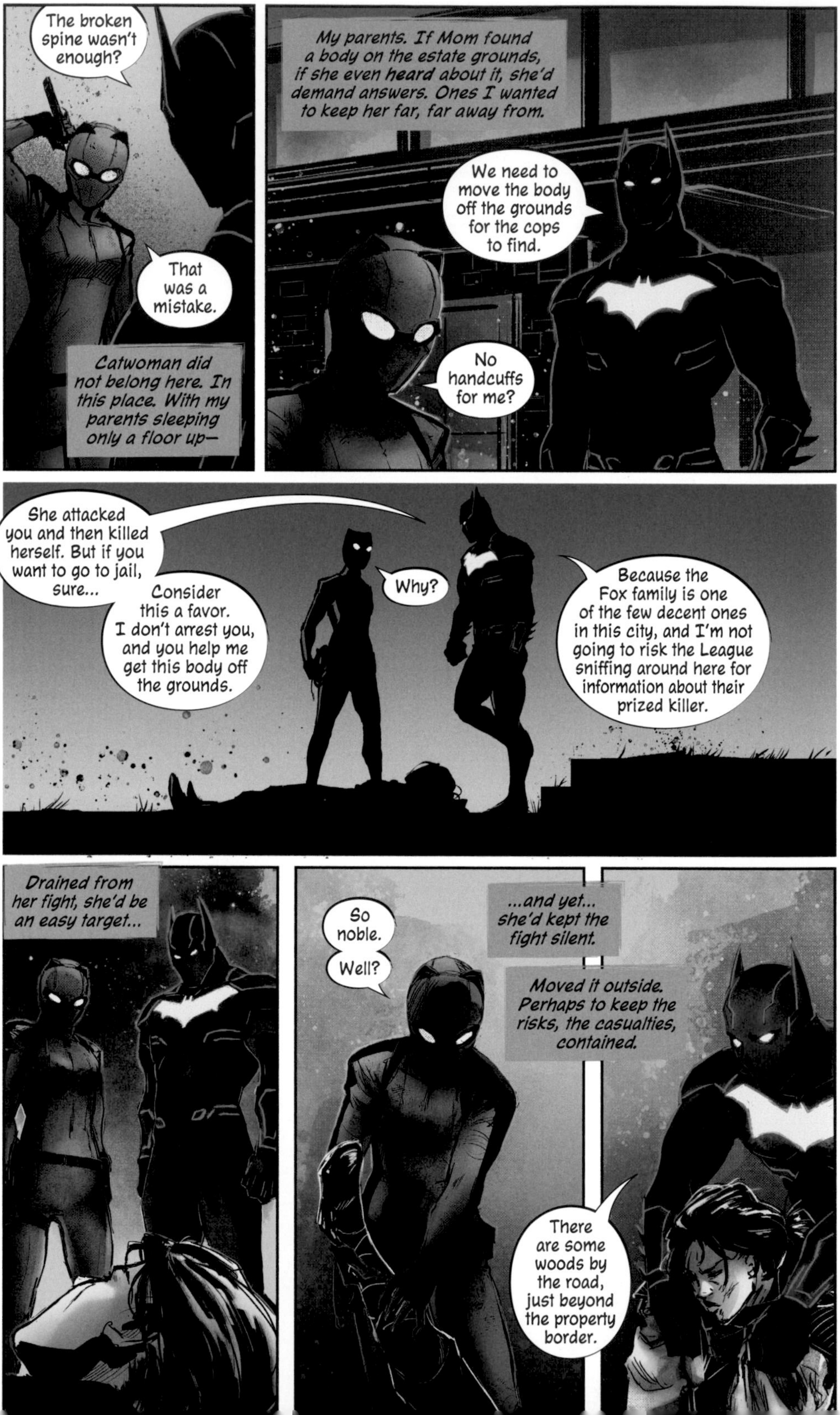
The broken spine wasn't enough?
That was a mistake.
Catwoman did not belong here. In this place. With my parents sleeping only a floor up—
My parents. If Mom found a body on the estate grounds, if she even heard about it, she'd demand answers. Ones I wanted to keep her far, far away from.
We need to move the body off the grounds for the cops to find.
No handcuffs for me?
She attacked you and then killed herself. But if you want to go to jail, sure...
Consider this a favor. I don't arrest you, and you help me get this body off the grounds.
Why?
Because the Fox family is one of the few decent ones in this city, and I'm not going to risk the League sniffing around here for information about their prized killer.
Drained from her fight, she'd be an easy target...
So noble.
Well?
...and yet... she'd kept the fight silent.
Moved it outside. Perhaps to keep the risks, the casualties, contained.
There are some woods by the road, just beyond the property border.

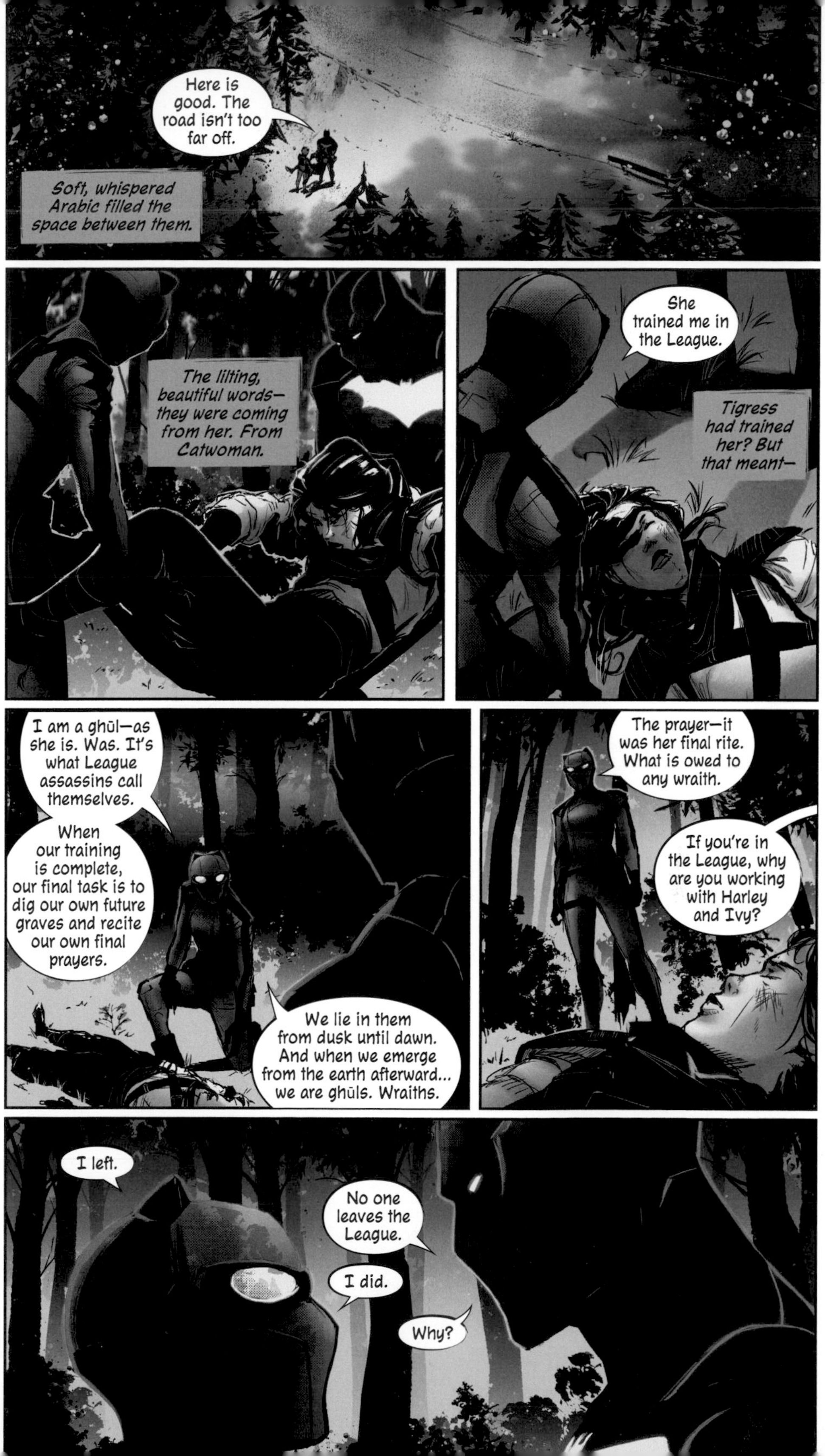
Here is good. The road isn't too far off.
Soft, whispered Arabic filled the space between them.
The lilting, beautiful words—they were coming from her. From Catwoman.
She trained me in the League.
Tigress had trained her? But that meant—
I am a ghūl—as she is. Was. It's what League assassins call themselves.
When our training is complete, our final task is to dig our own future graves and recite our own final prayers.
We lie in them from dusk until dawn. And when we emerge from the earth afterward... we are ghūls. Wraiths.
The prayer—it was her final rite. What is owed to any wraith.
If you're in the League, why are you working with Harley and Ivy?
I left.
No one leaves the League.
I did.
Why?

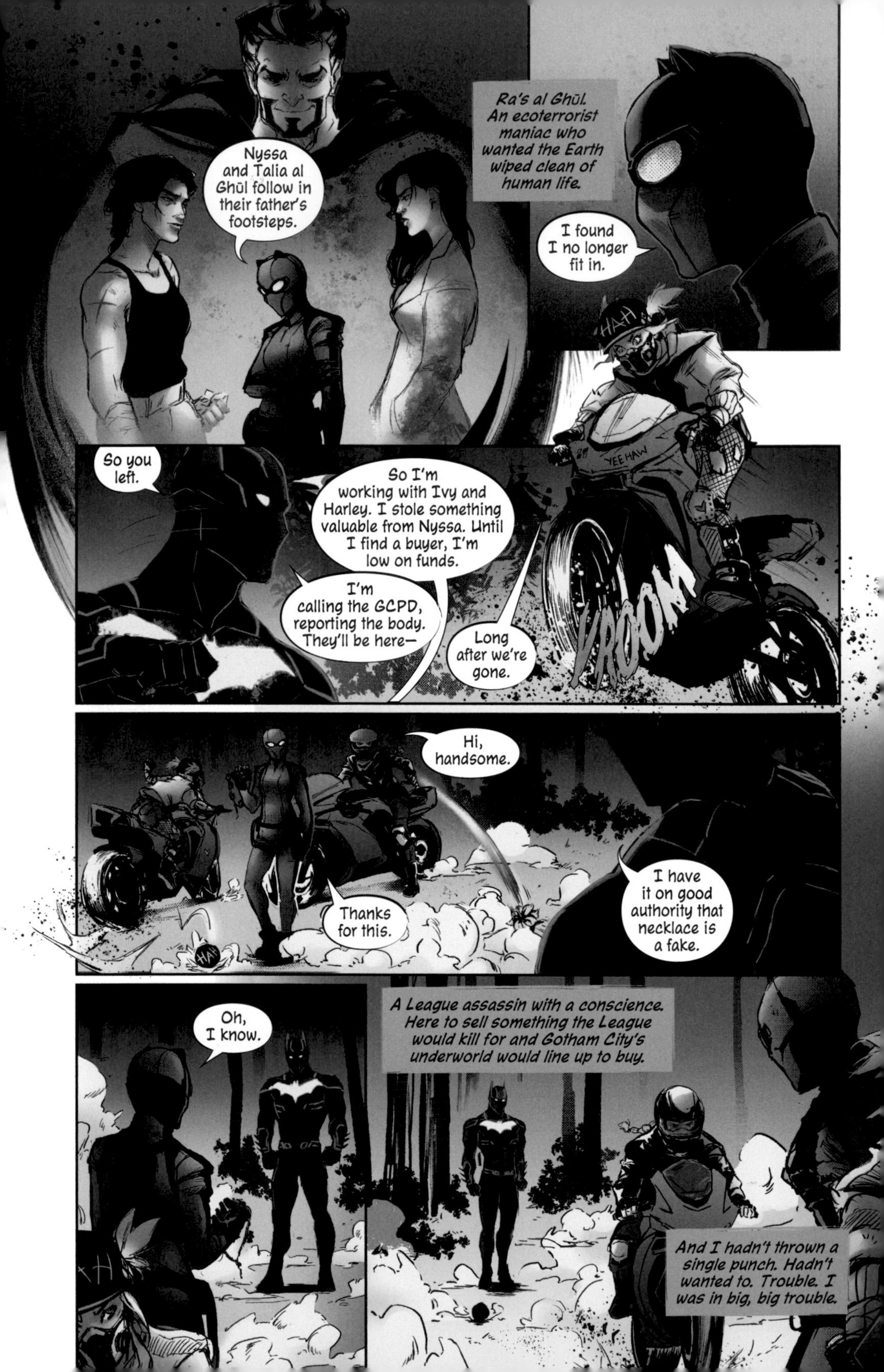
Nyssa and Talia al Ghūl follow in their father's footsteps.
Ra's al Ghūl. An ecoterrorist maniac who wanted the Earth wiped clean of human life.
I found I no longer fit in.
So you left.
So I'm working with Ivy and Harley. I stole something valuable from Nyssa. Until I find a buyer, I'm low on funds.
I'm calling the GCPD, reporting the body. They'll be here—
Long after we're gone.
YEEHAW
VROOM
Hi, handsome.
Thanks for this.
I have it on good authority that necklace is a fake.
Oh, I know.
A League assassin with a conscience. Here to sell something the League would kill for and Gotham City's underworld would line up to buy.
And I hadn't thrown a single punch. Hadn't wanted to. Trouble. I was in big, big trouble.

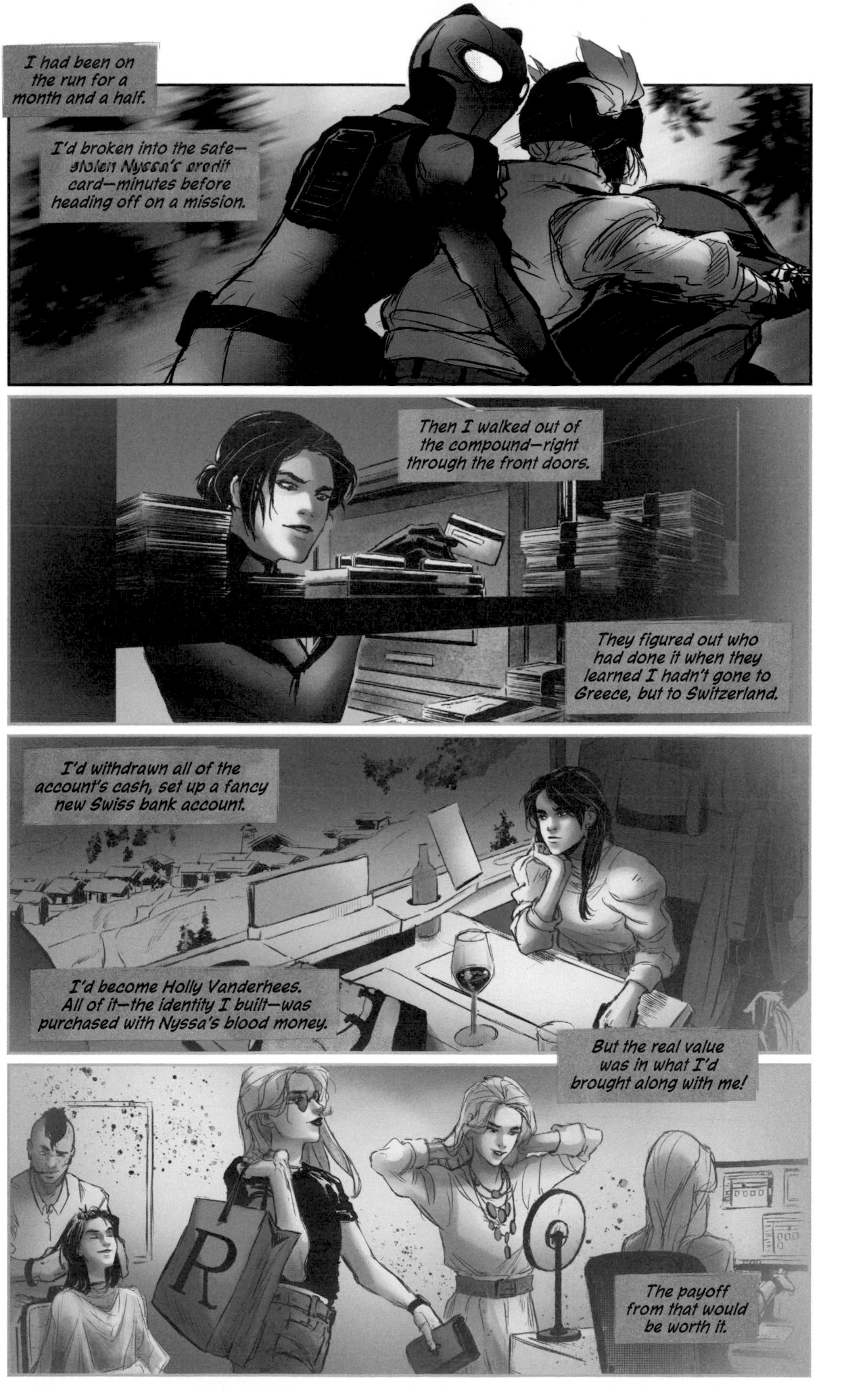
I had been on the run for a month and a half.
I'd broken into the safe—stolen Nyssa's credit card—minutes before heading off on a mission.
Then I walked out of the compound—right through the front doors.
They figured out who had done it when they learned I hadn't gone to Greece, but to Switzerland.
I'd withdrawn all of the account's cash, set up a fancy new Swiss bank account.
I'd become Holly Vanderhees. All of it—the identity I built—was purchased with Nyssa's blood money.
But the real value was in what I'd brought along with me!
R
The payoff from that would be worth it.

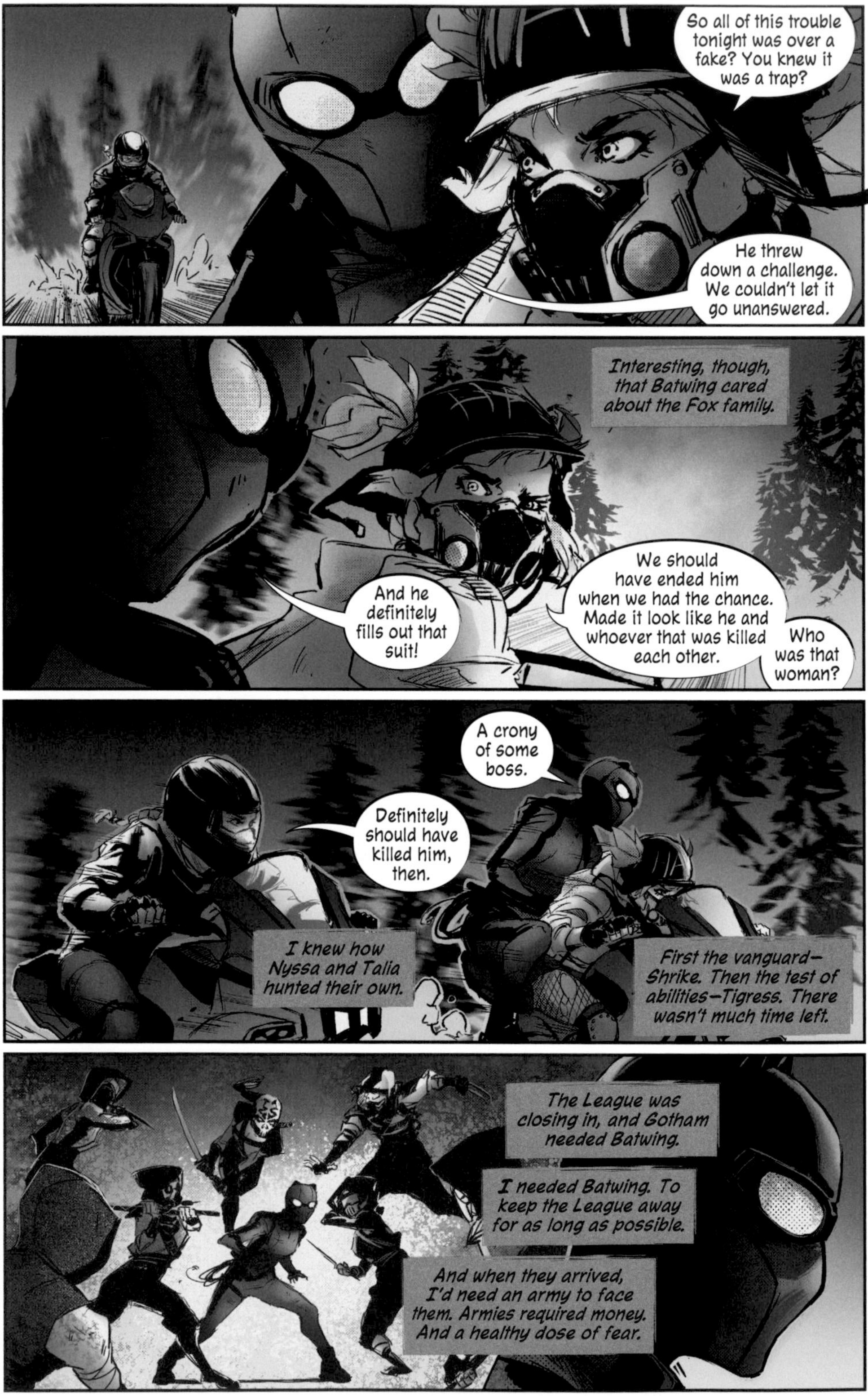
So all of this trouble tonight was over a fake? You knew it was a trap?
He threw down a challenge. We couldn't let it go unanswered.
Interesting, though, that Batwing cared about the Fox family.
And he definitely fills out that suit!
We should have ended him when we had the chance. Made it look like he and whoever that was killed each other.
Who was that woman?
A crony of some boss.
Definitely should have killed him, then.
I knew how Nyssa and Talia hunted their own.
First the vanguard—Shrike. Then the test of abilities—Tigress. There wasn't much time left.
The League was closing in, and Gotham needed Batwing.
I needed Batwing. To keep the League away for as long as possible.
And when they arrived, I'd need an army to face them. Armies required money. And a healthy dose of fear.

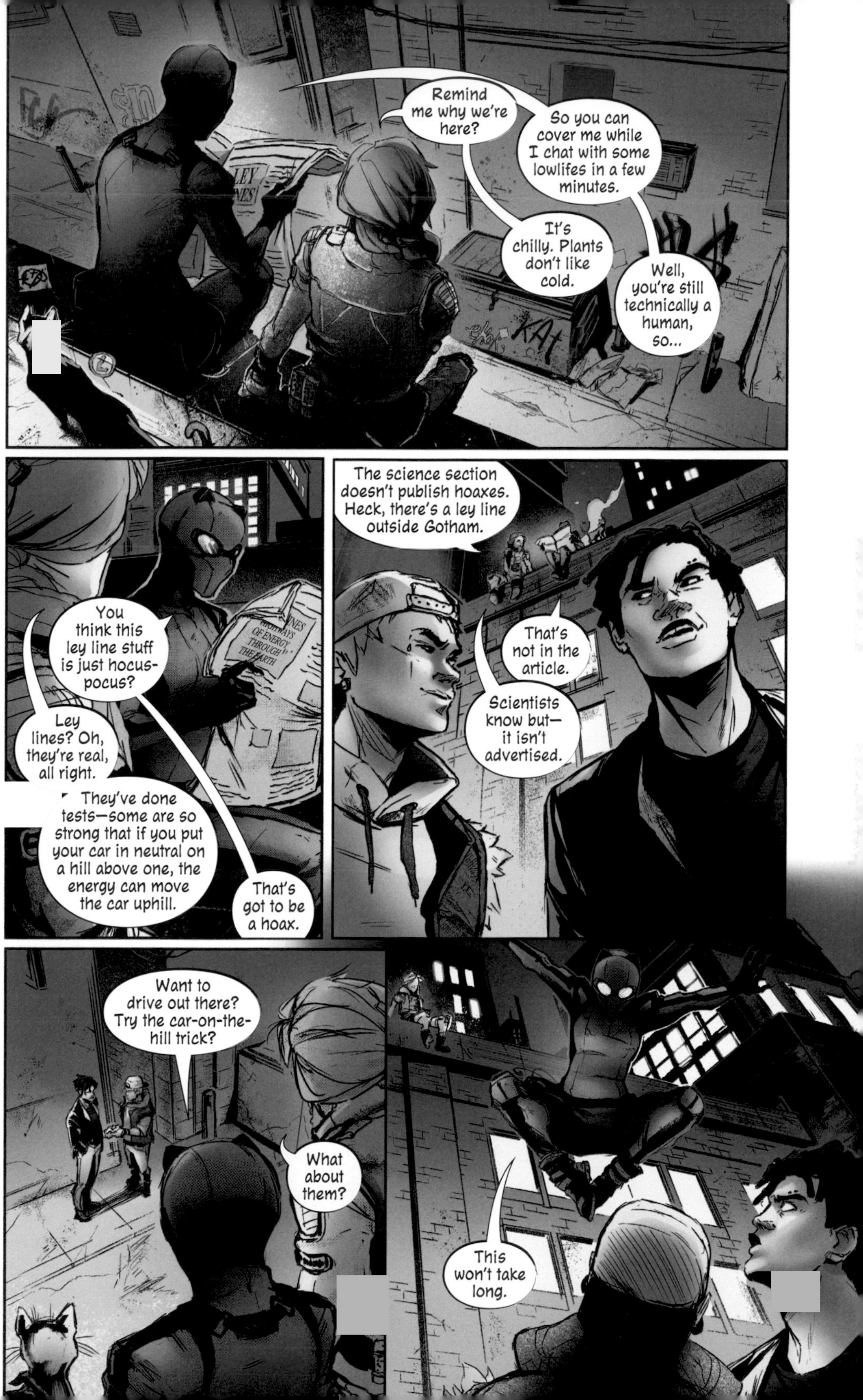
Remind me why we're here?
So you can cover me while I chat with some lowlifes in a few minutes.
It's chilly. Plants don't like cold.
Well, you're still technically a human, so...
You think this ley line stuff is just hocus-pocus?
Ley lines? Oh, they're real, all right.
They've done tests—some are so strong that if you put your car in neutral on a hill above one, the energy can move the car uphill.
That's got to be a hoax.
The science section doesn't publish hoaxes. Heck, there's a ley line outside Gotham.
That's not in the article.
Scientists know but—it isn't advertised.
Want to drive out there? Try the car-on-the-hill trick?
What about them?
This won't take long.

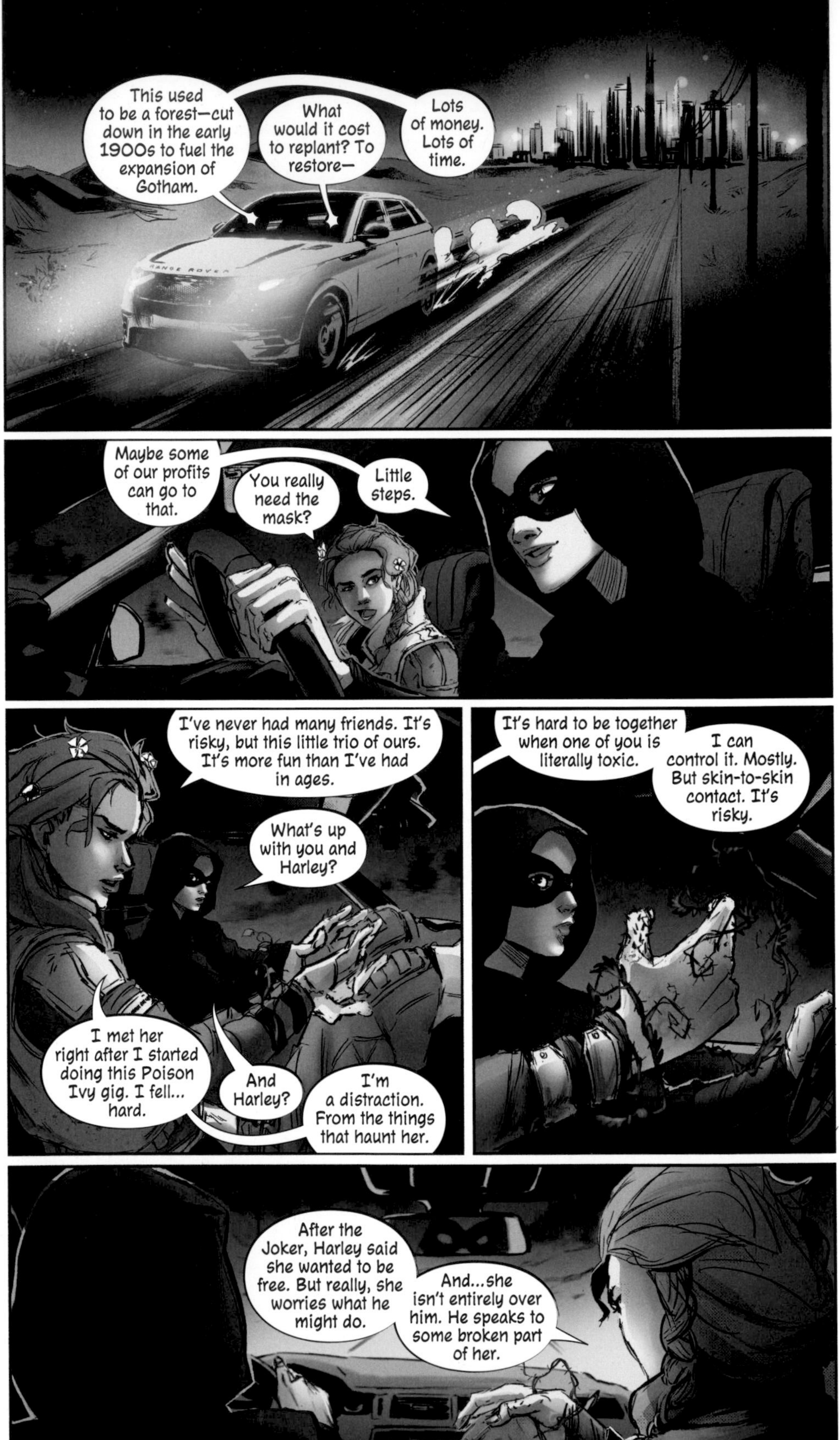
This used to be a forest—cut down in the early 1900s to fuel the expansion of Gotham.
What would it cost to replant? To restore—
Lots of money. Lots of time.
RANGE ROVER
Maybe some of our profits can go to that.
You really need the mask?
Little steps.
I've never had many friends. It's risky, but this little trio of ours. It's more fun than I've had in ages.
What's up with you and Harley?
I met her right after I started doing this Poison Ivy gig. I fell... hard.
And Harley?
I'm a distraction. From the things that haunt her.
It's hard to be together when one of you is literally toxic.
I can control it. Mostly. But skin-to-skin contact. It's risky.
After the Joker, Harley said she wanted to be free. But really, she worries what he might do.
And...she isn't entirely over him. He speaks to some broken part of her.

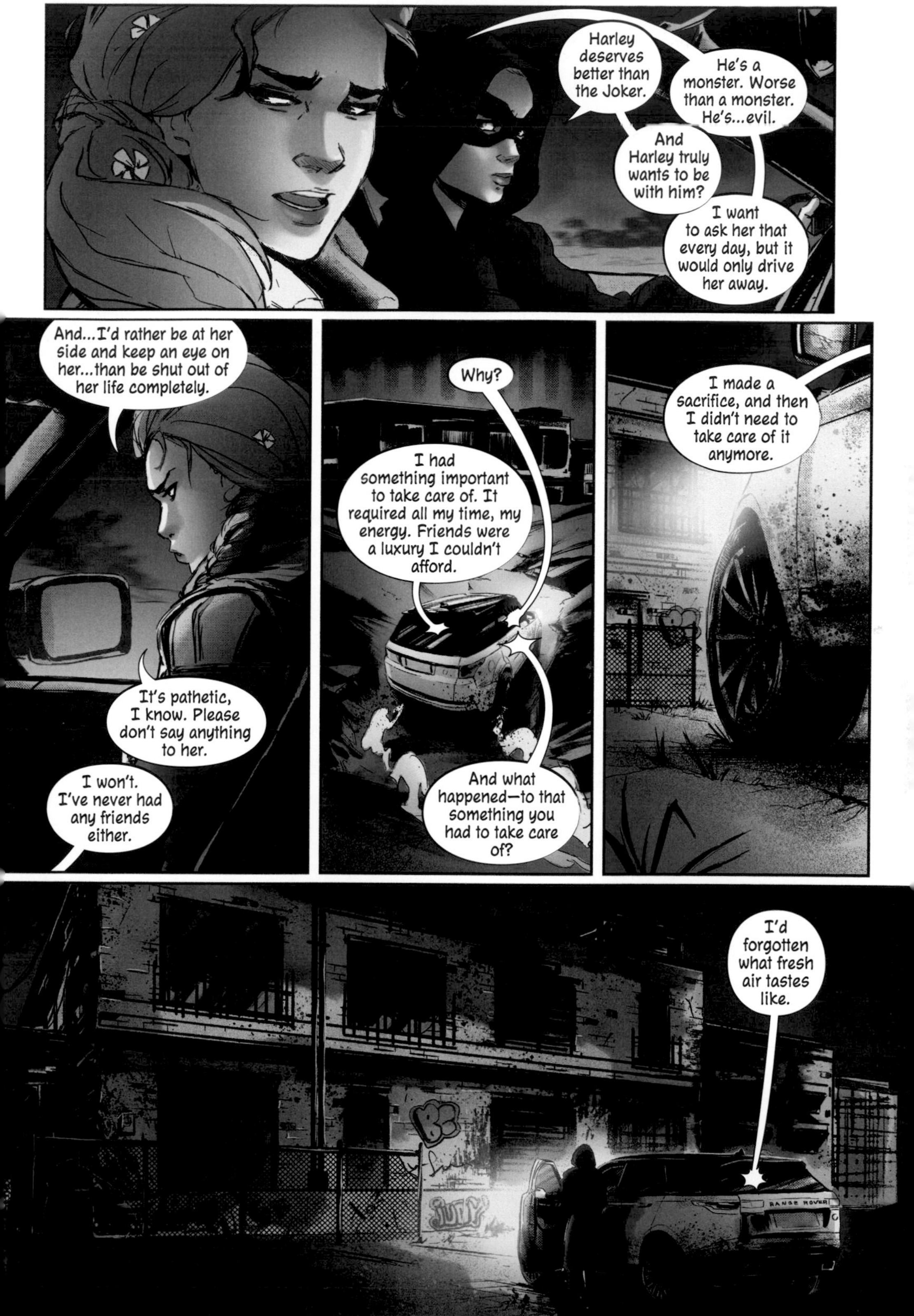

Harley deserves better than the Joker.
He's a monster. Worse than a monster. He's...evil.
And Harley truly wants to be with him?
I want to ask her that every day, but it would only drive her away.
And...I'd rather be at her side and keep an eye on her...than be shut out of her life completely.
It's pathetic, I know. Please don't say anything to her.
I won't. I've never had any friends either.
Why?
I had something important to take care of. It required all my time, my energy. Friends were a luxury I couldn't afford.
And what happened—to that something you had to take care of?
I made a sacrifice, and then I didn't need to take care of it anymore.
I'd forgotten what fresh air tastes like.

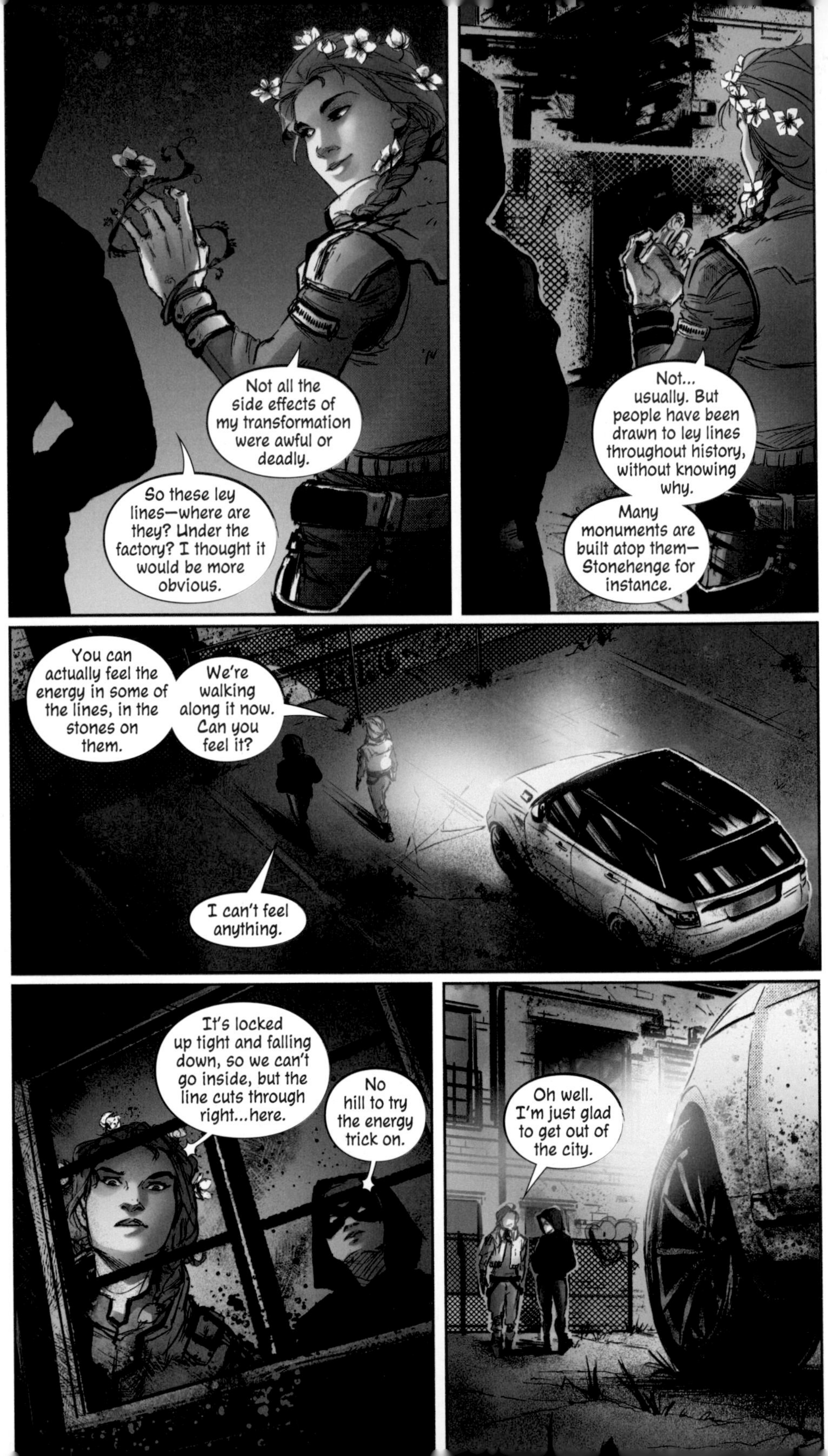
Not all the side effects of my transformation were awful or deadly.
So these ley lines—where are they? Under the factory? I thought it would be more obvious.
Not... usually. But people have been drawn to ley lines throughout history, without knowing why.
Many monuments are built atop them—Stonehenge for instance.
You can actually feel the energy in some of the lines, in the stones on them.
We're walking along it now. Can you feel it?
I can't feel anything.
It's locked up tight and falling down, so we can't go inside, but the line cuts through right...here.
No hill to try the energy trick on.
Oh well. I'm just glad to get out of the city.

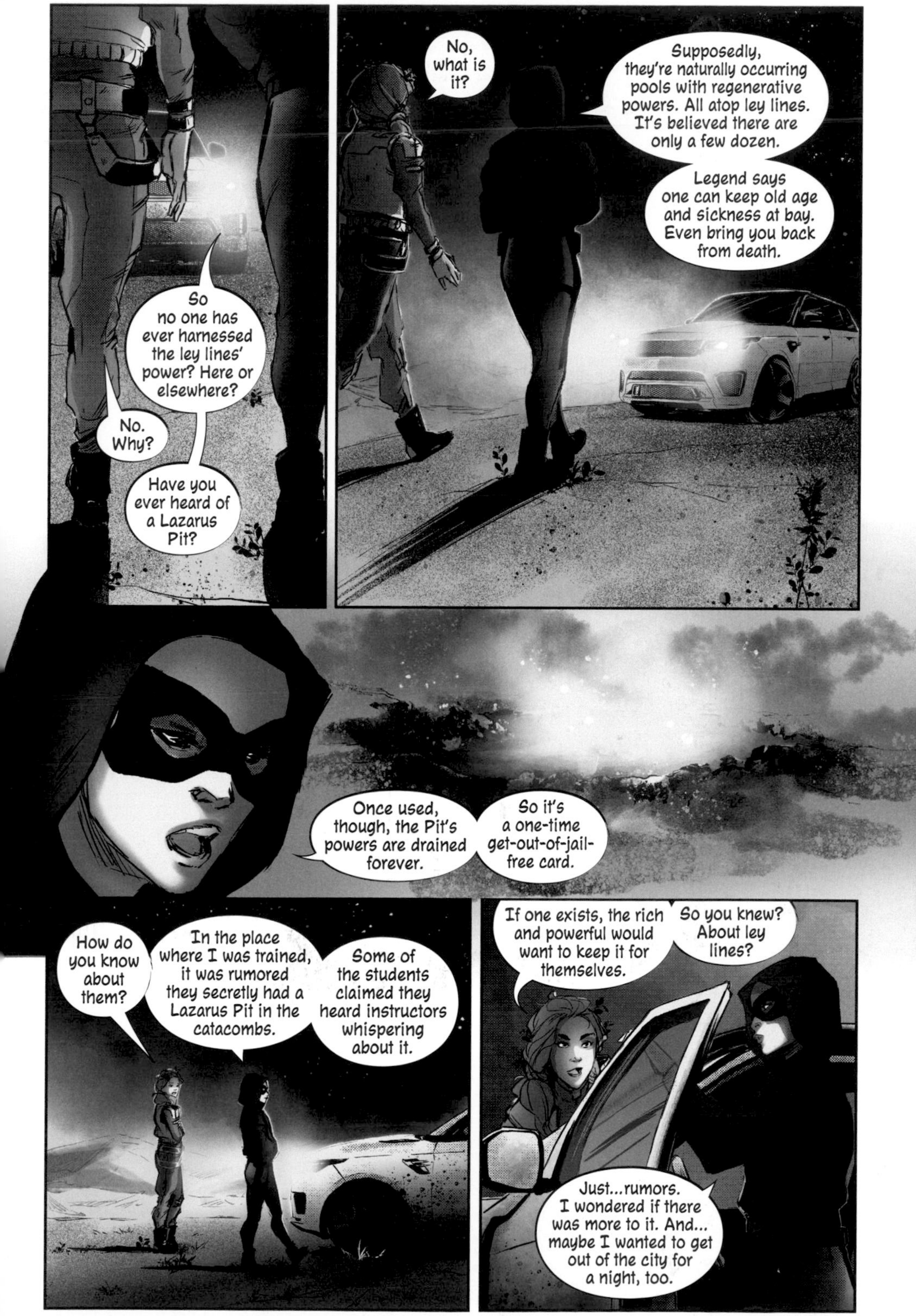

Have you ever heard of a Lazarus Pit?
No. Why?
So no one has ever harnessed the ley lines' power? Here or elsewhere?
No, what is it?
Supposedly, they're naturally occurring pools with regenerative powers. All atop ley lines. It's believed there are only a few dozen.
Legend says one can keep old age and sickness at bay. Even bring you back from death.
Once used, though, the Pit's powers are drained forever.
So it's a one-time get-out-of-jail-free card.
How do you know about them?
In the place where I was trained, it was rumored they secretly had a Lazarus Pit in the catacombs.
Some of the students claimed they heard instructors whispering about it.
If one exists, the rich and powerful would want to keep it for themselves.
So you knew? About ley lines?
Just...rumors. I wondered if there was more to it. And... maybe I wanted to get out of the city for a night, too.

PART EIGHT

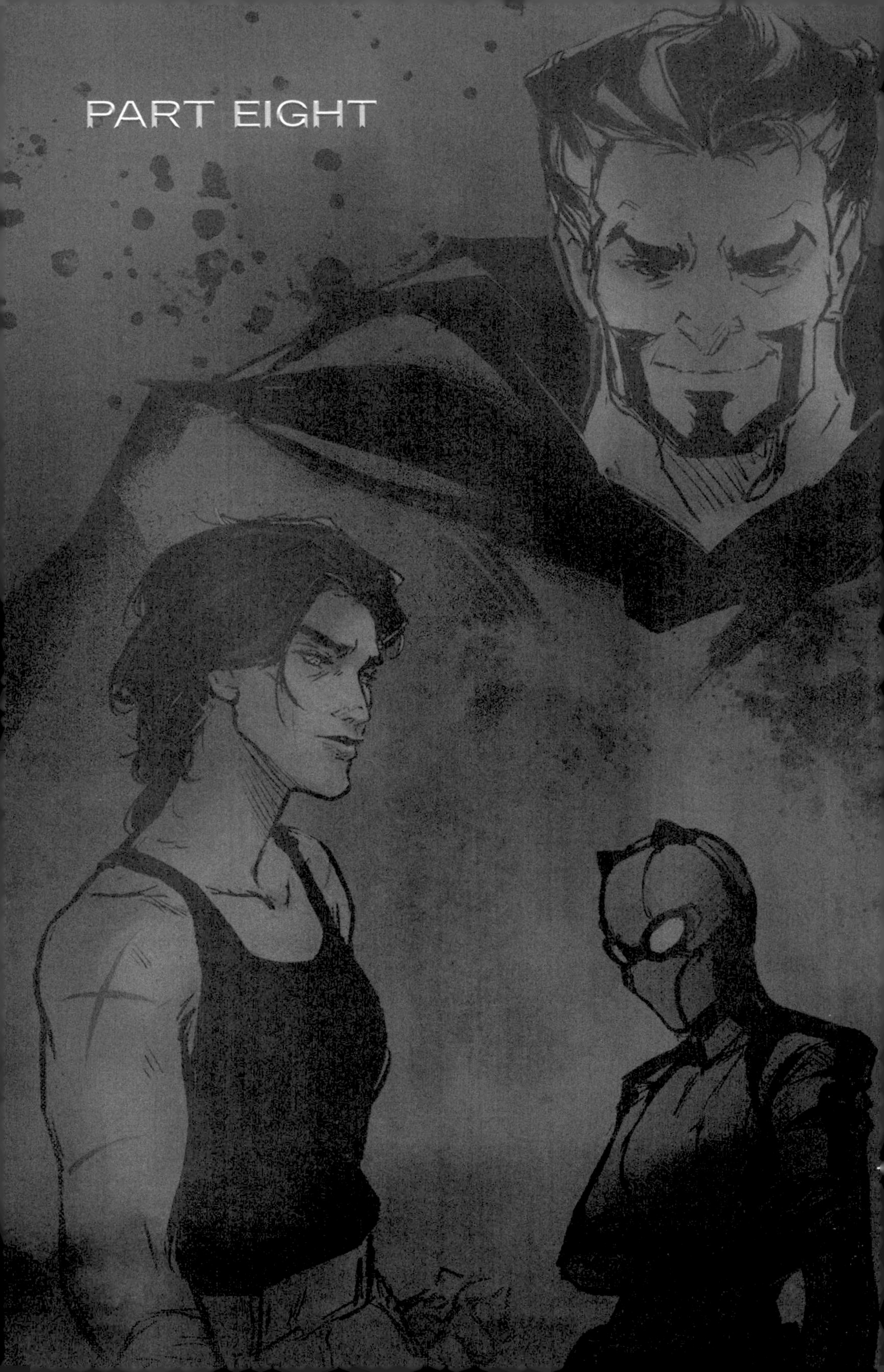

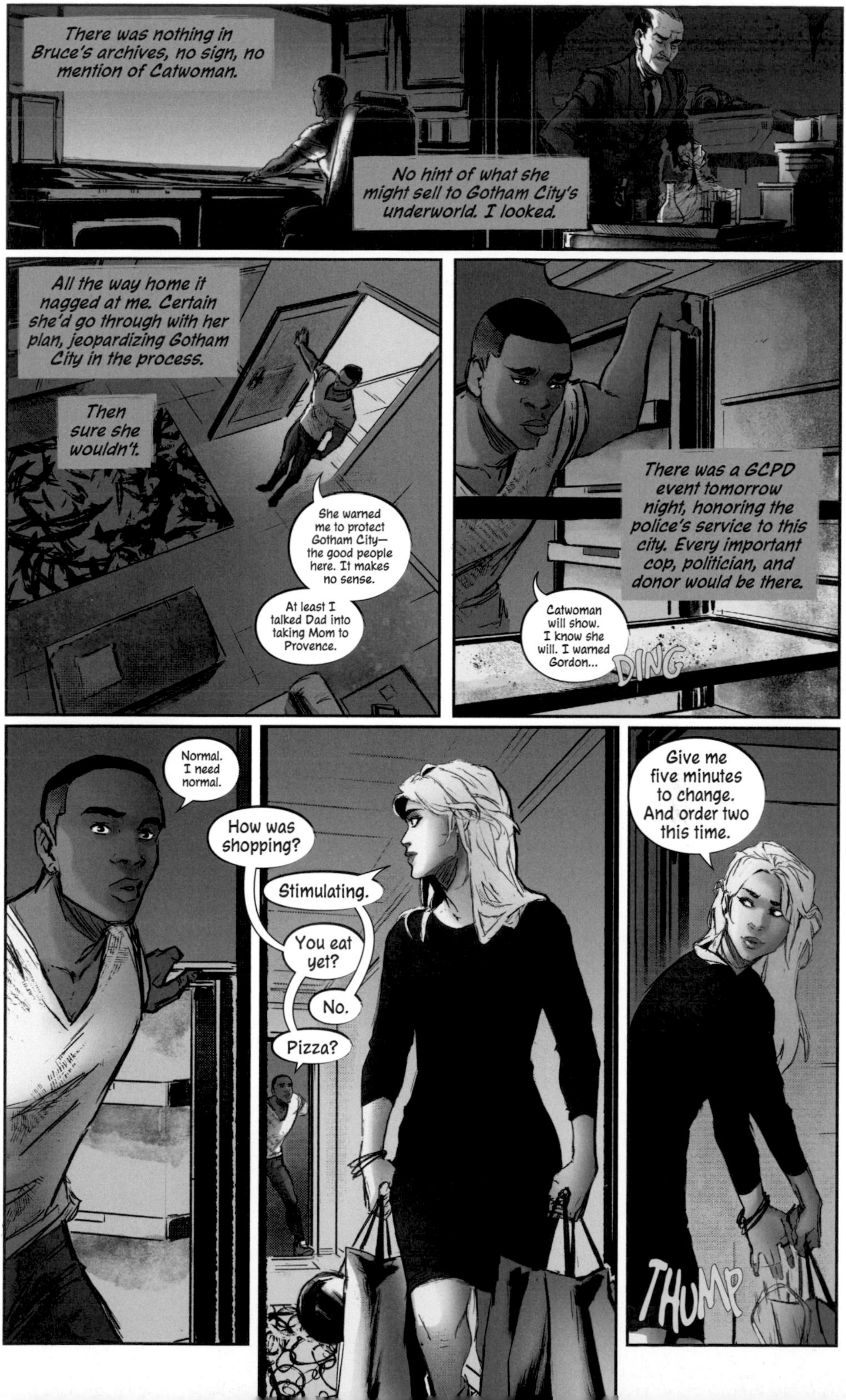
There was nothing in Bruce's archives, no sign, no mention of Catwoman.
No hint of what she might sell to Gotham City's underworld. I looked.
All the way home it nagged at me. Certain she'd go through with her plan, jeopardizing Gotham City in the process.
Then sure she wouldn't.
She warned me to protect Gotham City—the good people here. It makes no sense.
At least I talked Dad into taking Mom to Provence.
There was a GCPD event tomorrow night, honoring the police's service to this city. Every important cop, politician, and donor would be there.
Catwoman will show. I know she will. I warned Gordon...
DING
Normal. I need normal.
How was shopping?
Stimulating.
You eat yet?
No.
Pizza?
Give me five minutes to change. And order two this time.
THUMP

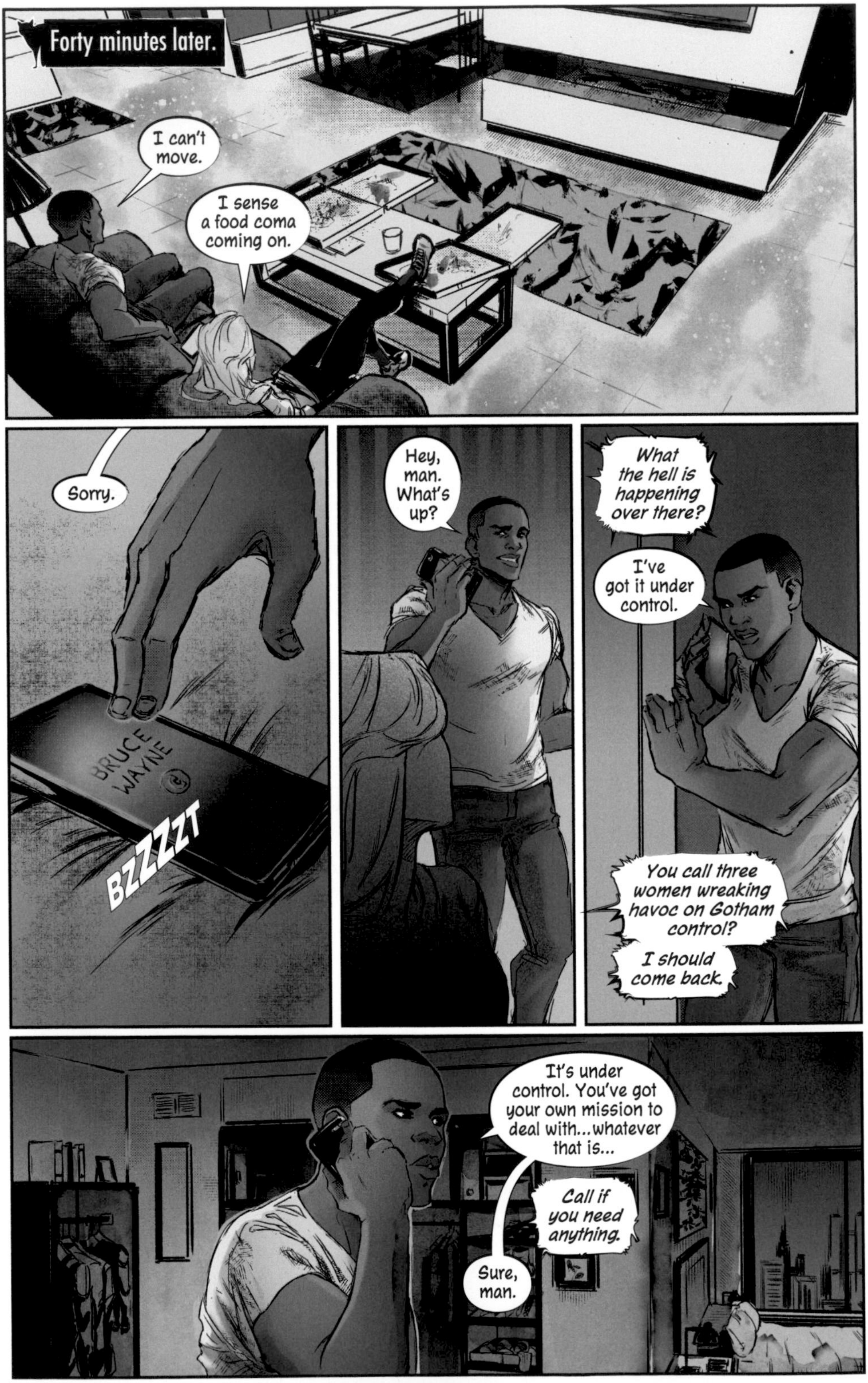
Forty minutes later.
I can't move.
I sense a food coma coming on.
Sorry.
BRUCE WAYNE
BZZZZT
Hey, man. What's up?
What the hell is happening over there?
I've got it under control.
You call three women wreaking havoc on Gotham control?
I should come back.
It's under control. You've got your own mission to deal with...whatever that is...
Call if you need anything.
Sure, man.

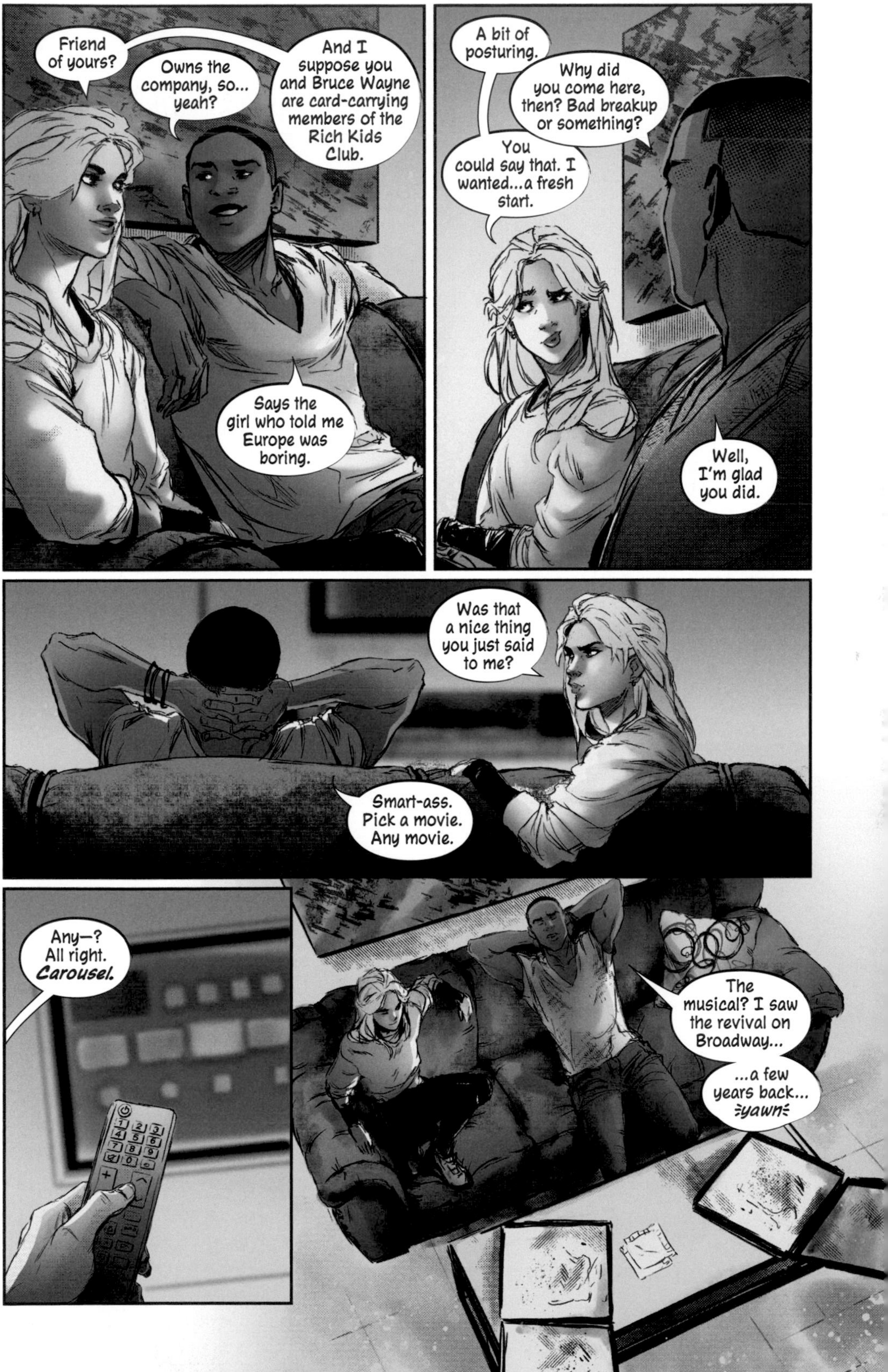

Friend of yours?
Owns the company, so... yeah?
And I suppose you and Bruce Wayne are card-carrying members of the Rich Kids Club.
Says the girl who told me Europe was boring.
A bit of posturing.
Why did you come here, then? Bad breakup or something?
You could say that. I wanted...a fresh start.
Well, I'm glad you did.
Was that a nice thing you just said to me?
Smart-ass. Pick a movie. Any movie.
Any—? All right. *Carousel.*
The musical? I saw the revival on Broadway...
...a few years back... *yawn*

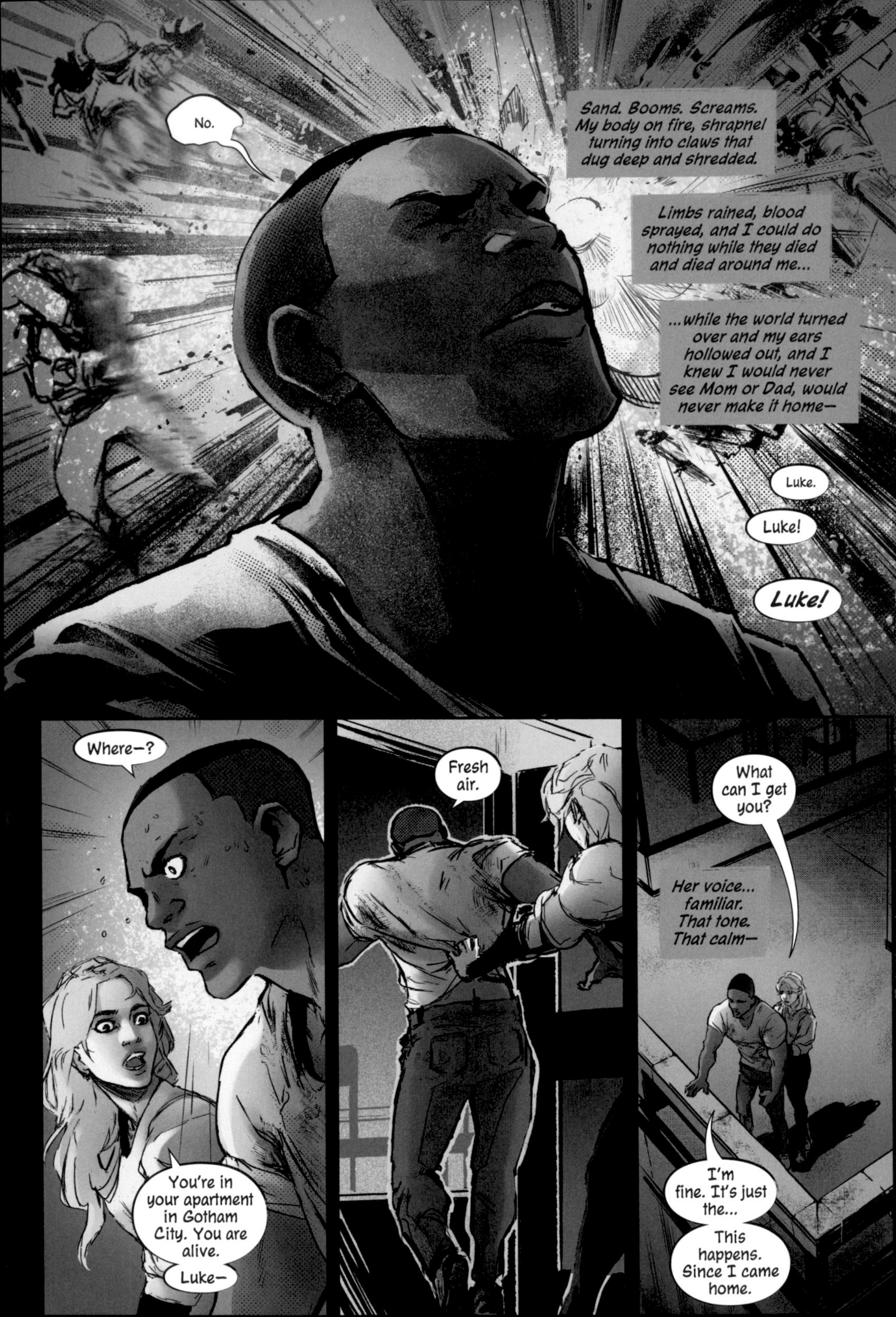
No.
Sand. Booms. Screams. My body on fire, shrapnel turning into claws that dug deep and shredded.
Limbs rained, blood sprayed, and I could do nothing while they died and died around me...
...while the world turned over and my ears hollowed out, and I knew I would never see Mom or Dad, would never make it home—
Luke.
Luke!
Luke!
Where—?
You're in your apartment in Gotham City. You are alive.
Luke—
Fresh air.
What can I get you?
Her voice... familiar. That tone. That calm—
I'm fine. It's just the...
This happens. Since I came home.

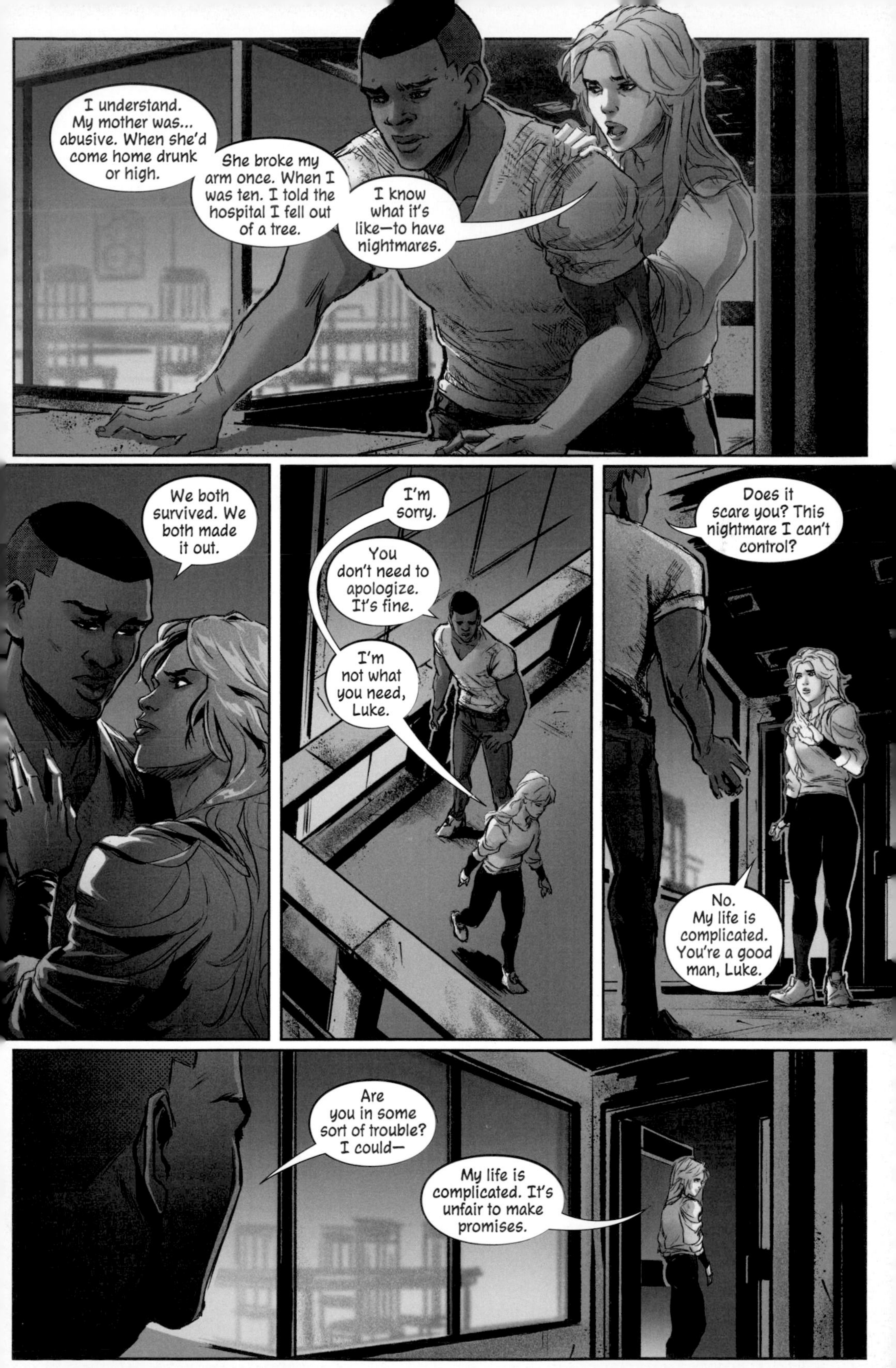
I understand. My mother was... abusive. When she'd come home drunk or high.
She broke my arm once. When I was ten. I told the hospital I fell out of a tree.
I know what it's like—to have nightmares.
We both survived. We both made it out.
I'm sorry.
You don't need to apologize. It's fine.
I'm not what you need, Luke.
Does it scare you? This nightmare I can't control?
No. My life is complicated. You're a good man, Luke.
Are you in some sort of trouble? I could—
My life is complicated. It's unfair to make promises.

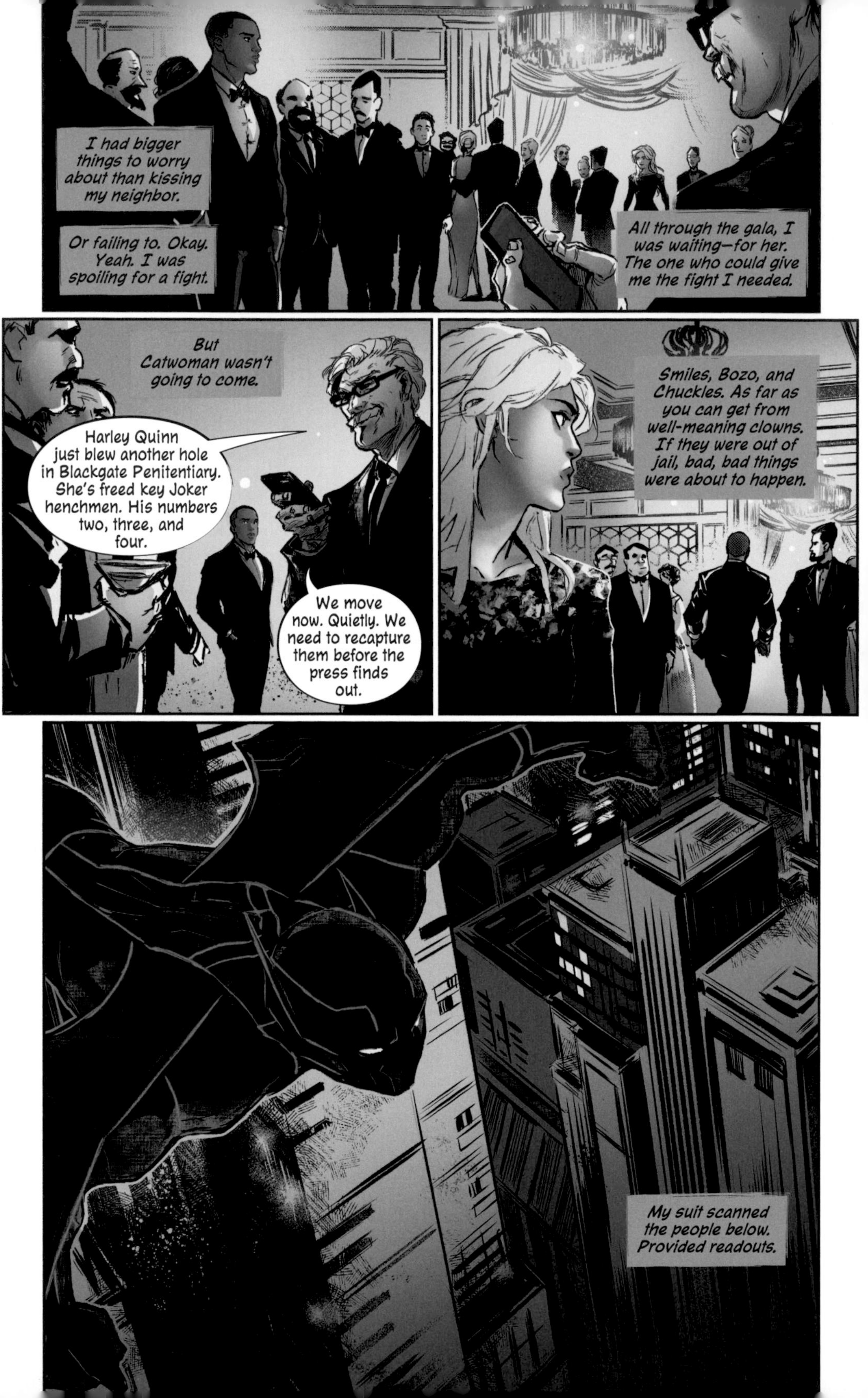
I had bigger things to worry about than kissing my neighbor.
Or failing to. Okay. Yeah. I was spoiling for a fight.
All through the gala, I was waiting—for her. The one who could give me the fight I needed.
But Catwoman wasn't going to come.
Harley Quinn just blew another hole in Blackgate Penitentiary. She's freed key Joker henchmen. His numbers two, three, and four.
We move now. Quietly. We need to recapture them before the press finds out.
Smiles, Bozo, and Chuckles. As far as you can get from well-meaning clowns. If they were out of jail, bad, bad things were about to happen.
My suit scanned the people below. Provided readouts.

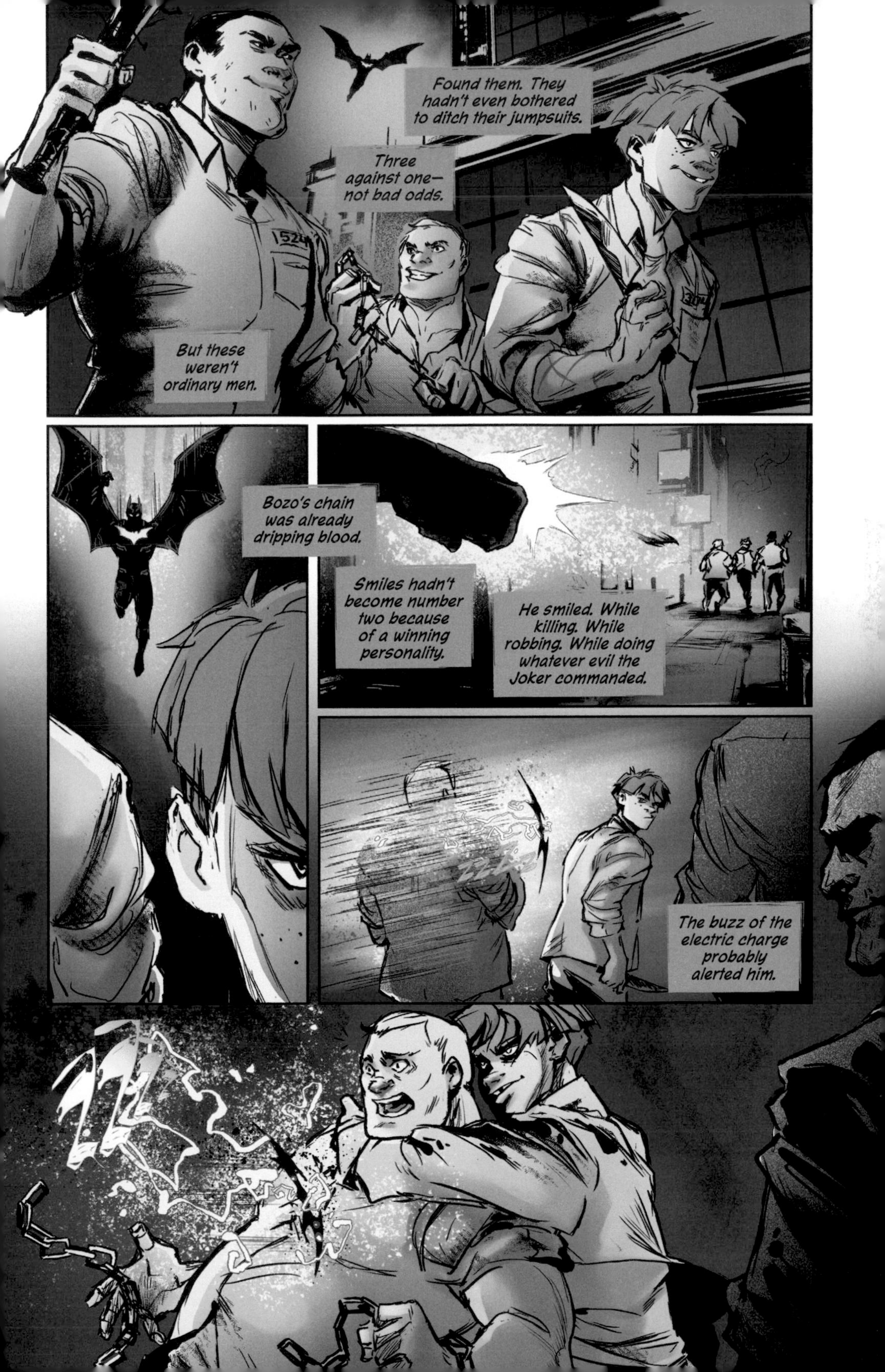
Found them. They hadn't even bothered to ditch their jumpsuits.
Three against one—not bad odds.
But these weren't ordinary men.
Bozo's chain was already dripping blood.
Smiles hadn't become number two because of a winning personality.
He smiled. While killing. While robbing. While doing whatever evil the Joker commanded.
The buzz of the electric charge probably alerted him.

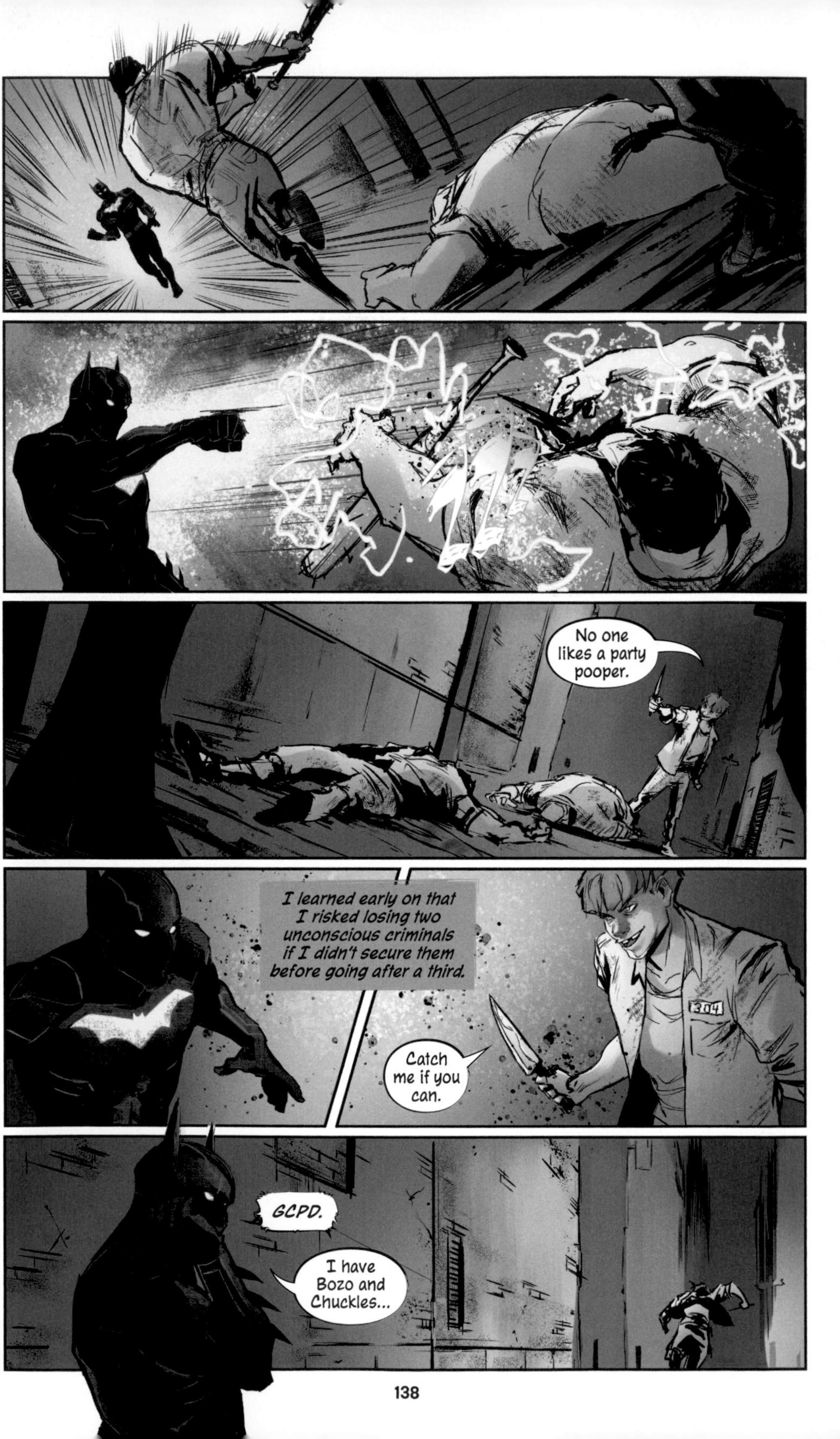
No one likes a party pooper.
I learned early on that I risked losing two unconscious criminals if I didn't secure them before going after a third.
Catch me if you can.
GCPD.
I have Bozo and Chuckles...

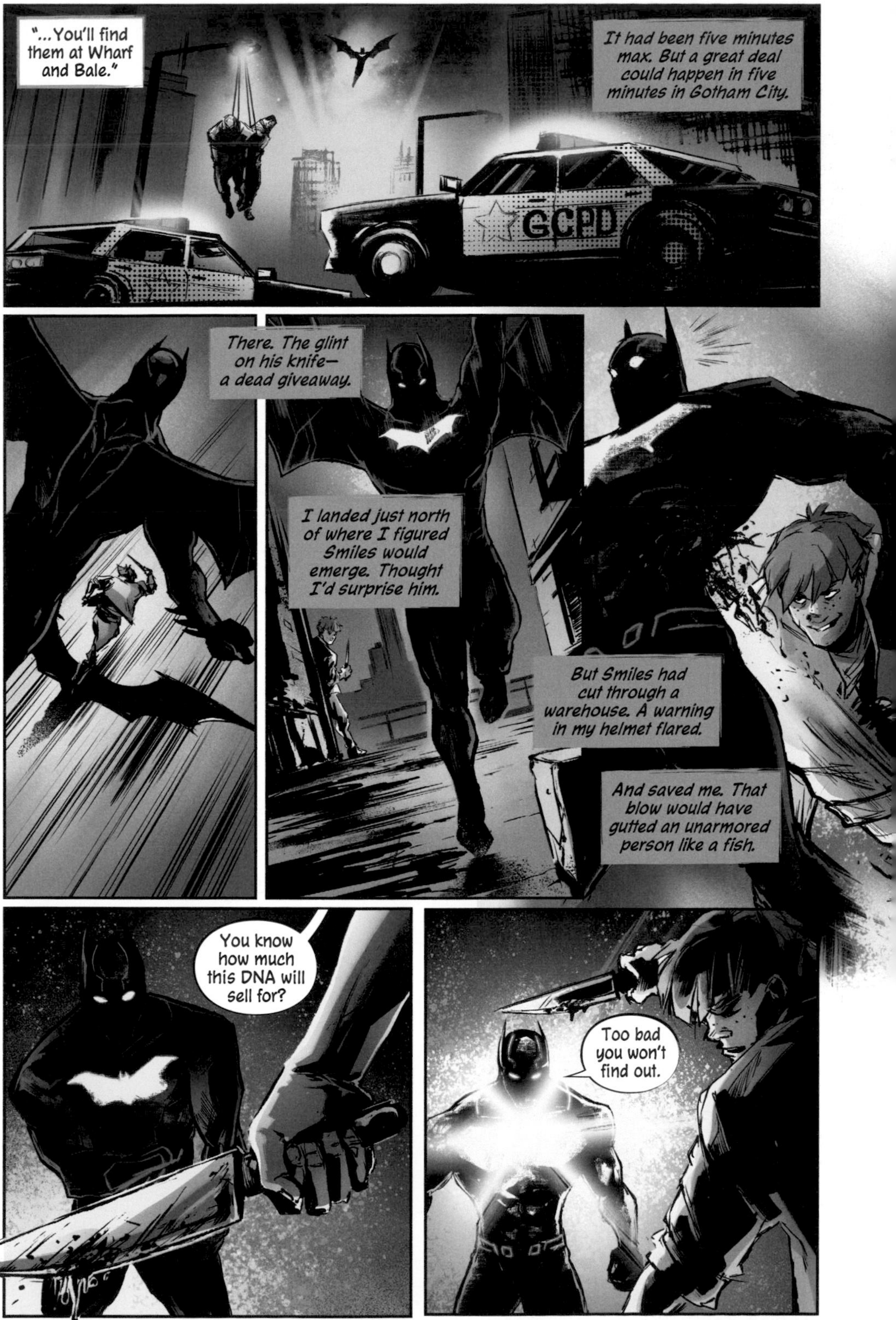
"...You'll find them at Wharf and Bale."
It had been five minutes max. But a great deal could happen in five minutes in Gotham City.
GCPD
There. The glint on his knife— a dead giveaway.
I landed just north of where I figured Smiles would emerge. Thought I'd surprise him.
But Smiles had cut through a warehouse. A warning in my helmet flared.
And saved me. That blow would have gutted an unarmored person like a fish.
You know how much this DNA will sell for?
Too bad you won't find out.

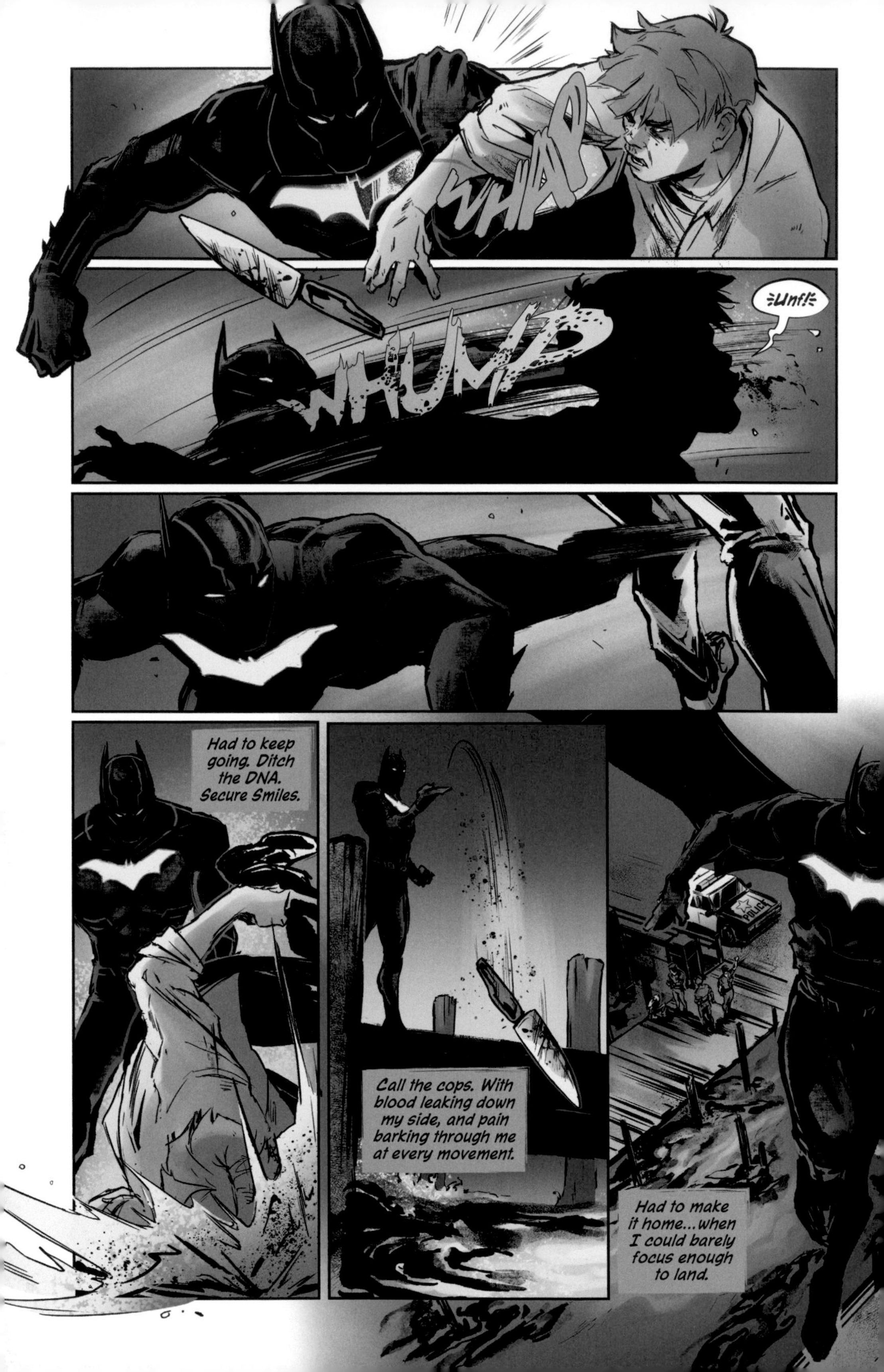
WHAP
WHUMP
Unf!
Had to keep going. Ditch the DNA. Secure Smiles.
Call the cops. With blood leaking down my side, and pain barking through me at every movement.
POLICE
Had to make it home...when I could barely focus enough to land.

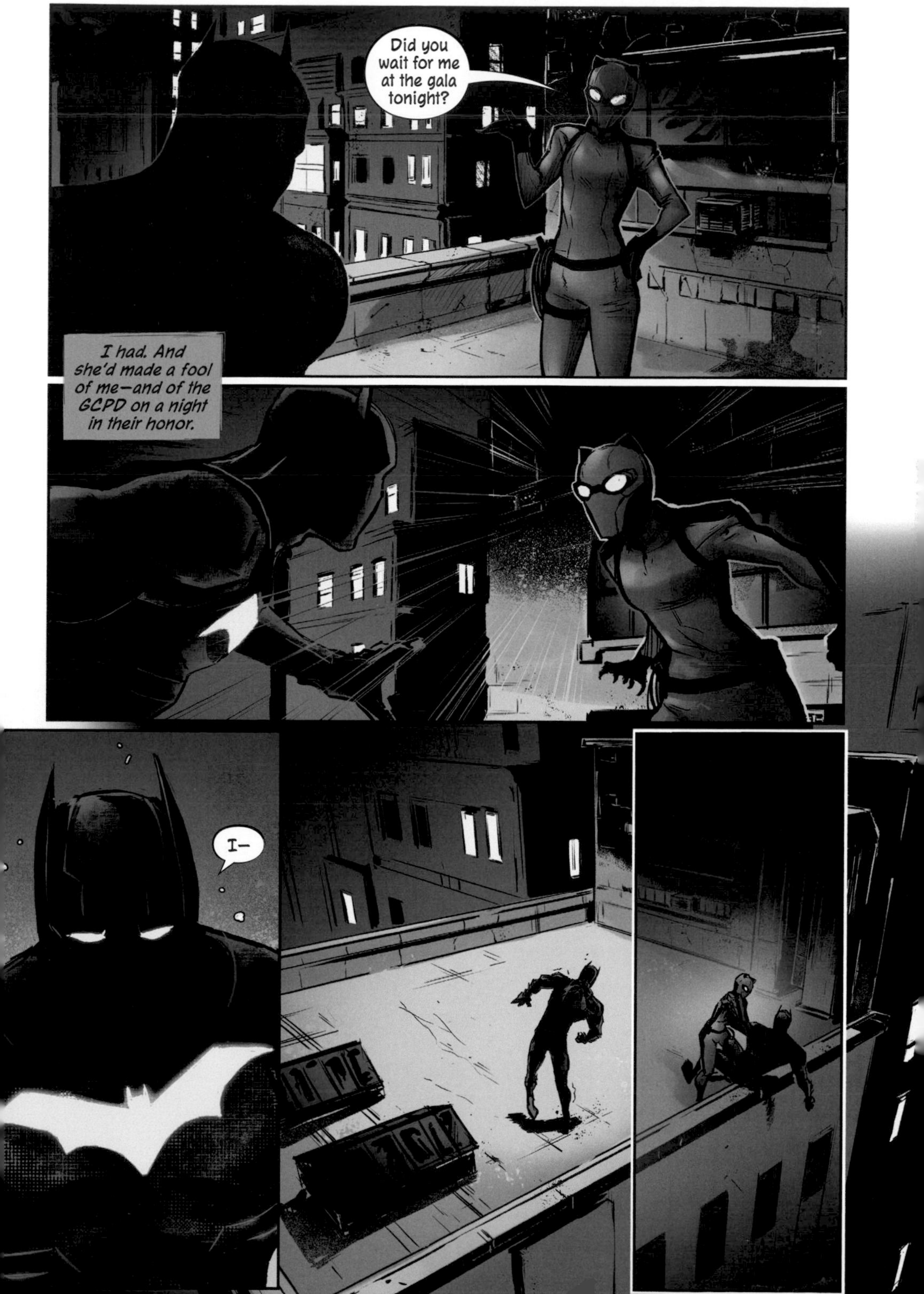
Did you wait for me at the gala tonight?
I had. And she'd made a fool of me—and of the GCPD on a night in their honor.
I—

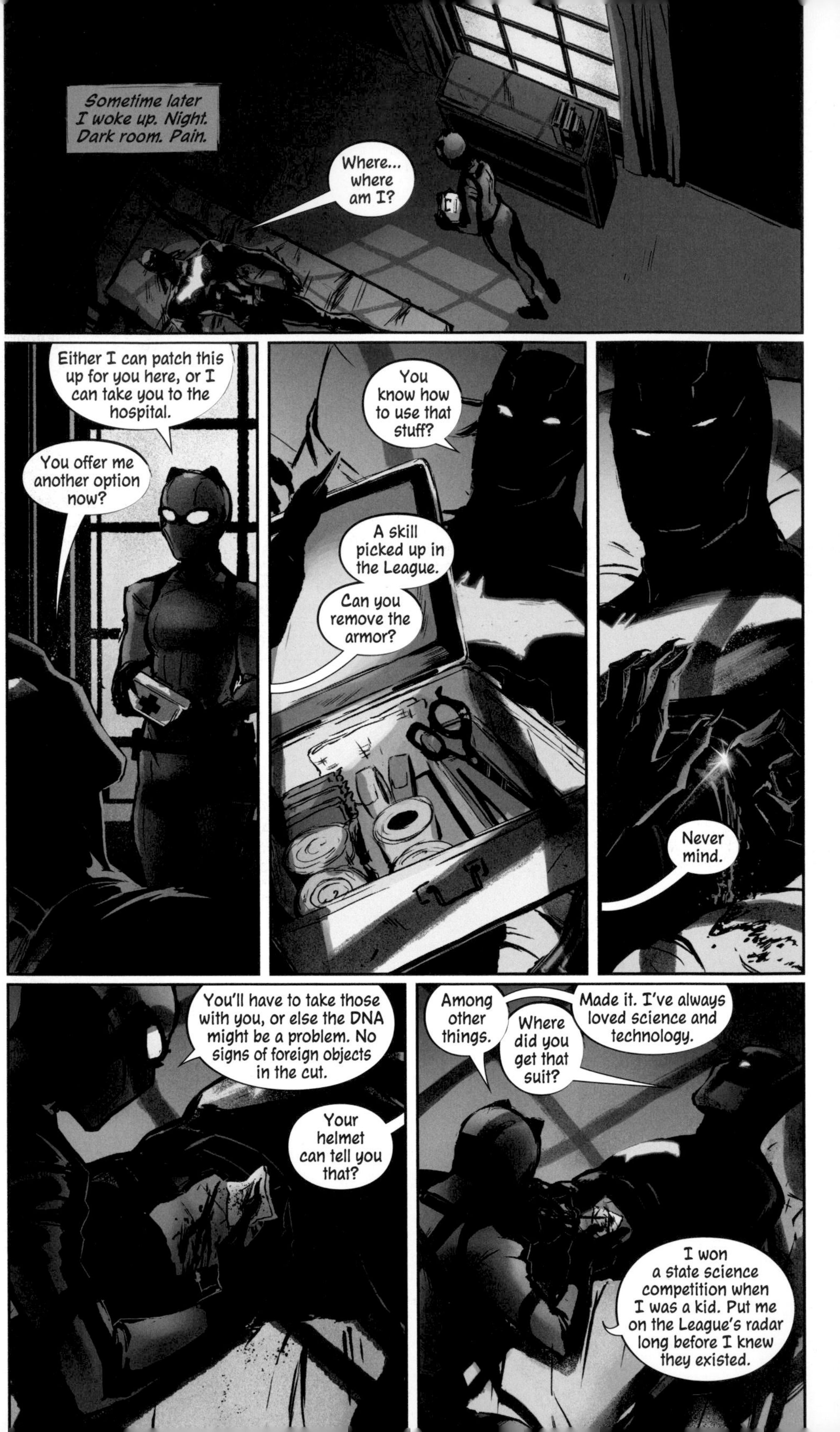

Sometime later I woke up. Night. Dark room. Pain.
Where... where am I?
Either I can patch this up for you here, or I can take you to the hospital.
You offer me another option now?
You know how to use that stuff?
A skill picked up in the League.
Can you remove the armor?
Never mind.
You'll have to take those with you, or else the DNA might be a problem. No signs of foreign objects in the cut.
Your helmet can tell you that?
Among other things.
Where did you get that suit?
Made it. I've always loved science and technology.
I won a state science competition when I was a kid. Put me on the League's radar long before I knew they existed.

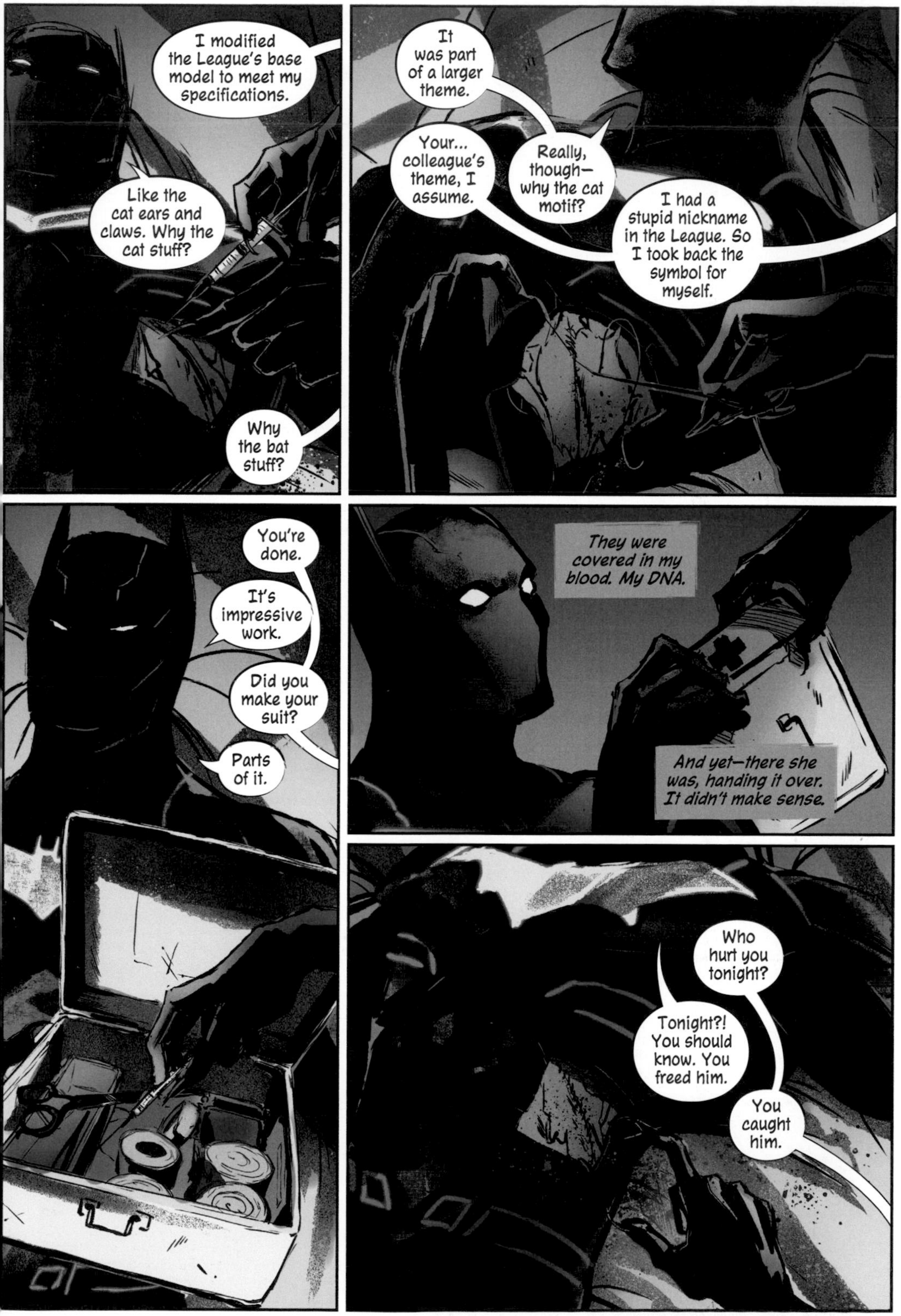
I modified the League's base model to meet my specifications.
Like the cat ears and claws. Why the cat stuff?
Why the bat stuff?
It was part of a larger theme.
Your... colleague's theme, I assume.
Really, though—why the cat motif?
I had a stupid nickname in the League. So I took back the symbol for myself.
You're done.
It's impressive work.
Did you make your suit?
Parts of it.
They were covered in my blood. My DNA.
And yet—there she was, handing it over. It didn't make sense.
Who hurt you tonight?
Tonight?! You should know. You freed him.
You caught him.

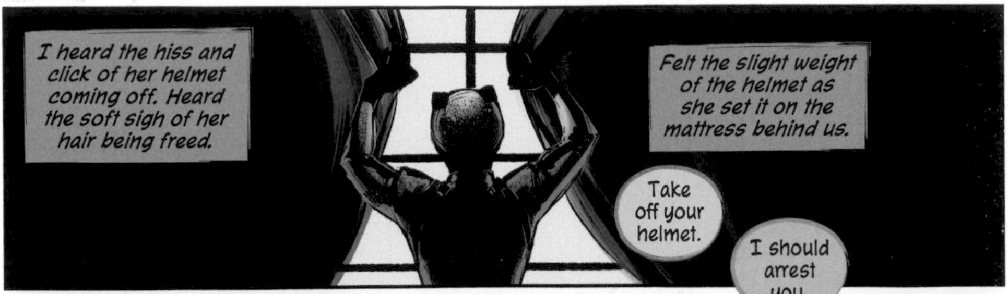
I heard the hiss and click of her helmet coming off. Heard the soft sigh of her hair being freed.
Felt the slight weight of the helmet as she set it on the mattress behind us.
Take off your helmet.
I should arrest you.

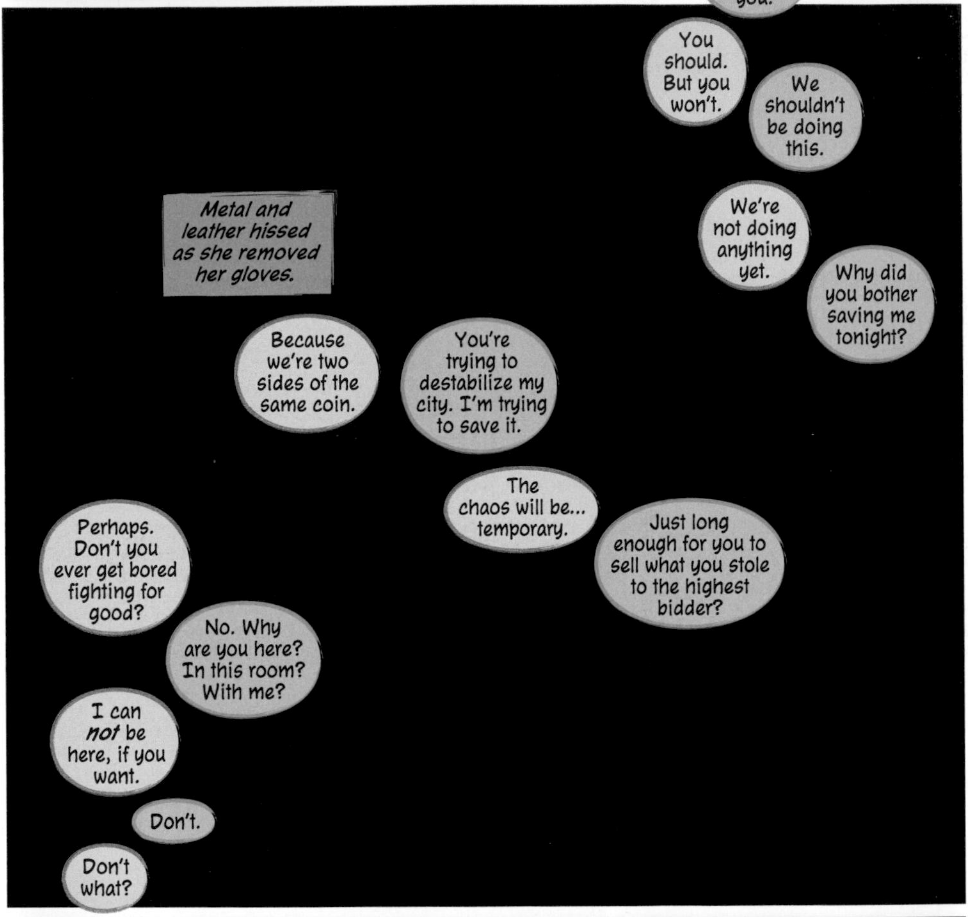
You should. But you won't.
We shouldn't be doing this.
We're not doing anything yet.
Why did you bother saving me tonight?
Metal and leather hissed as she removed her gloves.
You're trying to destabilize my city. I'm trying to save it.
Because we're two sides of the same coin.
The chaos will be... temporary.
Just long enough for you to sell what you stole to the highest bidder?
Perhaps. Don't you ever get bored fighting for good?
No. Why are you here? In this room? With me?
I can *not* be here, if you want.
Don't.
Don't what?

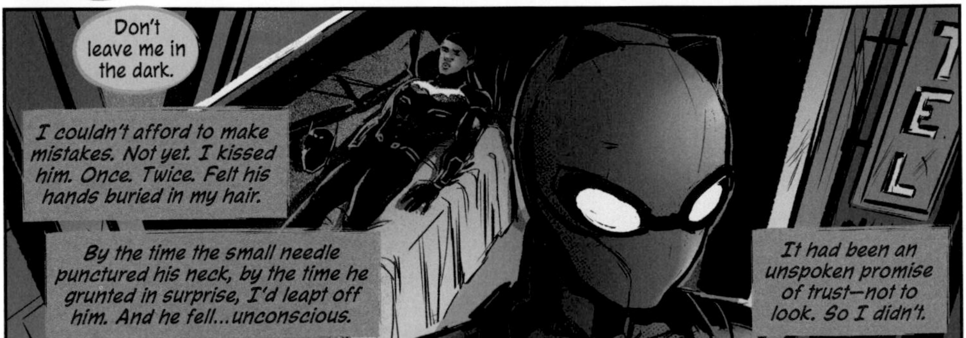
Don't leave me in the dark.
I couldn't afford to make mistakes. Not yet. I kissed him. Once. Twice. Felt his hands buried in my hair.
By the time the small needle punctured his neck, by the time he grunted in surprise, I'd leapt off him. And he fell...unconscious.
It had been an unspoken promise of trust—not to look. So I didn't.
TEL

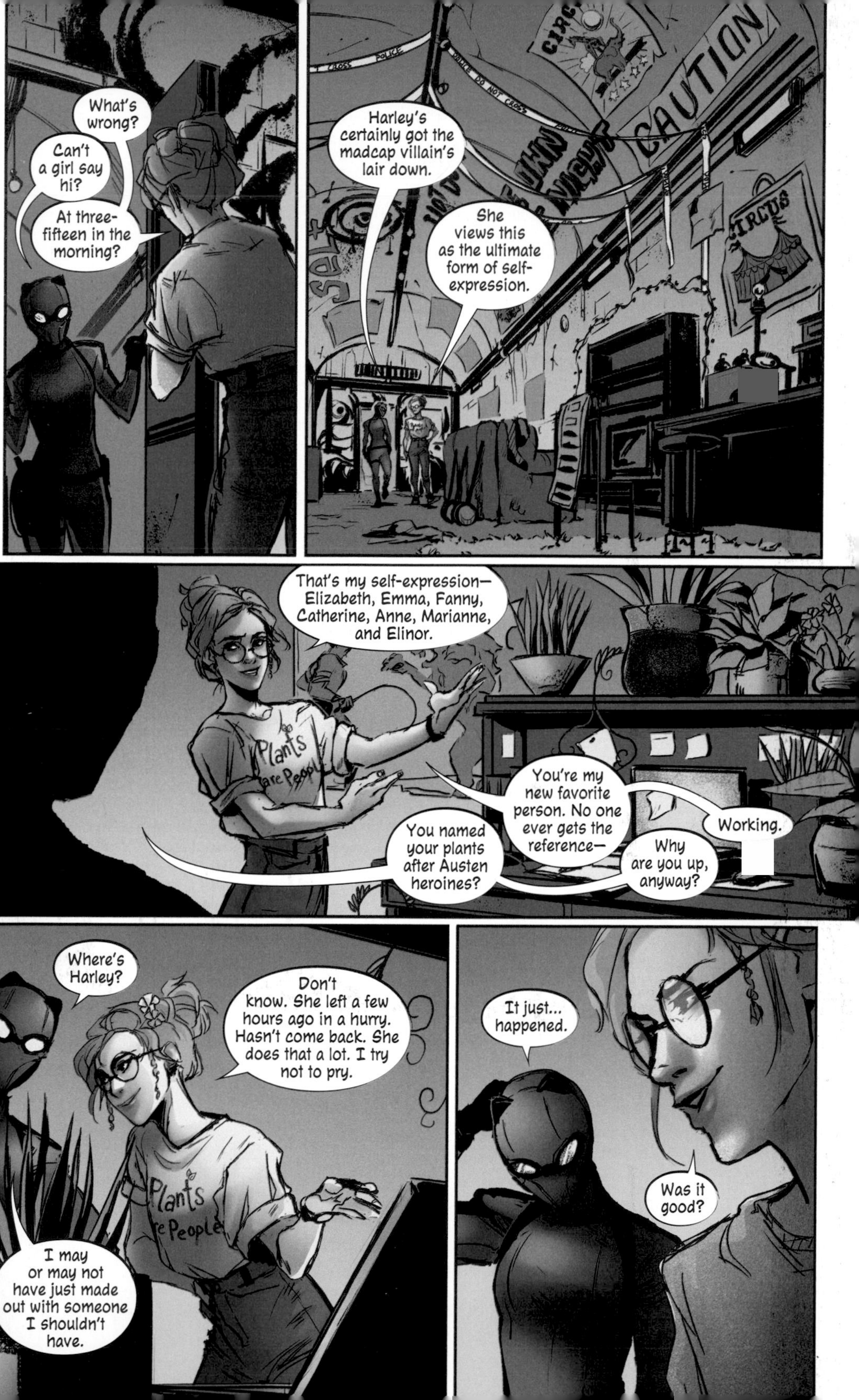
What's wrong?
Can't a girl say hi?
At three-fifteen in the morning?
Harley's certainly got the madcap villain's lair down.
She views this as the ultimate form of self-expression.
CAUTION
CIRCUS
That's my self-expression—Elizabeth, Emma, Fanny, Catherine, Anne, Marianne, and Elinor.
You named your plants after Austen heroines?
You're my new favorite person. No one ever gets the reference—
Why are you up, anyway?
Working.
Plants are People
Where's Harley?
Don't know. She left a few hours ago in a hurry. Hasn't come back. She does that a lot. I try not to pry.
I may or may not have just made out with someone I shouldn't have.
It just... happened.
Was it good?

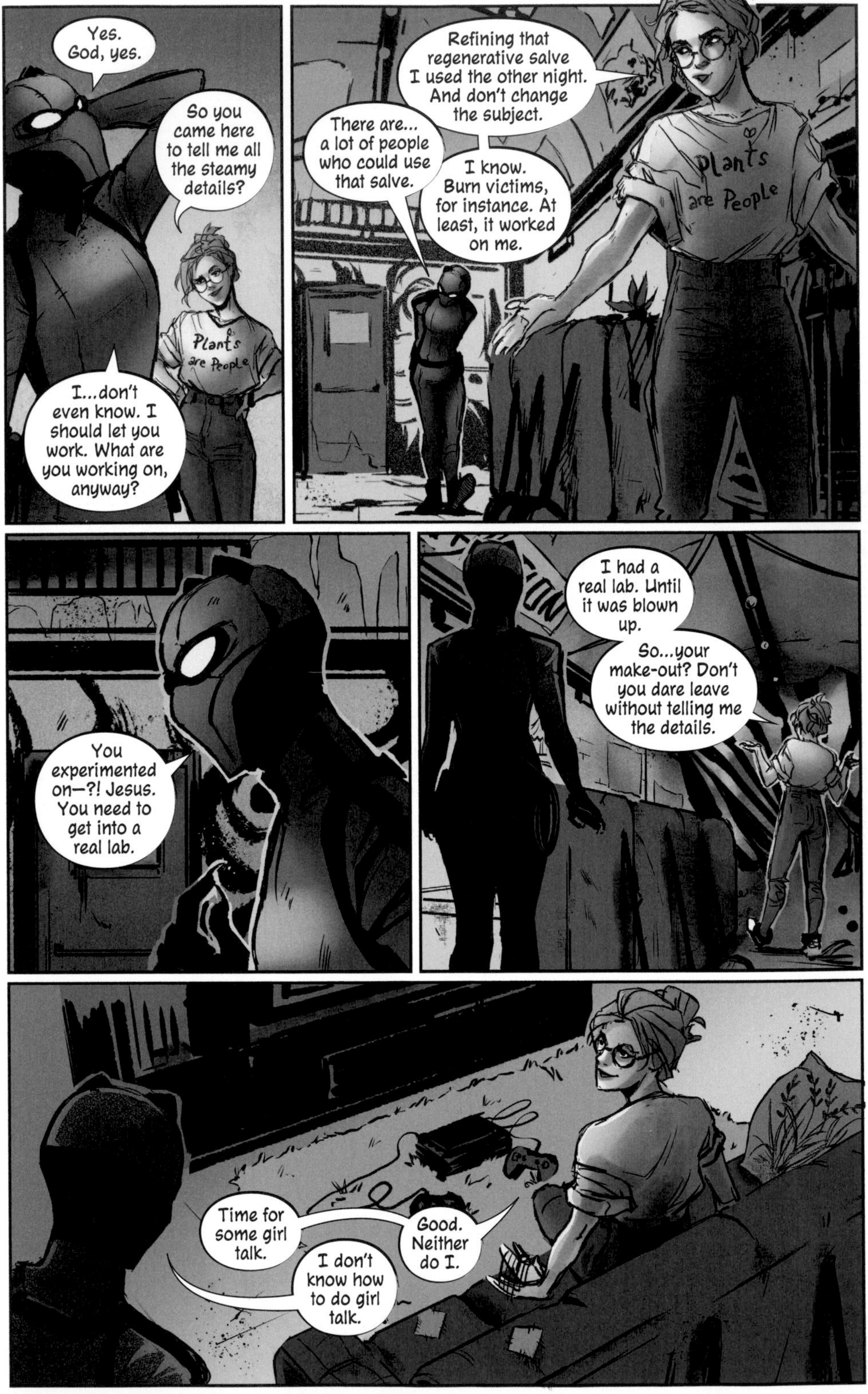
Yes. God, yes.
So you came here to tell me all the steamy details?
I...don't even know. I should let you work. What are you working on, anyway?
Refining that regenerative salve I used the other night. And don't change the subject.
There are... a lot of people who could use that salve.
I know. Burn victims, for instance. At least, it worked on me.
Plants are People
You experimented on—?! Jesus. You need to get into a real lab.
I had a real lab. Until it was blown up.
So...your make-out? Don't you dare leave without telling me the details.
Time for some girl talk.
I don't know how to do girl talk.
Good. Neither do I.

She drugged me... left me.

Also left the scales of armor... the stitching kit.

But where the hell was I?

Batwing!

Good morning.

Are you all right?

Jesus—

I'm fine. Just making sure all is well in the neighborhood.

She'd known precisely whose apartment she'd brought me to. I didn't know whether to be furious or amused.

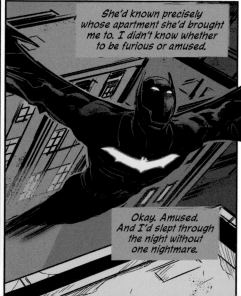

Okay. Amused. And I'd slept through the night without one nightmare.

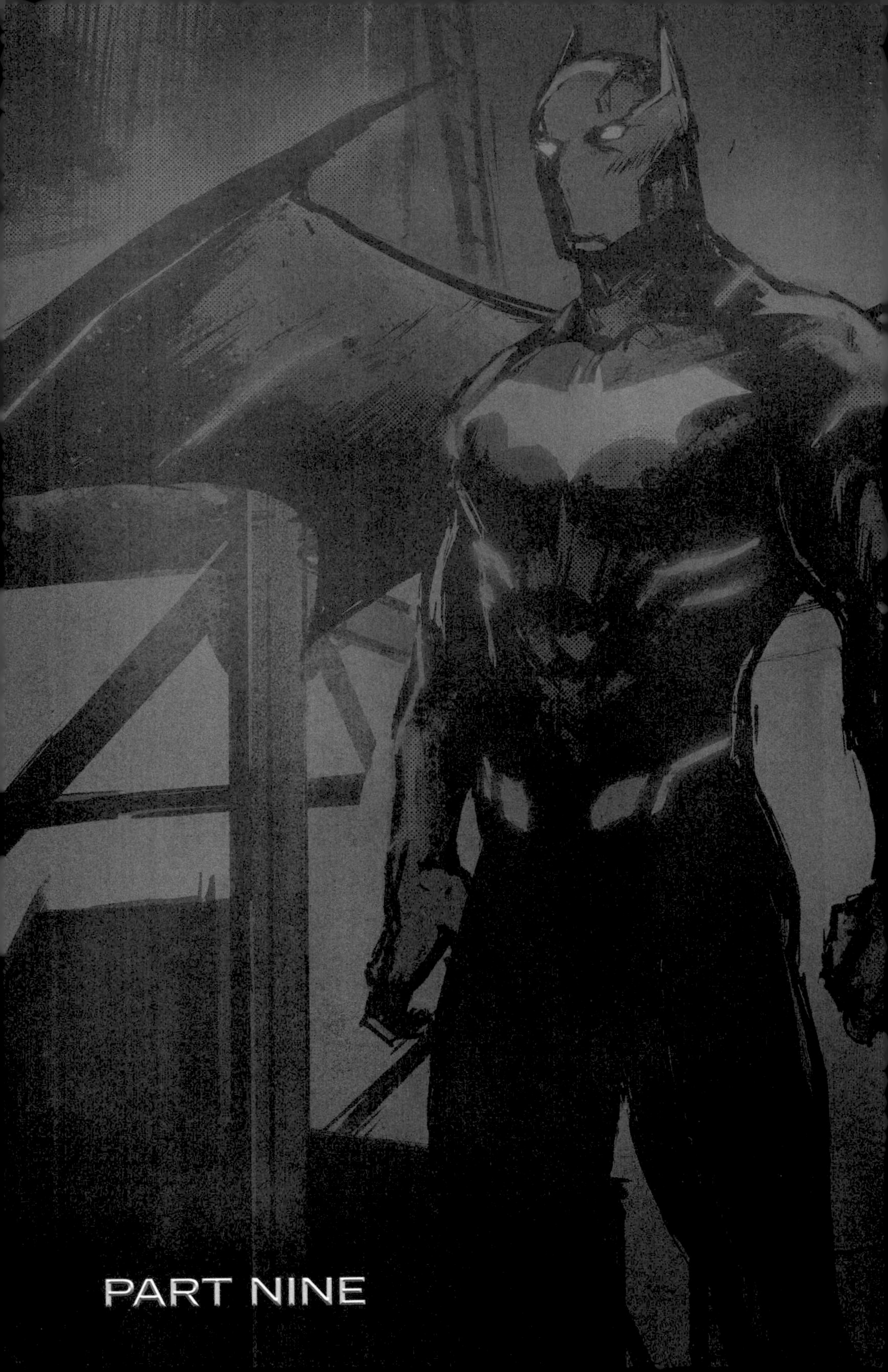

PART NINE

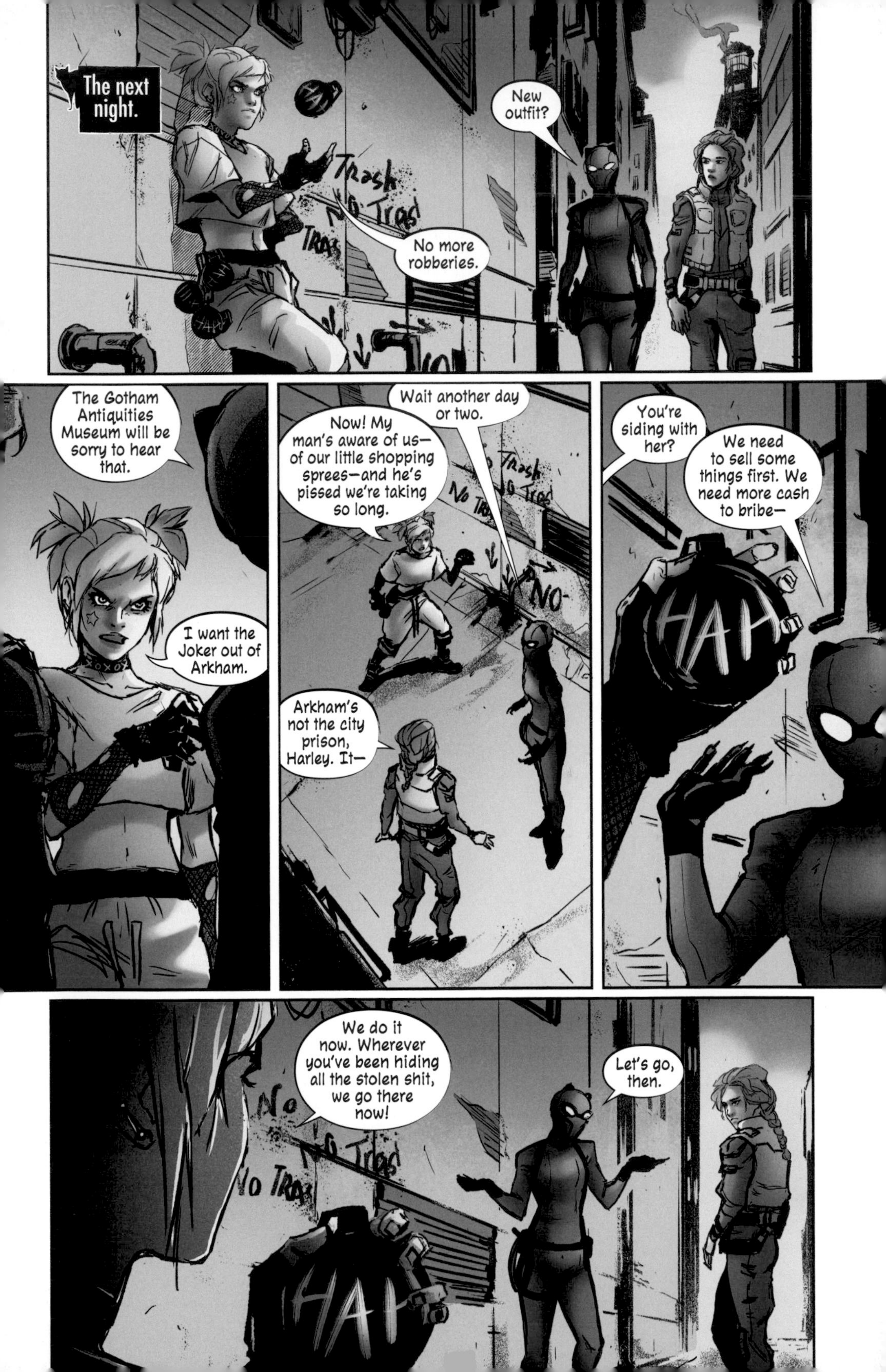

The next night.
New outfit?
No more robberies.
The Gotham Antiquities Museum will be sorry to hear that.
I want the Joker out of Arkham.
Wait another day or two.
Now! My man's aware of us— of our little shopping sprees—and he's pissed we're taking so long.
Arkham's not the city prison, Harley. It—
You're siding with her?
We need to sell some things first. We need more cash to bribe—
We do it now. Wherever you've been hiding all the stolen shit, we go there now!
Let's go, then.

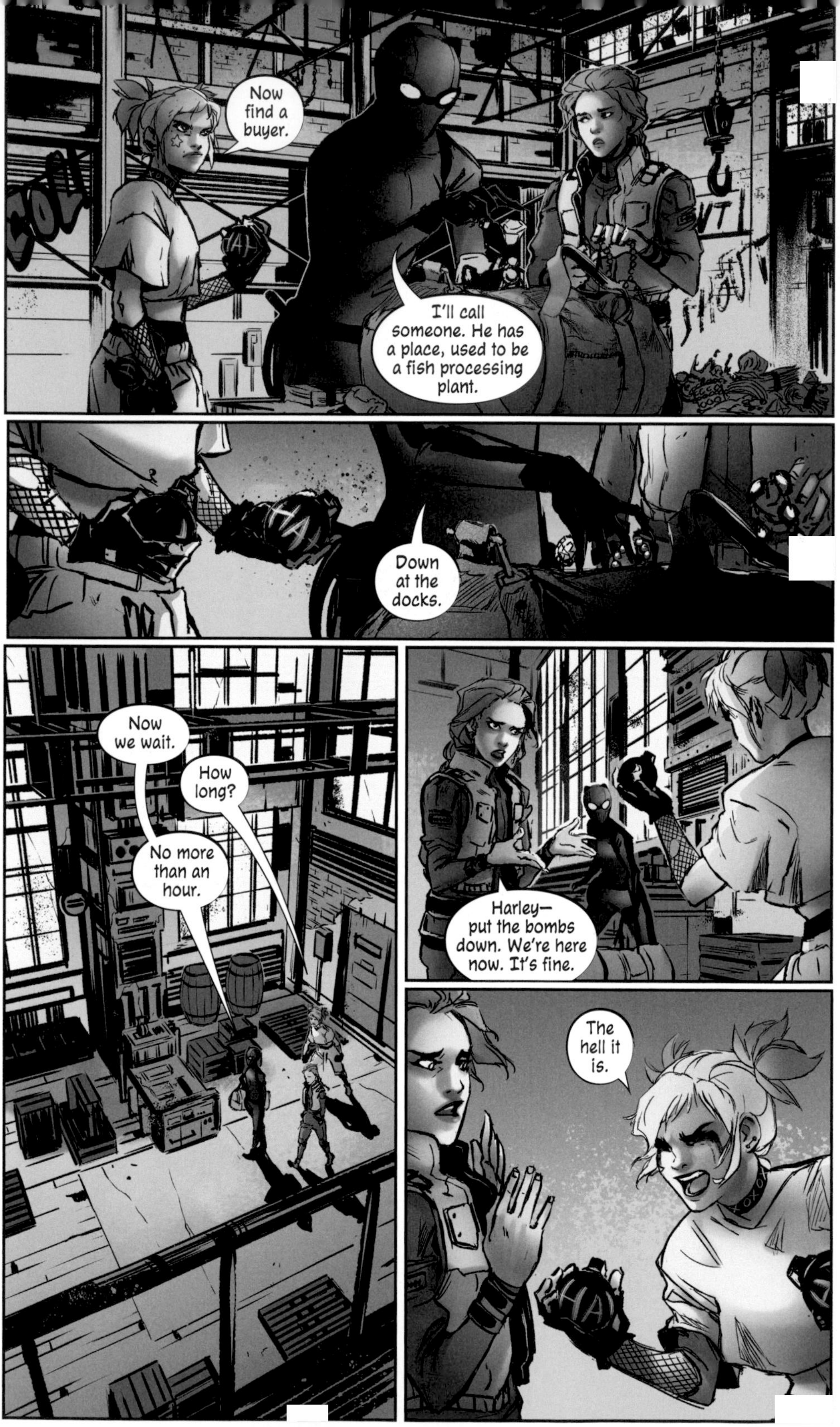
Now find a buyer.
I'll call someone. He has a place, used to be a fish processing plant.
Down at the docks.
Now we wait.
How long?
No more than an hour.
Harley— put the bombs down. We're here now. It's fine.
The hell it is.

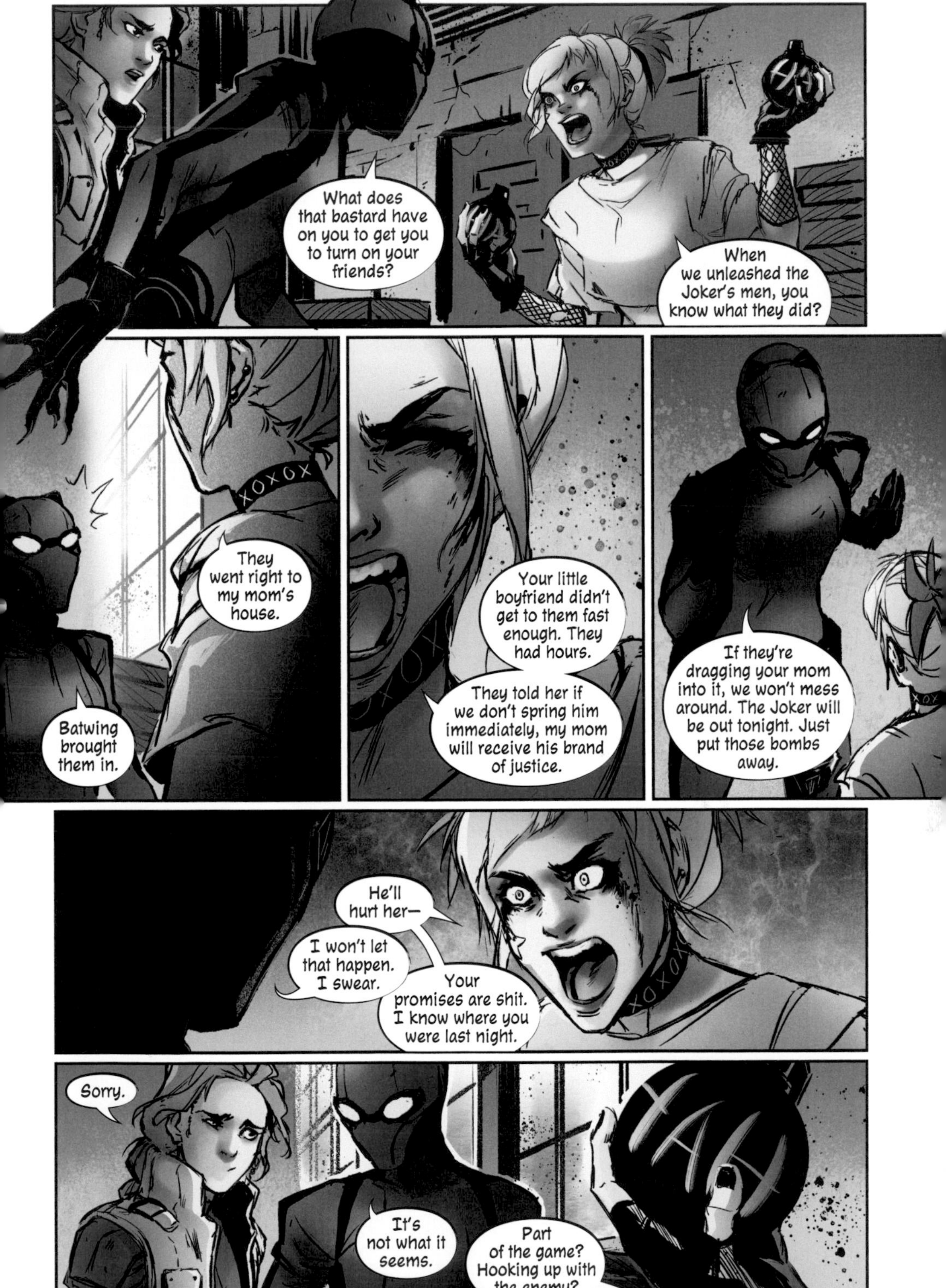
What does that bastard have on you to get you to turn on your friends?
When we unleashed the Joker's men, you know what they did?
XOXOX
They went right to my mom's house.
Batwing brought them in.
Your little boyfriend didn't get to them fast enough. They had hours.
They told her if we don't spring him immediately, my mom will receive his brand of justice.
If they're dragging your mom into it, we won't mess around. The Joker will be out tonight. Just put those bombs away.
He'll hurt her—
I won't let that happen. I swear.
Your promises are shit. I know where you were last night.
Sorry.
It's not what it seems.
Part of the game? Hooking up with the enemy?

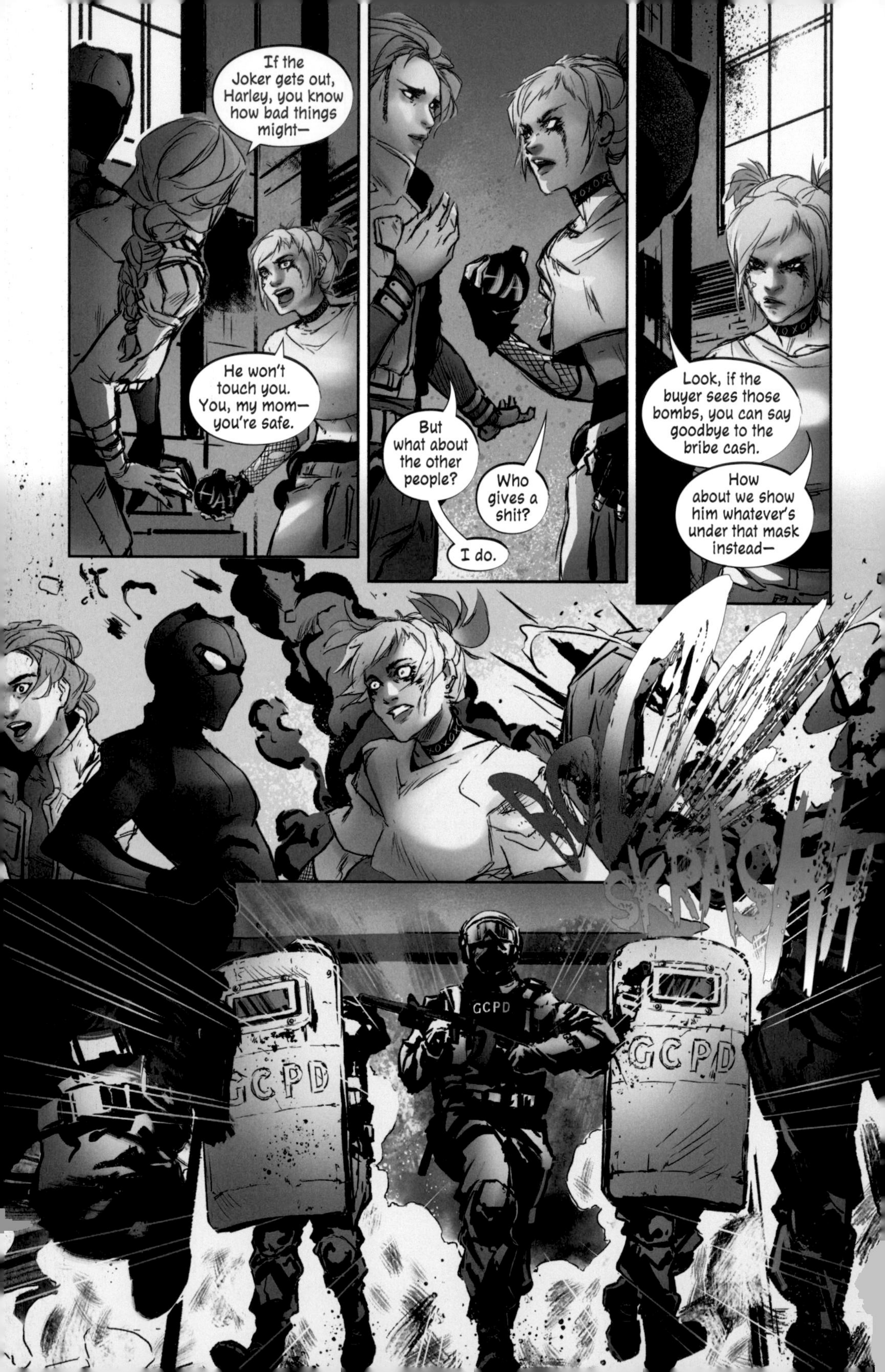
If the Joker gets out, Harley, you know how bad things might—
He won't touch you. You, my mom— you're safe.
But what about the other people?
Who gives a shit?
I do.
Look, if the buyer sees those bombs, you can say goodbye to the bribe cash.
How about we show him whatever's under that mask instead—
GCPD
GCPD
GCPD

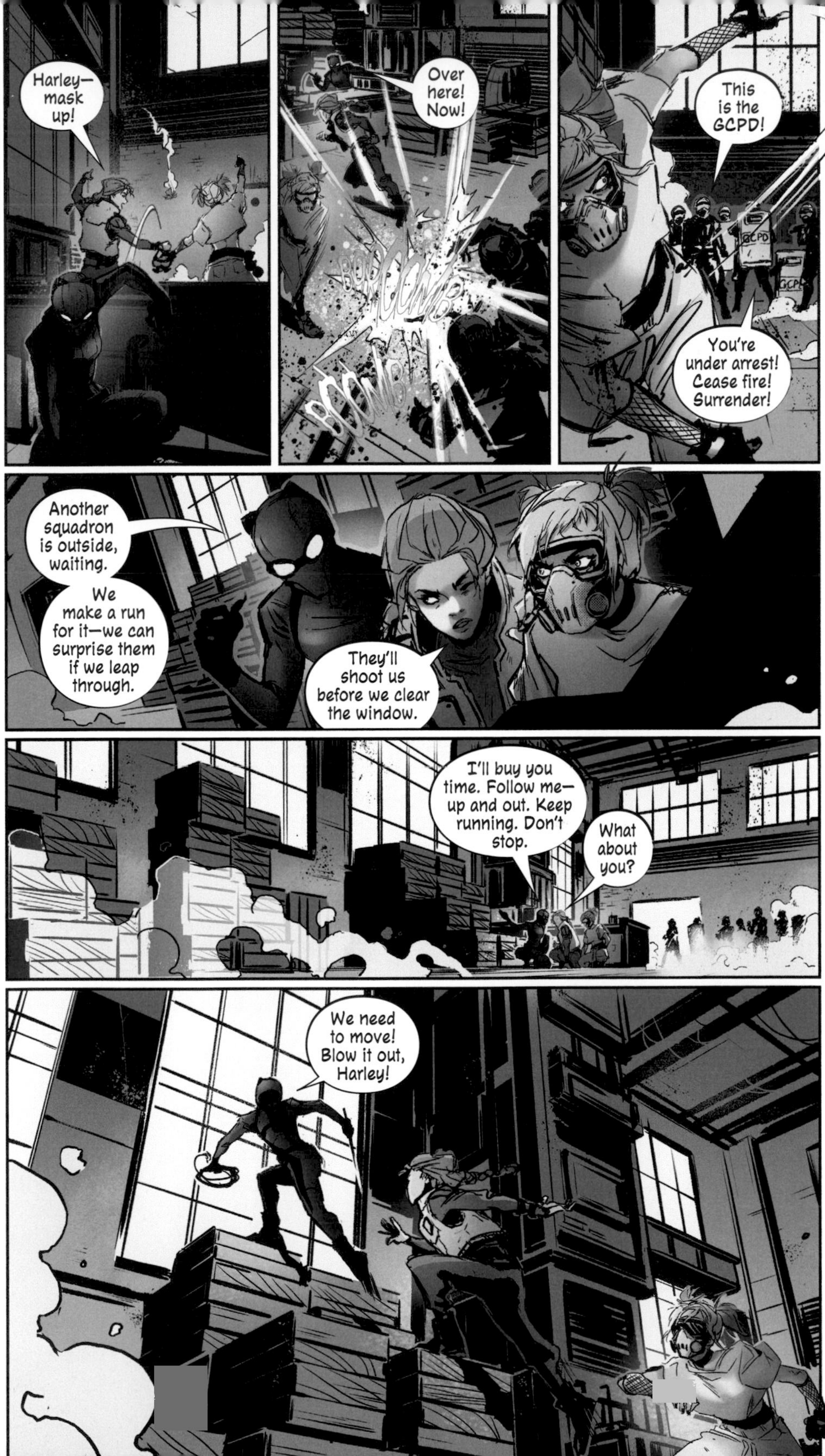
Harley—mask up!
Over here! Now!
This is the GCPD!
You're under arrest! Cease fire! Surrender!
Another squadron is outside, waiting.
We make a run for it—we can surprise them if we leap through.
They'll shoot us before we clear the window.
I'll buy you time. Follow me—up and out. Keep running. Don't stop.
What about you?
We need to move! Blow it out, Harley!

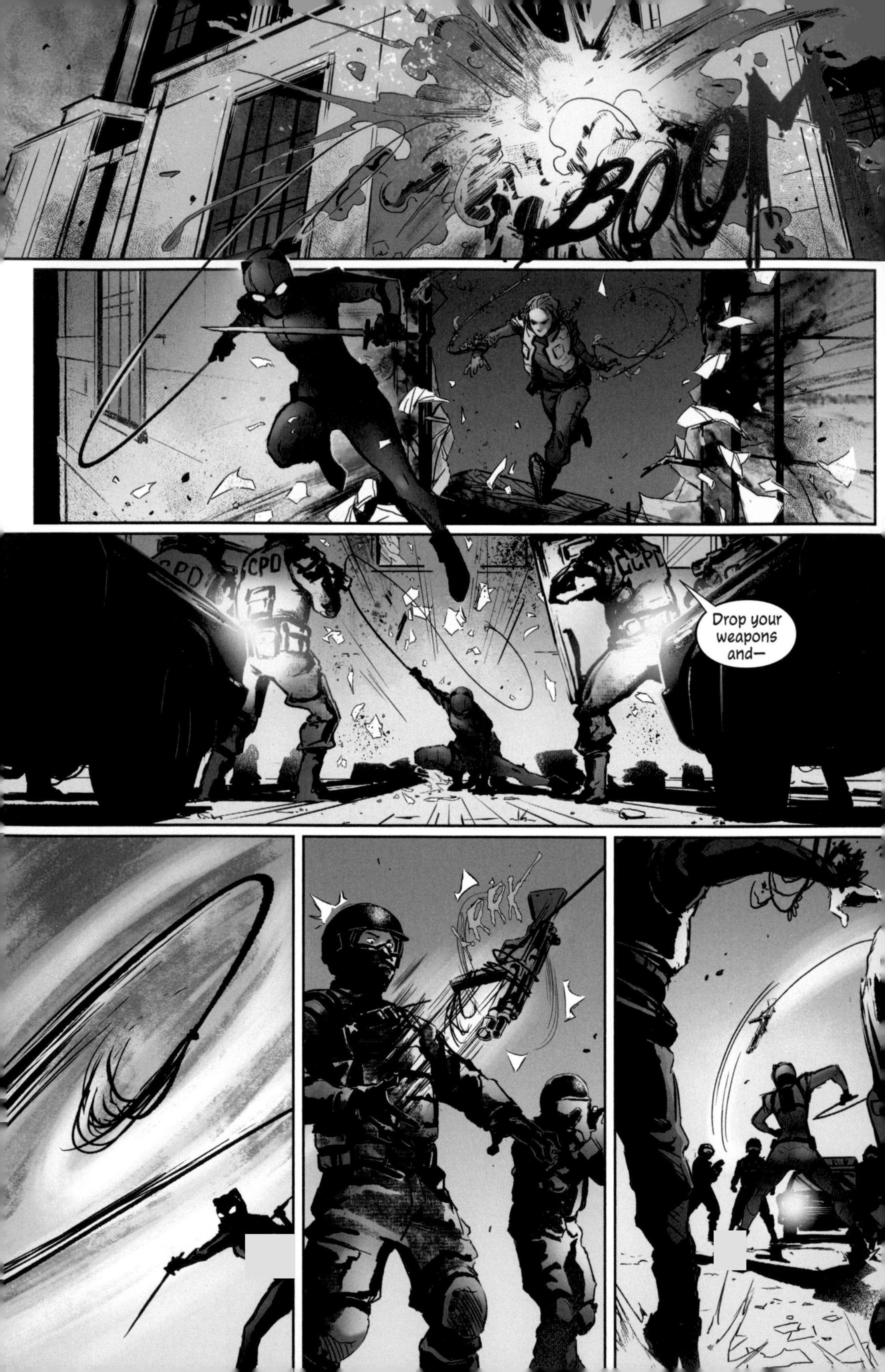
BOOM
CPD
CPD
GCPD
Drop your weapons and—

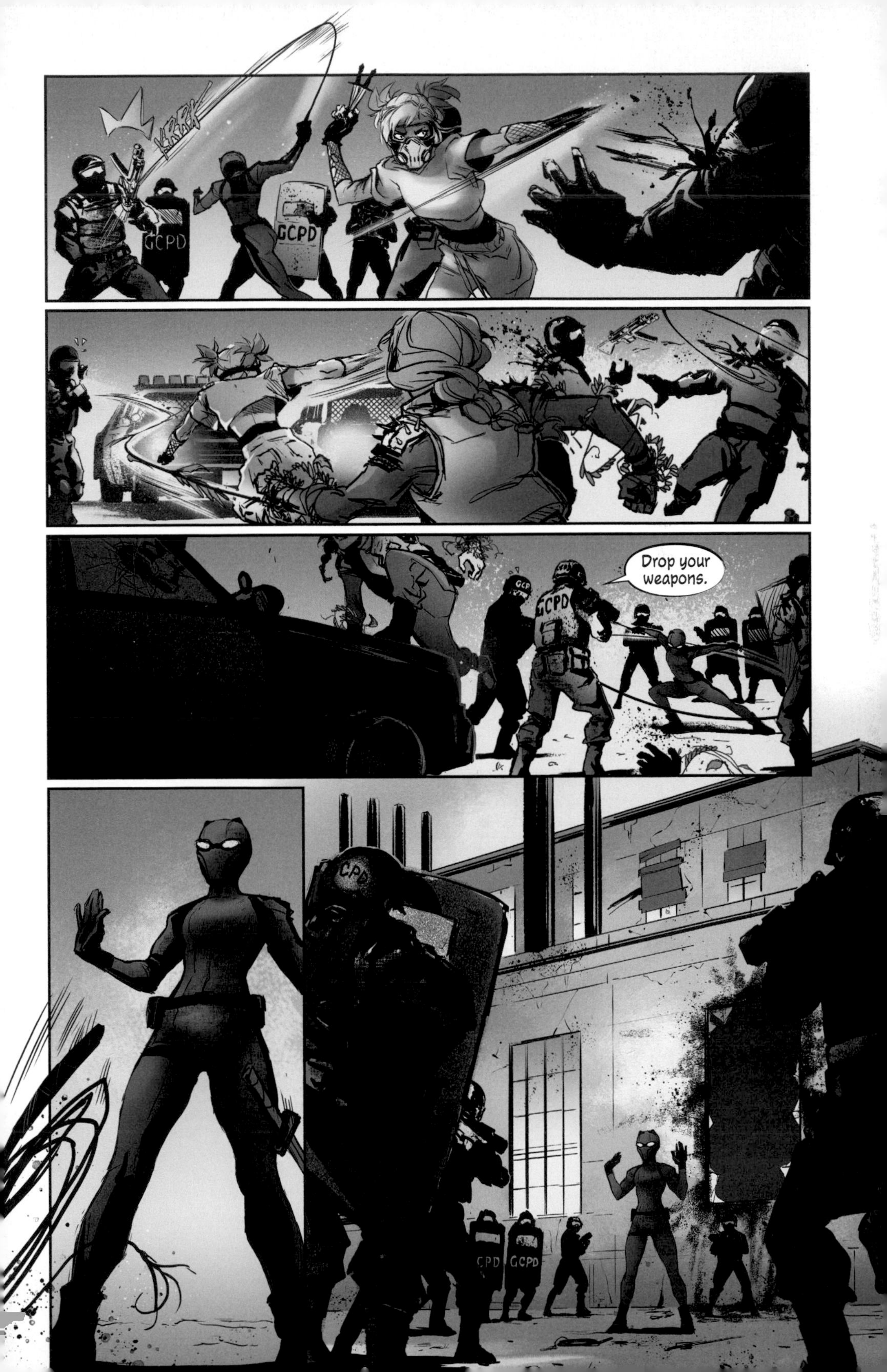
KRRK
Drop your weapons.

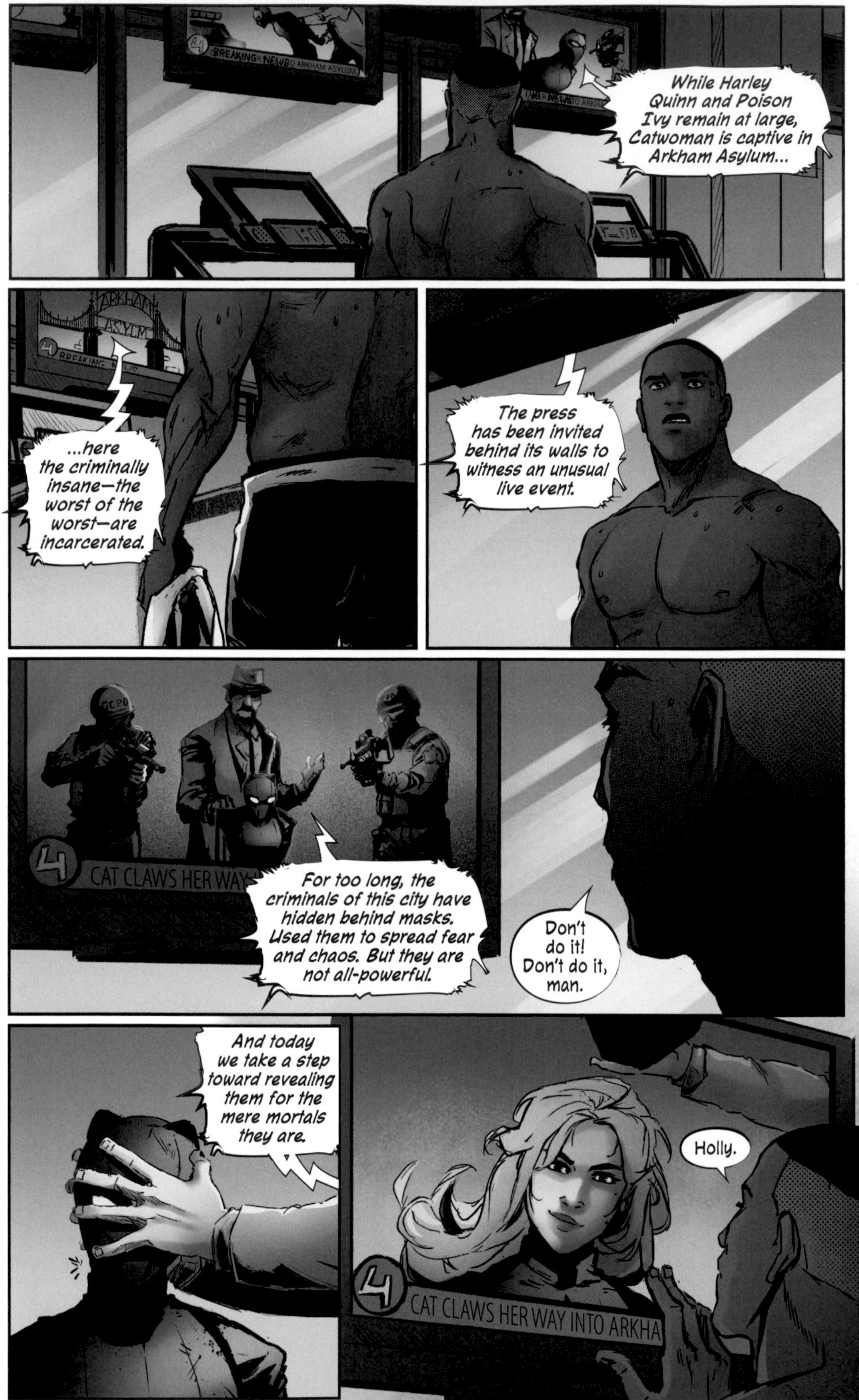
BREAKING NEWS ARKHAM ASYLUM
While Harley Quinn and Poison Ivy remain at large, Catwoman is captive in Arkham Asylum...
ARKHAM ASYLUM
...here the criminally insane—the worst of the worst—are incarcerated.
The press has been invited behind its walls to witness an unusual live event.
GCPD
CAT CLAWS HER WAY
For too long, the criminals of this city have hidden behind masks. Used them to spread fear and chaos. But they are not all-powerful.
Don't do it! Don't do it, man.
And today we take a step toward revealing them for the mere mortals they are.
Holly.
CAT CLAWS HER WAY INTO ARKHA

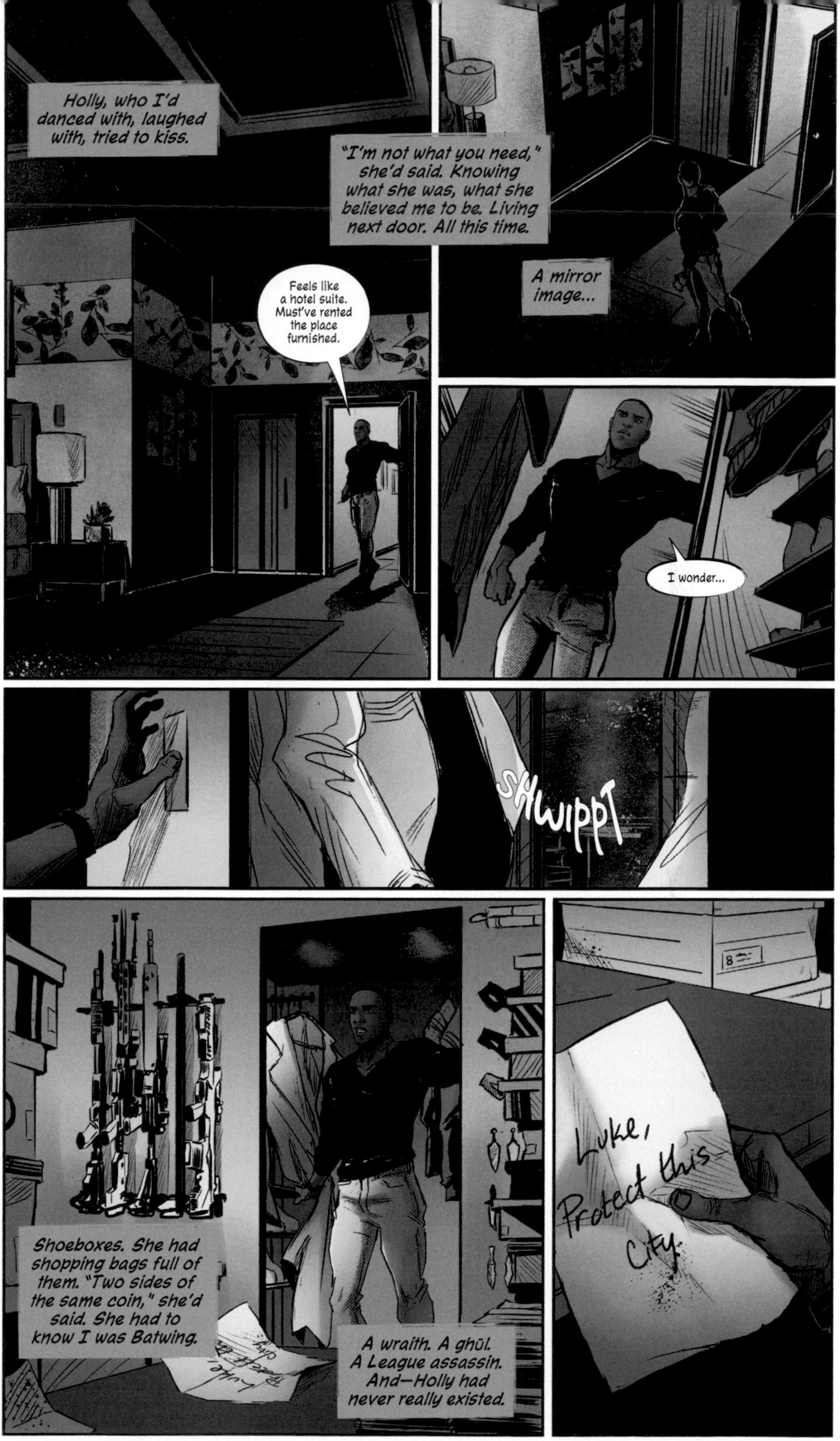

Holly, who I'd danced with, laughed with, tried to kiss.
Feels like a hotel suite. Must've rented the place furnished.
"I'm not what you need," she'd said. Knowing what she was, what she believed me to be. Living next door. All this time.
A mirror image...
I wonder...
SHWIPPT
Shoeboxes. She had shopping bags full of them. "Two sides of the same coin," she'd said. She had to know I was Batwing.
A wraith. A ghūl. A League assassin. And—Holly had never really existed.
Luke, Protect this City.

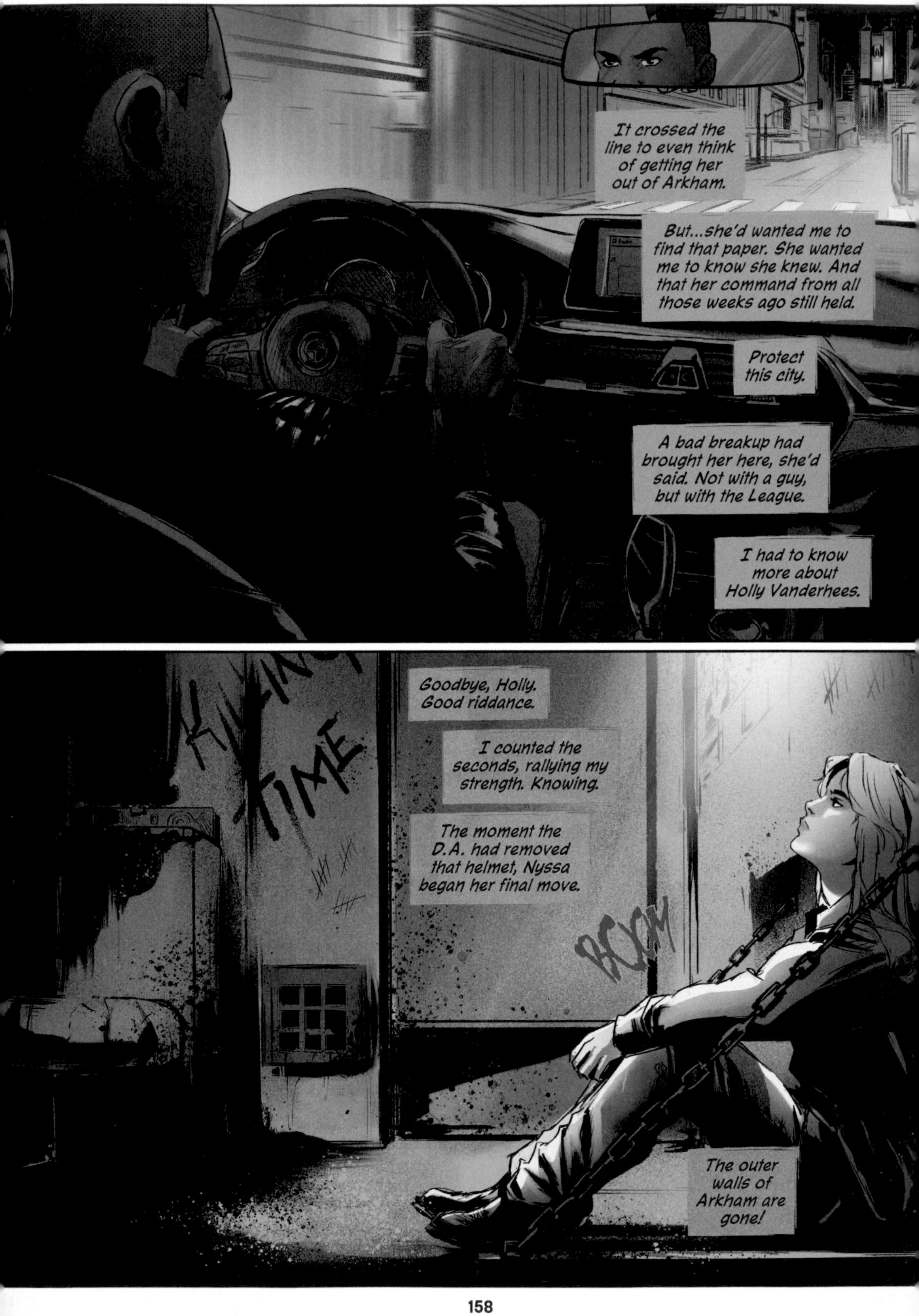
It crossed the line to even think of getting her out of Arkham.
But...she'd wanted me to find that paper. She wanted me to know she knew. And that her command from all those weeks ago still held.
Protect this city.
A bad breakup had brought her here, she'd said. Not with a guy, but with the League.
I had to know more about Holly Vanderhees.
Goodbye, Holly. Good riddance.
TIME
I counted the seconds, rallying my strength. Knowing.
The moment the D.A. had removed that helmet, Nyssa began her final move.
BOOM
The outer walls of Arkham are gone!

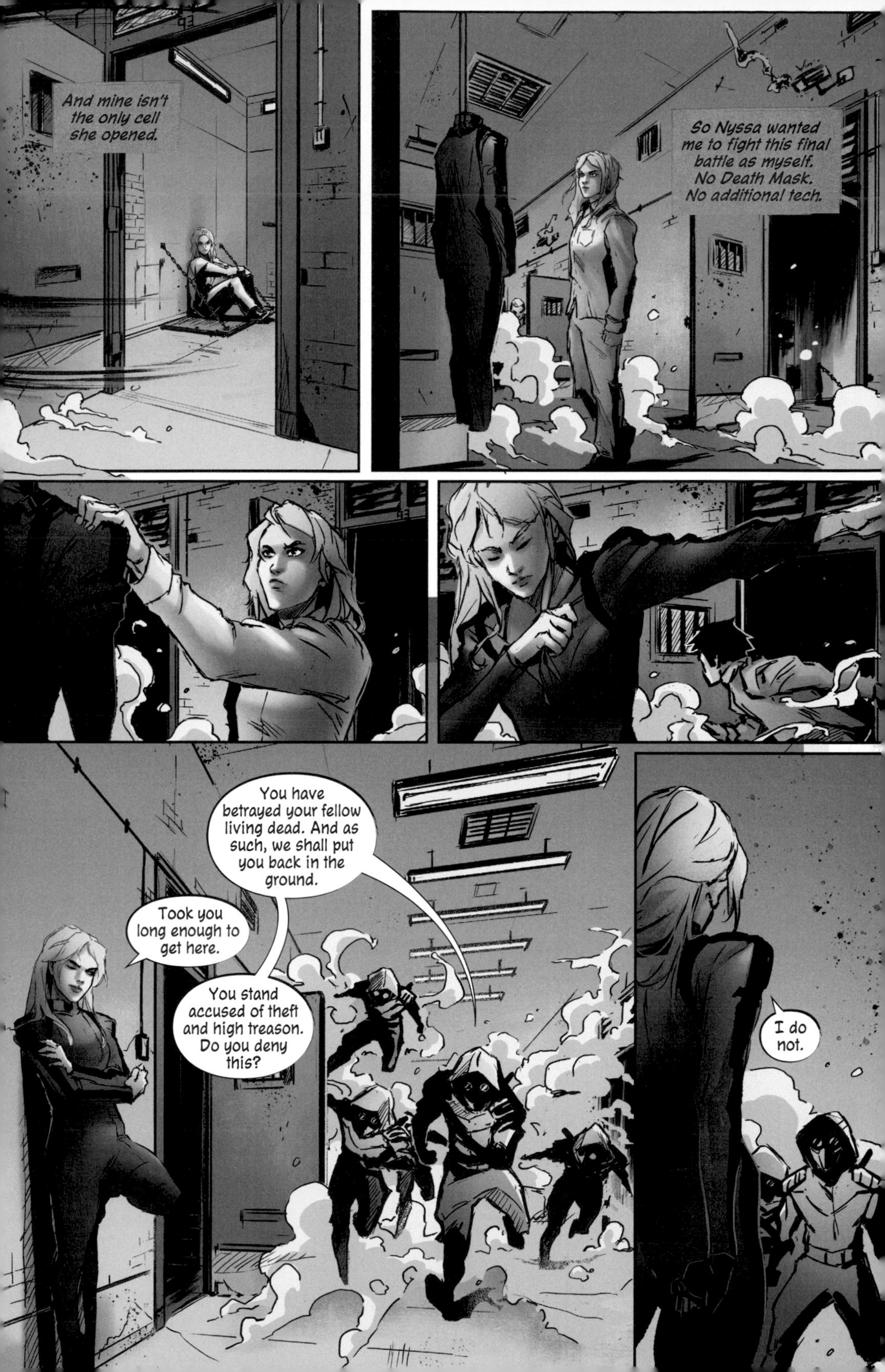

And mine isn't the only cell she opened.
So Nyssa wanted me to fight this final battle as myself. No Death Mask. No additional tech.
Took you long enough to get here.
You have betrayed your fellow living dead. And as such, we shall put you back in the ground.
You stand accused of theft and high treason. Do you deny this?
I do not.

Return what you stole, what you have come here to sell to these godless fools, and the League will make your death swift.

And what did I steal, exactly?

You will not delay this with foolish questions. You know what you stole.

You can't mean to tell me that Nyssa doesn't remember her little formula? Perhaps she should have paid attention to those scientists she kidnapped.

If she hadn't had us execute them...

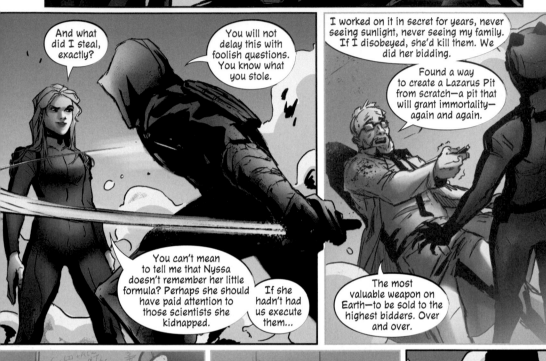

I worked on it in secret for years, never seeing sunlight, never seeing my family. If I disobeyed, she'd kill them. We did her bidding.

Found a way to create a Lazarus Pit from scratch—a pit that will grant immortality—again and again.

The most valuable weapon on Earth—to be sold to the highest bidders. Over and over.

I've hidden the data...here. My password. Free me. Don't let her unleash this thing upon the world.

Why aren't you—?

CRAK

Done.

Give us the formula. Now.

It's too late.

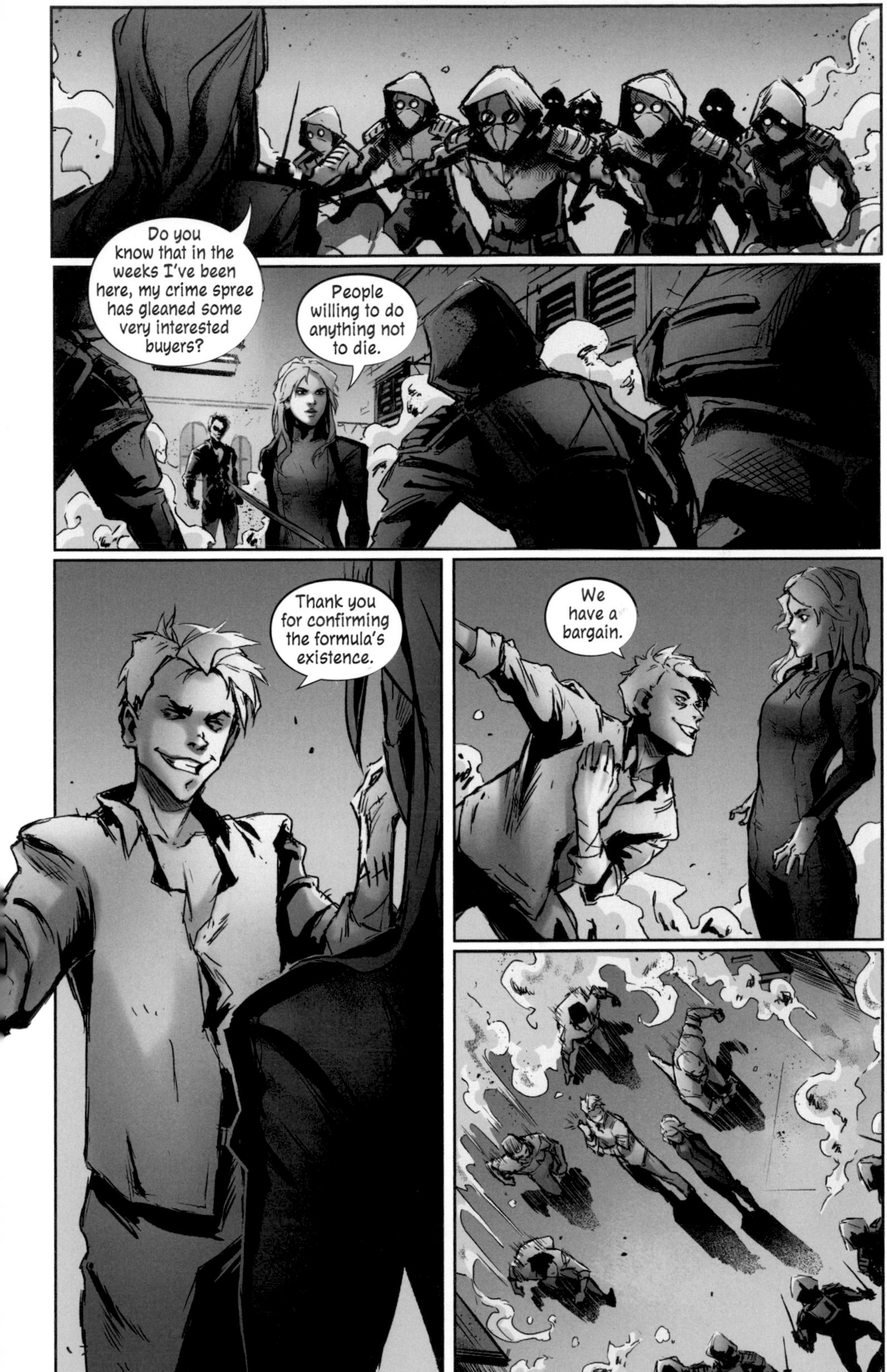

Do you know that in the weeks I've been here, my crime spree has gleaned some very interested buyers?
People willing to do anything not to die.
Thank you for confirming the formula's existence.
We have a bargain.

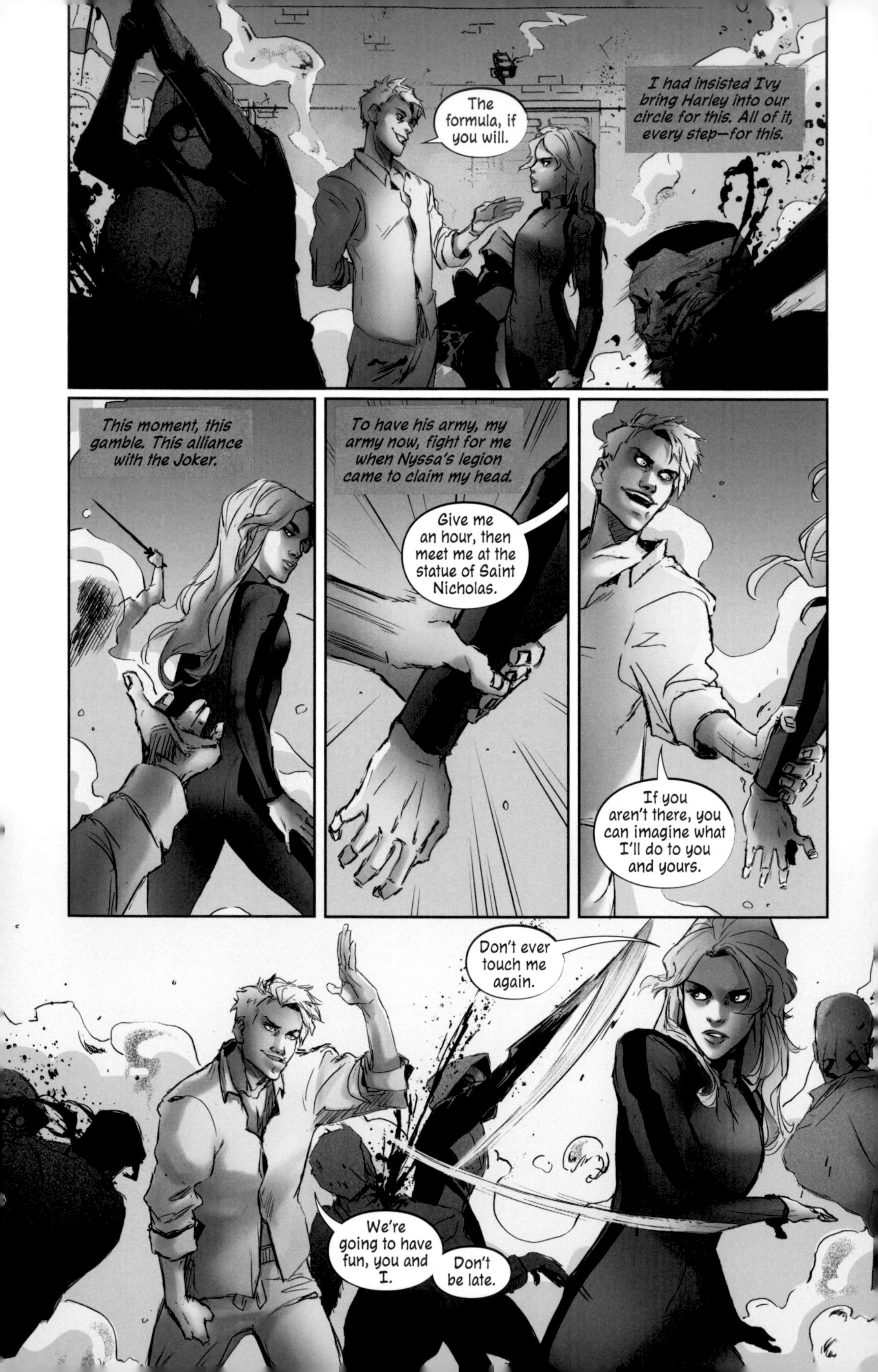

I had insisted Ivy bring Harley into our circle for this. All of it, every step—for this.
The formula, if you will.
This moment, this gamble. This alliance with the Joker.
To have his army, my army now, fight for me when Nyssa's legion came to claim my head.
Give me an hour, then meet me at the statue of Saint Nicholas.
If you aren't there, you can imagine what I'll do to you and yours.
Don't ever touch me again.
We're going to have fun, you and I.
Don't be late.

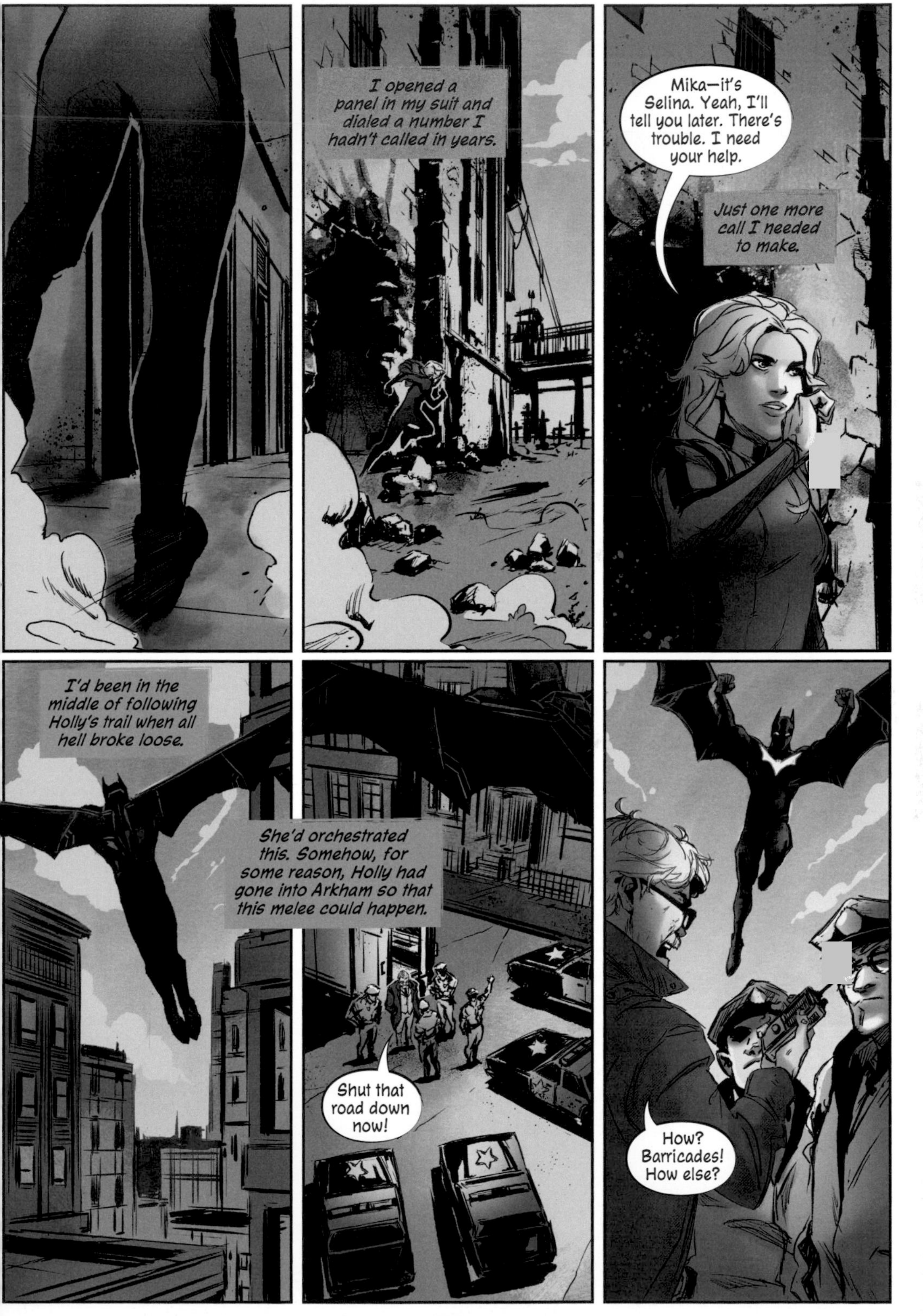
I opened a panel in my suit and dialed a number I hadn't called in years.
Mika—it's Selina. Yeah, I'll tell you later. There's trouble. I need your help.
Just one more call I needed to make.
I'd been in the middle of following Holly's trail when all hell broke loose.
She'd orchestrated this. Somehow, for some reason, Holly had gone into Arkham so that this melee could happen.
Shut that road down now!
How? Barricades! How else?

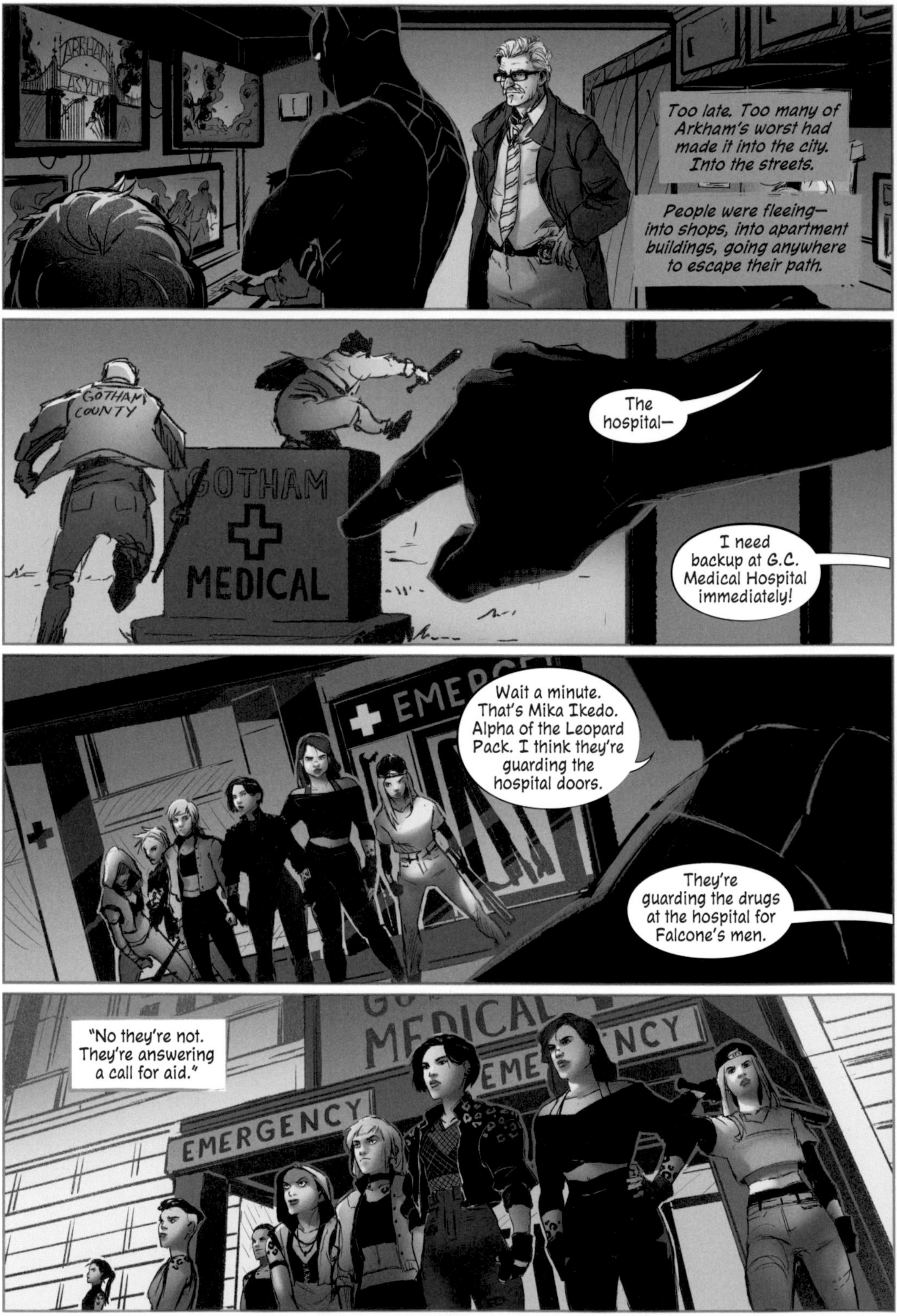
ARKHAM ASYLUM
Too late. Too many of Arkham's worst had made it into the city. Into the streets.
People were fleeing— into shops, into apartment buildings, going anywhere to escape their path.
GOTHAM COUNTY
GOTHAM MEDICAL
The hospital—
I need backup at G.C. Medical Hospital immediately!
EMERG
Wait a minute. That's Mika Ikedo. Alpha of the Leopard Pack. I think they're guarding the hospital doors.
They're guarding the drugs at the hospital for Falcone's men.
"No they're not. They're answering a call for aid."
MEDICAL
EMERGENCY
EMERGENCY

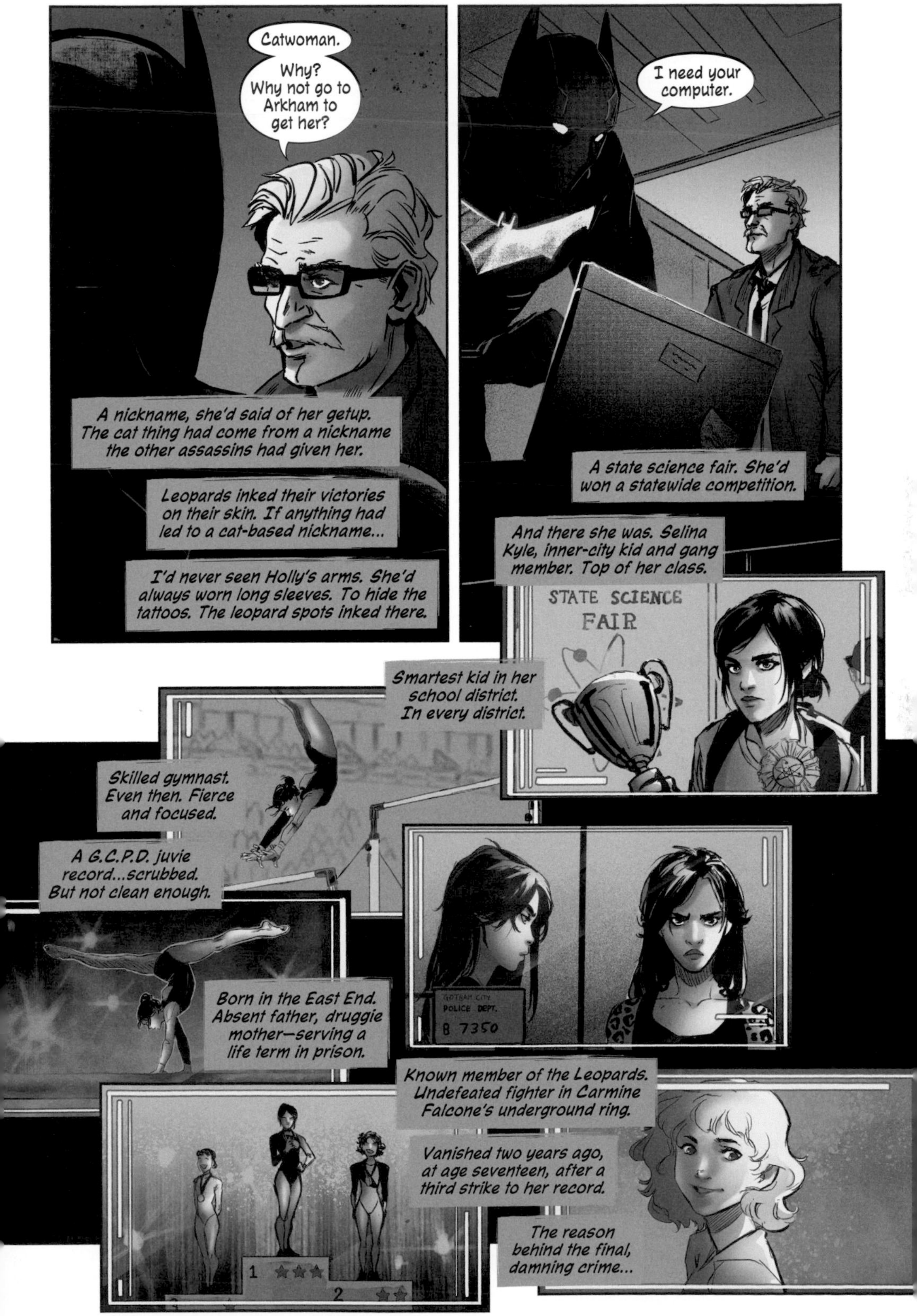

Catwoman.
Why? Why not go to Arkham to get her?
A nickname, she'd said of her getup. The cat thing had come from a nickname the other assassins had given her.
Leopards inked their victories on their skin. If anything had led to a cat-based nickname...
I'd never seen Holly's arms. She'd always worn long sleeves. To hide the tattoos. The leopard spots inked there.
I need your computer.
A state science fair. She'd won a statewide competition.
And there she was. Selina Kyle, inner-city kid and gang member. Top of her class.
STATE SCIENCE FAIR
Smartest kid in her school district. In every district.
Skilled gymnast. Even then. Fierce and focused.
A G.C.P.D. juvie record...scrubbed. But not clean enough.
GOTHAM CITY POLICE DEPT.
B 7350
Born in the East End. Absent father, druggie mother—serving a life term in prison.
Known member of the Leopards. Undefeated fighter in Carmine Falcone's underground ring.
Vanished two years ago, at age seventeen, after a third strike to her record.
The reason behind the final, damning crime...

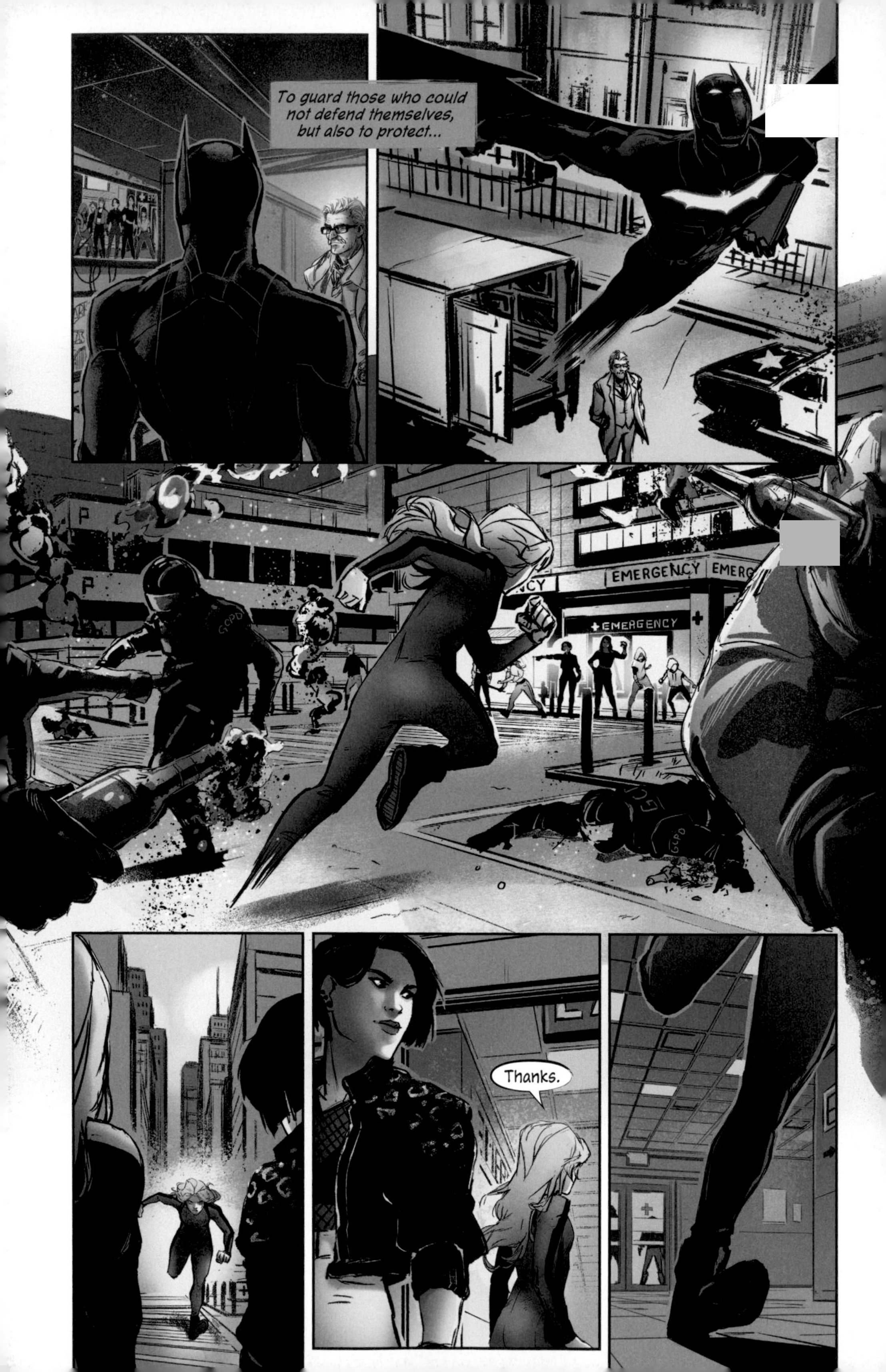
To guard those who could not defend themselves, but also to protect...
GCPD
EMERGENCY
EMERGENCY
+EMERGENCY
GCPD
Thanks.

PART TEN

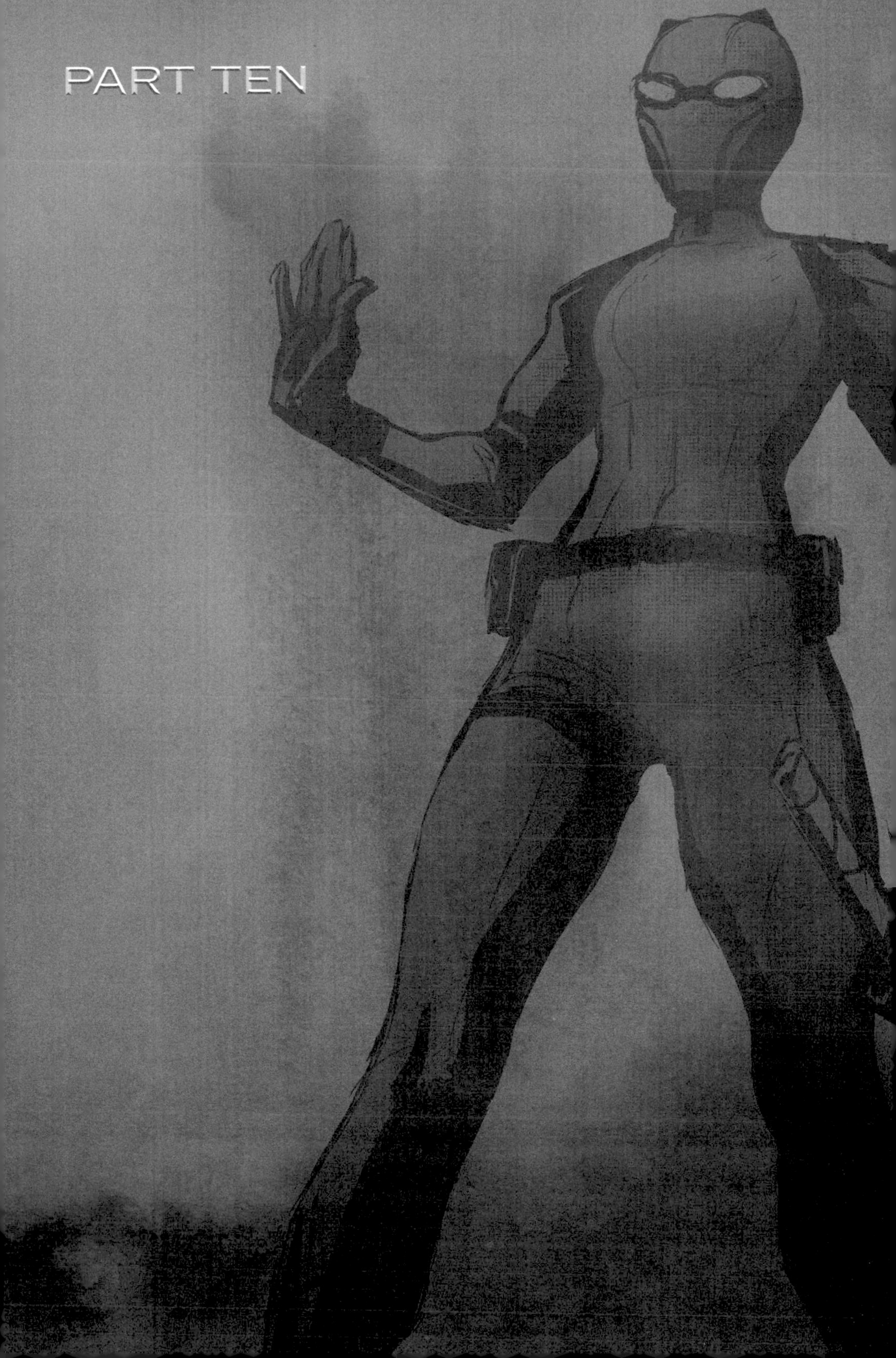

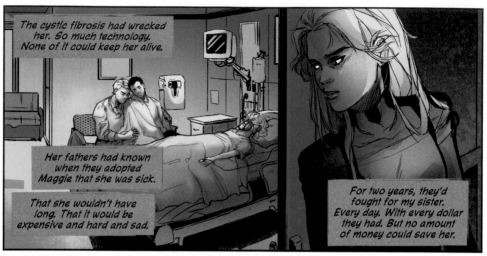

The cystic fibrosis had wrecked her. So much technology. None of it could keep her alive.

Her fathers had known when they adopted Maggie that she was sick.

That she wouldn't have long. That it would be expensive and hard and sad.

For two years, they'd fought for my sister. Every day. With every dollar they had. But no amount of money could save her.

I'd secretly been keeping tabs on Maggie—adoption status, medical records. My secret rebellion...

And then one night, six months ago, when I'd checked in...

LIFE EXPECTANCY: A FEW MONTHS AT BEST. IT IS NOW ABOUT MAKING MAGGIE AS COMFORTABLE AS POSSIBLE.

I'd given my life, my soul, my honor for Maggie's safety and happiness. In the end, it couldn't save her. But the Lazarus Pit could.

I had asked Nyssa to use the Pit to save Maggie. And Nyssa had laughed.

This is natural selection at work.

Even once the Pit is operational, it cannot be used on someone with so little value.

I remembered the scientist's password, his directions. How to access the formula. How to steal it.

I'd killed him. For this woman—this League. But I would make up for it. No, it would not fall into the wrong hands.

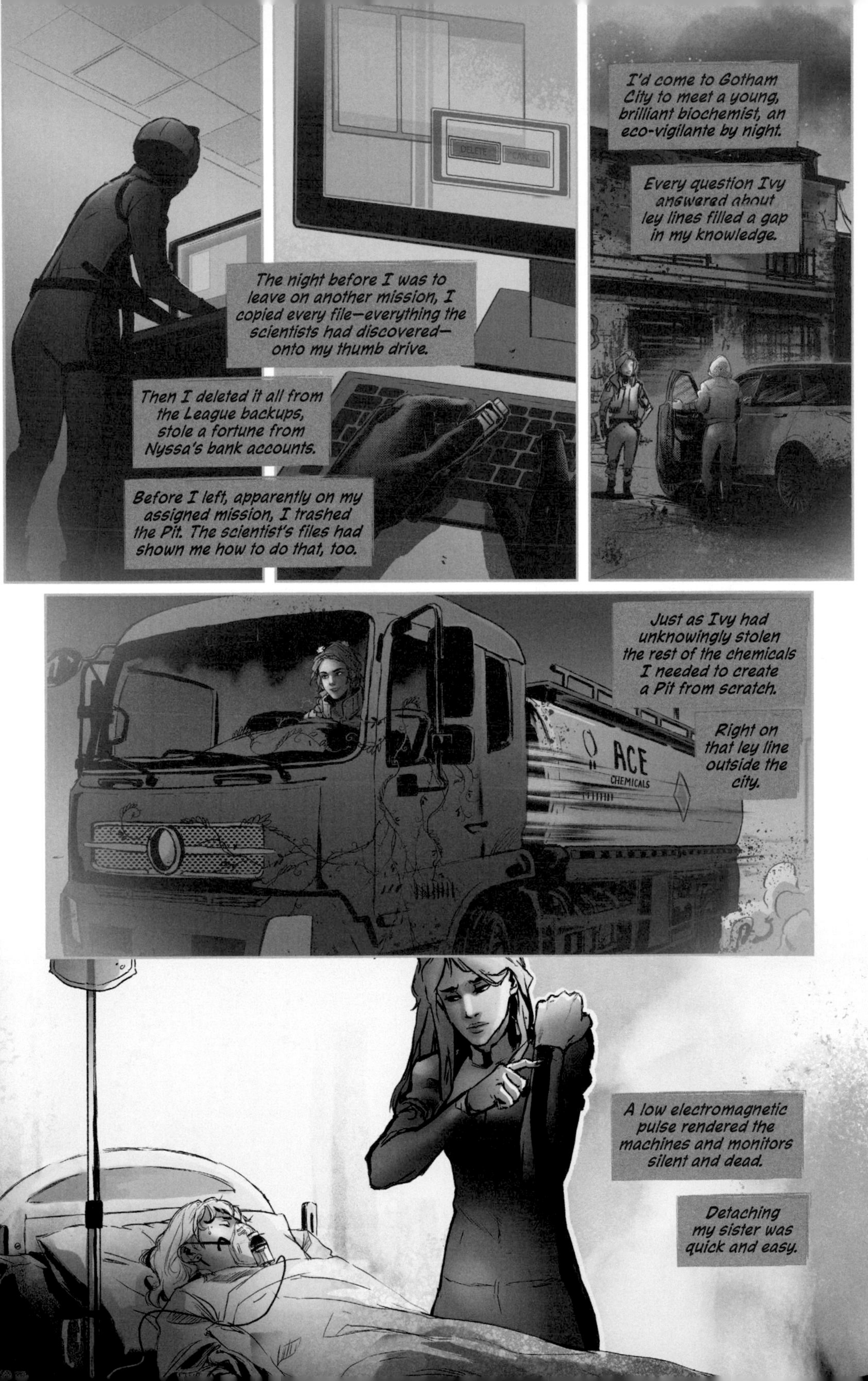
DELETE
CANCEL
The night before I was to leave on another mission, I copied every file—everything the scientists had discovered—onto my thumb drive.
Then I deleted it all from the League backups, stole a fortune from Nyssa's bank accounts.
Before I left, apparently on my assigned mission, I trashed the Pit. The scientist's files had shown me how to do that, too.
I'd come to Gotham City to meet a young, brilliant biochemist, an eco-vigilante by night.
Every question Ivy answered about ley lines filled a gap in my knowledge.
ACE
CHEMICALS
Just as Ivy had unknowingly stolen the rest of the chemicals I needed to create a Pit from scratch.
Right on that ley line outside the city.
A low electromagnetic pulse rendered the machines and monitors silent and dead.
Detaching my sister was quick and easy.

The hospital halls were deserted. Outside was chaos.

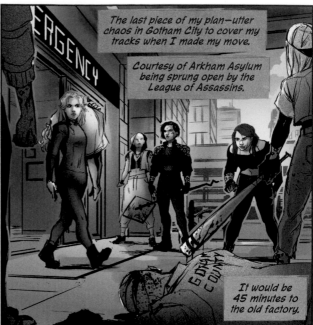

The last piece of my plan—utter chaos in Gotham City to cover my tracks when I made my move.

Courtesy of Arkham Asylum being sprung open by the League of Assassins.

It would be 45 minutes to the old factory.

That way. We kept it quiet for you. We'll stay, guard the hospital.

Thanks.

Several days back, I'd stashed my Mercedes in the hospital parking lot, the keys taped under the trunk.

Selina. Stop!

My own name... how had Harley figured it out?

I said, stop!

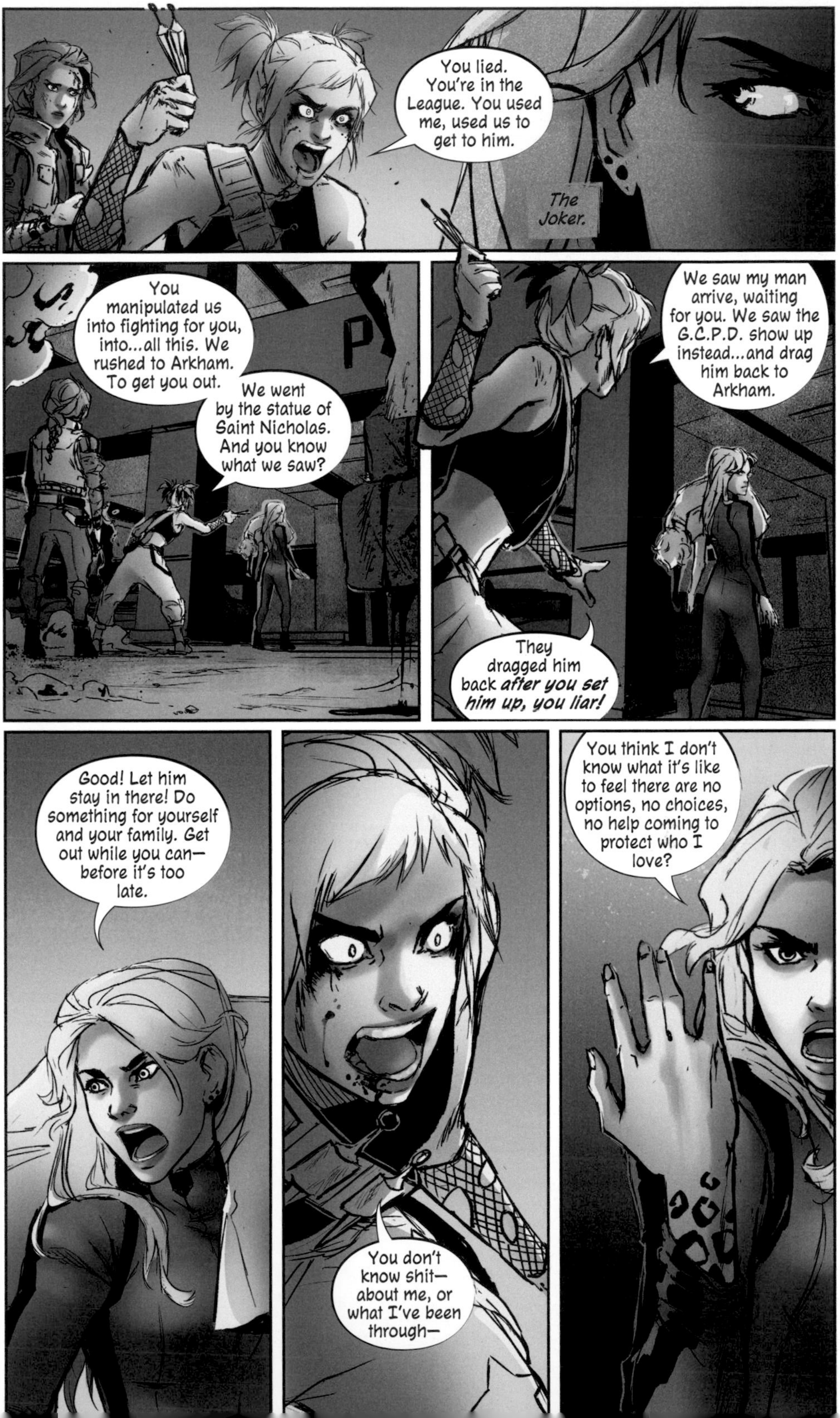
You lied. You're in the League. You used me, used us to get to him.
The Joker.
You manipulated us into fighting for you, into...all this. We rushed to Arkham. To get you out.
We went by the statue of Saint Nicholas. And you know what we saw?
We saw my man arrive, waiting for you. We saw the G.C.P.D. show up instead...and drag him back to Arkham.
They dragged him back *after you set him up, you liar!*
Good! Let him stay in there! Do something for yourself and your family. Get out while you can—before it's too late.
You don't know shit—about me, or what I've been through—
You think I don't know what it's like to feel there are no options, no choices, no help coming to protect who I love?

She's right, Harley. You and me—let's walk away. Even...help her.

That little girl is sick. Put the knives down. We'll figure something out, get you help—

Shutupshutup shutup! I don't need any—help...

The world is better off with him behind bars. And so are you, Harley.

BEEP BEEP CICK

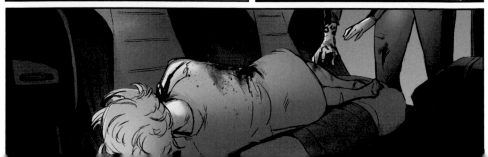

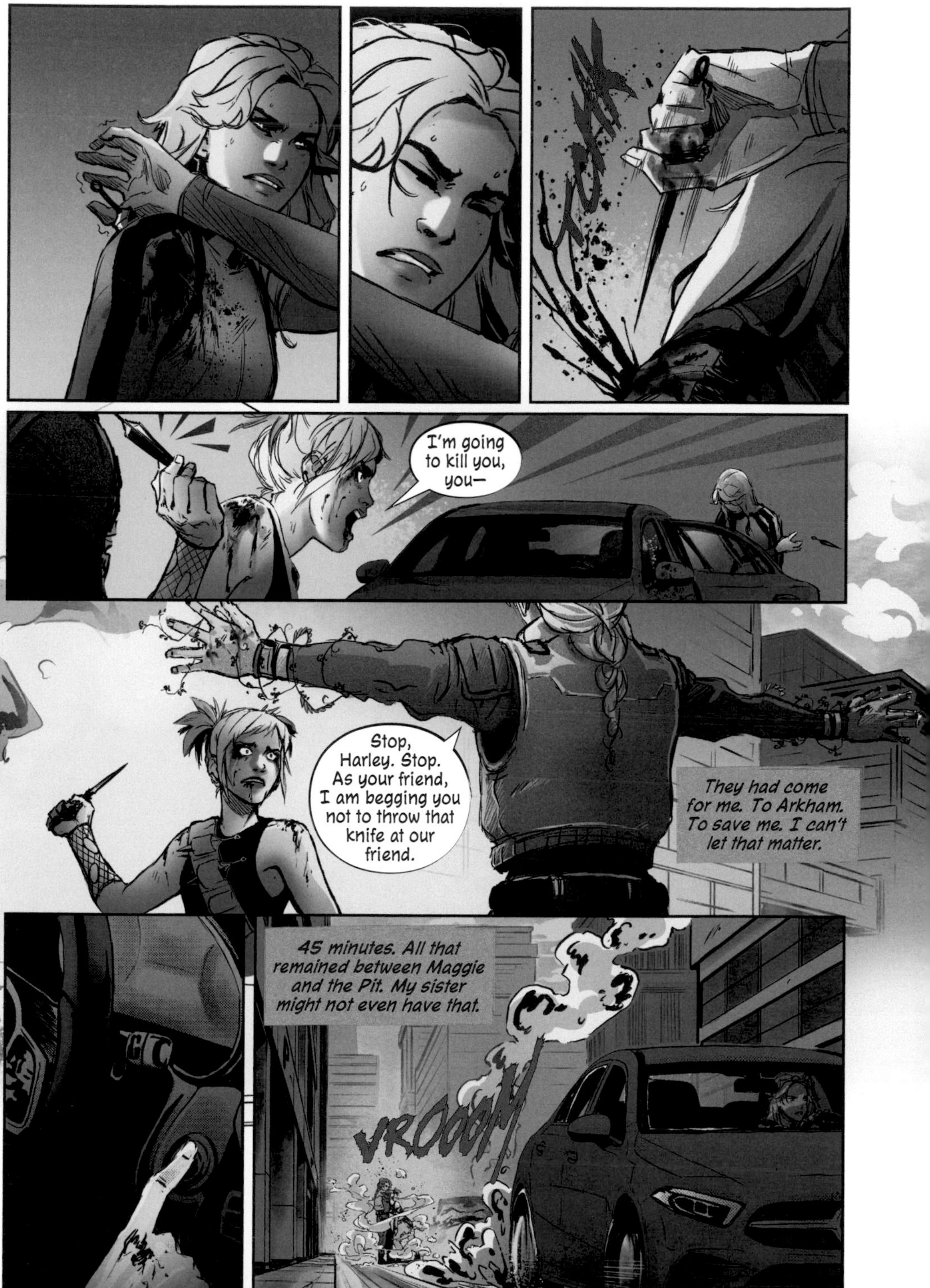
TCHK
I'm going to kill you, you—
Stop, Harley. Stop. As your friend, I am begging you not to throw that knife at our friend.
They had come for me. To Arkham. To save me. I can't let that matter.
45 minutes. All that remained between Maggie and the Pit. My sister might not even have that.
VROOOM

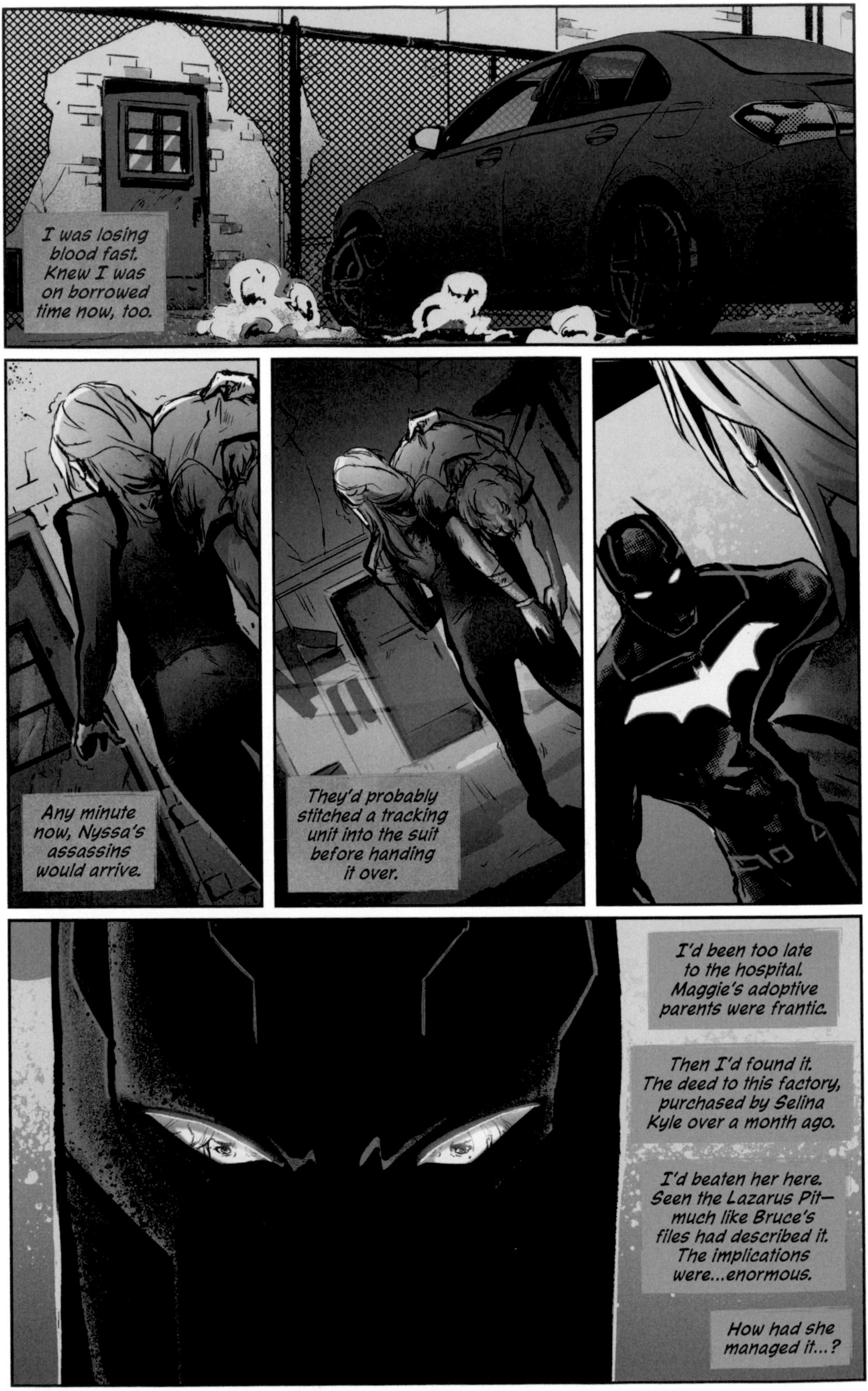
I was losing blood fast. Knew I was on borrowed time now, too.
Any minute now, Nyssa's assassins would arrive.
They'd probably stitched a tracking unit into the suit before handing it over.
I'd been too late to the hospital. Maggie's adoptive parents were frantic.
Then I'd found it. The deed to this factory, purchased by Selina Kyle over a month ago.
I'd beaten her here. Seen the Lazarus Pit— much like Bruce's files had described it. The implications were...enormous.
How had she managed it...?

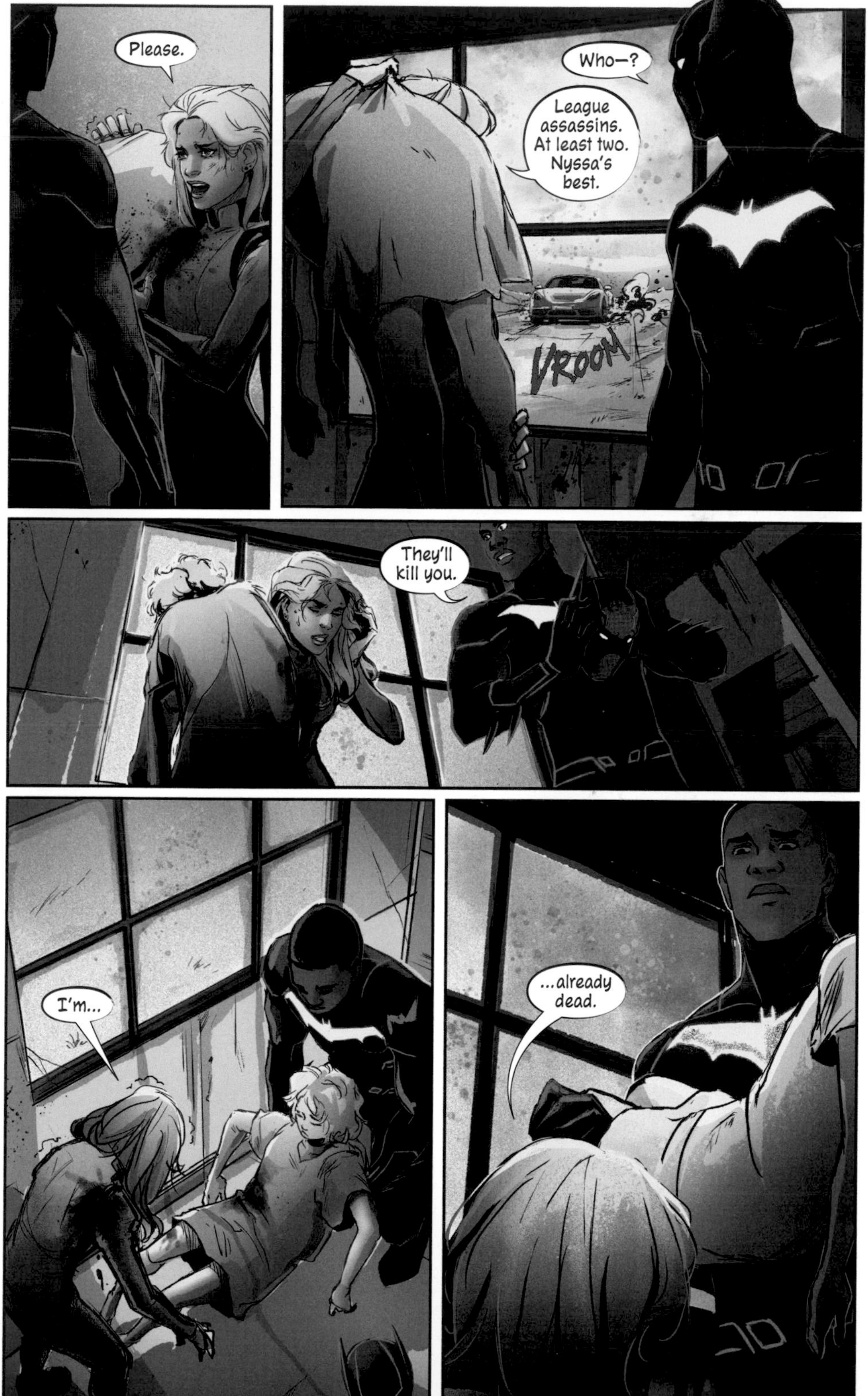
Please.
Who—?
League assassins. At least two. Nyssa's best.
VROOM
They'll kill you.
I'm...
...already dead.

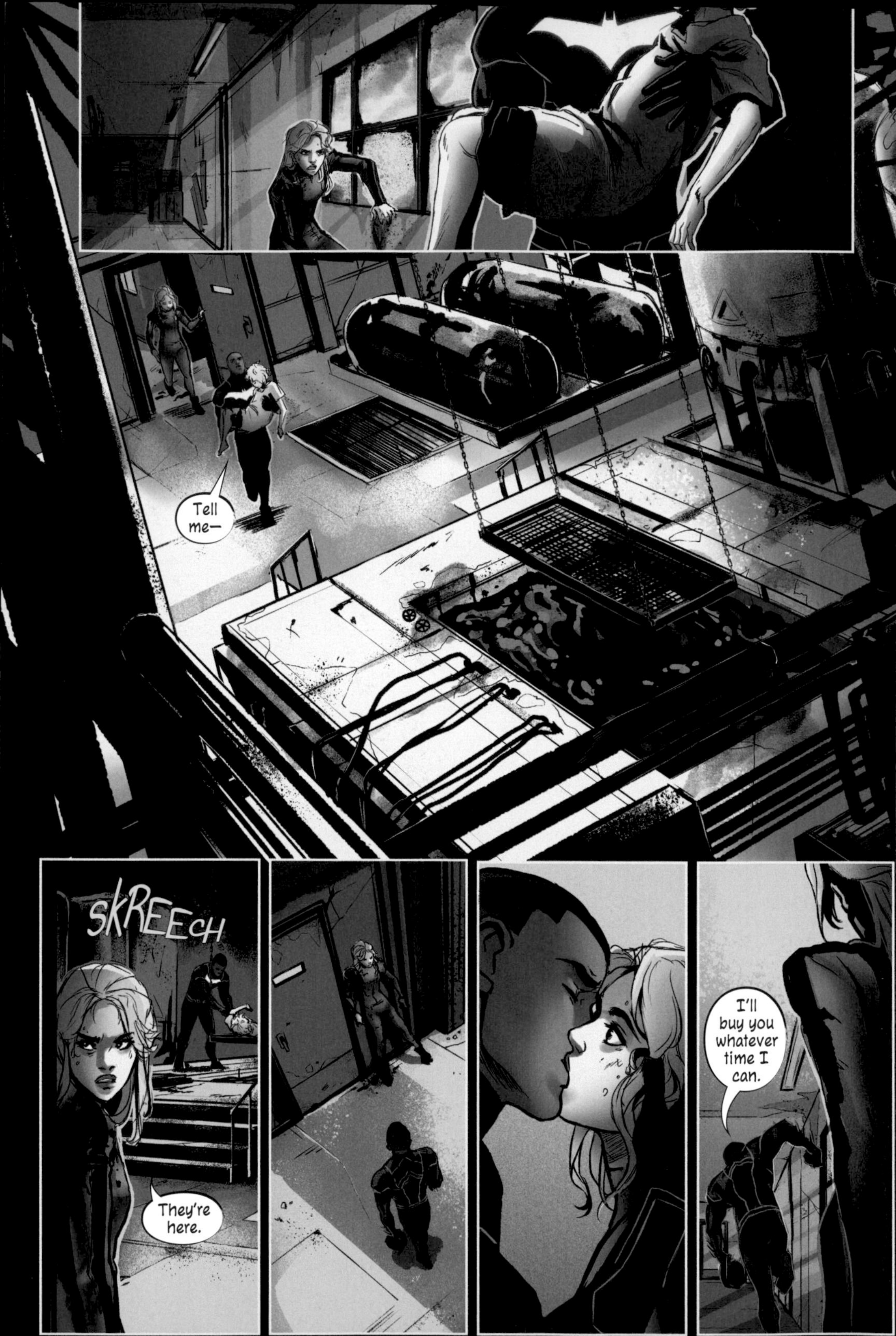
Tell me—
SKREECH
They're here.
I'll buy you whatever time I can.

I recognized them from Bruce's files. Nyssa al Ghūl's top three—Cheshire. Onyx. Rictus.

Three against one. I've faced worse odds, but my opponents hadn't been lethal killers built to take lives.

Blood.

Soon yours will join it.

I'd built it—following their directions.

CLACKETY CLICK CLACKETY CLACK CLACK

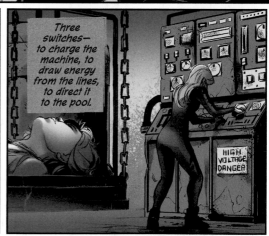

Three switches—to charge the machine, to draw energy from the lines, to direct it to the pool.

HIGH VOLTAGE DANGER

Green starts the chemicals mixing. Red stops it.

Luke can't last long out there. Neither will I. Just do... what needs doing.

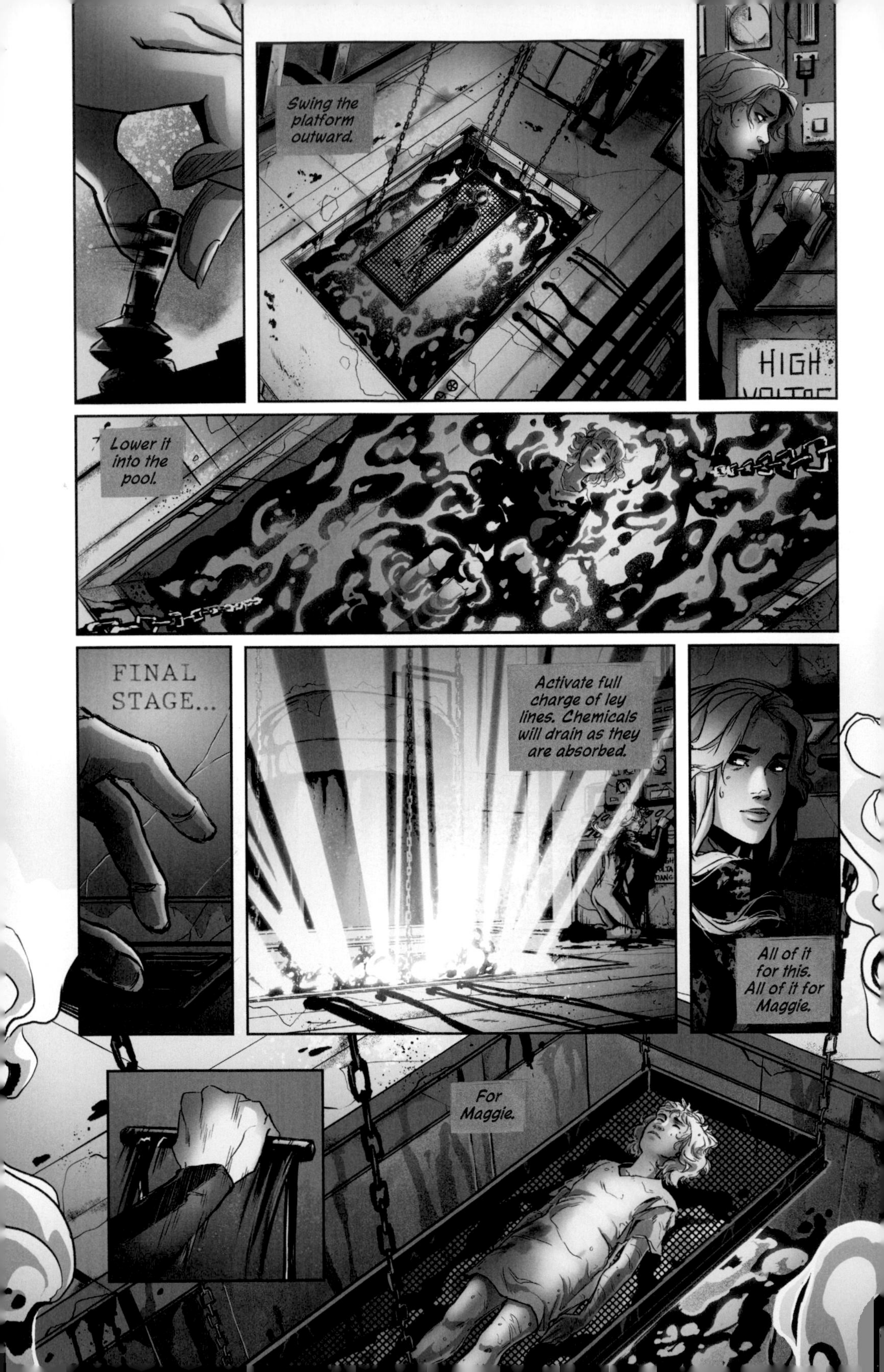
Swing the platform outward.
HIGH
Lower it into the pool.
FINAL STAGE...
Activate full charge of ley lines. Chemicals will drain as they are absorbed.
All of it for this. All of it for Maggie.
For Maggie.

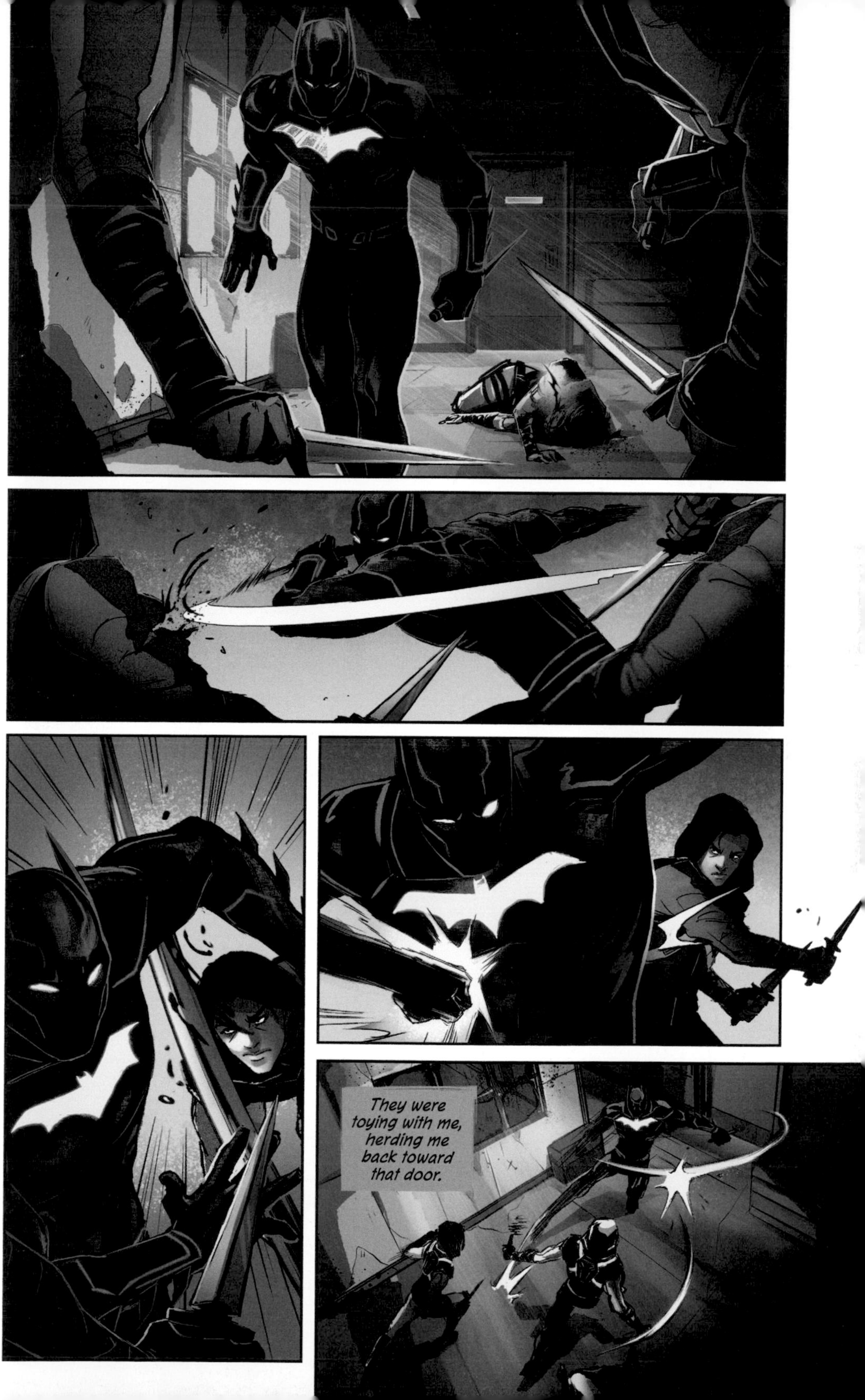
They were toying with me, herding me back toward that door.

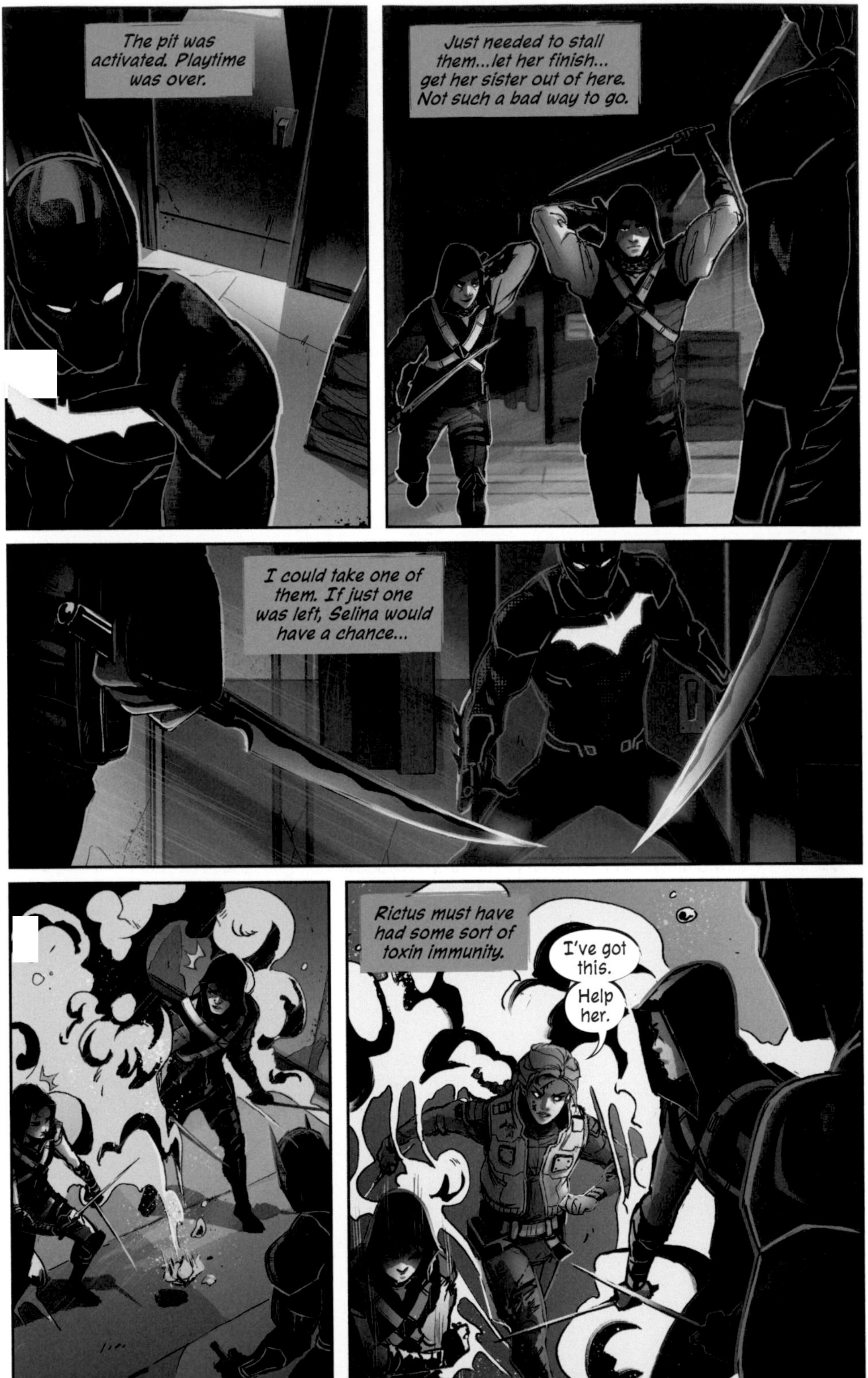

The pit was activated. Playtime was over.
Just needed to stall them...let her finish... get her sister out of here. Not such a bad way to go.
I could take one of them. If just one was left, Selina would have a chance...
Rictus must have had some sort of toxin immunity.
I've got this.
Help her.

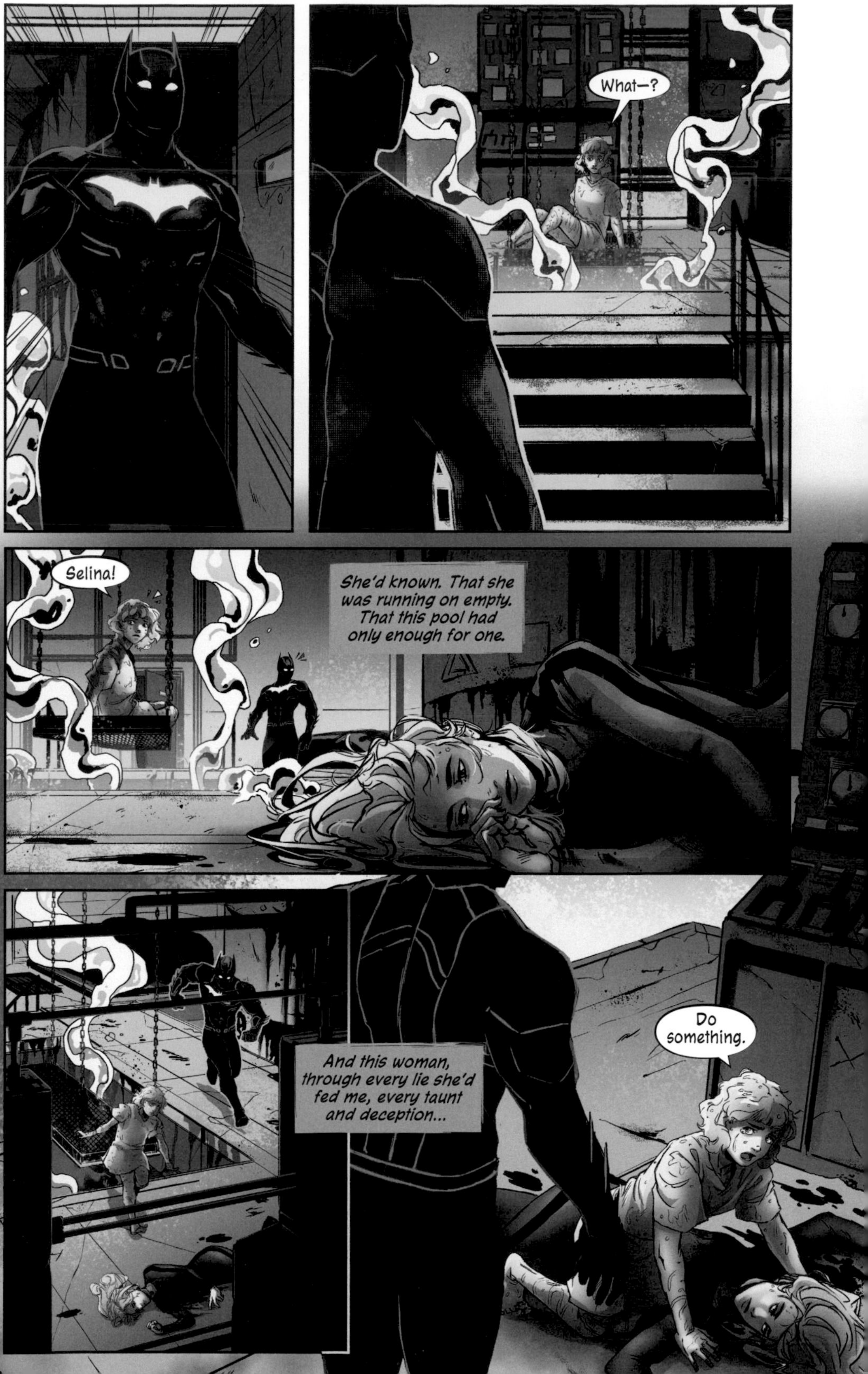
What—?
Selina!
She'd known. That she was running on empty. That this pool had only enough for one.
And this woman, through every lie she'd fed me, every taunt and deception...
Do something.

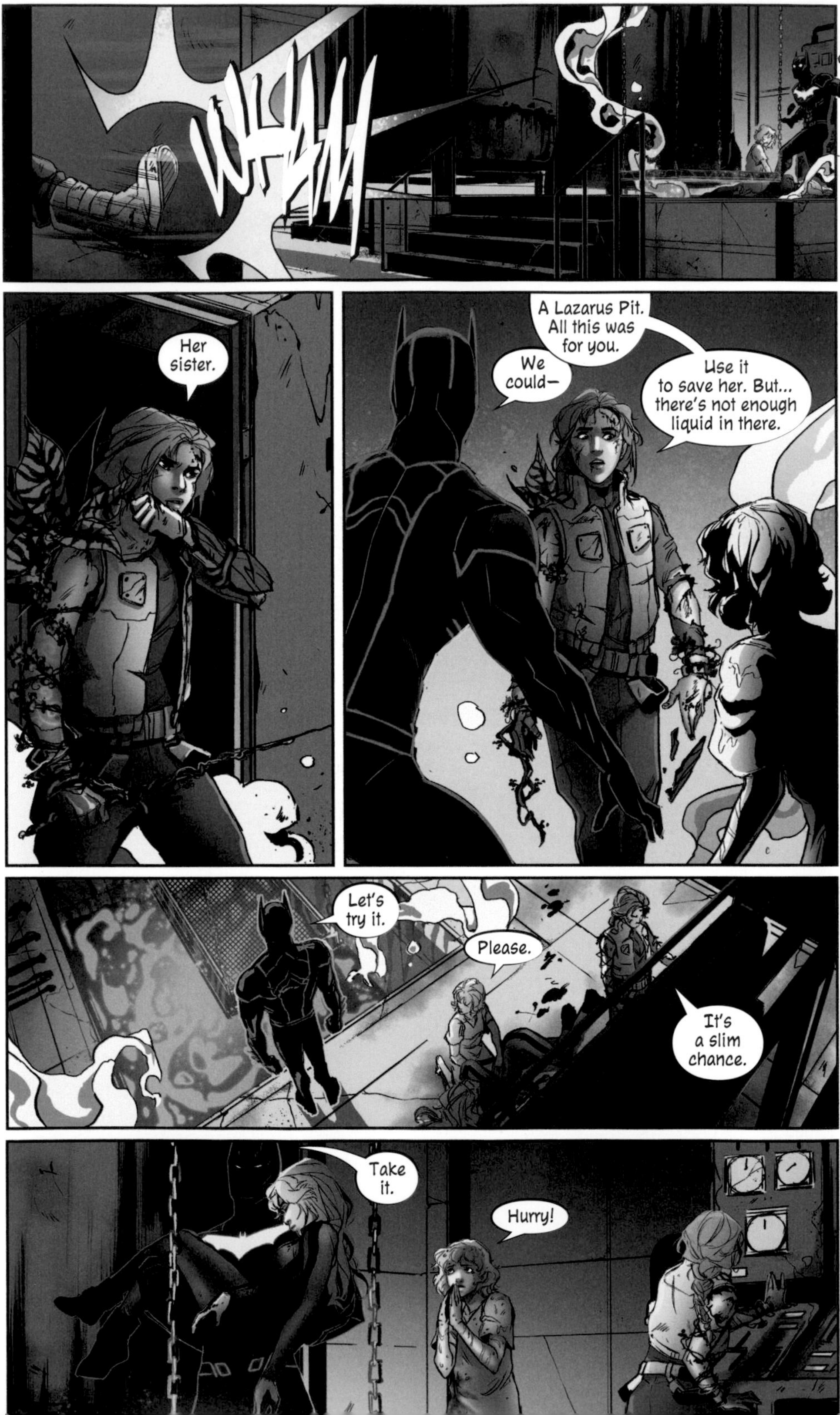
WHAM
Her sister.
A Lazarus Pit. All this was for you.
We could—
Use it to save her. But... there's not enough liquid in there.
Let's try it.
Please.
It's a slim chance.
Take it.
Hurry!

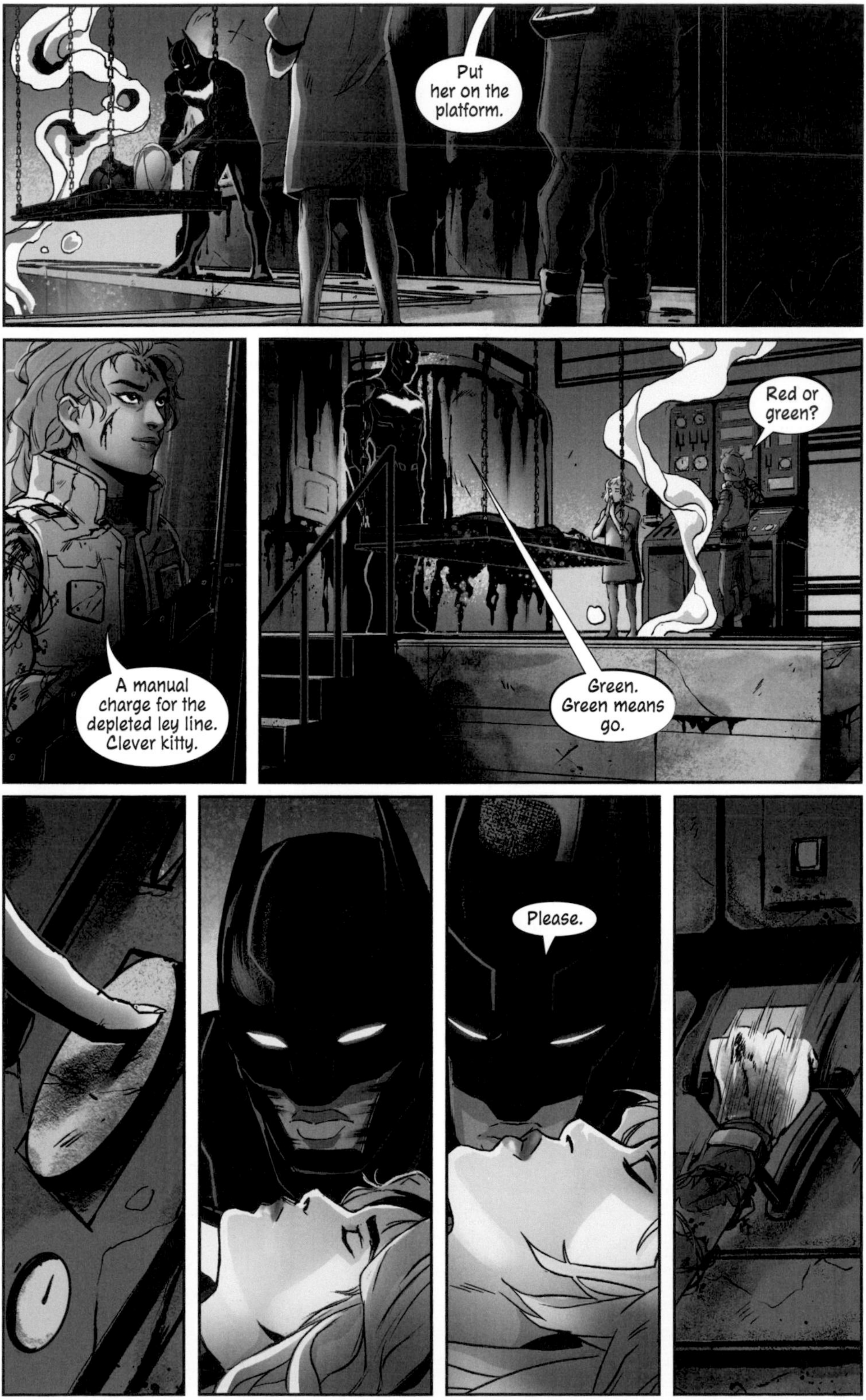
Put her on the platform.
A manual charge for the depleted ley line. Clever kitty.
Red or green?
Green. Green means go.
Please.

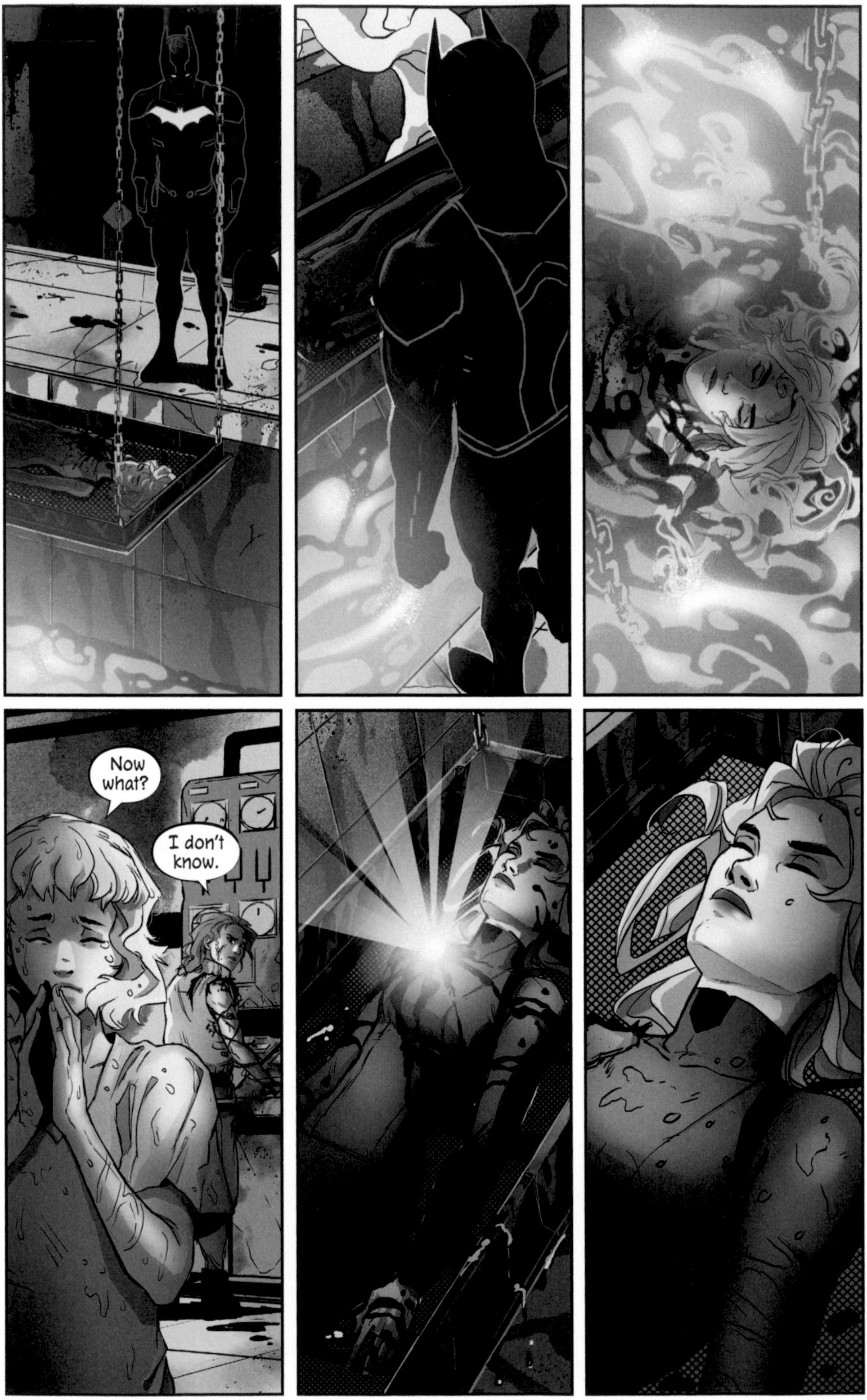
Now what?
I don't know.

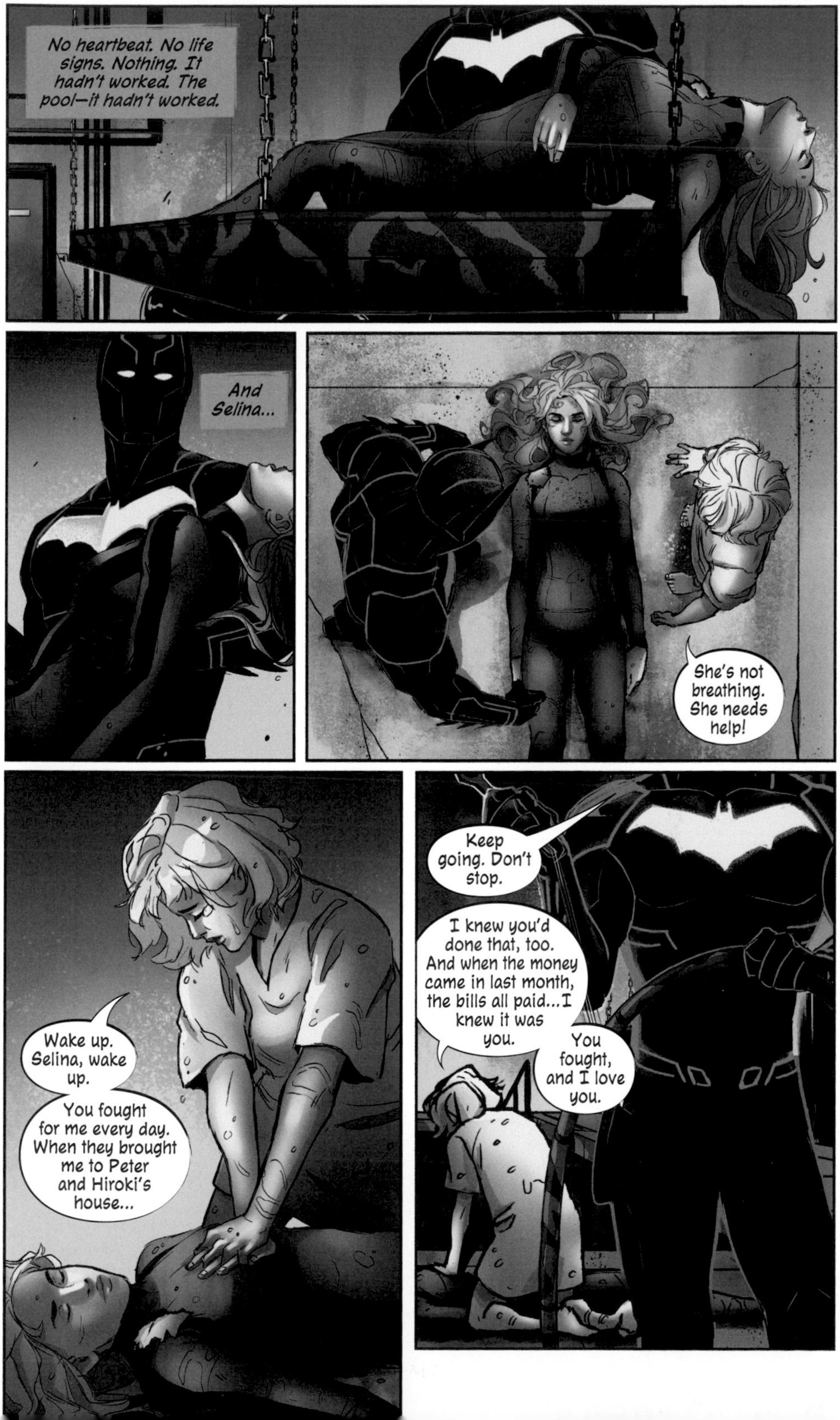
No heartbeat. No life signs. Nothing. It hadn't worked. The pool—it hadn't worked.
And Selina...
She's not breathing. She needs help!
Wake up. Selina, wake up.
You fought for me every day. When they brought me to Peter and Hiroki's house...
Keep going. Don't stop.
I knew you'd done that, too. And when the money came in last month, the bills all paid...I knew it was you.
You fought, and I love you.

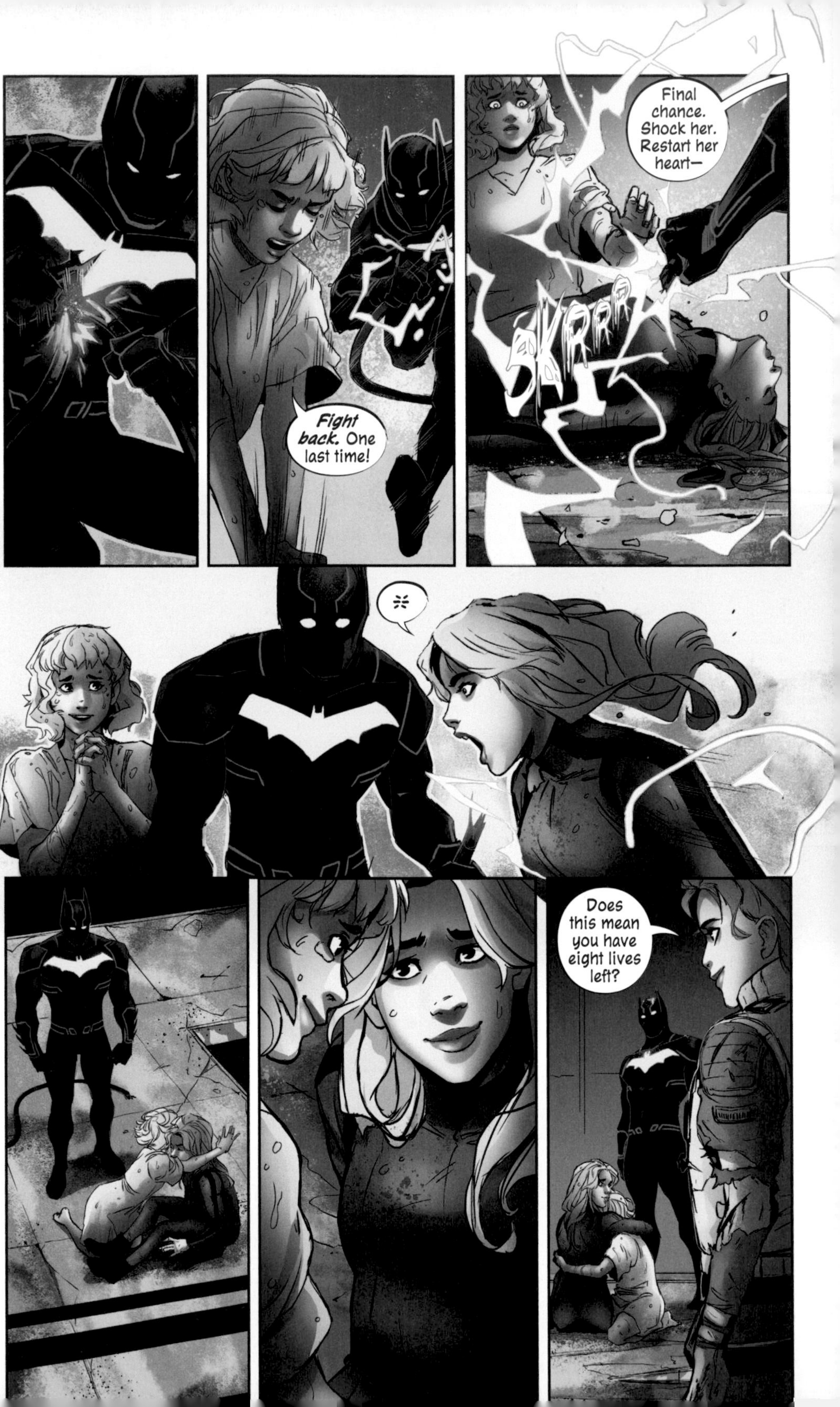
Fight back. One last time!
Final chance. Shock her. Restart her heart—
SKRRR
Does this mean you have eight lives left?

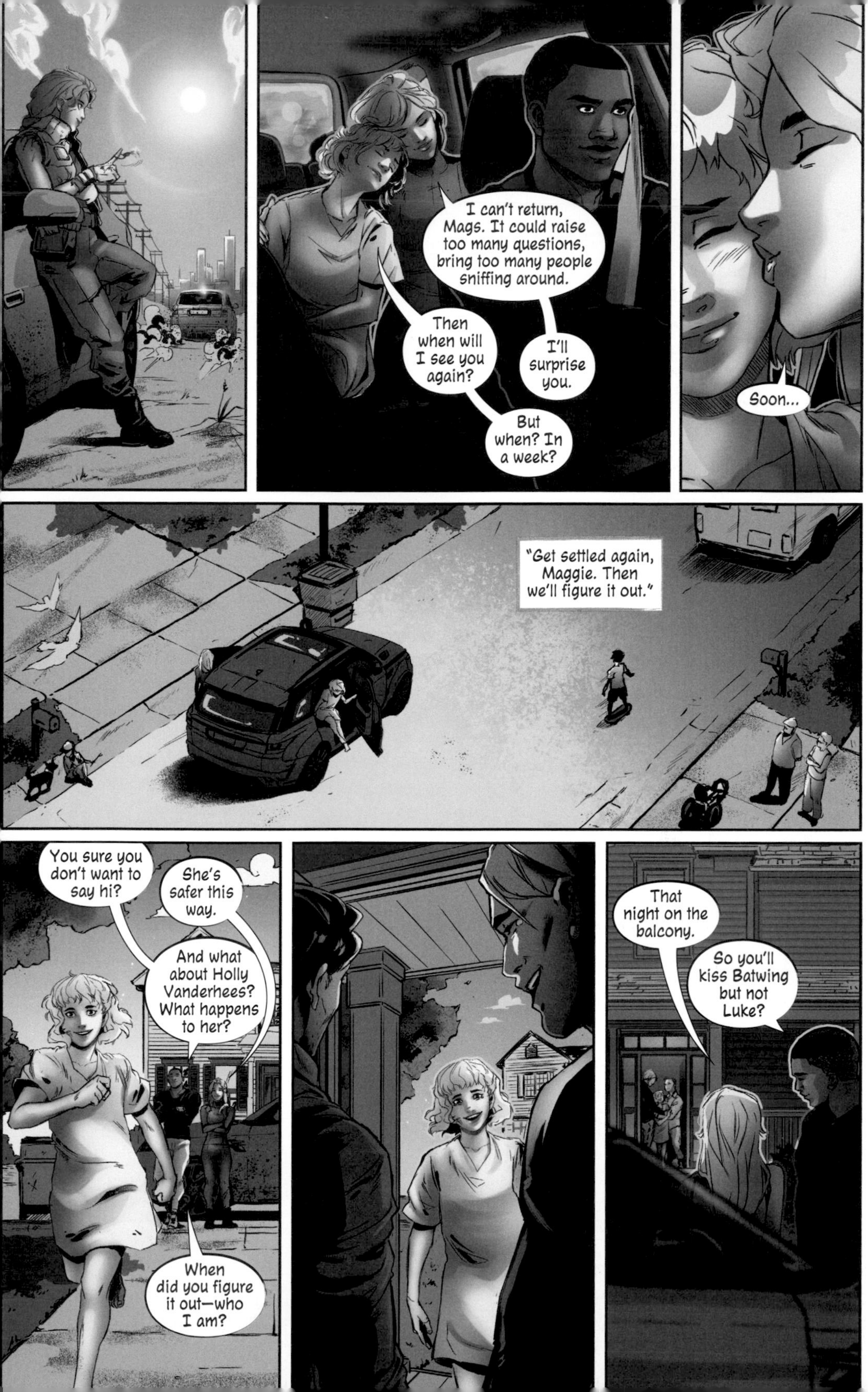
I can't return, Mags. It could raise too many questions, bring too many people sniffing around.
Then when will I see you again?
I'll surprise you.
But when? In a week?
Soon...
"Get settled again, Maggie. Then we'll figure it out."
You sure you don't want to say hi?
She's safer this way.
And what about Holly Vanderhees? What happens to her?
When did you figure it out—who I am?
That night on the balcony.
So you'll kiss Batwing but not Luke?

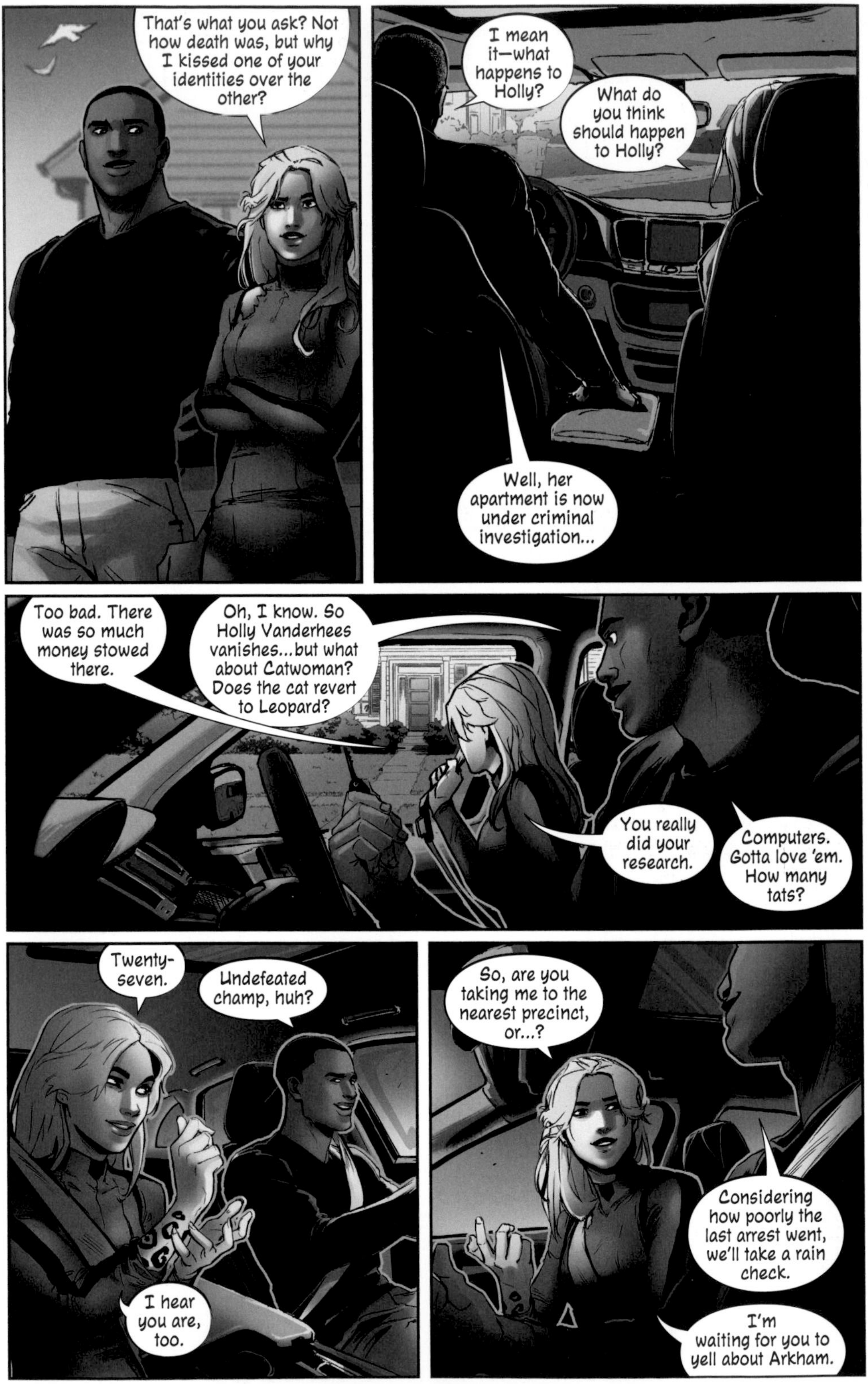
That's what you ask? Not how death was, but why I kissed one of your identities over the other?
I mean it—what happens to Holly?
What do you think should happen to Holly?
Well, her apartment is now under criminal investigation...
Too bad. There was so much money stowed there.
Oh, I know. So Holly Vanderhees vanishes...but what about Catwoman? Does the cat revert to Leopard?
You really did your research.
Computers. Gotta love 'em. How many tats?
Twenty-seven.
Undefeated champ, huh?
I hear you are, too.
So, are you taking me to the nearest precinct, or...?
Considering how poorly the last arrest went, we'll take a rain check.
I'm waiting for you to yell about Arkham.

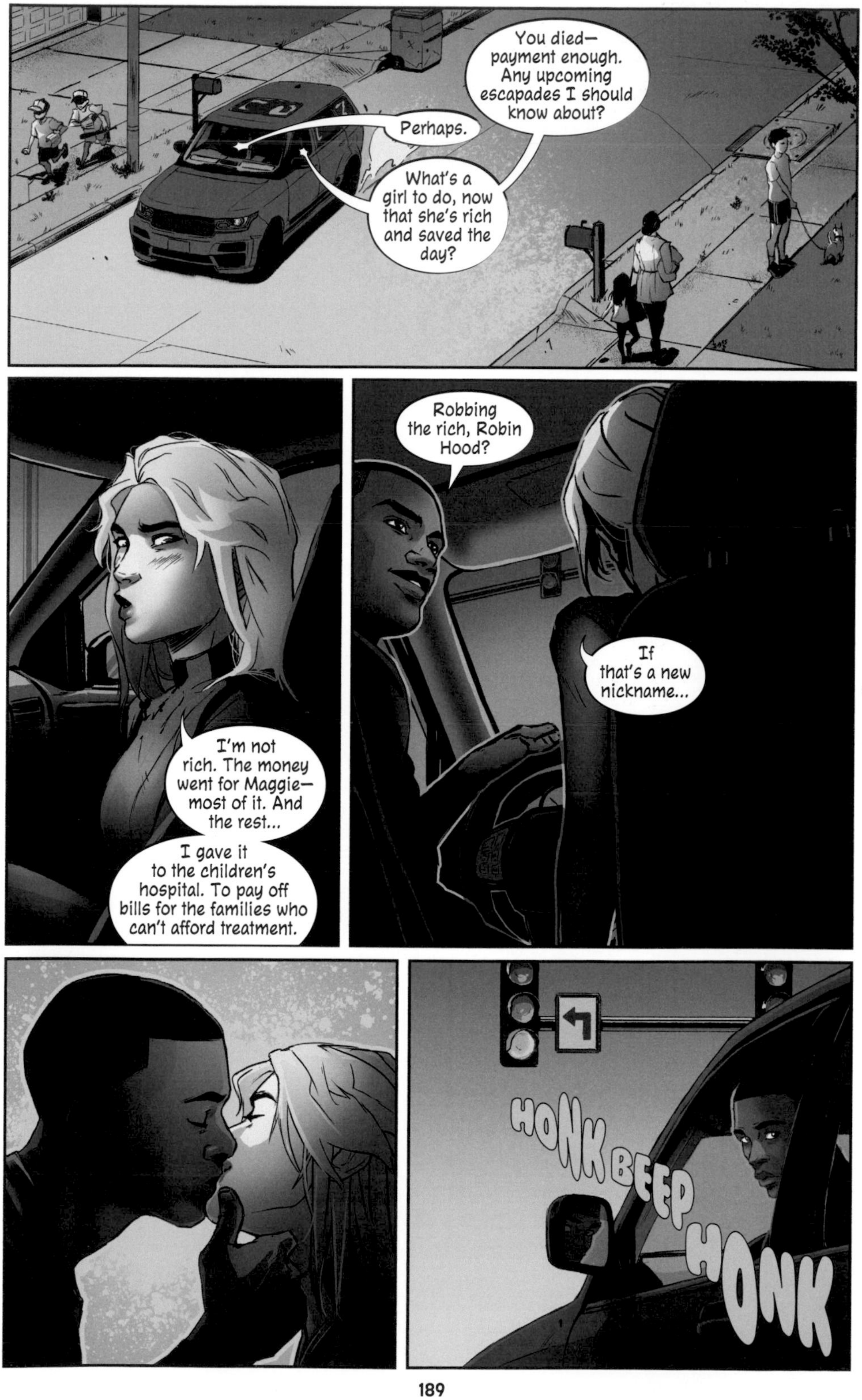

You died— payment enough. Any upcoming escapades I should know about?
Perhaps.
What's a girl to do, now that she's rich and saved the day?
I'm not rich. The money went for Maggie— most of it. And the rest...
I gave it to the children's hospital. To pay off bills for the families who can't afford treatment.
Robbing the rich, Robin Hood?
If that's a new nickname...
HONK BEEP HONK

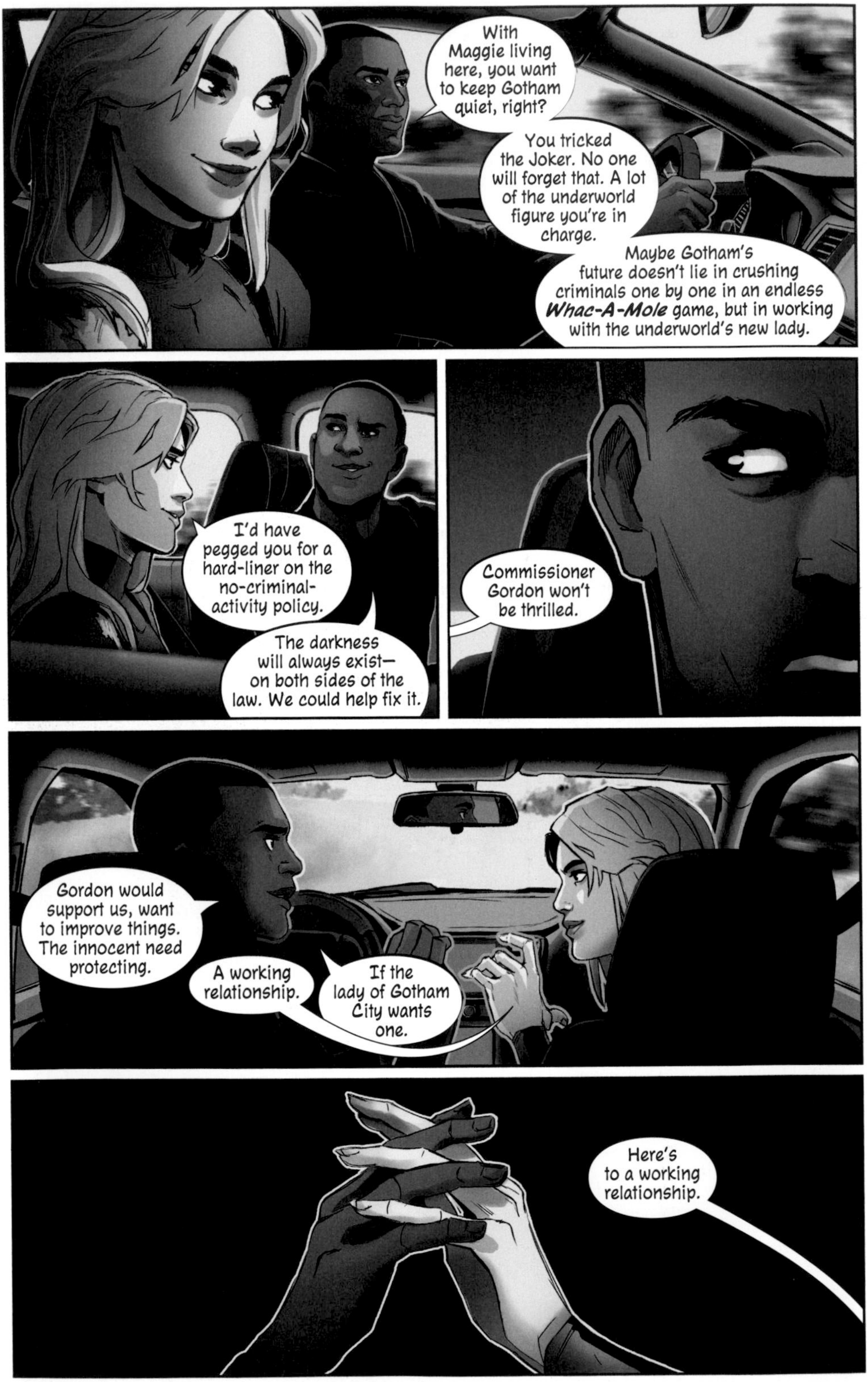
With Maggie living here, you want to keep Gotham quiet, right?
You tricked the Joker. No one will forget that. A lot of the underworld figure you're in charge.
Maybe Gotham's future doesn't lie in crushing criminals one by one in an endless *Whac-A-Mole* game, but in working with the underworld's new lady.
I'd have pegged you for a hard-liner on the no-criminal-activity policy.
The darkness will always exist— on both sides of the law. We could help fix it.
Commissioner Gordon won't be thrilled.
Gordon would support us, want to improve things. The innocent need protecting.
A working relationship.
If the lady of Gotham City wants one.
Here's to a working relationship.

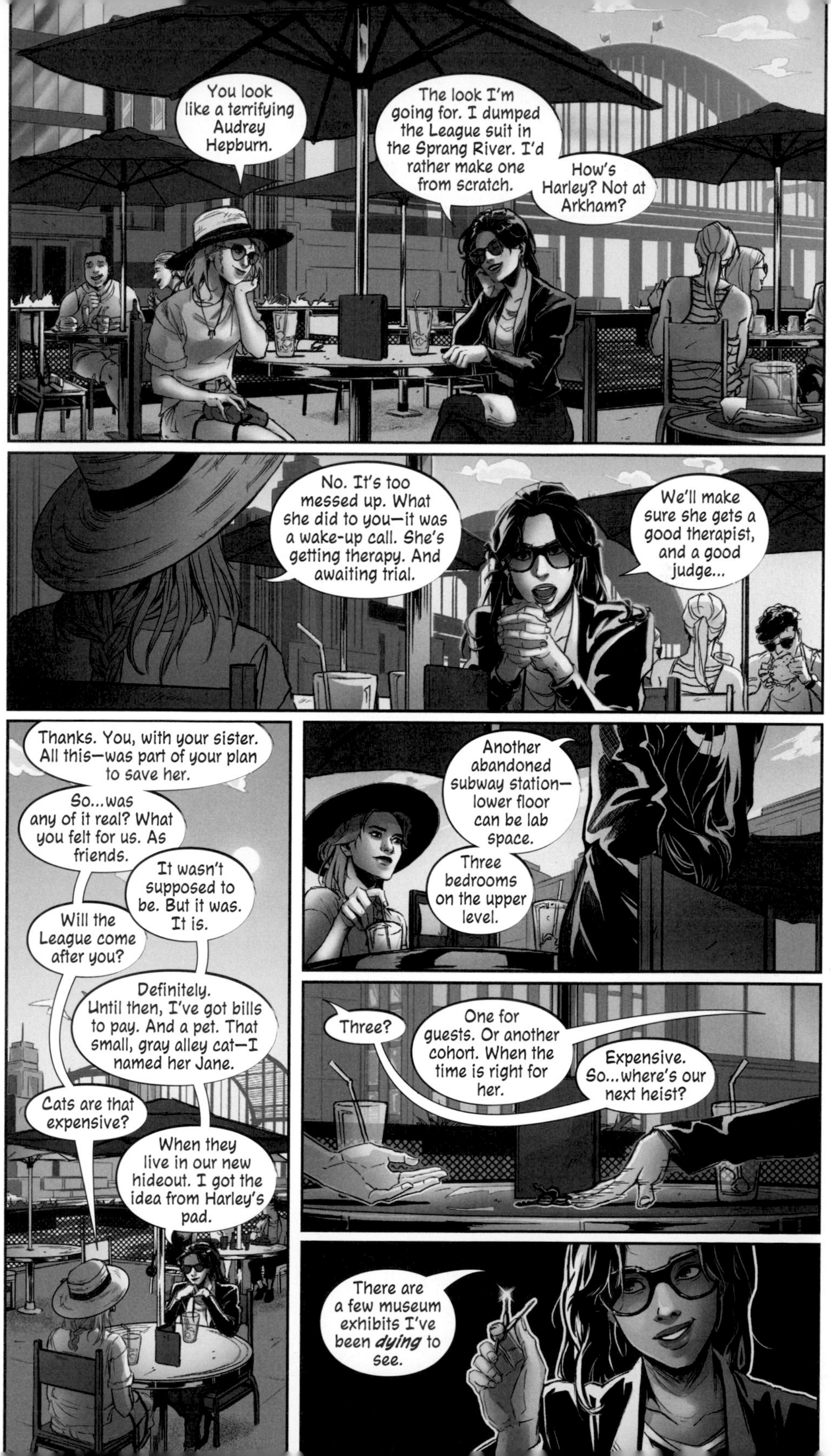
You look like a terrifying Audrey Hepburn.
The look I'm going for. I dumped the League suit in the Sprang River. I'd rather make one from scratch.
How's Harley? Not at Arkham?
No. It's too messed up. What she did to you—it was a wake-up call. She's getting therapy. And awaiting trial.
We'll make sure she gets a good therapist, and a good judge...
Thanks. You, with your sister. All this—was part of your plan to save her.
So...was any of it real? What you felt for us. As friends.
It wasn't supposed to be. But it was. It is.
Will the League come after you?
Definitely. Until then, I've got bills to pay. And a pet. That small, gray alley cat—I named her Jane.
Cats are that expensive?
When they live in our new hideout. I got the idea from Harley's pad.
Another abandoned subway station—lower floor can be lab space.
Three bedrooms on the upper level.
Three?
One for guests. Or another cohort. When the time is right for her.
Expensive. So...where's our next heist?
There are a few museum exhibits I've been *dying* to see.

SARAH J. MAAS

is the #1 *New York Times* bestselling author of the Throne of Glass series and A Court of Thorns and Roses series, as well as a *USA Today* and international bestselling author. Sarah wrote the first incarnation of the Throne of Glass series when she was just 16, and it has now been sold in 35 languages. A New York native, Sarah currently lives in Pennsylvania with her husband and dog.

LOUISE SIMONSON

writes comics about monsters, science fiction, superheroes, and fantasy characters. She wrote the award-winning *Power Pack* series, several bestselling X-Men titles, and *Web of Spider-Man* for Marvel Comics and *Superman: The Man of Steel* and *Steel* for DC Comics. She has also written many books for kids. She is married to comics writer/artist Walter Simonson and lives in the suburbs of New York City.

SAMANTHA DODGE

trained at Savannah College of Art and Design and started out designing interactive animations for 2D games. *Catwoman: Soulstealer* is her first DC Comics project. She loves drawing superheroes reacting to humorous or awkward real-life situations. Although her childhood "ultimate superhero pick" is a tie between Wonder Woman and Xena, Catwoman and the Gotham City Sirens will always be a close second. Her other favorite fandoms include *Avatar: The Last Airbender* and *The Legend of Korra*, Harry Potter, *Killing Eve*, *Star Trek*, and *Doctor Who*.

SHARI CHANKHAMMA

is a comics artist, illustrator, colorist, flatter, game assets maker (she did it once, still counts), and general artist for hire. Hire her for whatever—if she tries it, chances are she can do it. Notable work includes *Codename Baboushka*, *Sheltered*, *The Fuse*, and *Kill Shakespeare*. She was born and lives in Thailand, where the average temperature is 90 degrees Fahrenheit. It's very hot.

SAIDA TEMOFONTE

is a Los Angelena at heart currently based in Florida. She's been lettering and designing since 1997 with all major comic book players. When she's not missing California mountains, she can be found fishing in Florida.

RESOURCES

If you, or a loved one, need help in any way, you do not need to act alone.
Below is a list of resources that may be helpful to you.
If you are in immediate danger, please call emergency services in your area
(9-1-1 in the U.S.) or go to your nearest hospital emergency room.

National Suicide Prevention Lifeline
Available 24 hours a day, 7 days a week.
Phone: 1-800-273-8255
Website: suicidepreventionlifeline.org
Online chat: chat.suicidepreventionlifeline.org/gethelp/lifelinechat.aspx

The Jed Foundation
A nonprofit that exists to protect emotional health and prevent suicide
for our nation's teens and young adults.
Text "START" to 741-741 or call 1-800-273-TALK (8255).
Website: jedfoundation.org

International Hotlines
The above hotlines are based in the U.S. and Canada.
A list of international suicide hotlines is listed at
suicide.org/international-suicide-hotlines.html, compiled by suicide.org. Another list can be
found at iasp.info/index.php, compiled by the International Association for Suicide Prevention.

Safe Horizon
The largest provider of comprehensive services for domestic
violence survivors and victims of all crime and abuse including rape
and sexual assault, human trafficking, stalking, youth homelessness,
and violent crimes committed against a family member or within
communities. If you need help, call their 24-hour hotline at
1-800-621-HOPE (4673) or visit safehorizon.org.

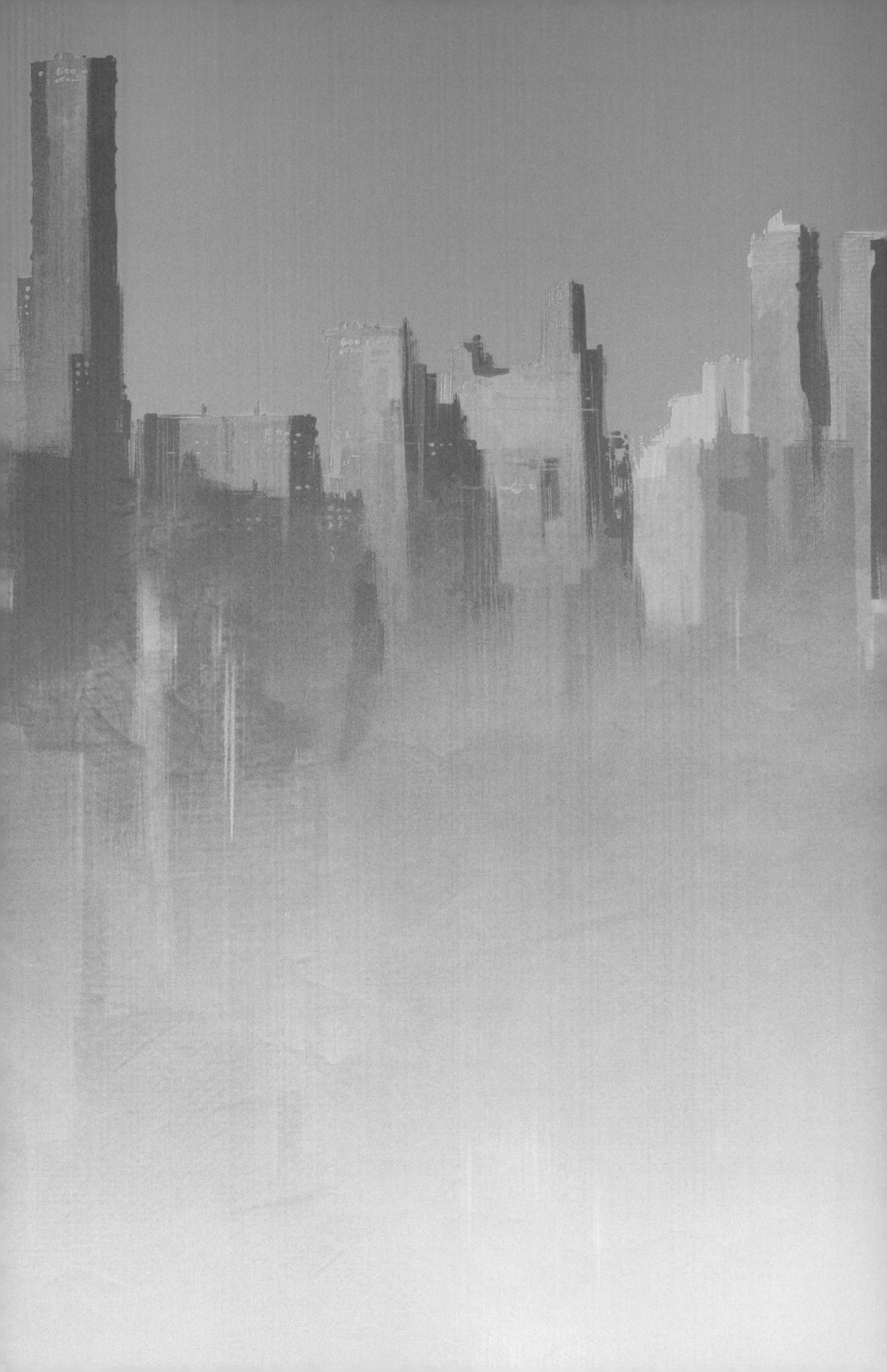

GOTHAM IS A DANGEROUS PLACE— AND EXPENSIVE.

A NEW GOTHAM CITY HERO
DC
"Empowering and unforgettable. E. Lockhart gives us a heroine worth rooting for."
—Kami Garcia, #1 *New York Times* bestselling author of *Teen Titans: Raven*
NEW YORK TIMES BESTSELLING AUTHOR
E. LOCKHART
Whistle
ILLUSTRATED BY
MANUEL PREITANO

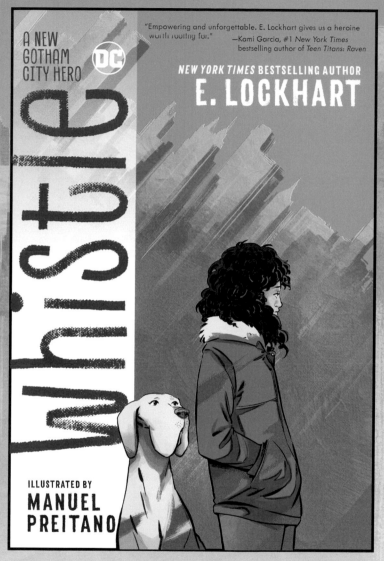

Willow Zimmerman has always known the city is dangerous, but when her mom gets sick and needs expensive care, things come to a breaking point. Just recently, an old friend of her mom's offered to help, and all Willow needs to do is follow E. Nigma's commands. Is this the assistance she needs, or just another trap? *New York Times* bestselling writer **E. Lockhart** and artist **Manuel Preitano** introduce a new hero to Gotham.

Keep reading for a sneak peek at *Whistle: A New Gotham City Hero.*

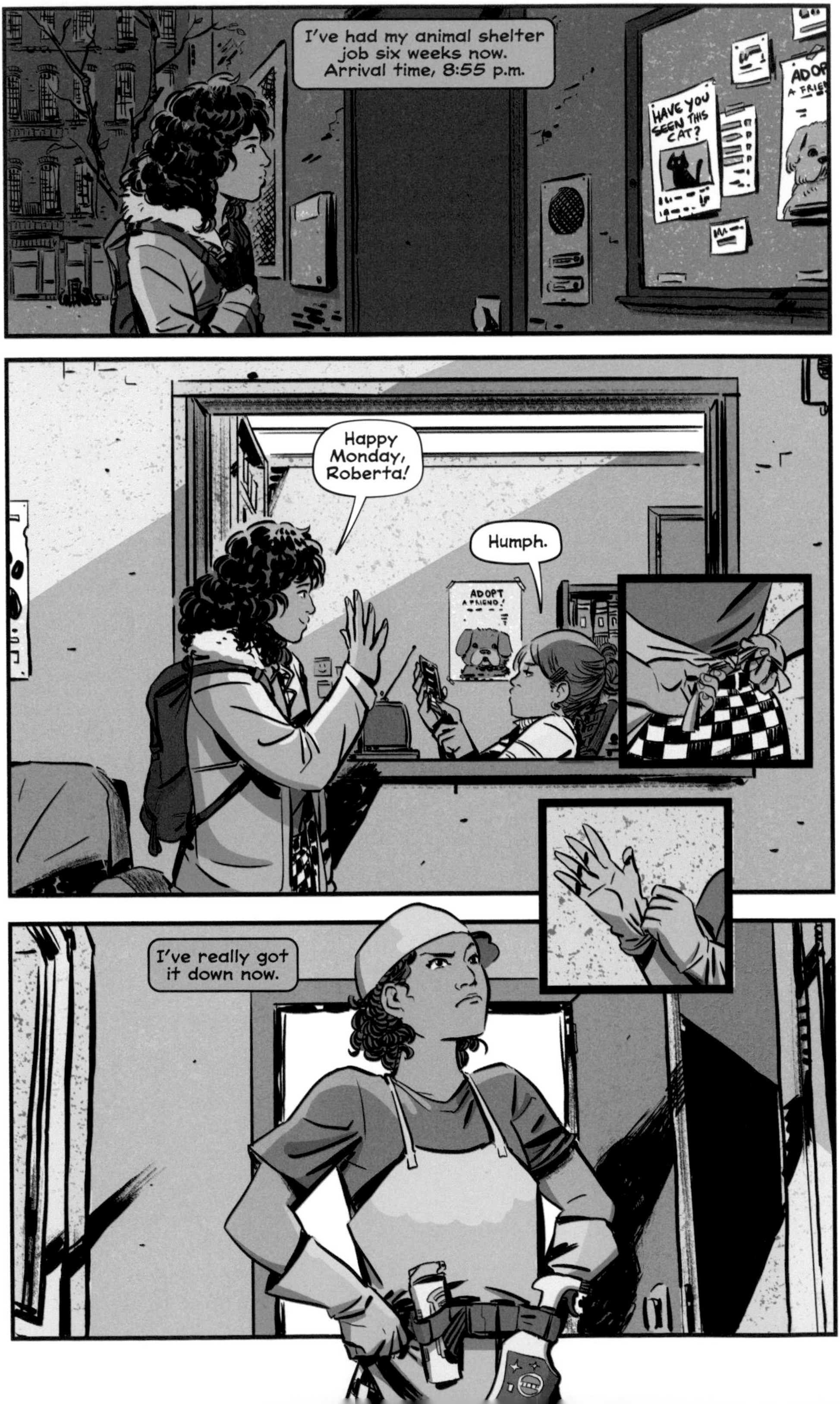
I've had my animal shelter job six weeks now. Arrival time, 8:55 p.m.
HAVE YOU SEEN THIS CAT?
Happy Monday, Roberta!
Humph.
ADOPT A FRIEND!
I've really got it down now.

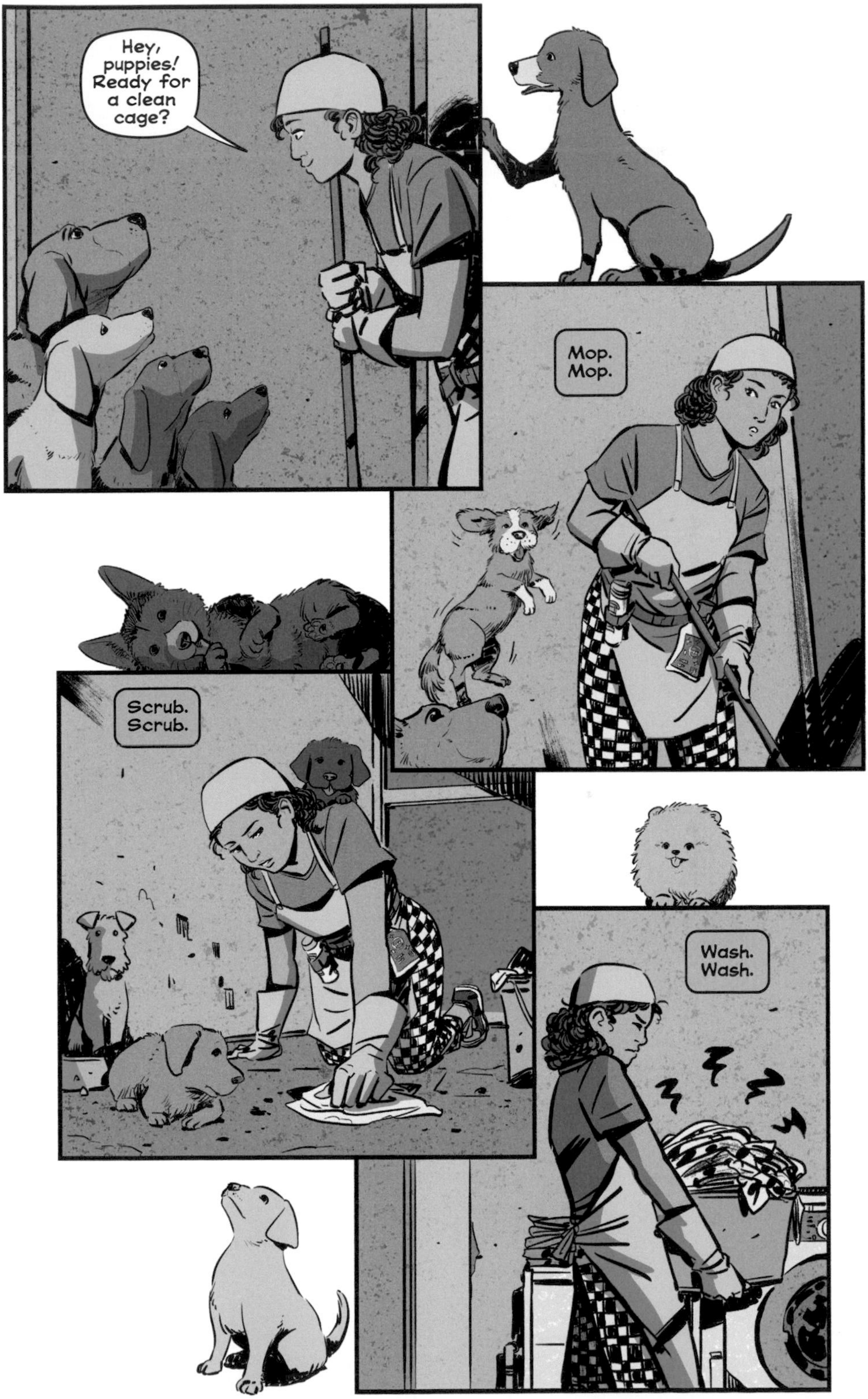
Hey, puppies! Ready for a clean cage?
Mop. Mop.
Scrub. Scrub.
Wash. Wash.

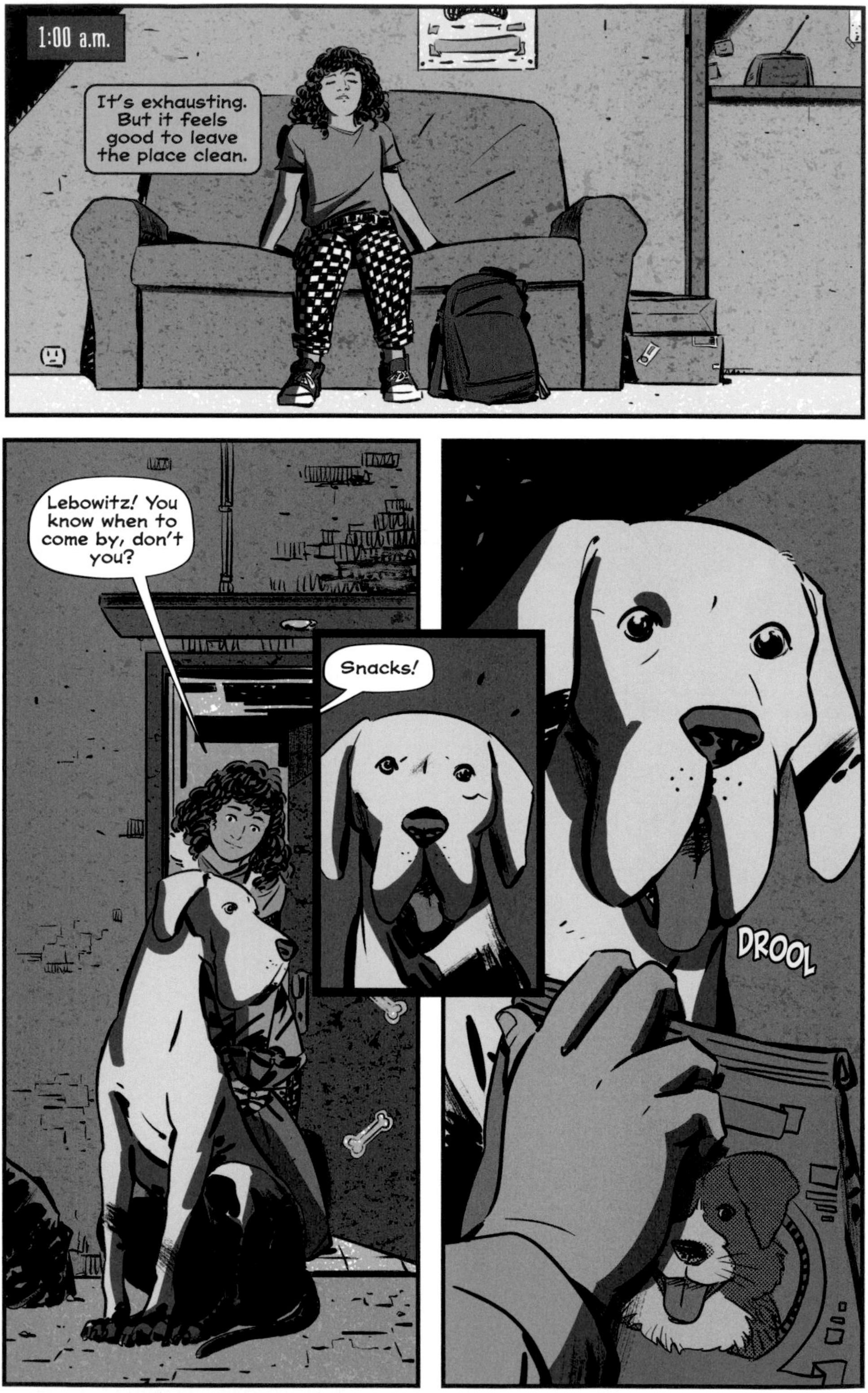
1:00 a.m.
It's exhausting. But it feels good to leave the place clean.
Lebowitz! You know when to come by, don't you?
Snacks!
DROOL

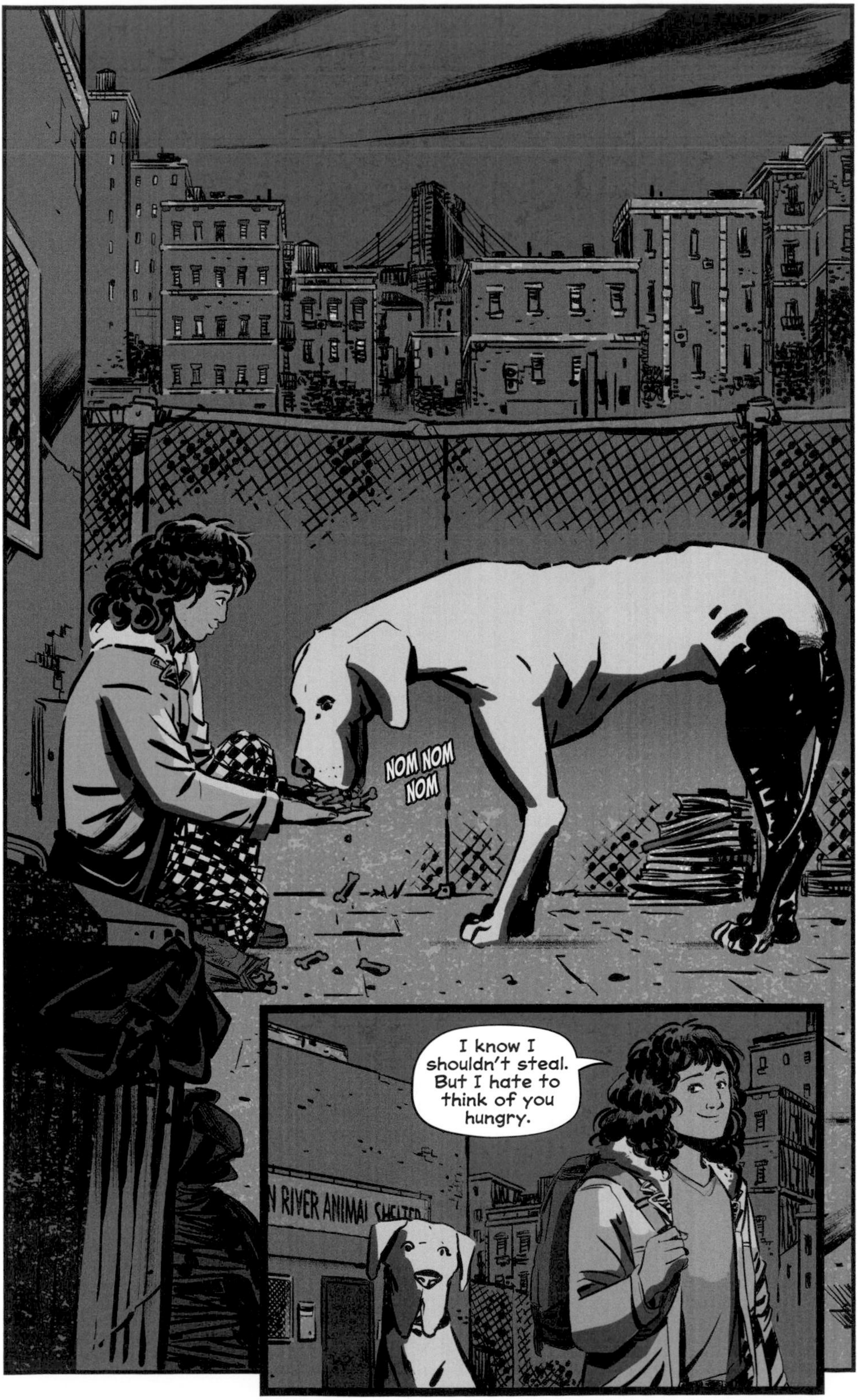
NOM NOM NOM
I know I shouldn't steal. But I hate to think of you hungry.

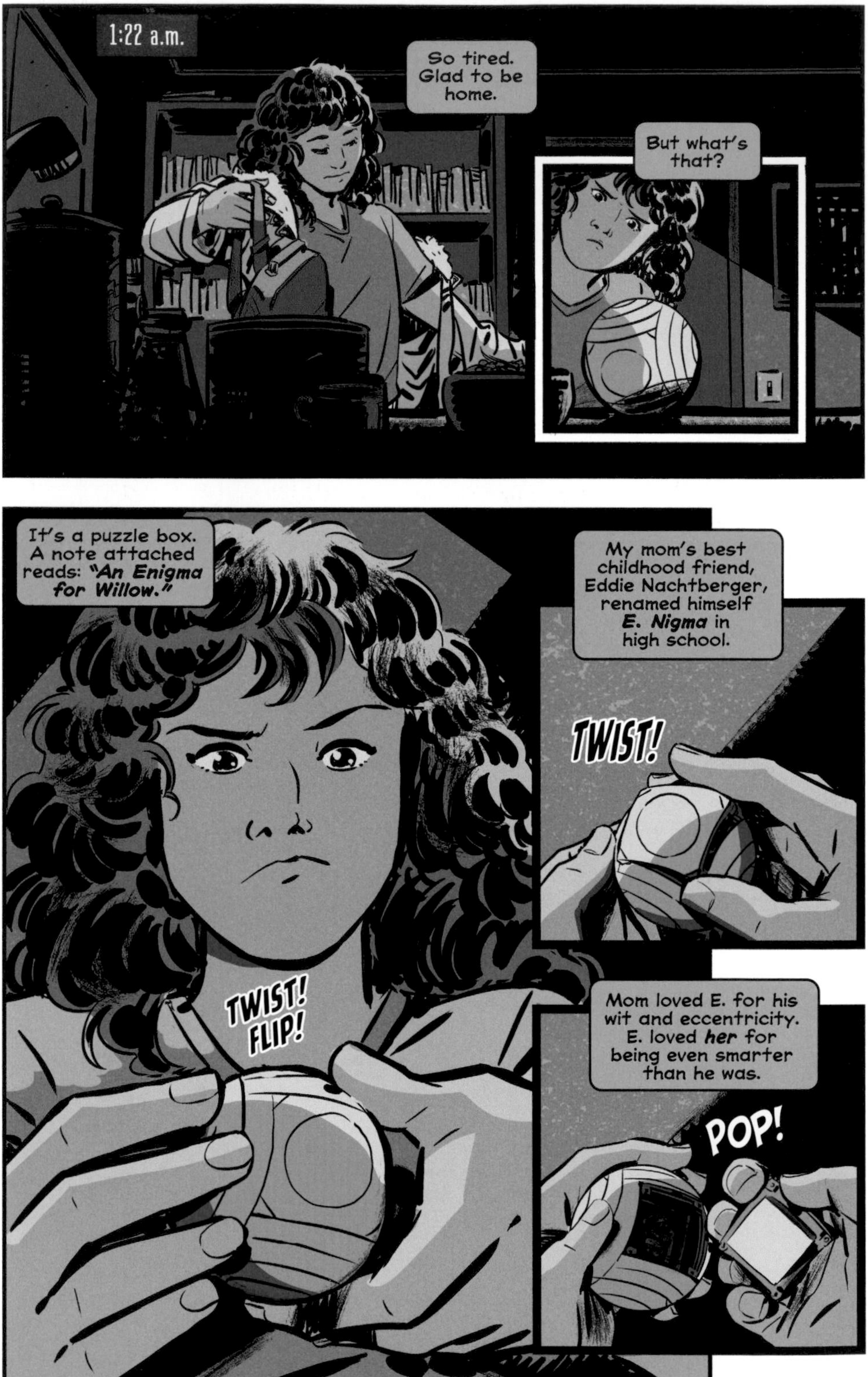
1:22 a.m.
So tired. Glad to be home.
But what's that?
It's a puzzle box. A note attached reads: ***"An Enigma for Willow."***
My mom's best childhood friend, Eddie Nachtberger, renamed himself ***E. Nigma*** in high school.
TWIST!
TWIST! FLIP!
Mom loved E. for his wit and eccentricity. E. loved ***her*** for being even smarter than he was.
POP!

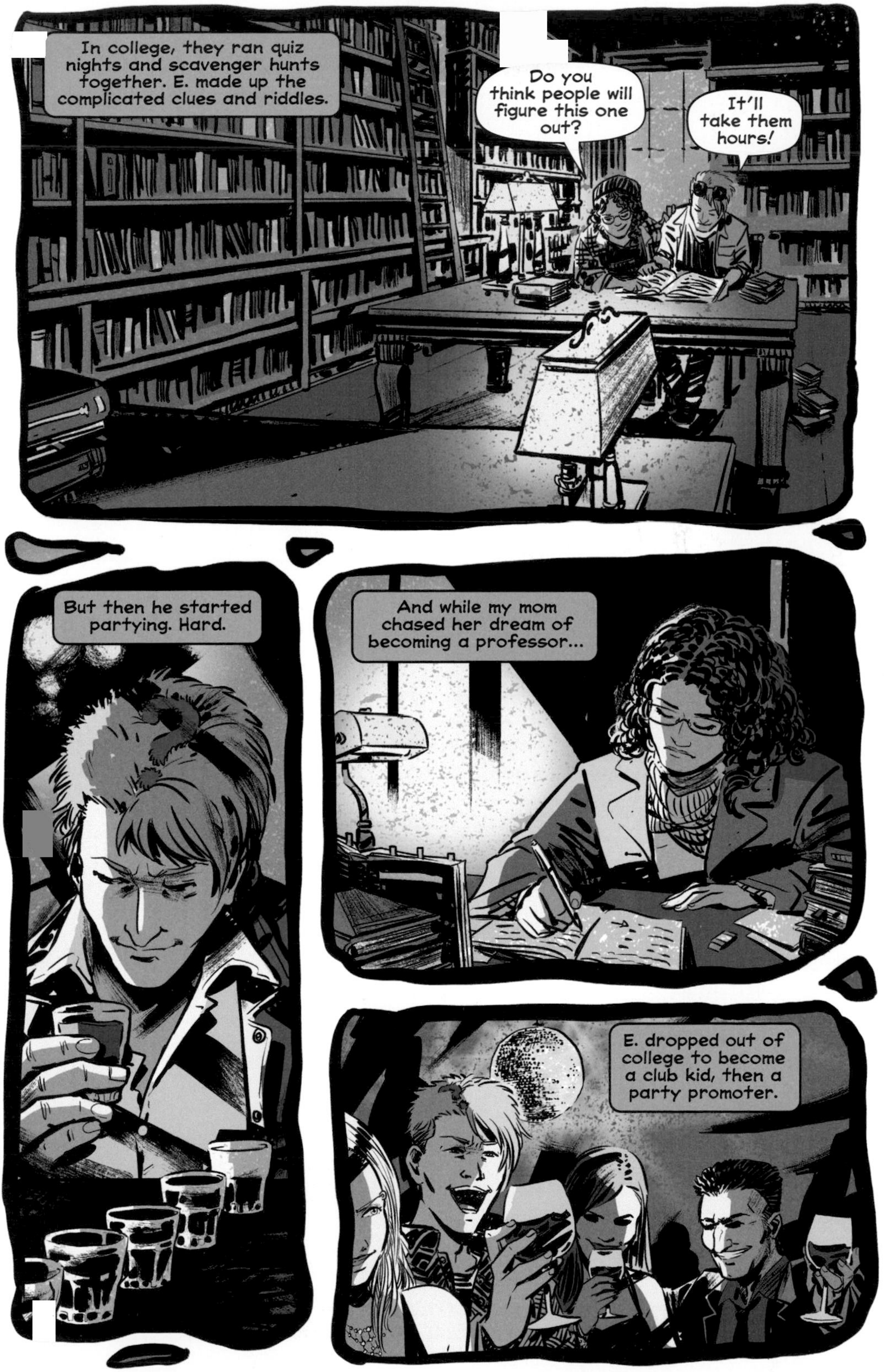
In college, they ran quiz nights and scavenger hunts together. E. made up the complicated clues and riddles.
Do you think people will figure this one out?
It'll take them hours!
But then he started partying. Hard.
And while my mom chased her dream of becoming a professor...
E. dropped out of college to become a club kid, then a party promoter.

BOING!

E. Nigma still came around a lot when I was a kid. He'd take us to shows and restaurants.

He brought me puzzle boxes, like this. And cherry cough drops, too.

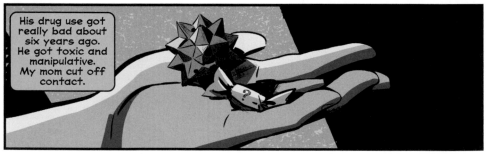

His drug use got really bad about six years ago. He got toxic and manipulative. My mom cut off contact.

Unfolded, the origami has a message.

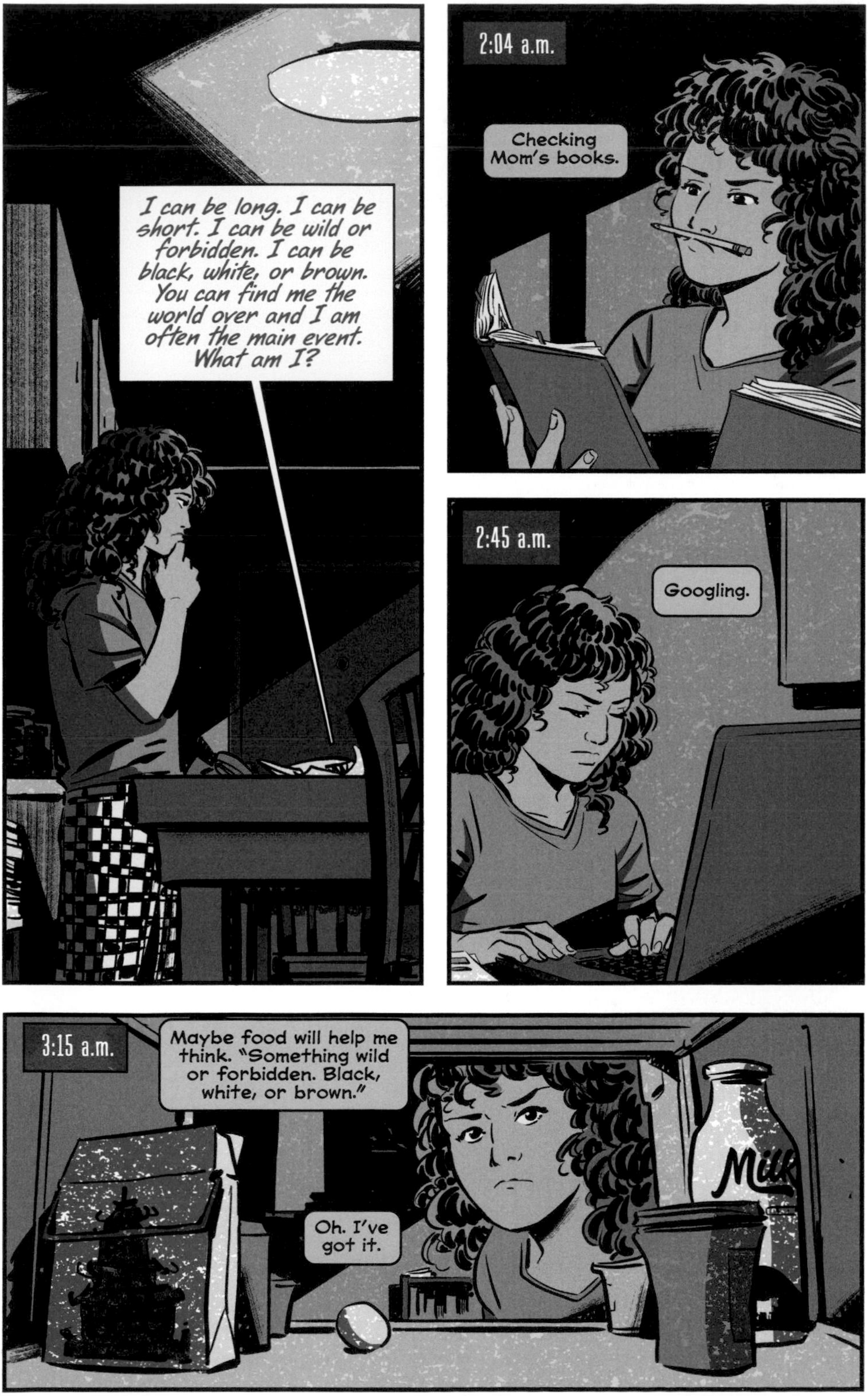
I can be long. I can be short. I can be wild or forbidden. I can be black, white, or brown. You can find me the world over and I am often the main event. What am I?
2:04 a.m.
Checking Mom's books.
2:45 a.m.
Googling.
3:15 a.m.
Maybe food will help me think. "Something wild or forbidden. Black, white, or brown."
Oh. I've got it.

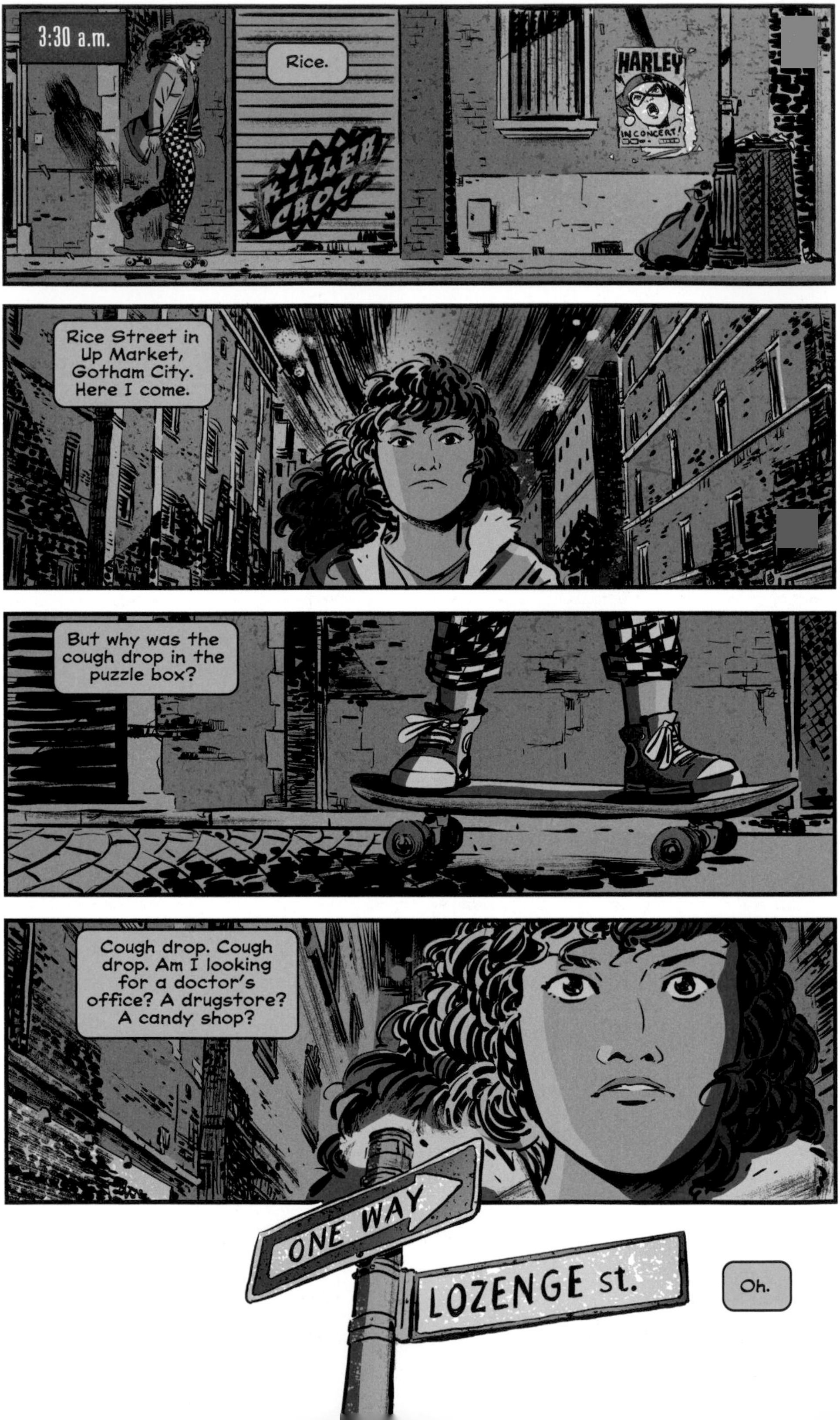
3:30 a.m.
Rice.
KILLER CROC
HARLEY
IN CONCERT!
Rice Street in Up Market, Gotham City. Here I come.
But why was the cough drop in the puzzle box?
Cough drop. Cough drop. Am I looking for a doctor's office? A drugstore? A candy shop?
ONE WAY
LOZENGE st.
Oh.

The Quandary. This has got to be his building.

THE QUANDARY

T. Wang, R. Sutcliffe, B. Klingenberg, W. Churchill.

But there's no *E. Nigma*.

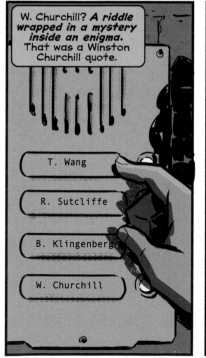

W. Churchill? *A riddle wrapped in a mystery inside an enigma.* That was a Winston Churchill quote.

T. Wang

R. Sutcliffe

B. Klingenberg

W. Churchill

Who is it?

Willow Zimmerman.

T. Wang

R. Sutcliffe

B. Klingenberg

W. Churchill

BUZZZZ

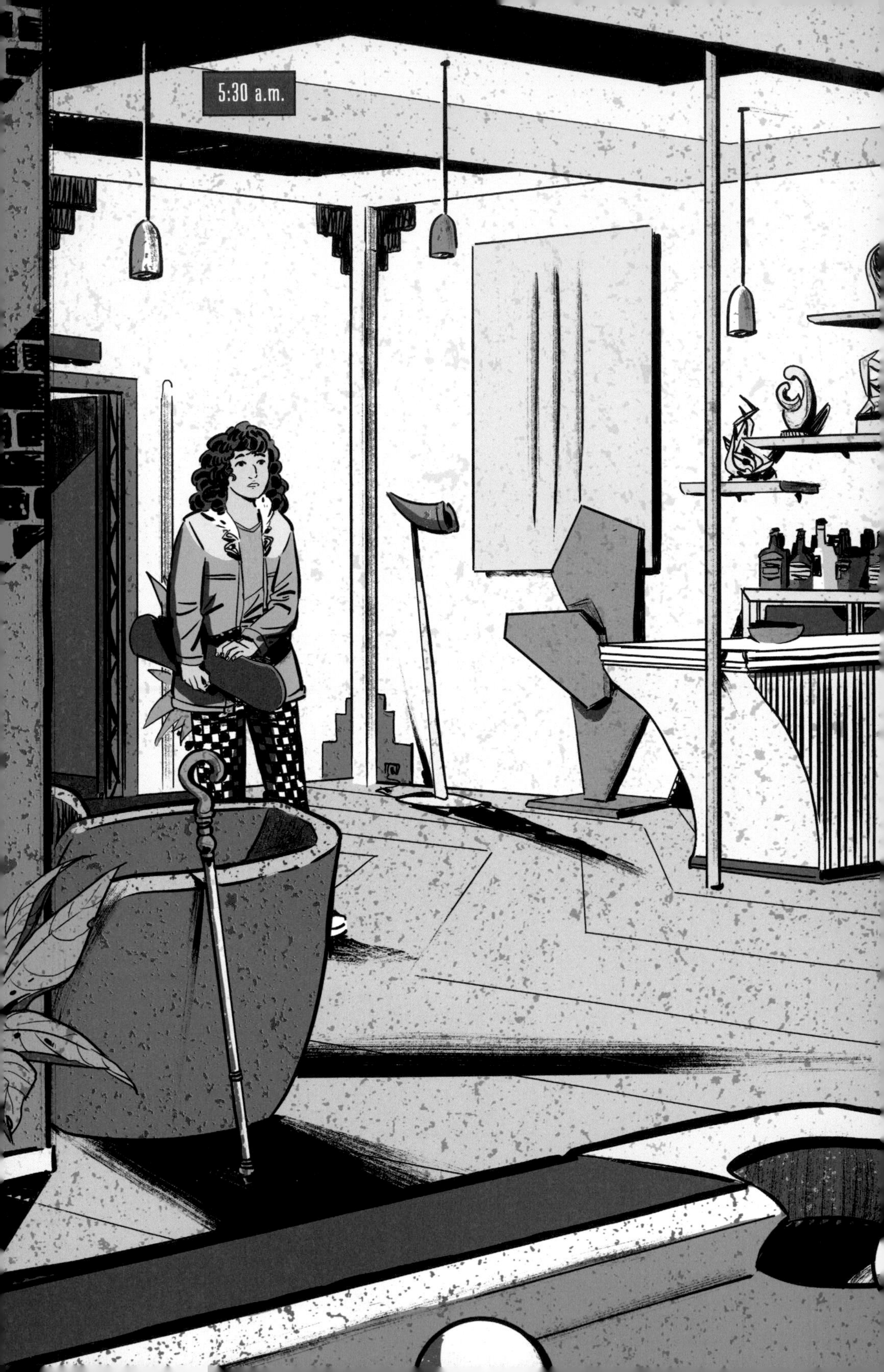
5:30 a.m.

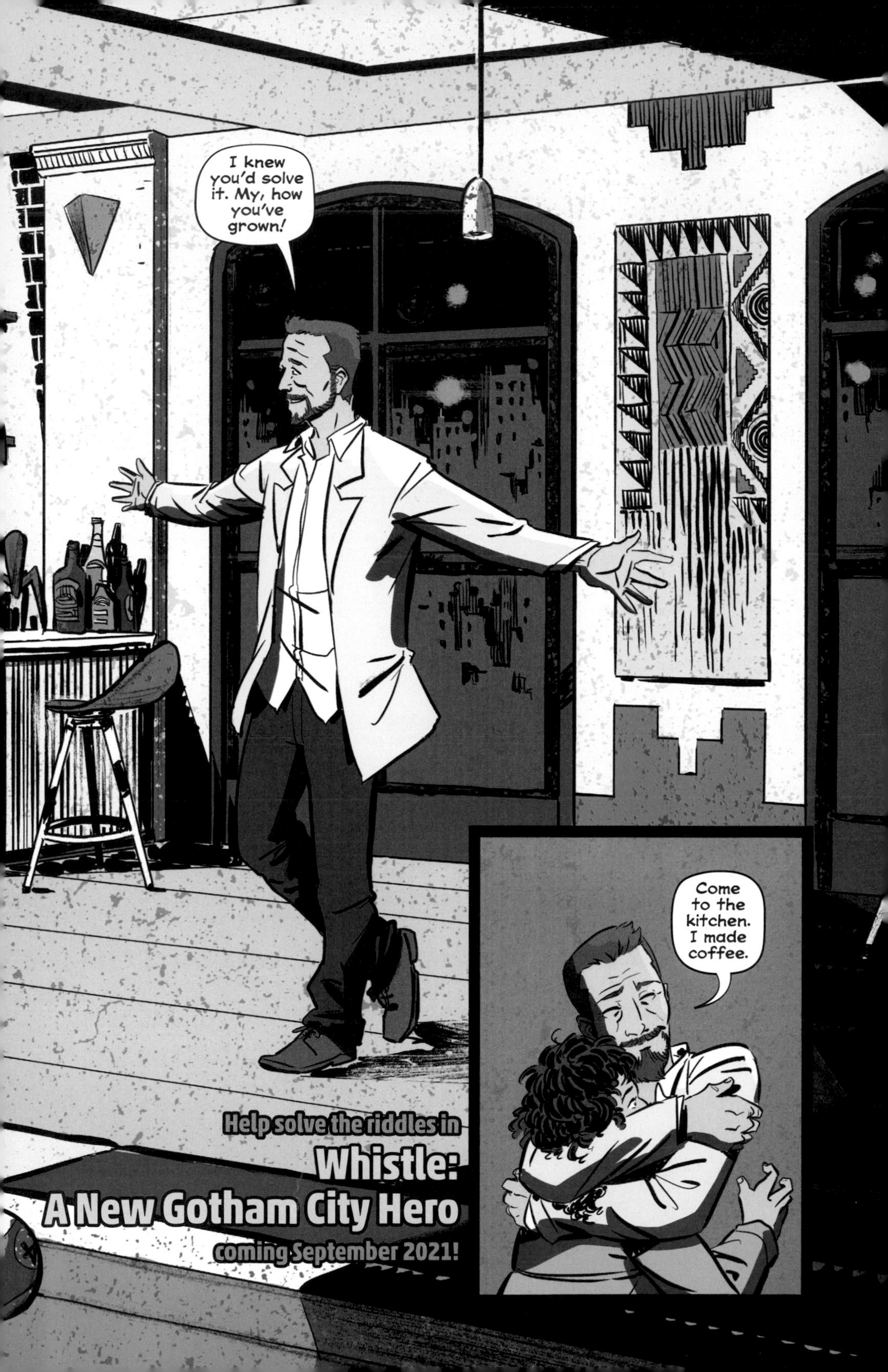
I knew you'd solve it. My, how you've grown!
Come to the kitchen. I made coffee.
Help solve the riddles in
Whistle: A New Gotham City Hero
coming September 2021!

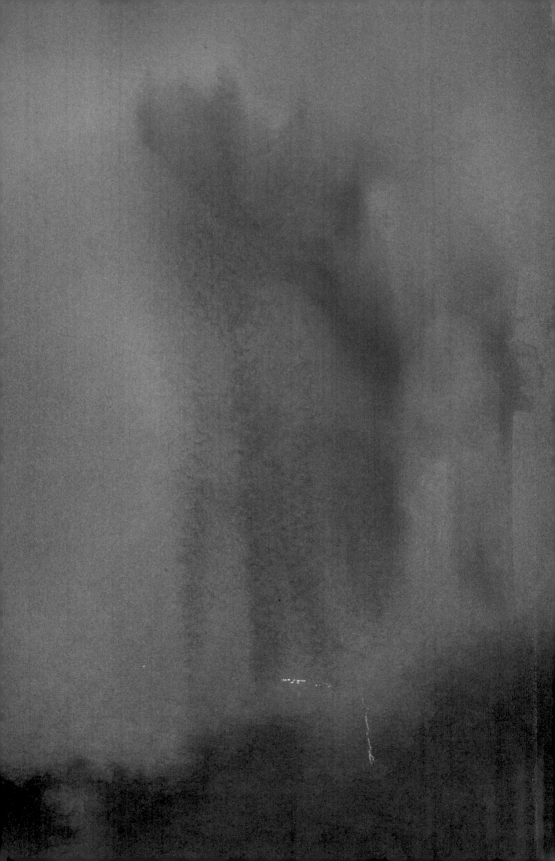